The Cold War was Heating Up . . .

Above and around them, the Arctic became a boiling cauldron. The sudden geysers of water were followed by immense waves that leaped into the air as great chunks of ice tumbled back into the sea.

It was preferable to face *Imperator* alone than to face elements that were beyond understanding. The only option left to the captain was ninety-nine percent suicidal. As his submarine increased her depth, he ordered two-thirds speed ahead and turned in *Imperator*'s direction.

His tubes were loaded. Perhaps his active sonar might work. He wanted just one return "ping," just one confirmation of *Imperator*'s position, before he fired everything he could . . .

CHARLES D. TAYLOR
SILENT HUNTER

CHARTER BOOKS, NEW YORK

SILENT HUNTER

A Charter Book/published by arrangement with
the author

PRINTING HISTORY
Charter edition / March 1987

ISBN: 0-441-36934-0

Charter Books are published by The Berkley Publishing Group,
200 Madison Avenue, New York, New York 10016.
PRINTED IN THE UNITED STATES OF AMERICA

Acknowledgments

The undersea world of our nuclear navy is a strange and fascinating place—and also one that wisely keeps to itself. I learned much about the Arctic environment from my friend, Steve Young, and his Center for Northern Studies, from Dr. Charles D. Hollister of the Woods Hole Oceanographic Institute, and from Barry Lopez' *Arctic Dreams* (Scribners, 1986). While *Imperator* sprang from my own imagination, I have studied designs of such mammoth submarines produced by the American Society of Naval Engineers, The Society of Naval Architects and Marine Engineers, and the Electric Boat Division of General Dynamics.

Tom Shields was kind enough to assist me with initial introductions in New London. Others who then offered help were Vice Admiral N.R. Thunman (who initially brought Admiral McKee's statement about *George Washington* to my attention), Rear Admiral Virgil Hill, Lt. Commander Cherie Beatty, Lt. Tony Kendrick, Senior Chief Robert J. Zollars of the Submarine Force Library and Museum, and especially Lt. Commander J. M. Crochet. Mike Crochet spent untold hours of his own time helping an old "surface type" understand the world of the nuclear navy. The countless little details that should make readers feel they are really sailing under the ice are thanks to Mike's patience with me; the mistakes are distinctly my own. Those who have earned the right to wear the dolphins should understand that everything about their world does not belong in these pages; any breaches of trust or security are the end result of my own imagination.

It is important to remember those friends who helped in so many ways—Candy Bergquist, my favorite retired typist, Dan Mundy and Ted Magnuson, who criticize so well, Bill McDonald, still our captain, Dominick Abel, my agent, and Mel Parker, whose advice is wise.

The world's first atomic submarine, "underway on nuclear power" on January 17, 1955, was a fantastic deterrent, for she never fired a torpedo in anger. She now lies proudly alongside her own special pier by the Submarine Force Museum in Groton, Connecticut. Report aboard for your tour of USS *Nautilus* (SSN-571); then take a few hours to visit the Museum, a valuable part of our American heritage.

Once again, I want to dedicate one to my wife, Georgie—her love is sustaining and she encourages me to achieve.

. . . It is clear that the new expansionist ambitions of the imperialists on the oceans, directed against the countries of socialism, can be countered by our seapower which is capable of exerting a sobering influence on them.

. . . the growth of importance of submarine forces makes necessary the intensive development of submarine-hunting forces . . .

> —from *The Seapower of the State*
> by Sergei G. Gorshkov, formerly
> Admiral of the Fleet of the
> Soviet Union

George Washington, our first Polaris submarine . . . retired without fanfare after silently and effectively performing her mission of deterrence for more than twenty years. She never fired an armed missile. In the business of deterrence, that is the absolute definition of success.

> —Admiral Kinnaird R. McKee, USN
> Director, Naval Nuclear Propulsion Program
> on 6 March 1985 before House Committee
> on Armed Services

Prologue —————————————

A GRAY CHEVY eased to a dusty stop at a scenic turnoff on the coastal highway in Washington State. The man who got out and stretched as he rolled up his shirt sleeves might have been a salesman taking a midday break. The automobile was registered in the same name that appeared on his driver's license—Charles Pearson. He was of medium height, clean shaven, indistinguishable in a crowd, apparently an average working man stopping by the roadside for a breather during a busy day.

It was a rare sunny day for late winter. Ocean waves boomed with a never-ending rumble on the rocks below. A small sandy beach interrupted the unevenness of a rocky coastline. There, seals wiggled ashore to sun and frolic, their playful barking rising as the man's eyes methodically completed their second complete circuit of his surroundings. Satisfied, he reached in the driver's window and extracted a set of high-powered binoculars. They'd been adjusted to his eyes that morning in his hotel room. He again looked about cautiously before scanning the hills behind him. No one there, nothing unusual he could detect. As a matter of fact, there had never been any reports of lookouts anywhere in the vicinity. Yet his comrades continued to disappear.

Arkady Kovschenko—for that was his given name in his hometown of Tula, a city south of Moscow—swept the binoculars from the landscape behind him to the high pasture on the spit of land two miles down the coast. It sat on a bluff sloping sharply down to the water's edge. He had memorized the available charts for this section of coastline, and that entire spit of land seemed to have appeared out of nowhere in the last few years.

This was a remote strip on the Washington coast, barren enough that it had not been mapped by Soviet satellites for years. The spit's appearance had been noted a few years back by a minor operative who found it unusual. When he suffered a heart attack soon after, apparently no one in the KGB's cartographic division had considered the report significant. A little more than a year ago, another agent had provided sketchy reports on a strange consortium of military officers and defense contractors (mostly involved with submarines) that would meet on a monthly basis in Washington, D.C. They would also mysteriously disappear every few months after flying into the Seattle area. Strangely enough, covert checks at their normal offices would always indicate they were either temporarily unavailable to the caller or somewhere other than reported by the agent in the Northwest. When he died in an automobile accident, his carefully prepared reports seemed to have died with him. There was no correlation from the other sources that would have made his reports more important than first judged.

If the number of Soviet agents dying in the American Northwest hadn't finally attracted some attention in Moscow, the bureaucrats who administered these agents might have buried what would later prove to be one of the most vital intelligence coups in the United States.

That was why Charles Pearson/Arkady Kovschenko was peering intently through his binoculars at the pastoral scene before him. The powerful lenses brought the pasture and the spit to him as though they were next to the car. It appeared so natural that without his earlier training he would never have noticed the oddities he now identified. The coastline in that vicinity was punctuated by sharp grades running up from the waterline, broken only by the narrow flood plain of rivers and creeks flowing from the inland peaks. This spit sloped more gradually, taking on an unnatural appearance as he concentrated. The rocks seemed to have been placed there by man rather than nature. Then he noticed the grass in the pastures. Though there actually were cattle grazing there, the shading of the grass they consumed was slightly different, thicker and more textured than that nearby. It was almost as if it had been planted there to ensure that the cows remained.

The Russian studied the rollers ceaselessly attacking the shoreline. He had been trained in oceanography classes to study the action of coastal waters, and he now saw what convinced him that perhaps a giant American submarine wasn't just a rumor. The coloration of the water, the movement of the waves, even obviously shifted sandbars on either side indicated that a deep channel existed right to the base of that spit—and it was wide, over three hundred feet. This could be the monster's lair.

There was but one way to confirm his suspicions. After a final sweep of the surrounding area, he dropped the binoculars inside his car. Opening the trunk, he extracted a large, well-wrapped package, which he lugged to the edge of the slope, lowering it carefully by rope to the bench below. The curious seals wriggling over to sniff the foreign object scattered when he tossed the rope down behind it.

Hearing the sound of a distant motor, he closed the trunk carefully. Extracting a paper bag from the front seat, he neatly laid the contents on the hood. As the only vehicle in the past twenty minutes approached, the Russian was perched on the hood of his car munching on a sandwich, a Coke bottle in his other hand. Smiling and waving to the approaching car, he was just a salesman enjoying his lunch by a scenic turnoff. The driver of the other car waved and continued on his way.

The lunch had been an afterthought, but it tasted good. It wouldn't hurt him to finish it, and he remained on the hood of the car, pleased with his discovery and the few relaxing moments he was able to steal.

They would be his last for the driver of the other car had already alerted security.

High above, in an undetected orbit, a photographic satellite recorded his every moment. The images appeared quite clearly on a small screen in the security office situated well below the grazing cows. The watch officer was alerted early on to the car that stopped by the scenic turnoff. That spot had actually been constructed to provide the best view of this artificial headland, and a warning buzzer sounded in the security office whenever a car pulled off there.

The watch officer moved over to a periscope and studied his objective through a powerful lens that literally brought Kovschenko into the room. He depressed the automatic photograph button three times so that they would have clear pictures of the intruder, should he manage to elude them. Once the package was lowered over the edge to the sandy beach below, he then punched the alert button for the duty SEAL team.

The Russian finished his lunch, methodically bunching the sandwich wrappers and sliding them under the car seat with the empty Coke bottle. Then he moved back inside the car, unseen by either human or satellite. Quickly he dictated everything he had seen and would attempt to accomplish in the next few hours on a tiny recorder that fit in the palm of his hand. Finally, again checking to see that he remained alone, he removed his clothes down to a bathing suit under his trousers.

As he left the car, he placed a handwritten note under the windshield wiper—"out of gas will return." He then engaged a switch on the tiny recorder to radiate a signal that could be picked up only by a similar instrument. Another recording had been left in his hotel room explaining where he would be going that morning. His people would be able to trace every step if he disappeared. His

recorded words confirmed his impressions of the existence
of a lair for a giant submarine.

After slipping the compact recorder under a loose rock
at the edge of the cliff as he prepared to lower himself, his
descent to the seal beach was rapid. Detritus preceding his
approach irritated the seals until they finally moved offshore. The Russian removed a wet suit, breathing apparatus, diving mask, miniature underwater camera, and an
electric pulling motor from the package.

By the time he entered the water, the leader of the
SEAL team was in the security station watching. He'd seen
those motors before and knew how fast they could pull a
swimmer. Checking his watch, he calculated within minutes when the Russian would approach the thousand-yard
barrier.

There was little effort involved on the part of the SEALs.
When they unexpectedly appeared around him, the Russian
reached futilely for the knife in his belt. But before he
could remove it from the sheath, a dart with an explosive
head had already penetrated his chest cavity, disintegrating
his heart.

That night his body was towed out to sea and dumped,
along with his equipment, in a weighted bag. Before night-
fall, his car was a compact lump of metal in a junkyard a
hundred miles distant. The area surrounding the car had
been swept electronically.

Like those who had gone before him, there was no
evidence that he had ever existed. But the compact device
he had secreted under the rock had gone undetected. It
would be turned up a few weeks later by what appeared to
be a highway crew—a sweep team sent out by the Soviet
intelligence officer in Seattle. It would be confirmation
that the next man would utilize in the quest for a menace
the Soviets had yet to ferret out.

In an even more remote part of the world, an equally
determined individual was embarking on a similar quest.
He was an American but he was not masquerading as a

Russian on the forbidding Soviet Kola Peninsula. There was no need for such cover in the bitter arctic winter.

He was one of an elite few able to survive comfortably in that territory. His training was unsurpassed, primarily because he was the originator and instructor of the most rigorous cold-regions survival course. Swathed in white, not a centimeter of skin was exposed. His unique clothing was lightweight yet insulated against colder temperatures than he now faced, and his eyes were screened against the cold and the whiteness. A minuscule oxygen generator enhanced his breathing. Worldly needs were carried on his back, including an inflatable cocoon to protect him from the elements when he burrowed under the snow to rest.

The Norwegians had offered a miniaturized snowmobile, which had been politely rejected based on his assumption that the Russians guarded against such machines with sniffers capable of detecting the slightest trace of exhaust. Preferring to operate on his own, his training and stamina more than made up for any benefit a fallible machine might provide.

His mission was limited—a maximum of three days, he insisted. Longer would surely mean he'd failed. His superiors made one last offer, an honorable way to drop out. They would wait another month or so until the seasonal storms passed, then try satellite photography. He refused. The final transmission from one of his men—his closest friend—near Murmansk indicated the Soviets had been prepositioning tanks, artillery, and supplies near the Norwegian border under the cover of arctic storms. Only the Russians were capable of such large-scale movements that time of year. If the report was accurate, they would easily filter troops in to operate the weapons under the cover of the long arctic nights. Unanticipated, they could conduct a blitzkrieg-type sweep into Norway. His best man had died to relay that—he could not live with himself if he waited until the Soviets proved the report correct. The result could be Soviet occupation of the land mass controlling access to the Arctic.

The bleak landscape had been photographed repeatedly

the past year by satellite, and terrain models had been constructed. There were obvious locations to conceal vast numbers of weapons, easy to camouflage and perfect for launching an assault as the weather broke.

He slipped across the border on cross-country skis less than forty miles from two of the three most logical spots. He navigated with a compass and a watch, matching his pace against the distance. The darkness, the snow, and the cold, punctuated by the persistent winds, provided the gift of security as the hostile terrain enveloped him.

The initial cache lay in a depression, and the downhill slope he anticipated there was nonexistent. Instead, a fuel storage area had been established in its place. The camouflage cover combined with the drifting snow to create a smooth-appearing surface when he should have been moving gently downhill. Little time was required to estimate the amount of stored fuel. It would support a massive assault. A satellite recorded the data he flashed skyward in a short, simple code. Aware there were no guards, he then rested under the protection of the Soviet camouflage.

Two hours later, refreshed, he skied the track of a frozen river at a rapid pace. Pride and ego spurred him on through the frigid, never-ending darkness. No other man could accomplish what he was now enjoying. Single-handed, he was defeating the Russians at their own game.

Anticipation of success, the thrill of superiority, each played a part in his undoing. The prepositioning of such vast arms supplies could not go totally unprotected, regardless of the hostile environment. A small unit of KGB guards had been attached to a post near the tank depot. They had no need to patrol their position. Rather, they utilized electronics to monitor their surroundings. The American had no indication when he tripped the beams, but a red light and soft warning buzzer alerted the KGB duty team.

The Russians employed snowmobiles. They were protecting their own assets and had no reason to be elusive when the alarm was tripped. Each man covered a preplanned sector. With no idea of the cause of the warning or its threat, they traveled without lights. There was no wildlife able to trip their beams, so it was almost certain their quarry was human. And, in such a hostile locale, there would be only one purpose. The well-armed troops remained in constant radio contact.

The American had instinctively gone to the rear of the tank depot rather than following the ravine. Half a dozen KGB guards moved out to cover the approaches. Nothing. Then another light flashed on the security board in the guardhouse. It was relayed to the leader's machine. Someone was moving near the back of the depot.

The American found exactly what he was looking for. Cutting through the heavy camouflage cover, he briefly illuminated row after row of T-80 main battle tanks. Perhaps the mental effort of estimating the numbers so quickly decreased his alertness. Whatever the cause, the first sound he heard—small, high-speed engines—was much closer than he ever should have allowed.

Moving rapidly into the open, he flashed a rough coded signal of what he'd seen in the direction of the satellite, realizing the intelligence was now more vital than his life. However, every move he made at this stage now became guesswork, as his signal was aimed skyward in a direction he anticipated the satellite was located. His tank estimate also seemed jumbled as the sound of engines drew dangerously near, and he repeated his signal, adding a warning at the end to indicate he was in danger.

With still no confirmation of what he faced, the American skied quickly away from the approaching machines. There was no way he could outrun a snowmobile, but he might confuse them, then burrow in the drifts until they gave out. With long, purposeful strides, he increased his speed to the maximum. He knew his limits but he had maintained such a pace in training for as long as fifteen minutes at a time. No other human had ever been able to keep up with him. There was as yet no doubt in his mind that he was able to survive any challenge.

The KGB team leader carried an infrared detector. When a third beam was momentarily broken in an adjacent sector, there was little difficulty in locating a warm-blooded creature in the frigid Arctic. The Soviets closed their target like a pack of wolves. They could neither see nor hear their quarry, but they could track the minimal heat he was radiating.

The American knew his odds were limited when he recognized engines on either side and he accepted his fate when the roar of another was directly in front. The crack of the first rifle shot came to him through the chill blackness at the same time as the muzzle flash and the impact of the bullet in his thigh. He went down in a heap as more bullets cracked above him.

Rolling to his belly, he unhooked the lightweight, automatic rifle from his hip. There was no way a man could escape this godforsaken region with one leg, but he promised himself that others would remain with him as he brought the weapon to his shoulder. The firing subsided. They were moving closer, and at twenty yards they opened fire again. He selected the flash of two weapons too close together, set the selector on automatic, and squeezed the trigger, moving his gun barrel rapidly from side to side, then up and down.

There was no further response from that direction. He waited, hoping against hope that someone else might fire on him and miss. But they were too smart. Nothing.

Then a steady blast came from his right side, no more than fifteen yards away. His head moved in that direction and he tried to bring his weapon around, but he was unable to wheel fast enough. The firing continued long after the American had died.

Their leader came over and kicked at the body. Satisfied, he roped the intruder's feet, attaching the other end to the back of his snowmobile. He flicked on his homing device, and the vehicles raced back to their quarters. The American bounced along behind, face down in the snow.

The loss of two such superb operatives was not to be the last— for either side. The disc recording left by Kovschenko established beyond a doubt that a submarine of great magnitude was building on the Washington coastline. The

death of fine men before and after him would prove that
great sacrifice was necessary to learn the capabilities of
this immense submarine. Similarly for the Americans, the
knowledge that a prepositioned invasion force was developing near the Norwegian border was proof of Soviet
designs on the North Atlantic in the near future.

For more than a decade, the Russians had been designing
their ballistic missile submarines to operate under the arctic icepack. They reinforced their craft for surfacing through
the ice, improved communications gear to keep in touch
with their commanders, and developed navigational devices to perfect targeting from that region. Under the ice,
they were as close as necessary to their American targets
without the need to expose themselves to sophisticated
detection equipment by transiting to the Atlantic or Pacific. They could depart their own arctic ports and commence directly north to the safety of the ice. The only
method of locating them after that would be another
submarine—an attack submarine designed to seek them
out, without being detected first, and sink them before
they could fire their missiles. ICBMs raining down on
American cities from unknown sources in the Arctic were
almost impossible to defend against. The Russians were
converting the Arctic Ocean into a Soviet domain.

The American response had been to produce faster,
deeper-diving submarines, vessels so quiet they could sneak
up on their opposite number and fire before they themselves were heard. There were two direct routes to the
Arctic Ocean: one through the shallow Bering Strait between Alaska and Siberia, the other through the North
Atlantic and Norwegian Sea. The former could be easily
monitored by the Soviets; the latter presented a challenge.
The Kremlin determined that the only method of protecting
their territory—for they felt quite defensive about the waters north of the Scandinavian countries—would be to
eventually control Norway and convert the Norwegian Sea
into a high-threat environment. With naval bases in that
country and Soviet planes flying over the ocean between it

and Greenland, they were confident that they could protect their missile submarines under the icepack.

Soviet intelligence estimates indicated that they'd have to respond rapidly or the Americans would move additional attack submarines into arctic waters. Control of the Norwegian Sea appeared a necessity. The Norwegian Constitution denied quartering of foreign troops in that nation in time of peace. American and Canadian military supplies had been prepositioned there, but they would be useless if the land was in Soviet hands before troops could be landed. The Soviets moved their own prepositioned material for a blitzkrieg-type offensive into position in the dead of winter. The troops were less than a hundred miles away in Murmansk.

Wiser heads in the Soviet Union suggested that maybe an arrangement could be made with the U.S. to keep NATO ships south of a designated line in the North Atlantic. It might serve as a starting point to negotiations and withdrawal of Soviet forces near the Norwegian border. Some of the Politburo felt that talking was a better option than invading their neighbors.

In Washington powerful people on both civilian and military levels felt that nothing could be done before the prepositioned Soviet forces were completely withdrawn. Intelligence reports established that the arctic wasteland between Norway and Murmansk already possessed the greatest concentration of naval, ground, and air forces in the world. There were forty airfields, sixteen of them capable of all-weather operations, with close to fifteen hundred military aircraft. Two motorized special winter divisions were quartered in the Murmansk region along with an amphibious infantry division in Pechenga. And their Northern Fleet was now approaching one hundred fifty warships. Nothing should be negotiated with that threat. Attack submarines were ordered to additional positions under the icepack and counterinvasion plans were instigated to defend Norway. The final plan was an early release of the most powerful weapon devised in submarine warfare as a direct challenge to the Russians. Work in the secret submarine pen on the Washington coast was hurried.

While the politicians watched and wondered and schemed, intelligence reports on both sides expanded on the dire consequences taking shape, urging immediate action before the other side could move.

1

HAL SNOW HAD never learned to keep his mouth shut, nor was he concerned with the problem. That was the prime reason he was never nominated for the star that would have made him a flag officer. "I don't give a shit what they say in the Pentagon . . ." he responded.

"You are in the Pentagon," Admiral Reed interrupted.

"I know that, Andy. But you're not Pentagon military anymore than I am. You just as much as admitted you're not part of the in group right now."

Andy Reed was not, he knew, part of that elite that Snow referred to, but there were few these days who were welcomed to it. He did wear the two stars of a rear admiral, which carried about as much weight this moment with Hal Snow as . . . the hell with it, he said to himself. "Go on, Hal, I'm listening."

Snow was in civilian clothes—for security reasons. He had been requested to wear a uniform only when he was aboard *Imperator* in her pen. The navy preferred not to broadcast the fact that Hal Snow had returned to the navy. Studying him now in a tailored gabardine suit, Reed could see why the defense contractors fell over themselves trying

13

to hire Snow when he left the service a few years back. He was tall and slim. Finely chiseled features complemented a full head of close gray hair. Snow looked as sharp now in a three-piece suit as in a uniform and he spoke well and understood the language in both corporate boardrooms and Capitol Hill. He was exactly the type the civilian contractors wanted to carry their messages to legislators and speak before the television cameras—but as he often repeated, he didn't have to like it.

Admiral Andy Reed was also a very persuasive individual. He had been the one to convince Hal Snow to come back, "for one more ride." Reed remembered how he'd rehearsed that speech that day before Snow first came into his office, thinking of every word that might convince this superb submariner to return to uniform. Snow had let him go on, never once interrupting, which was very odd for Snow. And when Reed had finally come to the clincher and explained how badly the navy needed him now, Snow had said simply, "Okay." When Reed asked why the decision had been so easy, Snow responded with one of his classic statements: "It's simple, Andy. I feel like a goddamn transvestite, switching from the captain of a nuclear submarine to a huckster pleading for someone's tax money." Hal Snow, Reed realized, was never one for understatement.

Snow had taken over *Imperator* a little less than a year ago, while she was still on blocks. Taking over Reed's responsibilities, he'd accepted that unforgiving job of preparing a new construction ship for sea—and had done his usual superb job.

Now, Reed had to use the power of his two stars to convince *Imperator*'s commanding officer that she was going to sea ahead of schedule and that there was work that wouldn't be completed. It was nothing critical to her mission, but Hal Snow would know there were blemishes where a perfect ship should exist.

"You know, Andy, it's just like rape. I've got the largest, most powerful ship ever built, a goddamn secret weapon—the juiciest command ever—and these armchair admirals want to put it on the market just before it's ripe.''

"She'll be fully capable, Hal. No limitations in the engineering plant or weapons department—"

"The idea stinks,'' Snow added with finality.

"You want to turn her over to someone else?"

"Not on your life.'' Snow grinned for the first time. "Dumb sometimes. Big mouth a lot. But crazy? Not by a long shot. *Imperator*'s mine, Andy. She's a dream. . . .'' Then he paused, a quizzical look spreading over his face. "Yeah, dumb sometimes . . . maybe now, too. Why, Andy? Why do they want her out before she's finished?''

And when Reed gave the only answer he could—he didn't know exactly why he'd been ordered to prepare *Imperator* for sea ahead of schedule—that's when Snow had said, "I don't give a shit what they say in the Pentagon." The Pentagon mentality—that's what outsiders called decisions that appeared to have no reasons, or at least no reasons given. So now Reed sat there while Snow got everything off his chest. Listening was easy because he knew there was no one else to replace Snow.

Snow continued on about officers with too many scrambled eggs on their hats for their own good, and decisions that weren't well thought out, and then he finally concluded by saying, "Okay, Andy, what can I do to help you? I know it's not your idea. I'm not going to give her up."

"You can spend the rest of the day going over these work orders with me. They say they want her ready in eight weeks. I figure twelve may be what they mean. Help me get everything you absolutely want in the next eight weeks, and I'll try to get you an extra month for cosmetics. How's that?"

Snow shrugged. "Aren't we all supposed to say: I'm ready now?'' He murmured with another grin. Then he cocked his head a bit to one side and added curiously, "You going to send me up under the ice before I have a chance to shake her down good?"

"Come on. Cut it out. You're shaking her down right

now. The computer can do better than any human being with a ship like that. And you've got the prime specialist in the country handling it— ''

Snow interrupted, ''That broad—''

''That broad designed that system,'' Reed said emphatically. ''Carol Petersen knows more about that computer than you'll ever know in a lifetime.'' He pointed a finger in Snow's direction. ''You promised, and I'm holding you to it.''

Andy Reed was not what the navy would consider the recruiting-poster type. He was of medium height, not short but certainly not the type that appeared to have been born to a uniform. His shoulders were broad, but sloped, and his legs were short and thick. His double-breasted navy jacket used to look smarter, but his spreading mid-forties waist pulled it out in the front and left it baggy in the rear. His posture was what his wife described as his saving grace. Andy Reed had military bearing before he had ever set foot in Annapolis; it was a touch that came with natural leadership ability. He was born to the job! His brown hair had become quite thin, but his black eyes were sharp and piercing and conveyed his every mood. Admiral Reed commanded respect naturally.

''Say no more. That broad,'' Snow added hastily, ''can do whatever you say she can and I'll keep my mouth shut.''

''Don't bring her up again,'' Reed concluded. From the outset, he anticipated Snow's contempt for a woman on a submarine. He was no different than any other submariner, maybe a little more explicit now that it was a fact of life. Carol Petersen was responsible for the design of *Imperator*'s computer. She had named it Caesar (''What better name for the machine that controls *Imperator*, soon to be the emperor of the seas?''). But no matter what her qualifications were—even mother of the computer—no submariner accepted the idea of a woman at sea with them. Most of the crew were navy types. They ran the reactor, controlled the weapons systems, and stood the watches. The only civilians were systems specialists, like Carol Petersen, who so far had been treated with disdain.

Later that day, as they went through the stacks of work orders they'd been numbering one to ten in importance, Snow looked up, his eyes as clear and positive as ever, and stated, "I'll bet we'll go under the ice right away, Andy. No time to get the feel of her before someone tries to sink us. I want to be so ready. . . ." Then his voice drifted off.

Reed knew how much Snow had grown to love that monster of a ship. That was another reason they'd given him permission to talk Hal Snow into coming back. Not only was there no submariner out there with the know-how to take on this job—the best had been promoted and were anchored to desks—none of them could handle a ship and a crew quite like Snow. If he was a lousy administrator stuck in his rank forever, he was the optimal commanding officer. Some of the brass hated to take him back in after they'd passed him over for promotion and driven him out, but he was the one man for the job. None of them could disagree. The navy worked in strange ways in peacetime.

As Reed and Snow determined how they would prepare *Imperator* for sea, senior flag officers in a room not too far away from their own struggled with another problem. They were now rescheduling assignments for attack submarines in New London and Norfolk and Charleston on the East Coast and San Diego and Pearl Harbor on the West Coast based on direct orders from the White House to the Joint Chiefs of Staff.

While some of the submarines would remain on assignments in other parts of the world, many would be directed to arctic waters—some as decoys, but most of them to counter the threat of Soviet ballistic-missile submarines lurking under the ice. It was considered by the White House to be a valid response to a valid threat from the Kremlin.

The orders were issued at the highest threshold of security, based purely on a need-to-know basis. Even Admiral Reed had yet to be included in these plans. Unfortunately, there was limited knowledge of the sophisticated Soviet intelligence network within the naval communications system. Penetration by the KGB had taken a generation of operatives, but it was superb. Before many of the squadron commanders reported their units ready for sea, this shift in strategy was already being analyzed in the Kremlin. They also were aware the mystery submarine was preparing for sea and intuitively they assumed it would be directed to Europe's Northern Flank.

Abe Danilov knew more about submarines than any other admiral in the Soviet Navy. He also was considered without a doubt the expert on American submarine strategy and tactics. No decisions were made without first briefing Danilov and probing his mind for a response. He understood challenges and he knew when there was a bluff.

"They're not bluffing this time. They've no choice. The weakest segment in their defense system is to the north, over Canada. With our SSBNs sitting up there under the ice, they see a significant threat." He turned to face Admiral Chernavin, his immediate superior. "If I was in their position, I would do exactly as they have done. They've no choice," he repeated again, his dark brows knit together so that curly, maverick white hairs projected at odd angles above his eyes.

The discussion continued through the morning. Options were considered, some tabled, some dropped, until they finally came back to what Chernavin knew they should have done much, much earlier. "What would you suggest, Admiral Danilov?"

The heavy eyebrows shot up. He'd been getting progressively more tired as the useless discussion continued and he knew eventually they would ask him. "You've already come up with much of the answer. You said yourself," he said, indicating his chief of staff, Captain First Rank Sergoff, "that there are only two doors to the Arctic for the Americans. Nothing can go through the Bering Strait without being tracked. Since you can't sink them, pick them up one by one and follow them as they enter the Arctic

Ocean.'' He shrugged. ''Simple enough.'' Then he looked
at Chernavin again, raising his dramatic eyebrows. ''The
North Atlantic is a different matter, eh?''

Admiral Danilov's heavy features presented a menacing
appearance at times like this. He was taller than many
submariners of his era, but was still under six feet. He'd
entered the service when no man over six feet was accepted on those small diesel boats. Because he had little
neck to speak of, his head appeared too large for his body.
Danilov was husky—wide shoulders, heavy but not fat
trunk, and arms that seemed to strain at his uniform seams.
His powerful, stubby fingers were a lie to the rest of his
body, for they were as nimble and quick as any quartermaster laying a course on a chart. Danilov's face was full
and square, and many said he looked enough like Brezhnev
to have been his brother. That in itself was enough to
contribute to his reputation. But beneath this gruff, bearlike
aspect was a superb tactical mind.

Admiral Chernavin waited silently for the other to continue. He was familiar with the dramatics and knew Danilov
loved the audience. Let him enjoy it now.

''You can't very well stop them from going up through
the Labrador Sea or the Denmark Strait or the Norwegian
Sea now, can you? That would be the devil's own time.''
He chuckled. He drew a deep breath and waited until all
eyes seemed to be fixed on his own. ''I guess you should
tell them they *can't* go up there.'' He enjoyed the silence
that greeted his response. ''Since we don't have the ability to
stop them any other way, I think that's by far the best idea.''

''Can you tell us how we ought to go about that?''
Admiral Chernavin asked, amused by his own response,
for he knew of no other answer either. Unlike most of the
others around the table, he knew that Danilov was not only
deadly serious, but was absolutely correct.

''That's for the politicians to figure out, Vladimir. I'm a
submariner and I think I'll keep it that way. I'd much
rather retire and go live in my dacha than be a politician
and die of a heart attack too young.''

Another younger admiral, one who was not a submariner and had designs on someday becoming a politician, inquired, "How would you convince them that they ought to listen to a suggestion so wild?"

"By making a deal with them. They love deals." Danilov would much rather have them make a deal for the time being. He had no desire to go to sea in the near future. His wife was seriously ill and he wanted to be at her side.

It was Admiral Chernavin's responsibility to carry Danilov's suggestion to the Kremlin and explain that it was the only solution that the best naval minds had been able to develop. He hadn't the least idea what kind of deal could be made but, as Danilov had explained, that was up to the politicians. The Soviet Navy had strong feelings that the evolving crisis had been created by the politicians.

Once Chernavin had stated his case, political minds pondered the situation and tried to imagine what the Americans might accept in exchange. It wasn't until the following day, when the American ambassador to the United Nations made a speech before the General Assembly concerning Soviet troops poised on the Norwegian border, that the solution appeared to them.

The following week the General Assembly heard from the Soviet ambassador. He concurred that the U.S. did indeed have a point. But, Moscow's intentions were not aggressive toward their neighbors to the west. The annual NATO exercises called Teamwork took place in the North Atlantic and extended well into the Norwegian Sea and beyond the North Cape. These exercises were structured around American carrier battle groups, and impressed upon the Soviets the need to maintain tight security in their arctic territories. After all, the U.S. and Canada over the last few years had prepositioned military supplies in northern Norway scant distances from the Soviet border. These Teamwork exercises were designed to support amphibious landings by NATO forces on Norwegian territory. The Kremlin was forced to interpret these exercises as preparation for an invasion on the Soviet Arctic. As the Soviet ambassador stated—prepositioning could be considered the first cousin to an actual declaration of war. And now, Teamwork!

Moscow had been so impressed with NATO's annual display that they had no choice but to devise a method for protecting their arctic lands. While admitting the prepositioning of small amounts of armor and supplies, they denied any massive buildup. Not only were there no troops available to utilize this equipment, but much of their own effort had been only an exercise in prepositioning. The explanation was logical.

Further, the ambassador explained, Moscow feared the return of American carrier battle groups that summer. Because the Scandinavian countries remained neutral, the Soviet government was ready to offer a solution—they would remove what limited matériel had been prepositioned near the borders if the U.S. would agree not to send any of their naval forces north of the Arctic Circle, approximately the sixty-seventh parallel, that year. By naval forces, the Soviets meant surface, air, and subsurface units. It seemed a small enough gesture on the part of both nations toward international peace.

This olive branch was well received by members of the General Assembly.

"That speech was just so much unmitigated crap," the head of the CIA stated to the others around the table. "Too many good men have been lost in the past couple of months to accept that kind of baloney. We have the lists of divisions and their commanders who are scattered near Murmansk just waiting to move out." He slid a sheaf of papers toward the middle of the table. "Anybody care to look at that? Pretty close to an invasion plan if you ask me. That's so goddamned different from what that clown claimed at the UN . . . it would make the devil blush. . . ." He sputtered on about orders of battle and numbers, but it was all unnecessary. Each man around the table understood the purpose of the Soviet offer all too well.

But in another part of Washington, the possibilities of

the situation were scrutinized more carefully by ambitious politicians with eyes on reelection. There had been a great deal of logic in the Soviet offer. Instead of an eye for an eye, they were presenting a solution where it seemed neither side had to lose either an eye or even a shred of dignity. The concept also appealed to many of the more liberal members of the NATO community.

Those powerful but short-term members of Congress blissfully unaware of the extent of Soviet expansion along the Norwegian border, were impressed with the idea of cooling off an area that appeared to be bubbling over. Extensive debate followed in both the Senate and the House. White House advisors appeared caught up by the positive aspects of the debate.

Within days, the Russians provided proof of their goodwill by commencing the removal of the matériel they had admitted to. Though it would be inconclusive that time of year, they even invited satellite confirmation of their efforts. U.S. intelligence sources knew, however, that the vast majority of matériel remained hidden under camouflage.

Once the Kremlin had made their first move for the sake of goodwill, they went right ahead and set a date a few weeks hence that American naval forces should remain south of the Arctic Circle. Since American naval units generally operated in the Mediterranean or warmer waters during the winter months, there was nothing north of that line other than a few submarines conducting normal operations. The timing in the Kremlin had been superb.

A week later, poised at the same table, the CIA director turned to the senior naval officer after completing his diatribe about the extent of Soviet forces that remained poised on the Norwegian border. "We don't have a choice, do we, Admiral?"

The admiral shook his head from side to side.

"I'll be making my recommendation to the White House shortly. We have to test them—we have to send a ship north of the line. . . .

"If the Soviet Union is able to keep us out of the Arctic—turn it into their own bathtub . . ." The admiral was again shaking his head. "If they control Norway, that means their SSBNs are as secure as a baby in mother's arms. . . ."

Another admiral opened his briefcase and took out photographs that had been enlarged for release to the news media. Some were clear, some dark and grainy, but they all displayed exactly the same subject—Soviet ballistic-missile submarines. Included were the older, smaller *Yankee* class; the ten-thousand-ton *Delta*s with their longer-range missiles; and the massive, twenty-five-thousand-ton *Typhoons*—each more menacing than the next. The *Typhoons* could hit their U.S. targets without ever leaving the dock. They hid below the icecap only for their own protection. To allow the Soviet Union to control Norway and the Arctic would create a "bastion for these marauders," as the admiral put it.

While a special ambassador was dispatched to Moscow to discuss elements of the offer with his counterparts, one of the deepest American plants in the Soviet apparatus observed discreetly as the Soviet military dismembered its prepositioned force—at least the amount that had been admitted to. The withdrawal was the beginning of a complete circle, with tanks, artillery, and supplies first being loaded on trucks or trains headed south. At a point a few hundred miles south of Murmansk, they began a wide turn, eventually heading back to the Murmansk sector.

The CIA clarified the situation to the White House, and various senior members of the military were called in for advice. At the same time, Congress was encouraged to continue their debate. It seemed wiser that the general public and the Soviet Union understand that the offer was still being considered.

Another interested party in Washington was that same deep Soviet plant in the naval communications system. There were two types of orders issued in the following weeks to the various submarine commands—those under a clearance weak enough to reveal that the submarine squadrons would revert to normal operating status, and others at the highest classification that maintained exactly the same orders as before. The Kremlin understood this implicitly. It was no different than the methods they often employed themselves. So they allowed their special ambassador to continue negotiations, blissfully unaware of military preparations. He entertained his American counterpart like visiting royalty, which provided excellent press.

But the decision seemed already to have been made on both sides.

As often as Andy Reed had been inside *Imperator*'s enormous pen on the Washington coast, he never ceased to stare in awe at his surroundings. The "fishbowl" was the nickname for the underground cavern, which had served as both the birthplace of this magnificent submarine and now the technical center for her shakedown.

It appeared from the inside as if a mountain had been hollowed out, which was partially true. In actuality, a high section of the coastline had been excavated and the dirt dumped well out to the sea by dredges. A man-made cocoon was then constructed over it and extended seaward to complete the fishbowl effect. The area selected was sparsely populated and little traveled. There was minimal concern among those few natives who noticed the unusual changes. The dredges dug out a channel over a two-year period from the open sea into the fishbowl. Every few months sections of a floating dry dock were moved inside to be joined together. Generators were delivered. A miniature shipyard evolved.

When the fishbowl was done, navy tugs would appear towing sections of the hull constructed at various locations on the West Coast. Most shipments to the fishbowl came in this manner, and usually in the middle of the night. The skilled workers who made *Imperator* a reality also came by sea. They worked intense twelve hour shifts for a week at a time, then would depart as they came, returning two weeks later to resume their shifts. Their paychecks sealed their mouths.

Reed remained enthralled with the fact that such a project could continue as secretively as this one. There was no doubt in his mind that it would not have occurred this way if *Imperator* had been constructed with government funds. The fact that she was spawned by private funding through a consortium of defense contractors made her secret existence possible. There had never been a name for the organization, at least not one known on the outside. They simply had been known among themselves as the "consortium" when the project began, and the name had stuck. Retired officers became covert advisors, involving only active-duty personnel whose assignments would conceal their time at the fishbowl.

"She looks like she could slide out tonight, doesn't she, Andy?" Hal Snow cut a recruiting-poster figure in his uniform.

"Yup. But how long do you think it would take if I said get ready for sea now?"

Reed had often compared *Imperator* to an aircraft carrier, for the giant submarine was longer and would displace more tonnage when fully loaded and submerged. Yet the comparison wouldn't stick. Most of an aircraft carrier rode above the surface for the whole world to see, while *Imperator* was like an iceberg on the surface. Ninety percent of her bulk lay below.

"It's just a matter of final testing from the main reduction gears aft." Snow smiled knowingly. "The computer says everything's hunky-dory, but I just want to make sure for myself. I've got my engineers making personal inspections now—the old submariner in me." The old guard were not opposed to computers: they simply had greater trust in a human being than an electronic wonder. "The reactor's been on line without a whimper for so long that we hardly pay attention anymore. Auxiliary engineering's been double-checked until they can repeat the status of each unit in their sleep. Every pump and valve has been through each test at least three times. The only thing I can't guarantee is weapons. Haven't fired a one," he joked.

"Then you could get underway tonight if you had to?"

Snow peered out of the corner of his eye. "After I've run my final tests on the shafts . . . I suppose so."

"Don't bet that it might not be soon."

"I thought you said I could probably squeeze out twelve weeks."

"I said eight—that I'd try for twelve. Now I doubt it."

"I still have a lot of incomplete job orders that are close to ten on our list."

"Make sure you have the parts on board if you have to get underway beforehand. You've got the talent to do that at sea."

Hal Snow paused thoughtfully. "You know, I don't think you could find a better man than me for this job right now, but I hope you've got someone else in mind after this tour. I think I'm from another generation . . ."

"We both are."

They were standing near the stern, looking forward. The sail structure was larger and higher than the bridge on a destroyer, yet it appeared a last-second thought on a submarine longer than four football fields. Andy Reed had yet to be included totally by the inner circle, whose evolving strategy was based on arctic confrontation. It was only after a late-night meeting two days before that he was informed orders might be coming any day.

"There's just one item holding me back now, Andy."

Reed turned curiously to his friend.

"That broad, Andy. Every damn day someone comes in to see me with only one thing on his mind—is the navy really crazy enough to send her off with us? I'm not losing my grip on this crew, but I've never run into anything tougher. They still won't speak to her."

"Do you?"

"Of course I do. I don't have any choice. She controls the brains of the ship. Without her, that computer might be useless at the wrong time. She's got me by the shorts!"

"Do you get along?"

Snow shrugged disconsolately. "I suppose so. She's polite, understands the navy, does her job . . . and she doesn't take shit from anybody."

"Doesn't have to either," Reed said, as he smiled and gestured for the other to follow while he meandered along the dockside. It was no different than the first female astronaut. The consortium wanted to exhibit some element of liberalism. Not only was Carol Petersen one of the most talented computer designers, she was destined to succeed, for she was their display piece.

"I wouldn't be surprised that, if there was some guy just as qualified as Carol Petersen, the navy still would have had to accept her. The times they are a-changing," he added wistfully.

As they strolled beside *Imperator*, Snow returned to a question he'd asked before. "You expect I'll head directly for the ice?"

"Couldn't say. But it looks more like it to me each day."

"Still too bad you can't go with me."

"I'd give my right arm but they want to see what you can do alone. I'll catch up." Reed stopped and turned to the other man. "You've never been worried about anything before in your life. Are you starting now?"

"Negative. Nothing of the sort. I imagine it's more like the first man in space, or Armstrong stepping out onto the moon. When the greatest thing that will ever happen in your life is about to take place, you're not scared or worried. You have to be excited about the unknown. It's just that I'd like to know when and where—a normal human reaction, I think the shrinks would agree."

Nothing more was said until they reached the head of the dock and looked down the length of *Imperator* from the bow. She's beyond comprehension, Reed thought to himself, yet there she is. Sleek and black, the giant submarine lay silently in the water, waiting to emerge from her cocoon. Many of her weapons had been delivered in the past few months—torpedos, missiles, tanks, helicopters, everything that could be stored deep within her hull except her marine contingent. Troop movements were watched too closely by the media. When they came aboard, they'd be transferred at sea.

"I envy you, Hal, more than anyone ashore can imagine," Reed said quietly.

Abe Danilov rarely invited guests to his apartment. It was not so much that he disliked social contact; rather, he was selfish about saving all his wife's time for himself—and giving all he could spare of his own to her. Anna Danilov was ill. Her days were numbered, and those close to her knew it. Her husband intended to fill those days with as much love as he could afford, and he begrudged every minute of his time that the navy required.

The guest was Captain Sergoff, his chief of staff, who was part of the family, in Anna's opinion. He'd been with Danilov much too long to be considered a guest anymore. While he was simply called Sergoff by the admiral and others senior to him, she knew he had a first name, and it was one that appealed to her—Pietr. Danilov would look up with surprise every time Anna used the man's first name.

Captain Sergoff had no family. He was an only child whose parents had died in the last of Stalin's purges. Sergoff had been lucky at that early stage in his life, for his grandparents had survived the purge and raised him. Sent off to a naval school at an early age, he knew no other life but the service and he had never been married. Abe Danilov recognized his military talents at an early stage and Anna Danilov was the one to recognize his loneliness, treating him more like a son. Even in the final stages of her illness, she often asked her husband to invite Pietr Sergoff home. His tall, blond appearance was almost patrician in comparison to her husband's compactness.

"No, thank you, I think not," she replied when Sergoff extended a platter to her politely. "I had too much at lunch," she lied. Anna Danilov rarely ate, and was usually sick when she did partake of food.

Danilov's eyes clouded over as she continued her small talk with Sergoff. Discussion around the ministry that day had been about the imminent departure of a hunter/killer group of submarines for duty in the Arctic. He knew they would not be leaving immediately, for he would be their commander, but he dreaded the approaching day, for he feared leaving Anna. Staff members came to him often to ask if they would be involved since rumors surfaced or changed each day. He would smile and say that if anything were about to happen, he knew nothing about it. The latter was true—nothing was definite. But something would break soon. That was for sure.

Now Sergoff turned from his conversation with Anna Danilov. "Isn't that correct, sir? The Americans seem to be cooperating with us. There's no sign of any of their ships moving northward."

"I think for once," he replied, smiling at his wife, "that you can believe everything you read in the papers. There is no immediate threat. The negotiations are continuing briskly." But Danilov was one of the few who knew exactly what was taking place. He was aware that the armament being withdrawn from near the Norwegian border was taking a circuitous path back toward Murmansk, and he also knew that the original orders to the American submarine squadrons had not actually been revoked. He had been in this business long enough to realize that neither side really could anticipate what would happen over the next month or so. It was not so much the firm plans that brought nations to the brink, but the ones that seemed minor at the time.

Their small talk continued until it became obvious that Anna was growing tired. Then Sergoff volunteered, as he often did, to put some music on the record player. Anna Danilov loved the ballet and the opera. She had been a tireless patron during their years in Moscow, and now she asked Sergoff to pick something for her. When the music began, her face lit up. He had remembered her favorite Tchaikovsky ballet.

Even the admiral smiled to himself as he helped her to the sofa. His chief of staff was as invaluable to his wife as he was to his admiral. It was strange how relationships developed. If only he could depend on Sergoff to help Anna when it came time to leave for the base at Polyarnyy.

But that would not be the case because he desperately needed Sergoff. Perhaps, with a stroke of luck, there would be a meeting of the minds and he would not have to leave her. Yet he doubted that more each day. The intelligence reports from the American Pacific Coast indicated that the U.S. was preparing to release that submarine that had been building for years. And their Admiral Reed was known to be involved. He was to the Americans what Danilov was to his own navy. It became increasingly difficult to enjoy the music and Anna's pleasure in it as the implications of Reed's participation coursed through his mind.

For a few moments, with Anna and Sergoff engrossed in their music, Danilov's inner thoughts completely masked Tchaikovsky. *Reed—Rear Admiral Andrew Reed*—the foreign flavor of the syllables echoed back and forth across his mind, yet there was a familiar ring to them also. He knew the name as well as his own. If Reed had been born in Russia, and Abe Danilov in America, would they have assumed each other's bodies? Each other's position in life? Each other's . . . ?

There were so many similarities. While Danilov was older and therefore slightly more senior in their respective navies, their careers had followed remarkably similar patterns. Both had been involved in the early stages of nuclear propulsion; each had worked with the designers of new classes; each had commanded the first of a class. And, the Russian concluded, they were both simple men . . . family men . . . they had been loyal to their wives. He respected that in a man.

Danilov knew all about the American. He'd studied Reed's career folder often, a standard procedure when operating in an area where your opposite could be expected to appear. Abe Danilov was sure they had played cat-and-mouse games—once with their own submarines in the North Atlantic, later when they were squadron commanders evaluating their own commanding officers in the Pacific. The Russian admiral kept close track of his American encounters—especially with this Reed for some reason—and he hoped that his opposite would agree with him on the score: there had been no winners on either occasion.

A sense of respect had evolved from their brief competition. Often, when the hierarchy in the Kremlin was boasting of the superiority of their submariners, Danilov hoped he would never have to face Admiral Reed. It wasn't fear of the other man by any means; it would be the contrary— the challenge of a lifetime! But deep inside the burly, gruff facade that was Abe Danilov, there was also a man who did not want to take the life of one who could almost be his brother . . . nor did he want to hurt the family that must have been as beautiful as his own.

Fear often has a momentous influence on decisions. Among most people in leadership positions, it is not the gut-wrenching fear of failure or death. It is the fear of the unknown, or, more aptly, the fear of failing to challenge the unknown.

In Washington it was accepted that Soviet ballistic missile submarines lurked under the arctic icecap waiting for a signal all hoped might never come. It was known that the Russian threat was there and that they could be located by American attack submarines given enough time. Instead, it was the unknown that created a rising anxiety within the Washington power structure—the Soviet threat concerning an American warship crossing that arbitrary line, the Arctic Circle. Would the Kremlin enforce their threat, especially now that they were going through the motions of removing their prepositioned matériel on the Norwegian border? Or, presented with the challenge, would they back down, considering the retaliation an attack on an innocent ship might bring?

The Kremlin decision makers found themselves faced with the same gnawing concerns. They expected American submarines to seek out their missile boats under the icepack. Each country had been attempting to ferret out the other's missile threat since the game began twenty-five years before. Their greatest fear had been that the U.S. would send

a ship—just one lone ship—on a mission beyond the Arctic
Circle to test their seriousness. To back down would be to
admit defeat on a major issue they themselves had created.
And the submarine building on the Washington coast was
almost certainly nearing completion. The power of the
weapon wasn't nearly as much a concern as how it might
be utilized. All weapons had eventually been countered or
matched in the history of war, but the method of employ-
ing it was the single unknown that carried the greatest
threat. They knew that Washington had hurried its completion once the Kremlin determined to solidify its arctic
bastion.

In Washington certain hawks favored sending a carrier
battle group into the Norwegian Sea immediately. That
would show the Russians how much the U.S. regarded such
threats. The final decision was reached without consulting
many of the doves, who would opt to trust the Soviet
withdrawal agreement and in return would stay to the
south of the Arctic Circle for the time being. The doves
might have had more influence if American intelligence
hadn't been able to trace a withdrawn Soviet tank battalion
back to a railroad siding no more than twenty miles south
of Murmansk. Since that city was less than a hundred
miles from the Norwegian border, it was less than a two-
hour trip by high speed tank. In the final analysis, testing
the Soviets was necessary, but wiser heads agreed that the
sacrifice should be minimal.

Moscow's decision was no easier. Would the destruction of a single ship, when it crossed that invisible line,
justify the chances of retaliation? They could not back
down, nor could they stand tall before the world for what
most likely would amount to an assassination of a small
ship. The debate within the Kremlin consumed no less
time than that in Washington. When Soviet intelligence
intercepted orders directing an American marine amphibious unit to a point near the Aleutian Islands for transfer,
concern increased. Though the orders made little sense,
the security surrounding the directive was in conjunction
with the orders issued to U.S. submarines destined for the

Arctic. The message was also limited to exactly the same high-level individuals in the U.S. involved with that mysterious submarine.

They had no choice but to sink any American ship that crossed that line.

Carol Petersen climbed up through the aft hatch onto *Imperator*'s deck. She paused for a moment, looking down the vast expanse of rounded black hull before crossing the gangway to the dock with a tired smile on her face. For a woman whom none of the crew would speak to, she still smiled a great deal. Carol decided soon after reporting that it would accomplish nothing to be equally rude. Instead, she had a cheery greeting for everyone and became a favorite among the yard workers. She managed to make coveralls look neat and appealing with her efficient, short brown hair, brown eyes, and high cheekbones; and there was always a trace of makeup, even at the end of a long day. When she smiled, her eyes sparkled.

But she was tired now. The engineers had been conducting manual and visual checks in the after engine spaces and three times she had to override the computer's emergency alarm. She continued to run headlong into invisible lines she couldn't cross and rules that wouldn't bend where she was concerned. Now she learned to her dismay that naval engineers maintained an inbred distrust for safety checks other than their own. There was no possible way she could convince them that the master computer, Caesar, was as closely in touch with their machinery as they were—for twenty-four tireless hours a day and with an unerring capability of reporting the tiniest flaw, one unnoticeable to a man, within milliseconds.

She would be going to sea in this behemoth and she relished the idea, especially since she was breaking another tradition. She could accept the shunning now, as long as the men would eventually come to realize one inevitable fact. That neither *Imperator* nor Snow nor the crew could get along without her.

• • •

In the weeks that followed, the final events careened irretrievably into place. A small guided-missile frigate in the reserve force was dispatched toward the Arctic Circle. Admiral Andy Reed designated the rendezvous point for the screening group of submarines that would eventually join *Imperator*. She possessed the firepower of a carrier battle group and was capable of landing marines on the north coast of Norway if that became a necessity.

Admiral Abe Danilov, much to his dismay, received final orders that would send him away from his Anna. He would take command of a hunter/killer group of attack submarines in Polyarnyy. It was a foregone conclusion that the American submarine preparing to depart the Washington coast would transit the Arctic Ocean for Europe's Northern Flank, and Danilov was considered the best man to intercept it. Before his departure, he was called into the office of the commander in chief of the Soviet Navy. His old friend reviewed the behind-the-scenes negotiations of the past few weeks, emphasizing their futility. Now, the preservation of the Arctic as a Soviet domain for their ballistic-missile force appeared to rest on Abe Danilov's shoulders.

Fahrion rolled sharply to starboard, her bow plunging deep into the Atlantic. Green water swept back over the deck of the little guided missile frigate, swirling about her launcher before the high sharp angles of her bow reappeared. The ship shuddered, rising against tons of water gullying back on either side of the deckhouse. Heavy spray leaped to the pilothouse windows. The miserable, freezing lookouts, drenched within seconds of stepping out to the open bridge, ducked heads as the water lashed about them.

"Combat has a bearing on that contact, Captain." The voice of the officer of the deck—the OOD—was steady. "That type of signal belongs on those big Russian bombers, but they're jamming us like hell."

"No other signals yet?" the captain inquired casually. He had told his officers that their training mission had been altered by Washington, that they had been designated for a special mission that could be hazardous. But he could tell them nothing beyond that. The original Soviet warning concerning the frigate's voyage had been delivered verbally to the White House by the Soviet ambassador—*Fahrion* must reverse course. There had been no public dissemination of the threat in either Washington or Moscow. The Kremlin would not announce that they were about to annihilate a sacrificial cow in international waters any more than Washington would admit that the ship's fate might already have been sealed without opening it up for debate on Capitol Hill. Soviet resolve had to be tested. Both sides were well aware of that. The threat had not been an idle one. Its impact on superpower strategy could be immense.

"Nothing yet, Captain. Should they be searching any particular band?"

The captain had looked it up the night before in the privacy of his sea cabin. "J-band. Just tell them to search J-band for now."

When the OOD relayed the request to combat, he overheard a voice in the background mutter that J-band was missile-homing radar. But he said nothing to the captain. The watch standers held on tightly as *Fahrion* rolled heavily from side to side, continuing to dig her bow deep into the trough before shaking the water off like a puppy.

For the captain, each minute grew more agonizing as he awaited the inevitable. Everything that he could possibly do to protect his ship had been done in drills the previous day. There was little defense available to these ships, but he'd promised himself that everything in his power would be attempted to get his crew and himself home safely to their families. This cruise had begun innocently enough as an annual two weeks at sea, a training period for reservists. There had been no bands or parades as they pulled away from the pier at Newport. Though a training cruise was odd this time of year, most of them had been doing this for years and it was an enjoyable change from civilian life.

"Captain." A voice from combat echoed out of the speaker above his head. "We have contact with a J-band radar . . . it's steady." There was a pause. "Captain, it appears to be a homing device . . . but the book says what we have seems to be a Soviet missile. I'm checking the book again."

The captain raced for the general quarters alarm himself, pressing down the ship's PA button at the same time. "Damage Control, this is the captain," he shouted breathlessly. "Prepare for missile attack . . . prepare for missile attack." His voice echoed throughout the ship to a stunned crew before it was drowned out by the general alarm.

There was so little time. The AS-6 missile would climb steeply to achieve cruise level and would travel at Mach 3 before diving sharply at its target. It was difficult to pick up on radar, even harder to defend against. And *Fahrion*'s only real defense was her Phalanx Gatling gun, a last-ditch effort when the missile was already plunging downward.

"High-speed contact!" The frantic voice echoed through the bridge speaker. "Intermittent . . . there's no aircraft like that."

The captain blanked out the last words from combat. He was already giving orders to his weapons officer to activate *Phalanx*. That meant that when the Gatling gun's fire-control radar locked on the missile—if it ever did—it would spew heavy bullets at more than five tons of high-speed missile dropping down on them. The intent was to destroy a warhead containing more than eleven hundred pounds of high explosive—if the bullets could penetrate it.

"I have a second contact . . . slightly behind the first." *Fahrion*'s captain silently noted to himself that there was one *Phalanx* and two missiles now targeted on his ship.

"Fire chaff . . ." Time seemed to stop until the chaff canisters burst in a final effort to decoy the oncoming missiles. With an ear-splitting chatter, *Phalanx* automatically opened fire. An overwhelming din filled the pilothouse, silencing any last thoughts.

The first missile plunged through the pilothouse, detonating a split second later on the deck underneath. There was a flash, but no one in the pilothouse heard the sound for the entire forward deckhouse lifted into the air, disintegrating. Seconds later, the other missile plunged into the engineering spaces. That blast split *Fahrion* in two.

Just beyond the Arctic Circle, icy, stormy waters ripped at the burning remnants of *Fahrion*. The bow section had drifted a few hundred yards from the stern before turning turtle. After the disintegration of the entire superstructure, there was little left to identify it as part of a once-proud guided-missile frigate. The after section lit up in a brilliant gout of flame as the final storage tank for the helicopter's avgas exploded. Diesel fuel spread in an ugly, brown patina to merge with the foamy North Atlantic. Great rollers tore at the exposed engine room. Here and there desperate survivors struggled for a handhold in the wreckage. There were few of them, and their numbers dwindled rapidly as the cold, gray sea claimed them one by one until there was no longer any sign of life.

In the command post deep within the Pentagon, electronic devices aboard a satellite continued to record the scene. A large screen displayed the death throes of the little frigate and her crew with a clarity that froze the soul. Since the detonation of the first missile within her superstructure, not a word had been uttered by the assembled officers. The awesome split-second power of the cruise missile left them stunned. More than two hundred men had vanished before their eyes.

The unanimous decision at this point was no different than the one made hours earlier in Moscow. There was no turning back.

— 2 —

LUCY REED WAS a perfect admiral's wife. "One of a kind" was the cliché many of Andy's seniors often used with a trace of envy. The overlying reason she understood her husband so well rested with the fact that she was a navy brat. When her father retired as an admiral, he chose to settle near Annapolis. It was there she met Andy. The old man had also been one of the early pioneers in submarines and that allowed her to understand what drew her soon-to-be husband to the boats.

For as long as Lucy could remember, even before she ever attended her first day of school, moving had been a regular part of her life. New orders meant new friends, new schools, and a different part of the United States (sometimes even another country) to get accustomed to. Unlike her mother, she thrived on the vagabond life. She eventually became more independent than her big brothers. As she grew older, Lucy found that foreign languages came easily to her and she received good grades regardless of the language used in the classroom. It was easy to understand why she was the apple of her father's eye. What the old man also appreciated was her ability to understand when he packed his bags to be away for long periods of time. Eventually, though, her mother grew more distant with each new set of orders. She dreaded the family's making another move or her husband's being away for an extended period. The result was that Lucy began to organize the others. By the time the children were ready to leave home, Lucy ran the family while Lucy's mother drank. "Navy brat" had pleasant connotations when anyone referred to Lucy.

When she married Andy Reed soon after his graduation from the academy, the young ensign was the envy of the men who knew Lucy's father well. It was a marriage they all predicted would last because she understood the life. When Andy was accepted for sub school, it was predicted that Lucy would help to make his career. Not only was the navy life ingrained in her soul, she possessed that pert, fresh look—petite, short hair, constant smile, the consummate ensign's wife.

Near the end of his final day in Washington before taking command of *Imperator*'s screening group, Andy Reed called Lucy. "I'm going to be a little late, honey . . . and it looks like I might have to be gone for a while."

She paused momentarily to get rid of the catch in her voice. She'd been following the progress of negotiations with the Russians each day in the *Post*, and she knew the reports were too optimistic, hollow, without a sound basis. She sensed that her suspicions were correct the past few weeks whenever she discussed them with Andy. He'd been arriving home later each night recently and that made her even more skeptical about the news behind the headlines.

"Gone a long time?" she responded.

"Hard to tell. Could be. I really can't be sure."

"Want me to pack a suitcase for you?" Lucy had always packed for her husband since the first day he'd gone to sea. There were times that he would be awakened in the middle of the night and would have gone with only the clothes on his back if she hadn't prepared his suitcase for him.

"That would be great, honey."

"Civilian clothes, too?"

"No, just uniforms—mostly work type."

"I bought you some new work clothes last week. Couldn't get the stains out of the old ones anymore. Or are you going to insist on a couple of sets of the old stuff?"

"The old ones might be more comfortable, I guess."

"Off to sea again," she stated flatly. "Okay, I know exactly what to pack, old fellow. Been doing it for years. How about dinner? Can you spare a couple of hours for the old lady before you're off to see the wizard"

"You know I wouldn't miss that." Reed had missed exactly one dinner with his wife before any extended deployment and that had only been because she'd been rushed off to the hospital to give birth. When he returned home on that only night, he found a note containing the instructions for how long he should keep the meat loaf in the oven. The other kids had the table set when he arrived.

"You want the same old chateaubriand, or will you put up with some meat loaf and macaroni and cheese?" Teasing him with that same question was part of their pattern.

"I'll take the latter, if it's all the same to you." His answer never varied. It was his favorite dinner.

"Sometime you're going to surprise me and ask for the beef . . . and I won't know what to do with it." Her voice almost cracked again. Their conversation never failed to follow the same track whenever the time came for him to leave. But somehow this time seemed so different. She was scared. Too much was left unsaid, both by the papers and the government—and her husband could be trusted never to leak a word about what he was involved with at any time.

"I'll call when I'm ready to leave, hon. Don't forget the jug of red."

"Never have yet." Lucy hung up before she heard his last words. "Bye for now," she whispered to herself. He would call just before he left the office; he always did. That was the signal to slip the meat loaf in the oven. Andy never had a drink before leaving for sea—just the bottle of wine they would share.

• • •

Andy Reed smiled across the table and raised his wine-glass in a toast to the woman he was sure looked no different than the day they were married. He could sense from the way Lucy had been talking that she knew he was going off for much more than an exercise. But she'd never cried or complained before. He knew she wouldn't start now. "I think it should be noted that the finest meat loaf chef in the entire fifty states still holds her title. Since I can't tell the whole world about it right now, would this simple compliment do?"

She raised her glass, touching his gently, and they drank, looking into each other's eyes. Another tradition. He emptied the last of the bottle in their glasses. "I'll accept the compliment. Want me to send the recipe along so you can have it at sea?"

"It wouldn't be the same. No candlelight, no wine, different atmosphere somehow. And I don't think we'll be too excited about the menus." He took a deep breath, exhaling slowly. "You know, you've been a good trooper for so long, I'm going to have to take you on a vacation soon." He paused, then added, "Maybe we're both getting a little old for these things. Think I ought to get out of this racket . . . maybe run a charter boat, or something like that?"

"Who do you think you're kidding? I may be on the other side of the fence, but I've been in this submarine business longer than you and I think I can put up with it a few more years. I still don't ask questions and I learned to keep my mouth shut when I was a little girl. We navy broads are a tough group." She stopped what she was saying and looked at him through the candles. "Now I don't know why I was starting off like that. That's the speech I give to the new wives every year." She put a finger to her lips and stared back at him curiously.

"You said that because it's a normal reaction." He reached over and took her hand. "Since you've been a little girl, you also have never asked where we're going in our submarines. Your father couldn't tell you, and I've never been able to either. And it seems to me that at a certain point in your life you ought to be able to either ask and get an answer . . . or go along, too. It's getting a little tougher each time to tell you what a good trooper—I don't even like that word—but you are. Believe me, I know what's going through your head right now, and I wish I could say what I want to.''

"What you're going to do instead is make me cry. And I've never done that before."

"Let's do the dishes then. No one ever cries doing the dishes."

"I do—sometimes after you're gone, I do."

"We should have had another bottle of wine," he concluded uncertainly.

"That really would have done it. Women always cry at times like this if they've had too much wine." She blew out the candles. "I have no intention of crying now if I've been able to hold off for so many years. Let's go to bed."

"I'll help you with the dishes."

"The hell with the dishes. They've waited till morning before. Let's go to bed. Do you need me to spell it out?" She laughed huskily. "You'll be out of the house before anyone's awake so we only have a couple of hours . . . and I plan to have you for some of that time myself. Remember that we have some other very pleasant traditions around this house that I don't plan to let slip." She reached her hand out to him. "Bedtime, my dear. Come on. I've never had to coax you before."

He took her hand. "Not tonight, either."

When Anna Chuikov married the young naval officer, Abram Danilov, in Sebastopol, she had been considered much too good for him. Her father had been a hero during the Great Patriotic War, and it was assumed that the general's daughter would marry a rising army officer at least, if not a wealthy party official. She was everything that Abe Danilov wasn't—tall, graceful, well educated, schooled in the arts, said to be the most beautiful girl in the new society struggling out of the ruins of Moscow after the war.

No one, not even her parents, understood that Anna also had a mind of her own. When she chose to run away to Sebastopol and marry a young naval officer who served in the unknown world of submarines, her own family threatened to disown her. The general even had the dread KGB detain Danilov for hours, but that only set Anna's mind more firmly.

In the ensuing years, the general and his wife learned to accept their daughter's husband. Chuikov even attempted to assert some influence to ensure timely promotions for the naval officer but, to his surprise, that wasn't necessary. Abe Danilov was making it on his own. His mentor was Sergei Gorshkov, soon to be appointed commander in chief of the Soviet Fleet.

While Abe Danilov was rising through the ranks, Anna was unknowingly cultivating the cultural and social strata that would ensure his rise to power. As the years passed, Anna Danilov grew from a lovely, young girl to a radiant woman.

While the other senior officers took advantage of the privileges that came with power—the dachas, the cars, the mistresses—Abe Danilov remained faithful to his wife. He never forgot that he really didn't deserve her when they first met, nor did he fool himself into believing that it was he alone who secured their position in the upper levels of party society. She was the source that kept him in touch with the real world beyond the power structure of the Kremlin. Her love nourished a spirit hidden deep under his military facade until there were two Abe Danilovs. The visible one had spent the past three days in the Kremlin devising a plan to destroy the American mystery submarine before it passed the North Pole. The invisible Abe Danilov had been driven to their city apartment where Anna was spending her final days. On the way, he ordered the driver to stop at one of the private stores reserved for the wealthy and powerful in Moscow. When he came out, the man behind the wheel was sure he had never seen so many beautiful flowers in wintertime Moscow, and certainly never roses like that.

"They're beautiful . . . so beautiful."

Her husband could not be sure whether the tears in her eyes reflected joy or pain.

"But they cost so much, Abe," she added reproachfully. The dark eyes that had danced into his heart more than thirty years ago still sparkled, though now they were red-rimmed and deep, and dark circles lay under them. Then, grimacing, she sat up in bed and smiled broadly, tilting her head to one side just as she had the first day he met her. "I should also say thank you. I can't think of anything nicer, other than your being here. How . . . how long will you be able to stay?" she added hesitantly.

"I'm here. I'm finished with my work. Tomorrow, very early, I have to fly to Murmansk, but I have nowhere else to go before then."

"That's wonderful . . . so wonderful," she concluded wistfully. "I've been looking forward to having you to myself for an evening." Then she remembered, "Oh, but there's so little in the kitchen to eat, Abe. You know, I have no appetite now. So, when Natalya comes in to help me, I tell her not to bring anything. It just goes to waste."

He knew she wasn't eating. Though the drugs for cancer had bloated her body, her nose and cheekbones stood out in sharp contrast to the once elegant face. Her arms and hands were skinny, the flesh hanging in folds. She said that when she ate, the food didn't taste good. And more often now, she couldn't hold it down.

"Well, now, you have nothing to worry about as far as food is concerned," he beamed. "I made another stop on the way. Tonight, I prepare the dinner. I have a bottle of the best vodka—I know you won't have any," he added quickly, "but some for me and some for Natalya tomorrow since she's managed to drink what I left last time—then I have smoked sturgeon and salmon and caviar, and"—he smiled, patting her hand—"some of that trout you used to enjoy so much—"

She interrupted him with a sad smile, placing her hand

on top of his. "If I were the type who believed in prayer, I would thank whatever god I was praying to that Abe Danilov was my husband." She raised her hands to his face and drew him to her, kissing him gently on the lips. She pulled away, almost as if she had been stung, for she realized how cold her own lips must feel to him. But he knew why she had drawn back. It wasn't the first time. He leaned forward, this time holding her face in both hands, and kissed her tenderly.

"There, that's more like a husband and wife should kiss," he said, rising and holding out his hands. "Now, let me help you get up. If we're going to have such a fine meal, you have to put on that new robe I bought you the last time. I'll help you comb your hair, and you can fix up your face."

In his last few visits, a ritual had evolved and Anna accepted it once she understood that he was not revolted by what she had become. There was no difference in his love. He treated her in the same manner, remembered the same personal quirks they both had laughed or complained about over the years. Whenever she claimed that a nurse should be helping her, Danilov's reply was always the same: "I hope that if our lives had been reversed, if it was me who lay in that bed, that you would go to the vodka shop for me, and buy all the little treats I always loved, and hold my hand when I was in pain." And Anna understood there was no effort in his love.

There was a small couch in the other room and he settled her there, wrapping a blanket around her legs. "Would you like me to lay out the fish now?"

"Not yet." She shook her head, the mere thought of the food sending a shiver down her spine. She truly appreciated the gesture to serve her needs but she also knew that he needed some time. She could recognize the exhaustion in his eyes. "Pour yourself some of that good vodka and tell me what you will be doing next. Then we can dine." She forced a smile.

Danilov had been prepared for her response. That, too, had been the same as before. He extracted the bottle from the small freezer that had been given to him because of his rank. He'd placed a snifter in the freezer at the same time and it became opaque on the outside when he set it on the table. Anna reached out slowly and with one finger etched a smile through the frost, exactly as she had done the last few times. He poured a few ounces in the glass and lifted it in her direction. "To you, my dear Anna . . . for your smile . . . and to us. I'll be able to stay longer when I return from this trip." He drained the glass, exhaling powerfully, feeling the frozen liquid burrowing down through his chest.

"How long?" She managed to hold traces of her smile but could feel it fading with that same old nagging fear . . . fear that she might not still be here when he returned.

"No more than ten days. Certainly no longer than that if everything goes right, and I have no reason to think it won't."

Her smile widened. She was sure she could last that long. There was no chance she would be as strong when he returned, but she wanted desperately to be waiting, just as she had each time in the past. Her excitement would bring a resurgence of strength whenever an officer would stop by to assure her that Admiral Danilov had called to tell her when she could expect him. Sometimes, they were old men who still revered the memory of her father, the general. Other times, there were younger naval officers who would go out of their way anytime for Admiral Danilov. They would stop by with a message, then stay to chat. Even one of the political officers, now an admiral himself, would stop by to visit her because he had once served under her husband.

Ten days! She could make it through ten more days! She had already written nine letters for him. While he slept that night, she would finish the tenth.

After three more glasses of vodka, he carefully laid out the foods he had selected. He placed the salmon, trout, caviar, and sturgeon neatly around a large platter to emphasize the colors and the textures, much as she had shown him so many years before. There were thin slices of the black bread made with cocoa that Anna treasured, and a variety of foreign crackers, and some cheeses radiating aromas that still managed to tickle her nose. Then he poured ice-cold champagne into crystal glasses. Anna remarked that she could have done no better herself.

He prepared a plate for her containing tastes of each of the delicacies and set it on her lap with a linen napkin so that she would not have to lean forward. Then he brought her glass to her, balancing it on a tray that he'd fashioned to hold firmly to the arm of the couch by her right hand. This all had become a ritual once she became too ill to venture outside.

As she nibbled halfheartedly at the food she once loved so much, occasionally sipping at the champagne, they talked of the past, the places they'd lived, friends, their children. Their only daughter, married to an engineer living in faraway Irkutsk, had not been back to visit her parents in two years. One son was also a submarine officer, stationed in Petropavlovsk on the Pacific coast. The other was a doctor who seemed to spend more time in special schools than his father thought necessary. The youngsters had their own lives to live and the Danilovs had decided not to trouble them yet. The two older people had been comfortable with themselves. But Abe Danilov had decided to send them each a message before he departed from Moscow. He could see in Anna's eyes that it was necessary for them to return home for a final visit with their mother.

Later that evening when he saw her nodding, he said, "I need a few hours of sleep before I go. I think I'll rest with you." That, too, had become a ritual once she was unable to leave the apartment. He would change into some old pajamas and a bathrobe, and would climb into bed beside her. They would talk for a while, mostly about their absent children, and then they would sleep for a short time.

This night, Danilov fell asleep long before he intended. Anna remained awake with her pain. Besides, she had one more letter to write him. There had to be ten if he was to be away ten days. As he snored peacefully beside her, she slowly penned the tenth letter, the last one before he would return to her.

Abe Danilov was unable to sleep for long periods. Three hours later he was dressed in a fresh uniform, unaware that Anna had not slept. As soon as she finished her letter, she had been satisfied to cradle his head on her shoulder. Just to have him asleep beside her, she could almost forget the pain. He'd awoken in her grasp.

When he slipped his arms through the sleeves of his greatcoat, she said softly, "Take these with you." She extended the packet tied with a red ribbon. "You said you would be gone for ten days, I have written you a letter for each of them. So, you see, you have to be back before the eleventh day."

Danilov smiled. "All right. I see I have no choice. I wouldn't know what to do with myself after the last one. I'll be back in ten days, and we'll dine again in the other room. The menu will be the same if that's fine with you."

She nodded. "I'll look forward to it."

He moved to the side of the bed and bent down to kiss her. His warm lips touched her cold ones briefly, then held them longer a second time while he stroked her cheek. "Ten days," he repeated as he stood erect. Then he was gone. Anna Danilov's eyes glistened with tears of love as she heard the door shut behind him. Abe Danilov's were dry until the door was closed. Then there was one deep, gulping sob of loneliness as he descended the dark stairs.

3

VICTOR ULANOFF'S DEAD eyes seemed fixed on a star light years way, twinkling brightly down on the Pacific coastline of Washington. With the inherent realization that it was too late, which was simultaneous with the knife slashing across his throat, Ulanoff had accepted his fate. He had been staring in wonder through the night binoculars that Abe Danilov had entrusted to him a few short weeks before. Just as the admiral claimed, they were turning night into day.

Until moments before, about the time the sensor under his upper arm had pulsed to tell him that the satellite was recording, Ulanoff had been extremely careful. As a matter of fact, he had survived longer than any of the others who had been sent out to infiltrate the *Imperator* project. But the emergence of the object in question, *Imperator* herself, was so exciting that his guard had dropped for just long enough. Watching that immense shape emerging from its pen would hypnotize any man . . . and it had.

It was not a submarine pen in the sense of the old covered piers built in the past to protect submarines. To anyone—whether they were studying a satellite picture accurate to six inches, or even walking across what appeared to the naked eye to be a part of the land jutting out into a small bay on the Pacific Ocean—this was solid land, scrub brush near the water's edge, apparently farmed recently inland. Waves broke over the rocks and whispered on the sand just as they had seemingly done for hundreds of thousands of years. It was idyllic, and peaceful.

But nothing can escape the space lenses of the intelligence community for long, and the formation of this peninsula encouraged the attention of a number of Soviet agents, though the disappearances of so many of them failed to create much concern in the Kremlin at first. That is—until it was pointed out that too many of those inserted into the West Coast defense industry were simply dissolving into thin air. The fact that the Americans had penetrated one of their most deeply imbedded spy rings was not nearly as disturbing as the curious reason so many agents were vanishing.

The Americans normally attended to concentrated infiltration by ferreting out the leaders, tracing the source, producing ugly trials, or initiating exchanges for some of their own. But this time it was so different. The agents simply disappeared without a trace. Occasionally, a job could be botched and a Russian agent could turn up very dead with accompanying publicity. Both sides accepted that. But what was occurring now was extermination, a solution not normally directed by the Americans. So there was reason to find out exactly what had altered their reaction. There had to be something big somewhere on their Pacific Coast, and it was just a matter of time until the Russians found out what.

In the meantime, the list of Soviet agents who simply disappeared grew longer, and the Kremlin became more impatient—with the lack of intelligence, not with the number of agents lost in the line of duty.

In the end, Kovschenko's persistence did pay off. The *Imperator* Project was discovered, though getting the details took a bit longer. The Kremlin anticipated a submarine well before Kovschenko confirmed its existence by his unfortunate demise.

Now, on his last night on earth, Ulanoff had been literally hypnotized by the sight of *Imperator* as she slipped from her pen into the dark, cold Pacific. The people who designed the binoculars for Danilov claimed they turned night into day. That wasn't quite true, especially when the object of curiosity was an immense, black-hulled submarine. The best way to place *Imperator* in perspective was by watching the sailors at their stations on her hull. What Ulanoff had seen was a vast expanse of low black submarine, slithering like a snake emerging from a log. The sail was well back on the hull—an awesome sight. The submarine was longer than an aircraft carrier, certainly wider at the waterline, and deeper by far between keel and top of deck . . . and there was so much that he could imagine but couldn't see.

As the stern of *Imperator* emerged completely from the pen, Ulanoff had swung his binoculars all the way back up to the bow to record the impressions of this craft permanently in his mind—which was when he felt the cold steel across his throat. There hadn't been a sound—or if there was, he was too involved in *Imperator* to hear it—just the hand from behind lifting his chin at the same time the blade slicked through his exposed neck.

In the end, Ulanoff was the only Russian ever to have seen the submarine. But the sight had also been recorded from above by an infrared-equipped satellite, and the signals from that inspection had been transmitted instantly back to Admiral Abe Danilov at the Soviet arctic base of Polyarnyy.

The voice persisted until it became almost part of Danilov's consciousness. "Admiral . . . Admiral Danilov . . ." The sailor would never think of actually touching the man. That was not only rude and ill-mannered, it would be considered intemperate by his seniors. However, the sailor had been with Danilov long enough to know his habits and he could tell that the man was slowly, very slowly this time, bringing himself back to a conscious state. "Admiral, we have satellite confirmation that she's underway now." The eyes flicked open, staring up with an intensity that would have shaken any man who did not know Danilov's habits.

Abe Danilov's subconscious fumbled with the distant voice, momentarily rejected it, then reached out instinctively as the sound became more insistent. His sleep had been heavy, with no dreaming. There was hardly a man who could achieve that depth of relaxation, almost trance-like, so quickly. Whenever he recognized approaching exhaustion, Danilov simply lay down on his office sofa fully clothed, arms across his chest, and sank into a deep, satisfying sleep. But coming out of that self-induced hypnosis was more difficult.

"How long ago?" There had been no movement; the arms remained folded across his chest, but the eyes burned now with an inner strength.

"No more than ten minutes, Admiral. The duty officer confirmed the infrared readings with one of the technicians first. No doubt about it, Admiral. . . she's underway on nuclear power."

With a sigh, Danilov stretched and eased into a sitting position on the edge of the leather sofa, raising his arms over his head and yawning deeply. "Nuclear power," he murmured. "I told them it would be . . . no doubt about it when you're sure of marine shipments up there. It had to be." He glanced at his watch. "They got underway in the dark, I see."

"Yes, sir. It's sometime after midnight on the American Pacific Coast."

"And Ulanoff, have we heard anything from him?"

"No contact, Admiral."

"Thank you. I'm awake now." He looked up and half smiled. "I won't fall back asleep. I promise." He stretched again. "Not now, not when she's finally underway. Ask the duty officer to try to raise Ulanoff again." The admiral stood and waved his hand to dismiss the other.

He splashed cold water on his face in the tiny head, and when he looked up to observe still baggy eyes, he did it again. He also accepted the improbability of anyone getting in touch with Ulanoff. Even drawing his last breath, Ulanoff would have attempted contact if there was a chance. As far as Danilov was concerned, it was quite probable that he was dead, just like all the others who had in any way been involved in what he had finally learned was the *Imperator* Project.

This must be similar to being born again, Snow mused in wonder. The immense gates leading to "the world"—that's what they eventually called everything beyond the submarine pen that had been their home for so long—had opened soundlessly after the pumps brought internal water level equal with the Pacific Ocean. With small tugs cautiously hovering on either side of the bow, *Imperator* had eased slowly from underneath her camouflaged land canopy into the night ocean.

Snow muttered the word "forever" (mostly to himself) because it seemed an eternity from the time the sailors on the bow first peered up at the night sky until he would see it. A thousand feet after those first sailors arched their heads back to search for stars, *Imperator*'s bridge finally inched into the open with a few hundred more feet of stern still to follow.

Once they were in the open and the dimmed lights in the cavern behind no longer cast a glow over the bridge, Snow removed his red night goggles and bent his own head back to marvel at the stars.

"Captain." The speaker on the bulkhead murmured quietly. "This is Carol Petersen. Permission to come to the bridge?"

"Permission granted." Glancing over his shoulder, he saw that the fishbowl's doors had swung shut. They would already be pumping the water out. *Imperator* would not return, would no longer remain a secret. It was time to begin construction of her sister. As the ship's foreman commented when they shook hands—"The king is dead, long live the king"—it was time for new life. *Imperator* was now part of another world.

The soft whisper of elevator doors behind him heralded Carol Petersen's arrival. Turning, Snow watched her step from the faint, red glow of the elevator compartment onto the bridge. The doors closed with a hiss and the elevator was on its way again, perhaps returning the full twelve decks where Carol had just been—the engineering guidance center.

"I take it Caesar has decided you're not needed," Snow commented as she climbed up to the piloting wing beside him.

"Caesar never did need me," she answered.

In every sea trial over the past three months, though *Imperator* never once left the fishbowl, the computer had managed the reactor/engineering complex and had yet to miss a beat. "I had to be there, just to watch it operate under actual conditions." She laughed quietly. "I never quite believed it myself, you know. I understand it, but it's still hard to believe."

"Don't for a minute imagine that I'll ever accept it completely," Snow remarked with a forced laugh. "Ships and men belong together." The tinge of bitterness in his voice was evident.

"They do. I agree. But this is a little too much ship for one man, I'd say."

Snow peered out at the sailors working on the smooth, wide bow. They were dim, unidentifiable figures a fifth of a mile away. He raised the night binoculars to his eyes and watched as they stowed the port gear in compartments along the outer hull. His brain silently acknowledged Carol's remark, agreed it was much too much ship, but his heart said *Imperator* was his and he could handle her.

At the sound of three soft beeping sounds from his parka pocket, he removed a compact two-way radio and responded, "This is Snow."

"Kimmelman here, Captain. I was right again. You owe me a sawbuck when you get back." It was the security chief on shore.

"No lights, huh?"

"No way. One Victor Ulanoff is resting very comforta-

bly at my feet . . . and you were right about the satellite
. . . infrared. I found the instrument package under his
arm. It told him when the eye had contact with you."
When Kimmelman confirmed the satellite waiting above
them, there was no doubt in Snow's or anyone's mind that
it was infrared. It was just waiting for *Imperator* to emerge,
ready to confirm the heat from her reactor.

Kimmelman couldn't resist kidding Snow one last time.
The captain had requested a call from shore by blinking
light if they found Ulanoff where they expected him. But
Kimmelman had laughed out loud and said the satellite
would easily record the light, too. Why tell the people
back in the Kremlin that we knew that they knew that . . .
he went on and on laughing. Eventually Snow had laughed
with him.

"The sawbuck is yours, Sidney. Consider it done. Think
I've been radiating long enough?"

"I think they'll love you in Moscow, Captain."

Snow turned to the woman at his left. "Time for the
heat shields, Carol. Maybe they'll think we're going under." He held the radio to his mouth. "Done, Sidney.
We've wrapped her up. Out."

Snow could see whitecaps lapping either side of the
black hull below the bridge, but there was no sense of
motion aboard the submarine. It would take one huge
storm to create any sea motion on *Imperator*. He could
hear the muffled voices as Carol Petersen conversed with
the computer room. It was his ship—yet was it really too
much for one man? He'd given the order, but it was her
computer seeing that it was carried out. A chill crept down
his back as he once again experienced that feeling—which
of them was more powerful?

"She's all zipped up, Captain. They might be able to
pick them up on infrared." She gestured toward the sailors
still working on the main deck. "But there's no sign of
heat from the ship now."

"Let them try to figure that one out," he responded,
looking up as if he could pick out the tiny satellite hanging

more than a hundred miles above. "We're going to wink out . . . just like a star."

"Just like a star," she echoed. They were silent, both imagining more than twelve hundred feet of submarine suddenly winking out like a star. That was but one of *Imperator*'s tricks, and there were so many more to come. It was a game of "catch me if you can," and Snow had deliberately given the first signal that he was ready to start the game. Soviet directives had also been intercepted the past few weeks. He knew who Abe Danilov was and he understood approximately what the Russian's orders would be. One of the critical factors of this cruise, the only one Admiral Reed had impressed on everyone, was that the transit be completed—regardless. That was the single, vital message that *Imperator* could send to the world—that the oceans and the meaning of seapower had changed forever. And that included defeating everything the Kremlin could do to sink her.

Abe Danilov glanced disinterestedly at the infrared prints, then tossed them on the table. It was all new and exciting to this watch section but it was of little import to him. It simply confirmed what he'd projected about *Imperator*, including her ability to effect heat shielding. Damn her captain! He'd dangled a teaser . . . on purpose . . . just to let Danilov and his superiors know there were to be more surprises. They're still one step ahead of us, Danilov thought . . . and arrogant as hell.

His staff officers, occupied with the mundane, made every effort to look busy. They awaited his reaction, never anticipating that his anger at the American captain would be directed at them. Then a chain of orders emerged, his voice increasing in pitch, and he later decided his reaction had been as nebulous as their efforts. His senior staff officer, Captain First Rank Sergoff, was once again plotting *Imperator*'s course, painstakingly laying out the same track that Danilov had done himself too many times.

"What have you found, Sergoff, that has changed radically since we laid out that track yesterday?" His voice dripped with sarcasm as his thoughts drifted back to the previous days. He had not wanted to leave Anna in Moscow.

"I beg your pardon, Admiral," Sergoff said, lost for a moment, "I'm not altering their course, sir . . . just determining their time of arrival off Seward Peninsula now that we have a departure time."

"And?" Danilov demanded. His telltale eyebrows were once again menacing those about him.

Sergoff considered all this as the admiral waited for an answer. The knit eyebrows reminded him for the thousandth time that Danilov utilized his resemblance to Brezhnev with tremendous effect. Sergoff was younger, taller, much better proportioned, more striking in uniform, and he'd been with Danilov for years—but he still reacted with awe to his senior's temper. Now, he responded to Danilov's question with a stuttered, "I . . . I'm not sure . . . sir. I'm still working on her speed of advance through the Bering Sea. You said that with the ice still heavy this time of year, she'd probably be reduced to a speed of . . ." It was spring and the ice was breaking up.

"Between eight to twelve knots, Captain," Danilov said, his expression changing to one of amusement. "And I believe we agreed to use the higher speed since we want to be waiting for her if she survives that long—rather than trying to catch up," he added nastily.

There was no point in discussing details with the admiral in that mood, Sergoff concluded, and returned to his careful plotting. There was no damned submarine with a draft of almost a hundred feet that was going to go charging through ice-clogged waters in depths that were sometimes only twenty feet below her keel!

Danilov moved about the room, a caged animal antagonizing each of his staff until he, himself, understood what he was doing: subconsciously blaming them for Anna's illness. Then, gruffly, with just a tinge of apology in his voice, he remarked for all their benefit, "Enough. There is no point in all this. It is my fault that we are waiting here." So he folded his huge arms across his chest. "Sergoff, we will have a staff meeting with the commanding officers, executive officers, and political officers of each submarine in twenty minutes at the officers' mess alongside *Seratov*. All officers to be ready for sea.'' They'd packed their duffels days before in anticipation of the great hunt. ''And, Sergoff, have each commander prepared to get underway within twenty-four hours. I expect to arrive at our Chukchi Sea station at least a day before they get to the strait.''

Sergoff knew there was no real reason for one more briefing, but he also understood that Admiral Danilov grabbed at every opportunity to enhance morale in each operation he commanded. And this was to be the most vital of all. *Seratov* and the two other submarines would be instantly ready. None of their crews had been ashore for the past seventy-two hours. Their reactors had been on thirty-minute standby. Supplies had been replenished each day they remained at the pier waiting for the admiral's orders. After so many hours of inaction, he decided Danilov was correct. Even if they'd allow the men off the submarines, there was little to do around the naval base at Polyarnyy except to get drunk. A pep talk would rekindle spirits that might have dwindled with the long wait.

When the ever alert Sergoff called for a sailor to take the admiral's duffel to *Seratov*, Danilov refused. There was one key element to the start of every great adventure, and that was when Abe Danilov hoisted his seabag over his shoulder and carried it himself down the pier to the boat that would be his home during the cruise. There would be sailors who might disagree with him, but Danilov had prized that little bit of tradition since he boarded his first sub more than thirty years before.

When the admiral once again emerged from his tiny quarters behind the operations room, looking even more the bear in his greatcoat, he was smiling. The gruff voice was replaced by happy laughter as he led them into the freezing, snow-filled arctic night of Polyarnyy base, his seabag balanced on his shoulder with one hand. His voice howled beyond the ice crystals that snapped at their faces as they grudgingly followed their leader down the main street of the base and out to the pier.

Seratov's outline hardened into evil, low sleekness as they waded through the soft, sculptured drifts. She would be Danilov's flagship. Her sisters, partially hidden alongside, were *Smolensk* and *Novgorod*. Each of these submarines was known to run faster and dive deeper than any undersea craft yet designed. The term "hunter/killer" applied well to Danilov's tiny armada.

A long, single story building along the pier served as both quarters and messing area for submarine officers in port. It was here that the admiral chose to give his inspirational talk to the officers who would sail with him. There was no doubt in any man's mind about their mission. But the admiral had his own way of transmitting enthusiasm to his subordinates so they might react in a manner entirely satisfactory to him. It was much more than morale building. It was molding men to sacrifice more than they ever imagined in order to carry our their orders—in this case, Abe Danilov's orders.

When the speeches were over and toasts had been drunk to their mission, Abe Danilov was the first one out the door, his duffel slung over his shoulder. He stepped out into the snowy night, feeling the wind drive the snow into his face, and led his men to their vessels. To each of them, this great bear of a man was the ideal leader for this mission.

Once Abe Danilov had unpacked his seabag and neatly stowed his gear as only he could do it, he lay back on his bunk and read Anna's first letter carefully. It brought him back to his early days as a junior lieutenant in Sebastopol.

It was 1960. Anna Chuikov had run away to marry him, though her family, especially her father, did everything possible to stop her. The general even threatened to shoot anyone who helped them. They'd expected her to marry the son of someone important—a government official, or perhaps the son of a war hero—anyone but this man. General Chuikov was sure that Abe Danilov was a Jew.

He took advantage of old contacts to send the KGB after the young naval officer.

Danilov's submarine was tied up at the pier and he was on watch when they came. They appeared in civilian clothes but he knew who they were as they came down the dock because a friend at the gates had called to warn him. Even though he was watch officer on the quarterdeck, they simply stalked aboard, established his identity, then handcuffed him. One of the sailors ran for the captain, who was furious but could do nothing about it. Everyone feared the KGB for none had forgotten the violent purges of their NKVD forebears.

When Anna came down to the submarine at the end of the day, the captain explained that Danilov had been taken away. He was afraid to contact anyone, claiming he didn't know anyone to call. Anna quietly asked him to take her to the building where the phones were because she wouldn't have to wait in line if the captain of a submarine was there.

Her father raged. Her mother said later that she never remembered him that angry, even during the war. But Anna Chuikov had inherited her temper from her father. It was the first time she had ever talked to him like that, and she claimed later that if the general could have seen her face, he would have given in more quickly.

She often reminded her husband in the ensuing years that she never minded that the general didn't want her to marry Danilov. That was Chuikov's right. But the idea that he would send those horrible people to haul her fiancee away like a common thug was too much. She never knew what convinced the old man—maybe that she would never speak to him again, maybe that she threatened to kill herself. The story mellowed so much over the years that eventually she wasn't sure she ever said that. But the general finally gave in and Danilov was freed in a couple of hours.

Admiral Gorshkov, Abe Danilov's mentor since his early days in higher naval school, came down from Moscow to the wedding. There was no one else Anna knew except for some of his navy friends. But the admiral treated her as if she was the finest woman in Russia—she would never forget that. Gorshkov, a naval hero in the Great Patriotic War, had just been awarded the Order of Lenin by Khruschev, and he wore it proudly during the ceremony when he brought Anna down the aisle. When the KGB saw that, the Danilovs were never troubled again.

As Danilov now lay in his bunk, savoring that first letter she had given him, he knew more than ever how much he owed to that woman. And now she was dying. . . .

The stars were as crisp and cold as night itself. Hal Snow cherished being alone with the sea at these rare moments. Such isolation enhanced the affinity between a man and his vessel, and there were so few opportunities. Now, solitary and at peace with himself, he intended to savor each moment. In a way, as he luxuriated in this rare moment of serenity, he also felt a sense of wonder at being the commander of a vessel designed to be one of man's most feared weapons.

But the latter feeling passed quickly. Most of his mature life had been spent aboard other such weapons. Although Snow had commanded attack submarines, he'd also done his time on the guided-missile boats, where there had never been any opportunity to experience this feeling. They dived immediately on leaving port, transited to an assigned position, and surfaced only at the end of a patrol. There had been a kind of rapport between him and his boats then, but it had been more a relationship with a single objective—his missiles.

The link between Snow and the stars, as close to spiritual as he would ever come, was broken by a blinking light on the nearby console. The elevator was about to arrive on the bridge. It would be Carol Petersen. When he mentioned fifteen minutes before how good coffee would taste in the crisp sea air, she insisted on bringing back some mugs since it was time anyway for one of her instrument checks.

She stepped out of the red dimness of the elevator, extending an oversized mug as she moved next to him. "Be careful. Still hot as hell . . . insulated mugs. I already burned my tongue."

"Thanks," he replied, his voice muted. It seemed a sin of some kind to talk too loudly when only the soft splashing of the whitecaps broke the still air. There was no sound from *Imperator*. She was as silent as the heavens. "See those stars up there." He pointed a finger to the northwest.

"Not quite. My night vision's still weak." She strained to look beyond his finger.

"You should have been wearing your night goggles."

"I was. But I had to take them off to read the instruments."

"Can we still be seen from up there?" His head arched back to look straight up above them.

"Just a little. We copied everything transmitted by their satellite from the time we got underway. The shield's almost a hundred percent effective. We picked up the men on the bow until everything was stowed. Now, other than you, everything seems to be secure. You stand out like a beacon."

"Me?"

"That's correct, Captain." She laughed lightly. "One thing no one seemed to think about was shielded clothing on the bridge. No satellite's sophisticated enough to pick up a nose peeking out from under the visor of a cap . . . or your icy breath," she added, noticing the frosty vapor as they talked.

"We could run on the surface at night with no one on the bridge, and no satellite could—"

"But if something was looking for temperature changes on the ocean surface, we'd sure as hell be making it."

For Snow, the allure of man and nature at sea was fast disappearing. Man and his technology would deny one of the last of his pleasures. Hal Snow had agreed to come back to command *Imperator* because he was searching for nights like this one. His final command in the regular navy had been a Trident submarine, and he retired when new orders would send him ashore. There was no way he'd ever have become an admiral. Both he and the senior officers in Washington knew he wasn't cut out to plan strategy while other men took the ships to sea.

Snow was a maverick, and made everything much simpler for many of his friends when he put in his retirement papers. None of them would have to feel guilty about his being passed over for promotion.

Snow gulped down the last of his coffee, then checked his watch. "I hate to say it," he sighed, "but it's about time to take her down." It was necessary to exercise the ship as she had been designed. *Imperator* would be in her natural element—submerged.

Peering toward Carol in the darkness, he remembered rather than perceived her features. She was attractive, not the most beautiful woman he'd ever known, but appealing enough when he considered she was a hell of a lot smarter than he was. That was the guideline he'd always utilized to consider women, and the fact that she was still interesting, regardless of her brains, had bothered him. When he realized she was a highly competent scientist, it was even more difficult to acknowledge a feminine charm that hadn't been overwhelmed by her intelligence. With two divorces behind him, and a mostly jaded outlook toward women in general, Snow found it doubly hard to acknowledge Carol Petersen.

"If you don't mind," she answered, "I'd prefer to stay on the bridge for the time being. Couple more readings I need to check, and besides, *Imperator* can't submerge with me still up here."

"Is that what you want to check?"

"Partially. A few other things, too. They worked in the fishbowl. I just want to see if a few hours of open ocean steaming has any effect on them."

"All right. I'll follow through with the normal dive procedures." Without another word, Snow was gone.

Carol Petersen had the unique position as the navy's only seagoing computer controls officer without ever having spent a day in the U.S. Navy. There had been arguments—strong, intemperate ones—that a woman never had, and never would, belong on a submarine. The consortium decided otherwise.

Her final check on the command control console tying the bridge to the main computer would confirm Caesar's ability to report readiness for diving of the entire vessel to the captain. Turning up the soft background light on the console, she pressed a variety of buttons. The results were instant responses to her queries. Then she turned to the blank screen at one side. Taking a pencillike instrument from her pocket, she printed a single word on the screen— SONAR. Her word glowed briefly before fading from the screen. It was replaced by a series of printed reports on the status of each of the many sonars installed on *Imperator*. Satisfied, she printed another word—DIVE. Again the screen glowed with a status report of current conditions throughout *Imperator*. Then Snow ordered preparations for diving. She watched as the reports began to change. The computer was now informing her as conditions altered around the ship. The navy had reluctantly sent her to sea on an attack sub to better understand the normal daily routine—she'd adapted as well as any man!

Every condition imaginable had been simulated in the fishbowl to ensure that *Imperator* avoided probable detection by going out on sea trials. The sub had functioned superbly then and there was no difference now.

A metallic voice rang across the bridge. "*Imperator* is about to submerge. It is impossible to complete all preparations as long as the bridge is occupied. Would you be so kind as to go below to the control room."

Carol smiled. That was the final test. Caesar was designed to sense human beings in any section of the ship, and a fail-safe mechanism halted diving preparations as long as anyone remained on the bridge. Snow's voice came through another speaker: "Carol, we've stopped the countdown for diving . . . or rather your friendly computer has. Would you care to join us?"

She depressed a button on the console. "I'm on the way." Another button dropped a waterproof shield over the console. She turned just as the elevator door slid open. Caesar had ordered the elevator to the bridge.

Stepping out into the control room two decks below, Carol was immediately fascinated by the passivity that existed before *Imperator*'s first dive. Though the submarine had been tested interminably through every possible simulation, never before had she actually dipped her wide nose below the waves. While the computer was programmed to coordinate the entire evolution, Snow's early decision was to take her down himself for the first time—to satisfy his own ego if nothing else.

Snow grinned at her from the diving officer's position. "Now that your monster has concluded that everything is safe, can we override it and begin the dive?" More times than she cared to remember, he reminded her how difficult it was for him to have an inanimate object considered more capable.

"Go ahead. You do it. Maybe Caesar ought to get used to you punching in the override. I can't imagine that I'll be in control that often."

Tentatively, Snow punched in his code name, then the override code, and took command of the dive. "Hatch secured?" he inquired of her caustically.

"Sorry." She should have known he'd be following the old system. "Last man down, sir. The hatch is secured."

"Very well." He was waiting.

"Captain . . ." She hesitated, then continued, remembering the status on the bridge console. "The ship is ready to submerge— sounding is four hundred thirty fathoms."

"Very well. Submerge the ship," he called out. Tradition had been upheld. His orders were really no different than they would have been in an attack submarine.

Situated more than two thirds of the way back from the bow, the angle of incline in the control room was unnoticeable. High speed pumps whirred away with hardly a murmur inside the ship as the ballast tanks flooded. Nothing would be heard outside. There was a slight vibration from the increasing weight. Though many of the joints had been muffled in the fishbowl during sea trials, the computer was now busy locating and recording the noisiest for additional silencing once they reached depth.

Carol closed her eyes. To imagine *Imperator*'s first dive, she pictured an aircraft carrier steaming with its flight deck right at the water's edge. Only the island superstructure rose above the surface. Then, the image to the observer would be of the flight deck slowly sinking below the surface, the water washing rapidly from bow to stern as the ballast tanks filled, until the stern disappeared. Then, quite rapidly, the island structure, leaving an eddy of white water behind, would quickly submerge until only the antennae remained in view. Finally, with a rush of foam, the entire ship would be gone.

With the keel at 120 feet, the final trace of *Imperator* became invisible to the naked eye. The only evidence that she continued to exist would be an evaporating trail of white water and foam. Then, for as long as her forward motion affected the surface, a satellite recording sea surface temperature alterations might detect her location. Soon, even that would be lost.

Snow was visibly excited now. His enthusiasm radiated throughout the control rooms as he leveled off at 250 feet and called for a systems check. Nothing was out of sync.

Increasing speed at five knot increments, Snow and his crew developed a feeling for their vessel. More than twice as large as any submarine any of them had ever sailed, *Imperator* responded in much the same manner as one of her smaller sisters, and her reactions were equally fast. Nothing so large should expect to dive, surface, accelerate, or reverse like an attack submarine, but *Imperator* adapted to her element like an immense fish. Snow took her down to a thousand feet, not as deep as she'd tested in the fishbowl, but enough to make her creak as she sped on her northwesterly course.

"How about trying out the computer?" Carol asked more than an hour later. "Let's see if Caesar can compete with you."

"I think I'll let my officer of the deck handle that."

Almost to himself, he added, "No need to let the computer know I've developed any trust. Mr. Lyford," he called to a younger man sipping at a mug of coffee, "She's all yours now. Give the computer control."

After punching the identifying codes into the machine, Lyford settled before a console next to Snow's diving station. The screen glowed green as a message appeared before him: "I have assumed control. Depth, four eight zero feet; speed, two eight knots; course, two niner two degrees true."

"Take her up to four hundred feet, Mr. Lyford, and add three knots."

The OOD poked at the keyboard before him, checking as his orders appeared on the screen. Satisfied, he waited.

"Sir!" A startled cry came from one of the men on the bow planes. "I've lost control. . . ." He turned toward Snow, who simply shook his head.

It was hard. The planesman had retired from the navy, too. But now he put his hands in his pockets as he'd been taught in the fishbowl. The computer had control and was responding to the OOD's orders, and the results came within the allotted time Snow would have given himself. *Imperator* reached the exact depth and speed indicated, with no sensation of change. It had simply happened as if Snow were still at the diving station. Propeller revolutions had increased just enough to bring the submarine up to thirty-one knots. The dials on the control console showed that the planes had been used. The trim pumps had activated. They were at four hundred feet, the pumps still adjusting for a perfect trim. And all with no human being involved. *Imperator*'s computer had reacted instantaneously to the orders of the OOD. A confirming report appeared on the screen before him when they had been carried out.

Training in the fishbowl had been exacting, and now, as the night turned to dawn above them, the crew adjusted to the consistency that had been simulated until that time. No flaws appeared in either the submarine or her people. When Hal Snow fell into his bunk fully clothed, he napped

with a feeling of security. Everything had fallen into place—
just as the consortium had intended.

Perhaps his senses reacted to someone's presence, or it
might have been the faint perfume, still so alien to a
submarine. Snow came awake automatically. Without ever
touching him, Carol Petersen drew her hand back in surprise. Snow rose instantly on an elbow, shading his eyes
against the overhead light.

"I'm sorry." She stepped back involuntarily. "I didn't
mean to startle you like that."

"Old habits are tough to shake," he muttered, rubbing a
hand over his eyes, then smoothing his hair. "What is it?"

"Nothing special. I noticed you had a call in for
now. . . ."

"What time is it?"

"A little after zero eight hundred. You've been sleeping
for three hours."

Snow sat on the edge of his bunk, blinking his eyes
against the light. "I don't usually do that at sea. Of
course, I don't ever remember a woman waking me up in a
submarine before, either."

There was no expression on his face and she stepped
back another pace, involuntarily. "I'm sorry," she said
again. "I hate to destroy habits."

"Different boat, different service . . . what the hell.
Might as well start something new at my age." He sniffed
the air like a rabbit. "How the hell am I going to maintain
discipline when you run around the boat smelling so good?
Pretty soon we're going to have to have flowers in the
wardroom." Snow ran his tongue over his teeth and reached
for his toothbrush.

"I'll leave if you want me to."

"Ever see a man brush his teeth in the morning?"

She nodded.

"Good. Stay. I haven't had a woman who cared enough
to watch me do it for a long time." He snorted. Leaving
the fishbowl behind brought a great sense of relief. And
Imperator had performed perfectly all night, through every

conceivable evolution . . . every one except weapons systems, and that could wait.

She could sense she'd made a mistake, and Snow wasn't going to let her forget it.

"Can you handle me washing my face and combing my receding hair without stepping outside?" The attitude was unpleasant, the treatment subservient—the direct opposite of hours before.

"Haven't seen anything that's bothered me yet, Captain."

"Good. This beats hell out of having some pimply-faced sailor barking at me to get up. I could get used to it."

"First thing you know, everyone would want to be captain for a day," she retorted.

"How about ordering me some scrambled eggs and whatever else they're dishing out, and I'll change and be up to the wardroom in about five minutes. Okay?"

"Consider it done, Captain," she answered grimly, stepping back into the passageway.

"Oh, by the way," Snow called before she'd taken more than a couple of steps, "did you tell anyone you were coming down here to get me up?"

"Just the messenger on watch."

"Wonderful. It's probably all over the ship."

Snow pulled the curtain across the entrance to his cabin. Long ago, he'd convinced himself not to grade any female over thirty on the scale he'd devised for himself, but Carol Petersen was well above average in looks as far as Snow's classification system worked. She must be late thirties, he surmised, maybe leaning pretty hard on forty. But she didn't really look it. She still had a fine figure. He learned she'd never been married soon after she reported to the fishbowl. She managed to make coveralls look neat and seemed to fill them out, even the baggy ones.

Until this morning, he rarely considered her as anything else but a senior engineer, a vital one, but still a critical member of his crew. But being awakened by her—now he was even sure that perhaps it was the smell of the perfume that he'd noticed—set his imagination to running.

• • •

The continued success of *Imperator*'s first day at sea was marred only by a single message: SOVIET SUBMARINES MONITORED VICINITY 48N 146W MOVING IN GENERAL DIRECTION YOUR TRANSIT AREA. ANTICIPATE INTERCEPT. OUR HUK WILL ADVANCE TO BLOCK. PROGRAM THEIR UNITS 24 AND 41, OUR UNITS 19, 39 AND 72.

Snow ordered the sound-library tapes for the numbered Soviet and American submarines inserted into the computer for passive identification and tracking.

The remainder of the day was without incident.

Andy Reed loitered against the shiny chrome railing in the control center, patiently waiting his turn at the periscope. It was the captain's responsibility to take the first look no matter how clear sonar reported the area. The periscope operated like a television camera, displaying exactly what appeared to the captain on remote screens. Glancing over his shoulder, Reed watched the scene shift on the unit mounted near the entrance to sonar. But it was not in color and Reed longed to see the Pacific as it actually was.

His thoughts drifted back a few short days to the moment they'd gotten underway from Pearl Harbor. It was so beautiful. Mornings like that were easily engraved in his memory forever after too much time behind a desk. Everything had been perfect that day: the water a deep blue to match the Hawaiian sky, wisps of cirrus on the horizon, a light breeze carrying the fresh aroma of flowers and mown grass, Diamond Head majestic to the east. As the picture came back clearly, he also remembered his good but failed intentions of immediately recording it in a letter to Lucy. But that had been forgotten as *Houston* exited the channel into the Pacific and the crew had made preparations to dive.

Caught up by the sensations of newfound freedom on the water, he had asked the captain's permission to take the conn as OOD. Once again he was the confident junior officer conning an attack submarine from the top of the sail, ocean water majestically foaming against the black hull. As *Houston* rolled casually in the soft swells, crew-

men secured the ship for that first day at sea. Reed watched
with pleasure as the men scurried about the rounded deck
attached to lifelines. Preparing for that first dive, sonar
always searched for the slightest rattle. All fittings were
double-checked, because there were no second chances
once they dived. In less than twenty minutes, much too
short a period from Reed's vantage point high above the
ocean, sonar pronounced the hull to be as secure from
sound as possible.

Houston was ready to dive and Reed found himself the
only man on the bridge, as command was shifted to the
captain down in control. Reed prepared the sail against his
own mental check-off list. The clamshells secured, he
dropped down through the hatch and reported last man
down. It was an exhilarating feeling to be back, yet momentarily disappointing to give up the sounds and smells
of the open ocean. Yes, he had spent too long behind a
desk.

He was brought back to the present by the captain.
"Admiral, care to take a look for yourself?"

The view through the periscope was so different from
the screen he'd been studying moments before, and *he*
could control it. Slowly circling, glued to the eyepiece, he
brought the vast beauty of the ocean swimming into perspective. In every direction, the sea was in constant motion, the horizon sharp in some places, setting off water
and sky, in other places merged by the meeting of clouds
at its edge. It was a singular beauty that he treasured. As
soon as he finished, Reed promised himself to sit down
and write Lucy—and include his recollections of the morning they'd gotten underway.

"Beautiful," he whispered silently to himself, stepping
back from the periscope. "Thanks for the look, Ross,"
Reed remarked to the captain. "About the only time I ever
see anything like that is when Lucy and I get away sailing
for a day—but even then there's always land in the distance," he added wistfully.

Houston's satellite antenna had been raised for daily
message traffic while they peered through the periscope.

Now, like any submariner, her captain was anxious to dive again. "Do you want to send anything to *Olympia* or *Helena* before we pull the plug, Admiral?"

"I guess not, thanks. Nothing's changed in the last twenty-four hours. We know where their submarines are in relation to *Imperator* and so do *Olympia* and *Helena*. I think I'll just keep her on the same track. She knows pretty much what to do if we lost contact at all. Let's keep radio silence and dive."

Ten minutes later *Houston* leveled off, speeding toward the rendezvous point that would place them between *Imperator* and the Soviet submarines sent out to destroy her. There had been no doubt of the Russian intent even before *Houston* departed Pearl Harbor. Their message traffic had been thoroughly analyzed. Other Petropavlovsk-based submarines had been detached, with orders to stop *Imperator* before she got through the Bering Strait to dive under the ice. That was the main reason Reed was to use *Houston* as his flagship—just in case the fates won out. His orders were to provide a screen until Hal Snow was ready to fight her. Then Reed was to analyze the competition.

And Danilov was leading the pack. Abe Danilov—that crafty son of a bitch, Reed mused affectionately to himself. It hadn't been so many years back that he'd first encountered the Russian when they were both commanding attack boats. It was all still so very clear in his mind. Intelligence had indicated before they departed New London that it was more than likely he might encounter Danilov among the Soviet boats operating off Greenland . . . and they'd been absolutely correct.

After his return, Reed had taken his sonar tapes to the library just to compare the sounds of that Russian against the others. There was no doubt about it. It had been Danilov. Everything he'd read seemed to indicate that it was the same man he'd met in that undersea dogfight over a three-day period.

The Russian had been the first to establish contact, a lesson Reed remembered. There seemed to be nothing nearby as he'd raced after that contact dead on their bow. About the same time that sonar identified it as a noise-maker, they also picked up the Soviet boat behind them. If they'd been at war, Andy Reed and his boat would have been at the bottom—with no warning at all until the whine of the torpedoes had been picked up.

Once the game had begun, Andy Reed confirmed what the navy had been claiming for so many years. The American boats were faster, quieter, more maneuverable, the Russians were noisier, slower, and they had to close their range more for accurate firing. But that didn't account for experience. Danilov was wily—that was the word that had come to him. He read the intelligence reports confirming that Abe Danilov would now be commanding the Soviet hunter-killer group—like a fox—no, a ferret was a more apt term.

Reed understood that any man who looked forward to combat was crazy, unfit to command, but what a challenge Danilov presented. There was no other submariner in the world whom he respected more.

__4__

ABE DANILOV'S EYES flew open as the sound of footsteps halted outside his stateroom. When the messenger snapped on the overhead light, after knocking politely, he found the admiral's eyes eerily fixed on his own. The sailor had been on the staff long enough to grow accustomed to such habits, yet this one continued to be disconcerting.

There was time for an automatic salute—but before the messenger could say a word, Danilov ordered, "Leave the message board with me. Please inform Captain Sergoff I will breakfast with him in fifteen minutes." He dismissed the sailor with a wave of his hand.

Danilov stretched in the manner the doctor had ordered. First he pointed the toes of his right foot, tensing the muscles of his leg, then did the same with his left. Next he stretched his arms in front of him, balling his fists as he raised his arms above his head. Satisfied, he allowed himself the luxury of the kind of catlike stretch that any man enjoyed in the morning. Lying still, his eyes searched out the comfortable, familiar facets of the tiny stateroom. Though it normally belonged to *Seratov*'s commanding officer, it would be his for the duration of this operation.

Finally, again following the doctor's instructions, he took three deep breaths, exhaling slowly before he sat up on the edge of the narrow bunk. It was maddening, this getting older, even though he felt perfectly fine, well rested with only two or three hours of sleep. Danilov admitted his body did not respond as it had when he was a fresh, young officer, but he was still disturbed on principle, if nothing else, that the young doctor's orders were supported by higher authority. Admirals were not to bound out of bed—he could go along with that. Engage the senses one at a time; allow the aging body the privilege of waking and functioning properly—that wasn't as bad as it sounded at first. Yet many of the habits that Danilov had enjoyed over the years had now been recategorized by official Moscow as abuses to the body—and only a fool, a simpering old fool, would allow someone to toss his beloved, bad habits out the window.

But Abe Danilov accommodated their purposes with good humor, even though there was one ailment his seniors could do nothing about— he was lonely. Danilov desperately wanted to be beside his Anna. She was much of the reason he had slept but a few hours that night. That first haunting letter of hers would not retreat to the back of his mind no matter how hard he willed it. He read it completely through three times the previous night and found that he understood his Anna so well that parts of it were almost automatically committed to his memory, while other sections brought tears to his eyes.

After pulling on his pants, he hung the message board to one side of the mirror, a routine Danilov followed every morning. While he brushed his teeth, washed, and shaved, he would study each message out of the corner of his eye, pulling them off the board one by one so that his routine never ceased. Danilov was uncomfortable without his habits.

The general messages intended "for flag officers only" related the movements of forces around the world over the last twenty-four hours. Some involved actual confrontation, others the day-to-day Cold War challenges of a bristling world. Each commander was made aware of the events that could affect his small part of Soviet national strategy. None of it really interested Danilov. If anything occurred that directly affected him, he knew he would be awakened by a messenger in the night.

But there was one noteworthy communication that caught his eye as he shaved—the hunter-killer unit dispatched a few days previously from the eastern submarine base of Petropavlovsk was approaching a sector on *Imperator*'s projected path. That *would* be interesting, he mused, just to be a fly on the wall . . . to watch what each of those units would do that day. He knew that *Imperator* would not be alone. The Americans would have their own submarines out in front while this massive new weapon experimented with itself. And what would they do with the Soviet submarines? Would they simply let them tag along recording each of *Imperator*'s capabilities? Danilov doubted that very much as he washed the shaving cream off his face. He expected that if they didn't turn away at a reasonable point in time that they might find themselves going down a drain . . . much like the shaving cream that disappeared from the metal sink before his eyes.

As he finished knotting his tie—Danilov always wore a tie until they were well away from the piers—he studied the local weather message. No change—the same stinking spring weather that constantly swept across the Kola Peninsula from the Barents Sea—snow, sleet, gusty winds. It would be an unpleasant passage to their diving point. He would probably be ill. He usually was when they got underway from Polyarnyy, even in midsummer. Too much time ashore these days, he realized, and fervently hoped no one, not even Sergoff, would notice that now he could only enjoy a voyage below the surface where the water was calm and his stomach could return to normal. The doctor was right, in a way, about age. When he was younger, Danilov never dreaded those first couple of hours on the surface. He was tough then.

He knew he was tough now, especially mentally. But this sense of loneliness was intruding and pervasive. It would take all of his willpower to put it aside once the hunt began.

There was room for only two people in *Seratov*'s tiny bridge as she departed the ice-choked harbor at Polyarnyy— Abe Danilov and the submarine's commander, Stevan Lozak. The younger man had been handpicked by his admiral the year before. His selection was much like Admiral Gorshkov's sponsorship of young Abe Danilov. Mentors were invaluable in the Soviet military.

They winced as the howling winds snapped sharp crystals of sleet into their faces. It bounced off their goggles with a crack, bit into their exposed cheeks, then dripped down through heavy mufflers onto their necks. The low sail area rose out of the hull like a knuckle. There was little protection as the wind whipped spray off the white-caps that swirled about the hull.

"Yes . . . yes, I have it," Danilov exclaimed. His words disappeared into the wind, but Lozak had caught them, noted the angle of the admiral's binoculars, and swung his on the same bearing. "Almost four points to starboard, maybe five hundred . . ." His last words were swept away by the winds.

Lozak steadied his arms on the bridge railing. A sheet of snow and sleet from a floating cake of ice swirled across his line of sight. For a moment the range opened to five or six hundred yards and he caught a glimpse of the sea buoy Danilov had pointed out. He bent to the speaker just below the bridge railing, "Come left two degrees." He knew exactly where he was, or he at least had a better idea than the radarman below who had reported at least three different locations for the sea buoy in the past sixty seconds. The channel was wide now. His only concern would be any other craft foolish enough to venture into Polyarnyy in this weather without informing the port control. "Increase your speed to seven knots," he ordered.

Danilov turned toward the captain and nodded. Even though the admiral's face was mostly covered, Lozak recognized that familiar smile of contentment that appeared

whenever they cleared the buoy and headed into the open
sea. Only Danilov's cheeks showed and they were a bright
red from the stinging sleet. But he nodded again, which
was also habitual at this stage of the cruise, and he leaned
over to Lozak's ear. "I'm going below now. You'll be
able to dive shortly after you're clear of the peninsula. It
should be soon." He clapped the other on the shoulder and
was quickly through the hatch into the control room.

The surface of the Barents Sea was no place for a
submarine on a day like this, and the bridge was certainly
no place to tarry. For perhaps the fifth time that morning,
Danilov found himself at the chart table, hands in pockets,
studying the thin red line signifying the path *Seratov* and
her two sisters would follow to a point in the Chukchi Sea
well north of the Bering Strait. They would take a northerly course that would bring them between Franz Josef
Land and Spitsbergen. An almost constant course would
take them within a hundred miles of the North Pole. At an
average speed of thirty-five knots, they would arrive at a
point slightly north and west of Point Barrow and about
five hundred miles north of the Bering Strait after three
days at sea. Sergoff had calculated that *Imperator* would
take about four days to reach a point south of the Bering
Strait if she was not intercepted before then. Though departing a day after *Imperator*, Danilov would be waiting
on the fifth day. That one day was designed to track
Imperator if she made it through the Bering Strait. Abe
Danilov wanted every possible bit of information fed into
his computers before their cat-and-mouse game began in
earnest.

"How long has it been dead in the water?" Snow
inquired.

"About three hours, Captain." The chief sonarman turned
a control switch to allow another of his operators to search
for the reported spy ship. If it could be found, the source
would be electronically isolated by the computer, then
transferred to the sonar console. "A maritime patrol aircraft picked it up on the surface due west of us and stuck

with it. It took a while to locate in the catalog after we intercepted their report. Classified it after a time as a Moma-class intelligence collector.''

''Never heard of them.'' Snow had given up his futile attempt at listening on the headphones.

''Neither did I, Captain. It was listed in there, but it was buried pretty deep. They were originally buoy tenders built in Poland. They're little bulldogs—about two hundred forty feet, fifteen hundred tons, two diesels, two shafts—the type that would probably just plow through a sea of cement if they had to.''

''Not a bad cover. Who the hell's supposed to pay attention to a buoy tender bobbing along?'' Snow shook his head in wonder. ''Except there's nothing out here to tend for thousands of miles. Christ, they're smart. Never miss a trick.''

The sonarmen hadn't paid much attention to searching for the little Soviet ship until the watch changed. One had been assigned to look it up in the intelligence manuals. It was a habit *Imperator*'s men had been taught at Snow's insistence—never take anything for granted. There's something hidden, he repeated time and again during their training, in everything you perceive until you prove otherwise. So one of them had looked up the Moma class and noticed that some, even though they'd been reclassified as intelligence ships, had retained their buoy-handling cranes. And the previous year, two of them had been equipped with a highly sophisticated passive sonar system. An immense hydrophone unit, not as yet classified in the West, could be lowered over the side with the crane. A structure had been built on their sterns that intelligence assumed was a computerized evaluation system for the sonar, along with a satellite relay to shore.

''No kind of sound from her?'' Snow inquired, as if he needed reassurance.

''Not a thing. She's stopped just about on top of our path of advance according to the position that patrol plane called into his base—probably using her engines to maneuver a little bit—station keeping, I guess.''

Snow considered the consequences. Given time, the Russians would record enough sound data on *Imperator* to thoroughly analyze this mystery ship. Without ever seeing her visually, they could construct a reasonably accurate picture of what they faced. There was no doubt in Snow's mind that right now those hydrophones were riveted on his bearing and that very picture of *Imperator* might be developing. Every sound radiating from her could be recorded on tape and relayed by satellite to a land station for final analysis. They could create such an accurate picture of *Imperator* that they'd figure out everything but the color of his skivvies. It was a very neat effort.

"What's the range now?" Snow asked.

"Nothing firm, sir, since she's not moving. I'd say, figuring our own advance the last few hours, that she's a little more than a hundred miles now."

"Fair enough. No reason to spread our legs and give them a free look. We'll take it out." As he left the blue-lighted sonar room, he added over his shoulder, "We'll see how our Tomahawks work in a few minutes, Chief." Snow's orders were to take out anything in his way—no need to create an international incident if he could solve the problem himself.

Submarines on patrol acted quite the opposite of other military units when they were out on their own. Their appearance when surfaced—evil and intimidating—became their personality when they dived. They became hoodlums cruising the depths, sneaking about the darkened abyss of the oceans seeking trouble. Communications with their bases, or any higher authority for that matter, were rare. Totally on their own, each decision by a commanding officer was an interpretation of his final orders before departing. No man could delve into the future to see what might challenge each mission, so the captain of a submarine became a god unto himself. The right or wrong of his actions would be considered when, or if, he returned.

General Quarters was sounded from the control room. Snow overruled the computer. He would run the attack himself. Caesar would run a dummy attack, and the results would be compared afterwards. Snow hoped that each new evolution could be handled totally by a human being and then matched with Caesar's solution before he would trust the master computer—Snow was still from the old school.

The process was no different from that on an attack submarine. The target was reidentified for weapons control. Approximate range was fed into the attack computer. The Tomahawk missile was selected, the tube flooded and pressure equalized with the outside, the door opened, presets entered in the missile. Standard reports were made verbally to Snow. His excitement heightened as he heard "weapon is ready" and then "solution is ready." Quite suddenly, Snow was aware that the control room was as silent as it had ever been. Each person was responding exactly as trained.

"Shoot on generated bearings," Snow ordered evenly, masking his excitement.

The weapons control coordinator's finger squeezed the firing key. A red light blinked, signifying weapons release. There was no sound, no sensation at all in the control room as a Tomahawk cruise missile leaped out from the forest of vertical tubes in *Imperator*'s hull almost a thousand feet ahead of them. Snow's brow knit—there should be something, some physical response, but, nothing . . . His brows knit in disappointment.

"Weapon's broken the surface," came from sonar.

Snow's expression relaxed. The Tomahawk was airborne. "Time of flight?" he queried.

"Eight minutes, four two seconds." There was a pause. "Caesar claims five two seconds."

Snow considered what could happen in the next eight or nine minutes on the targeted ship. They had to be totally involved in the details of their mission, locating then acquiring every sound emanating from *Imperator*. Did they consider that they could have been detected by that plane? Would they know the sound of a missile fired from below the surface? Most of the crew on those intelligence collectors were civilian. It was more than likely none of them had ever been aboard a submarine. What did they have on board to pick up electronic radiation? Would they be listening for a missile's radar homing? It seemed unlikely. Intelligence collectors weren't normally on the firing line. Why would they worry about being a target so far from any land? Or did they even realize the significance of what they were tracking? Negative on all counts, Snow was sure.

The minutes passed slowly, each one taking longer to tick away. The weapons officer reported with a cool detachment the various programmed evolutions the missile was passing through until it achieved active radar homing. That would be the crucial stage. A warship would have a good chance of detecting the electronic emissions and have time to prepare evasion tactics—fire chaff, emit false signals, activate antimissile weapon systems. But this small Moma-class ship was more than likely wallowing in the North Pacific wholly consumed in its tracking mission. They could have heard the missile emerge from the submarine, but it was probable they would have no one on board to identify the sound, or verify that they were being fired on.

Time magnified doubt in Snow's mind. Should he have fired another? There was so much that could go wrong—a malfunction, the missile detected and decoyed, or it could even hit and cause only minor damage to the target. He'd considered the latter and dropped the idea. Now, it again became important. A thousand pounds of high explosive should do the trick . . . but if it didn't, the Russian ship could get off a warning message. Christ, he'd be everybody's target once they knew he was allowed to fire at anything at any range.

Imperator continued on her course at a steady speed. She had a mission. There was no time for deviation as they waited for eight-plus minutes to elapse. The tension remained constant until a report came from sonar, "We have sounds on that bearing, Captain."

While the computer automatically initiated an analysis of these new sounds, it was the chief once again who reported solemnly, "That's the sound of a ship breaking up, Captain. I'll bet on it—even at that range. I'll put all my paychecks on a direct hit."

Another of the sonarmen listened intently as the chief identified the sounds of a ship in distress. When it was over, and there was only silence on that bearing, the younger man removed his headphones and murmured, "There's nothing out there now, Chief." He turned to look up at the man. "You get kind of used to something when you listen for hours. It almost takes on a special personality. Now it's gone."

Snow had sent a message to the Soviets with that missile, even more symbolic than the slaughter of *Fahrion*. The Americans had unleashed a lethal weapon that sailed with orders to remove anything in its path—and that would change the Soviets' approach to *Imperator*. They could no longer try to satisfy their curiosity. Now there was no choice but to destroy her. But unlike *Fahrion*, she was not a sacrificial lamb . . . she was a lion. . . .

Andy Reed was the kind of admiral sailors liked to have aboard, not so much because he was affable and pleasant to work for, but because he was the type who would always get them through. There were armchair admirals who plotted strategy and there were seagoing admirals who carried those plans through. Reed was the latter type. In an underwater world, each man on a submarine depended on the next. At the upper end of the chain, the only person left was the captain or, in this case, Andy Reed. The men in the three submarines of Andy Reed's hunter/killer group were content. Their admiral was a survivor.

Both Soviet and American strategists acknowledged that it was difficult to fool the other concerning ship movements. With spies roaming in port, spy ships offshore, and spy satellites, there were few surprises. Admiral Reed went to sea with specific orders to shield *Imperator* those first few days, especially while Hal Snow and his crew learned about their vessel.

The three submarines in Reed's group departed Pearl

Harbor days before at different times, allowing themselves
to be tracked in separate directions. Rabbits were then
detailed to shake their tails. *Houston*'s rendezvous with
Olympia and *Helena* was a sector one thousand miles due
south of Kodiak Island. Andy Reed's group would provide
the buffer line for *Imperator* to pass through the lower
Aleutians into the Bering Sea. Then, like a pulling guard,
they would join her as she headed north through the Bering
Strait.

In reasonable perspective, Reed could study the progress
of his own three submarines, of *Imperator* as she hastened
on the course that would take her through the Aleutians
near Dutch Harbor, and of the two converging Soviet
submarines. Reed doubted their intent was more than tracking for intelligence, perhaps even minimal harassment to
determine operational characteristics. Moreover, it would
be absolutely useless for propaganda purposes, since there
were as yet no news items concerning *Imperator* or her
mission.

Reed's objective was to place his small force between
Imperator and the snoopers. The Soviets had yet to invent
a computer that could separate and analyze sound through
the barrier he planned to create. Limiting their intelligence-
gathering activities was almost as important as guarantee-
ing *Imperator*'s progress.

Reed's tactical display was simulated by computerized
projections on a darkened board that created three-
dimensional depth with a little imagination. *Houston* and
her sisters, *Olympia* and *Helena*, formed a wedge in the
Pacific aimed between the two Russians and *Imperator*.
There were no communications between the American
vessels yet, nor would Reed break the silence until it was
absolutely necessary. He knew Hal Snow would be contemplating the identical picture in his control room, but he
would be using a three-dimensional holographic imager.
Reed had no doubt that his Soviet counterparts would
create much the same picture in theirs.

Initially, at ranges half a day apart from each other, the
six submarines appeared shy participants in a slow-motion

dance. Their speeds remained essentially the same, yet their pace appeared to increase as they drew closer. The Soviet boats split, one on a northerly heading to cross *Imperator*'s projected path, the other continuing on intercept approach. By a simple signal, Reed directed *Olympia* to impede the progress of the first one while *Houston* and *Helena* continued on a course to interpose themselves between *Imperator* and the second sub. She was one of the titanium hulled Alfas capable of diving deeper than any American boat. The choreography of this underwater dance now took form.

But nothing was instantaneous at those distances; the strategy evolved over three watches. Soon night cloaked the ocean surface when Reed ordered *Houston* to alter course, wedging her now between *Imperator* and the Soviet. Reed noted that the Soviet submarine approaching *Olympia* was rising to the surface at about the same time, and would be communicating with her base at Petropavlovsk—which was unexpected—indicating to Reed that she was seeking new instructions. Since the Russian submarines would be under specific orders regarding *Imperator*, the only purpose for communicating would be a change in those orders. He had no idea *Imperator* had already eliminated one problem in her path.

Carol Petersen was dozing on the wardroom sofa when someone dropped roughly onto the opposite end. She stirred but didn't open her eyes. It should have been obvious to anyone that she was sleeping. But whoever was on the other end obviously intended to talk with her. She waited, not moving.

Snow wondered whether she was playing games with him, or really was still asleep. He began tentatively, "Carol . . . Carol . . ." Then, more firmly, "Carol . . . I need the assistance of a computer genius . . . along with a little goodwill."

She smiled before opening her eyes. "Then it's just for business you're waking me out of a sound sleep, Captain?"

"Well, yes . . ." Men on submarines wouldn't think of

responding to their captain in that manner. He was very glad, perhaps relieved, that only the two of them were in the wardroom.

"Now what if I'd been in bed in my stateroom?" She was grinning to herself, but now there was no expression on her face. "Would you have called me . . . or would you have come in like you just did and bounced on the end of my bunk?" Her eyes remained tightly shut, but there were traces of amusement at the corners of her mouth.

"I suppose . . ." There was a moment's hesitation, then he continued, "I guess I would have called down to you."

Sensing the awkwardness in his last words, she was immediately sorry. She opened her eyes and smiled. "I'm just kidding." She ran a hand through her hair. "I hope I wasn't mean."

"No. Not at all." His words remained tentative.

She could tell by the expression on his face that he didn't expect to be treated this way aboard his own command. "I really am sorry. I guess I'm just punchy when I'm catching forty winks. Let's face it. You've never been at sea with a woman before. If it didn't make you uneasy sometimes, you'd be a very strange person."

Now it was Snow's turn to be wary. There was something enticing about Carol Petersen, something he'd toyed with since the day he'd first met her. One part of him, the part he desperately wanted to exercise right this moment, was pure submariner; there were some technical questions to discuss with a member of his crew. The second part was the hungry male who found this dark-haired woman more appealing than any he'd encountered in many years—was she that appealing? Or just the only available female? But in the back corridors of his mind lurked the Hal Snow he understood best, the one who had been divorced twice and was too street-smart.

"We've got company," he said. Her eyebrows rose in question. "Two Soviet boats, one an Alfa who's probably trying to get well under us, another Victor to the north trying to cut us off at the pass. Andy Reed's running some interference for us . . . and it is his game," he emphasized. "But I'd like to play some games of our own with that computer of yours. No telling when we might be on our own. Now's the time to see what your baby can do for us."

"Do I have time to grab something first . . . like a cup of coffee?"

"Sure." Then he added, "Having any second thoughts about Caesar?" He had to reassure himself of what that computer, or better yet Carol Petersen, could accomplish before they dived under the icepack. His reasoning never changed: the computer had to be double-checked—just in case. In his mind, no computer possessed the innate instincts of a true submariner.

"The only second thought I have is that I don't have someone else trained to handle that monster when I'm grabbing a nap."

"This is only the second day. Imagine when—" he began with a note of authority.

"Don't bother," she reacted. "I can imagine what it's going to be like after we've been at sea for a week. Come on, let's get it done."

Caesar was located on the lowest deck directly under the control room, and just forward of the reactor compartment in one of those sterile, doctor's office–looking rooms. Four remote units were located on the right as they entered. The opposite wall contained windows that looked in on the gray, upright boxes containing Caesar. The other wall was literally a giant cathode ray tube.

"Are we going to run anything serious from here, or just play?" Carol inquired as they stepped inside.

"Play," Snow answered casually as his eyes roamed about an area of his command that he knew less than he should about. "Play games, as in war games. But we're going to create the scenario here."

Carol switched on one of the remotes and punched in her code. "Are you concerned with the guests who seem to be joining us?"

Snow nodded.

"Okay. We probably want to use the big screen. I assume you want to move them around the ocean a bit?"

"There's one element that bothered me from the start of this whole operation, maybe because it never seemed to bother the consortium. I'm the target . . . or *Imperator*'s the target . . . for the Russians, whether you consider the boats coming in now or the ones who're going to be waiting under the ice. Andy Reed's commanding the operation, calling the shots, but I'm stuck here riding the target and I'm not often going to be able to talk with him or read his mind. I'm going to have to act independently under certain circumstances—Andy and I talked about this before—and I like to anticipate. . . ."

"You want to consider an infinite number of possibilities open to you by considering an infinite number of reactions available to your opposition." She grinned. "I could keep you here a week and Caesar here would keep spitting out possibilities until you cried for mercy."

"No, that's not it so much. I know pretty well what their boats are capable of and know how their captains are trained. I'll provide the probabilities, and Caesar can take it from there."

Carol Petersen glanced over her shoulder as she tapped basic data into the computer. "I thought you'd been programmed for every possibility, Captain Snow. Is there something they actually left out?" It was impossible to tell if she was serious or joking.

"Many submarine captains in the past who relied solely on themselves are resting comfortably on the bottom. But there's a number of us still alive and healthy who rely on what we know about the other guy."

There was a touch in Snow's voice that she remembered from that morning. It wasn't anything that bothered her specifically. It was more an undercurrent, a tonal quality that seemed to insinuate more than he was saying. He'd never shaken the belief that submarines were no place for women. Yet he was commanding one that carried a woman in a critical role. Snow had told the members of the consortium he saw no problem with a woman on a civilian ship during his initial interview with them. It was only after he'd signed the contract that he realized this bore no relation to a civilian operation. He was gradually coming to the understanding (though he tried to force it back in the recesses of his mind) that he was probably more affected by Carol Petersen than any of the other men aboard. It was disconcerting, and it was a situation he had to come to grips with before he could have *Imperator* fully under his command.

"Want me to key in the submarines in our vicinity?" she asked.

"First, let's get the big screen on a scale that covers the Aleutians. I want to include *Olympia* and that Russian heading in her direction. He directly affects the one heading for us."

"It's coming up now," she replied, looking over her shoulder at the screen. "Tell me if the scale's right."

Snow never ceased to be amazed by *Imperator*'s technology—so far beyond the submarines he understood. The huge screen, which almost completely covered the adjacent wall, took on a gray-green hue. There was no sound, nothing to indicate that anything had been energized. The screen changed color gradually and symbols for the various submarines were accurately defined in their relative locations. The Aleutian Islands hung in a half moon across the top of the screen.

"Put in their latest course and speed."

"Already there," she answered. "I just borrowed whatever's already in the memory. As long as we're tracking them, the computer updates all data every half minute." Her brows knit as she glanced over at him. "You really don't know a hell of a lot about Caesar, do you?"

"I don't need to if you're here." There was that subtle undertone again. Snow immediately regretted it as soon as he'd spoken. It seemed no different than a remark he might have made to his navigator while glancing at the chart. Yet there had been something implied that bothered Snow, more as *Imperator*'s commanding officer than anything else.

The exercise evolved much as he had anticipated. The deep-diving Russian attempted to position itself to force *Imperator* into evasive or protective maneuvers that would provide valuable data to the Russians. Anything they could relay by satellite to Danilov would be to their advantage.

Andy Reed's orders were to keep *Houston* ahead of *Imperator*, with *Helena* assigned to maneuver with the Soviet boat, moving into a blocking position, if necessary. The most dangerous possibility would be for the Russian to attempt a position underneath *Imperator*, between her and *Helena*, and realizing that, Hal Snow experimented with the idea of increasing depth if the Russian were directly under him. The idea might work initially according to the computer, but Caesar also pointed out the damage that could be done to *Imperator*'s underside, depending on the location of the much smaller Russian, if they made contact. So in the end, the idea was only viable in an extreme situation. And, according to the computer, a solution could only be delivered at the time events were actually taking place.

After studying Caesar's limited projections, Snow returned to paperwork in his cabin, and leafed through reports on spaces and machinery within *Imperator* that he'd never inspected himself. She was no different than an aircraft carrier in size, and Snow doubted that any man had ever toured every single compartment and void within a carrier. Her ballast tanks were greater in volume than the capacity of many tankers that still plied the world's oceans. To pass from *Imperator*'s bow to her stern involved a trip of much more than her overall length. There were ladders, catwalks over machinery, numerous watertight doors to open and secure, and passageways that would end with a sharp turn to port or starboard to bypass a secure space. Not only was an interior tour not a straight line, it was a maze, and so complex that no single individual could claim detailed knowledge of *Imperator*'s entire length.

Going through the reports, Snow found his mind wandering. The cause was Carol Petersen, but she wasn't the

immediate subject of his thoughts. Instead, he was contemplating the most unpleasant memories of his two wives.

The first, like him, had been much too young. They'd
married shortly after his graduation from the academy. It
had seemed the right thing and, in retrospect, they were
probably in love at the time. But she'd been as irresponsible five years later as she had been when they'd first met.
She loved the uniforms and the excitement of the military
life at first, and Hal Snow was the answer to a young girl's
romantic dreams—or so it seemed.

She was unable to adjust to the rigors of his nuclear
training, the reality of extended deployments, or the ensuing years on submarines without shore duty. There was no
romance in any of that. And those poor kids born in the
first five years had never been the answer either. In the
end, if there was one thing she considered revenge for the
romantic Hal Snow who never really existed, it was to
move away with the children so that he became a stranger
to them. Hal Snow never forgave her for that. He never
did know his children. Even today, if someone were to ask
him their birthdays, he'd often resort to the dates in his
wallet. Only on rare occasions could he admit to himself
what an irresponsible father he was—more often he was
able to convince himself it was their mother's fault.

His second marriage, to the girl who romanced him
shortly after he'd been given his first command, had been
short-lived. She came along for the ride, a social climber
from a military family. She intended to show off her
husband's dolphins, the scrambled eggs on his hat, and his
command-at-sea star to her set. She had been a lousy lover,
a lousy cook, a lousy homemaker—a dreary litany Snow
could still recite in his sleep. But what had bothered him
the most with her, the one thing that had really hurt
him—the only thing—was that she was a tramp. Sleeping
around was unacceptable enough, but the fact that she did
it in the confined submarine community was inexcusable.
Snow often wondered if she was much of the reason he'd
eventually resigned from the navy—partly because she'd
been screwing around with too many senior officers. Or

was it because he suspected the promotion boards knew
what she was doing? Either way, it had been time for him
to go.

After the second time around, Snow promised himself
that he was going to be a loner. It was much easier that
way. He'd had two wives that had made his life miserable,
and he had two kids he could lose track of for six months
at a time. Carol Petersen wasn't as good-looking as either
of them, but one thing he could say for sure—she was one
hell of a lot smarter than the two of them put together—
and she was a lady. For all the powers of concentration
that he prided in himself, here he was thinking about
her again, even comparing her to the others—while two
Soviet submarines were closing *Imperator* on an intelligence mission that could turn extremely dangerous any
moment.

At his age, things should fall into place in a logical,
systematic way. He knew they should. Then Snow sighed
and shook his head knowingly. But they never do. . . .

Lucy Reed was a devoted navy wife—one oriented exclusively to her husband and his career, in that order. There
had been times when she considered the idea of a job once
the kids were off to college. A lot of her friends were
doing that and they were loving it. One of them even
called it a reclamation project; she was reclaiming an
individual within herself that she'd all but forgotten. It
sounded good to Lucy at first, but then she had considered
the woman's husband and concluded that, given the same
man, she would have been walking the streets looking for
any kind of work long before.

Being Lucy Reed, the wife of a man tagged as "a bright
prospect" early on by the navy power structure, was quite
enough for her. But much of that realization could also be
called hindsight. She couldn't have gone back to work
when the last of the five kids went off to college because
the Reeds, quite unexpectedly, had been surprised by a
sixth child just when they were relieved that the toughest
teenage years were almost over. She'd often told her friends

that children were social animals, fun to compare to each other when you and all your friends in their twenties were surrounded by them all day. But when an infant appeared as you're nearing forty, and all your friends are enjoying a new lifestyle, you learn more about the individual child. Both Lucy and Andy Reed found the new addition both challenging and appealing from their advanced perspective. They were sure it forced them to remain young.

Puttering around her kitchen now, preparing lunch for young Kevin who was home from school with a cold, Lucy's thoughts circled for a moment, then centered on her husband. When he'd gone to sea as a junior officer, even as a captain, it seemed a perfectly normal thing. It was part of her life. Managing a large family with her husband often gone was standard for a navy wife—and she had been good at it.

But now, when Andy went to sea, without mentioning a word until just before he departed, it was something she couldn't get out of her mind. Tradition be damned! Admirals don't run off to sea like that!

At least Kevin wasn't difficult to handle yet. After five kids so close in age, managing him was still a breeze. His brothers and sisters had monopolized every waking minute at one time, not to mention any worries she might have considered when Andy had gone to sea in the past. Now with one child and so much time to speculate, a gnawing fear crept into her thoughts, something alien, frightening, a pervasive intruder that could not be dismissed. While young Kevin watched television from his bed, Lucy made herself a cup of tea and sat at the kitchen table staring out the window. The cherry trees were gorgeous, almost past their peak. She wanted desperately to be outside cleaning up the winter yard, but the thoughts taking hold in her mind blended into the headlines in the papers and on the nightly news.

There was no doubt in her mind that Andy was involved. She accepted that. But admirals normally worked from desks. Hers was at sea and he'd said nothing about returning. Momentarily, she wished her mind was occupied by one of those jobs her friends held. Then she remembered how often she and Andy had talked about how lucky they were to be together; they could have each other completely when a free day arose rather than living in two separate working worlds. When Andy needed a day off, they could sail together. With the kids at school they could pack a lunch and head for the boat early in the morning—while most of their peers were working in two separate worlds.

No, she didn't really yearn for the job that would occupy her leisure time. She relished the position she had in life, of being the partner of Andy Reed, who needed her so very much. She was satisfied to be a navy wife—and both of them were so happy that Kevin had arrived.

Then she thought about Kevin upstairs with that nasty cold and wondered how Andy was doing right now. One of his only complaints about late fatherhood was the childhood diseases that seemed so much easier to acquire as he grew older.

Andy Reed begrudgingly acknowledged the fact that he, too, was getting a cold. While most admirals managed to avoid the familial germs except for contact with their grandchildren, Andy and Lucy Reed learned to live again with the common cold as the result of their surprise arrival eight years before. While the rest of their family was in college or working, young Kevin could still seek out the most common germs in third grade and deliver them to his parents.

There was no place Admiral Reed would prefer less than a submarine when he was suffering from the common cold. At home, there was no one like Lucy to sympathize. While her willingness to break out the brandy at least improved his morale, there was no way he would ask the pharmacist mate for a tot from the locker. And with a runny nose, itchy throat, and plugged ears, it required all of his concentration to remain attentive to the unfolding tactical scene. The Russian submarines had made their move. There was little opportunity to sneak off for a nap, or even to feel sorry for himself.

Reed blew his nose and, trying to keep a reasonable distance from his operations officer, asked, "What's the time to intercept for the one headed toward *Olympia*?"

"If she maintains current speed, Admiral, I'd say about six hours . . . around zero-five-hundred tomorrow morning. But she's got the horses if she wants to get there quicker. She's waiting for something . . . I'm not sure what."

"Waiting for *Imperator* to get closer. That's what," Reed said hoarsely. "They probably figure their chances of getting some solid readings are better with two boats than one, but they're not taking any chances."

The ops officer studied Reed's face. "They'd just as soon take *Olympia* out as anything else I can think of. Is that what you figure, sir?"

Reed nodded, massaging his eyes slowly. They were sore and tired. "At this point, I think they figure *Imperator*'s important enough to go to just about any length." He cleared his throat and sighed. His head ached, too, and he needed some sleep. "If this was a normal situation, I'd have a better idea of what they'd do. They're usually predictable, but not now. Signal *Helena* to slip around to the other side of our guest. We're going to exercise a little intimidation of our own. Maybe that'll alter their movements up north."

"Admiral, why don't you try a couple of hours' sleep? That cold of yours is a pain in the ass, and we can take care of everything here. I'll wake you if—"

Reed interrupted, waving his hand. "That's exactly what I'm going to do. Maybe a couple of hours will change everything," he added, attempting to look cheerful. But he knew how long it took him to shake colds like this one. The next couple of days were going to be unpleasant.

Abe Danilov understood that he was treating Anna's letters with a reverance that bordered on teenage puppy love. But perhaps that was as it should be. He'd never forgotten his first feelings of love for his wife. Though that young Anna Chuikov bore little resemblance to the dying Anna Danilov, he saw her in his mind's eye as the same girl—only the outer wrapping had been altered.

The admiral's mind had been occupied that day with assumptions of what might be taking place in the northern Pacific. Any intelligence that could be gained by spy ships or other submarines would certainly be worthwhile, but he saw no reason to sacrifice any other ship. Danilov knew exactly what he wanted to do if *Imperator* made it through the Bering Strait and how he was going to go about it. Intelligence was nice, but not an absolute. He'd been in the submarine-hunting business for so long that he knew how the Americans operated. He understood Andy Reed's methods from their past encounters and he had studied the tapes on the man for hours. While a situation could arise that had yet to be inserted in the computer, Danilov was confident of his own ability. Long before there were computers, there were great submariners, men who survived on their own wits, and he was one of them. Danilov had also been familiar with Snow, but he had immediately filed the name when he retired from the U.S. Navy. Now that he was back, and admittedly in a unique position, the Kremlin had begun combing their computer files for details on the man. He was a maverick and Abe Danilov had no doubts that he was as capable as Reed.

A transit under the ice was a lonely journey for a man like Danilov. Some men enjoyed the quiet, the lack of communication, the tedium of watch standing, and the excitement of knowing that they were racing at high speed under uncountable tons of snow and ice. But Abe Danilov was not that type. The solitude, the not knowing what was happening above, the prospect of a dangerous face-off in the North Pacific—each of these became magnified in his mind. Without the steady flow of messages that he constantly reviewed when ashore, he was like a caged animal.

His only means of relaxation became Anna's letters. He could briefly return to times he had forgotten, to memories of Anna's over periods he'd been away from her. Danilov was reminded that he had not been present for the birth of his first son in 1962. That had been a difficult year for a young wife pregnant for the first time. Danilov had spent much of that year at sea, and when the baby was born in October he was in a submarine near Cuba. Much of his time was spent dodging American destroyers and pondering whether war would become a reality and he would die in foreign waters without ever knowing of his first child.

Anna explained in her letter twenty-five years later that for a very short time her husband was not the most important person in her life. He hadn't been around to share the wonder of those nine months, nor the miracle of birth that ended them. During those frightening days when war with the Americans seemed imminent, her only visitor after the birth of her son had been one of the busiest men in the Kremlin. The moment Anna saw Sergei Gorshkov's face, the youngster had been named after the commander in chief of the Soviet Navy. Sergei Danilov followed in his father's footsteps and eventually had gone into submarines. Even today, Danilov imagined, he could be on one of those now approaching *Imperator*. The thought was not a pleasant one.

Anna also had reminded him of how he'd spoiled his only daughter, Eugenia. Three years after the Americans had made fools of them in Cuba, Danilov was transferred to shore duty in Leningrad—and he hated it, afraid he would be passed by. It had been a transition period for the navy as well as for Danilov. Sergei Gorshkov had the opportunity to rebuild, to turn the outdated fleet humiliated off the shores of Cuba into a blue-water navy with the largest, most powerful submarine force in the world.

Abe Danilov had been so distraught at first at being put ashore, when he had hoped to command his own submarine, that he'd turned his complete attention to his infant daughter. Eugenia was the balm to his hurt ego and Danilov attempted to become both mother and father to her. Little Sergei, in the meantime, was just old enough to be jealous, and when Anna mentioned she was afraid he might hurt his sister, Danilov was so fierce with the boy that

Sergei cried in fear for hours. Anna reminded him in her neat handwriting that her husband had always seen other males as a constant challenge—even years later when he treated Eugenia's husband with disdain. Abe Danilov created a shell around himself as he grew older, and he had never realized until then how correct Anna had been. She'd chided him:

> You see, my real interest is in trying to remind you that the young heart of the old man still resides in the same place. I want to make sure that you understand that as you go off on this new mission. Search for the real Abe Danilov each night, and remember him the following day when you are approaching danger. Remember the man who loved that little girl so deeply, whenever the man in that shell who is so tough comes to the surface. Perhaps that will even save your life for me.

Abe Danilov reread her letter, then carefully folded it along the creases, replaced it in the envelope, and put the packet back in the drawer under his shirts.

The other letters had left him in tears, if not close to them, but this was completely different. Anna was searching for that part of himself that still lived in the recesses of his mind. He had stubbornly refused his blessing when his daughter married that engineer and moved to Irkutsk— Eugenia could have done better! And as he thought of that, he remembered what, so many years in the past, General Chuikov had thought of Abe Danilov.

How quickly our ideas change—how easily we forget those concepts that don't appeal to us, he realized now. In a concise way, Anna reminded him that Snow and his *Imperator* were not another challenge to his maleness. It was vital that he take the time to understand what he was facing, to take the rational approach that Anna counseled in her letter—so that he might return to her, she said.

Before he slept, Abe Danilov marveled at the immense

luck he had experienced in finding his Anna. Here, in his old age, or at least near the end of his career, his wife was reawakening so much that he had forgotten about himself. Somehow, she had sensed that she must do this if her husband was to return to her.

Never before had the eyes of the world been riveted so intently to the north. Quite suddenly the strategic value of the arctic regions captured the imagination. Troop and equipment movements about the Kola Peninsula, hitherto an unknown segment of the Arctic only days before, became a matter of vital importance. Newscasters found themselves routinely rolling such names across their tongues as Pechenga, Polyarnyy, and Severodvinsk. Once international attention centered on the Kola Peninsula, the Russian's circuitous routing of their prepositioned equipment was revealed overnight. While the area between Murmansk and Norway contained the greatest concentration of military might in the world, the sheer realities of numbers shocked the West. Preparation for major military movement cannot go unseen for long. There is simply too much involved in troops, tanks, artillery, and the supplies for the thousands of men and tons of equipment involved. All the disclaimers in the world would not convince observers that the Soviets were willing to negate their plans if U.S. ships would remain south of the Arctic Circle.

The Russians were just as vehement in their denunciation of American submarines ordered into arctic waters. The Kremlin knew they were approaching but it was another thing to prove. Satellite photos could not be made of their movements. For the time being, there was an advantage on the Americans' side.

Meanwhile, negotiations continued under a cloud of despair. The reality of an invasion on the Northern Flank would force a NATO effort to relieve a beleaguered Norway, and the conflict would expand. Others would gradually be drawn into the vortex.

The unknown factor remained *Imperator*. The Russians were as yet unable to explain exactly what her overall impact might be in the end. The massive submarine had been quickly shielded against satellites once she departed the fishbowl, but now they knew she must either be exposed or sunk. Her very presence posed a threat to any SSBNs that lay beneath the Arctic icepack, and quite possibly to Soviet offensive plans in Norway. For them it was frustrating enough simply being unable to articulate the magnitude and meaning of this superweapon to themselves and to the rest of the world.

__ 5 __

FOR A FLEETING moment, the skipper of *Olympia* was amused. Quite by accident, he realized his feet weren't cold—not that they necessarily should have been. But if he'd been wandering around his house in his stocking feet, they would have eventually become cold. Aboard *Olympia* there were no cold decks, no drafts leaking through cracks around windows and doors. A perfect climate. Any change in that specific temperature and humidity would indicate a malfunction. So there was no reason for his feet to be cold—none except the knowledge that he was both the hunter and the hunted.

The situation developed soon after *Olympia* approached the surface for her normal midnight messages. The strategy was as clear to her captain as it was to Hal Snow or Andy Reed. *Olympia* was alone, guarding *Imperator*'s approach to the Aleutian Island passage near Dutch Harbor. One of the Soviet submarines was closing her station. The coded, one-time message for the skipper's eyes only: "DESTROY SOVIET VESSEL."

Olympia's skipper imagined how simple it must all have seemed for those men in Washington to come to such a decision—sink a submarine and kill all the men aboard. The only alternative was for himself, and all of his men, to be killed by the Soviet. There was little doubt in his own mind and, he now realized, none in the minds of the men in Washington, that those were the very same orders the Russian was sailing under—destroy the opposition.

So, considering what would occur shortly, the realization about his feet provided a brief moment of amusement. Not a soul aboard *Olympia* was wearing shoes. It wasn't really that he was exercising an old trick passed down through generations of submariners. Rather, the captain had decided it was a way of uniting the crew in immediate understanding of how serious the mission actually had become. This was *not* a war game. None of them had ever fired a weapon in anger before. There had been many exercises, hours and days of hunting and being hunted, but the end result was always a critique back ashore. The simple act of each man removing his shoes, of seeing his counterparts, his officers, traipsing about *Olympia* in stocking feet, was a way of saying that the exercises are over. Though there was no declared war, there was only one option—the alternative was unacceptable.

Olympia hadn't moved since her captain settled in his preferred location, and in a case like this, the best offense was a good defense. Let the other guy come looking for you. It wasn't a matter of hiding. *Olympia* simply maintained her position, using minimal headway or as little as a nuclear submarine needed to hold her depth.

The Russian was still far enough away that there was no imminent danger. It was the Soviet's responsibility in this game to make the approach, otherwise he would not be in position to intercept *Imperator*. For the time being, this gave *Olympia* the advantage. To wait and listen, quietly, was much to be desired.

There was no pinging, no active sonar involved. A smart submarine, no matter on what side, either waited or crept toward its objective . . . and listened. That was the only way to find your target—wait until it made some noise. So *Olympia*'s skipper joined his sonarmen in listening. There were other sounds—shrimp clicking away nearby, the mournful sound of not-too-distant whales, the churning propellers of faraway surface ships. The passive ability of a submarine, the ability to listen to and identify ocean noises, was all part of this very serious encounter.

The first sound to come through *Olympia*'s listening device that might be identified as another submarine was instantly isolated by the computer. More time than any of them really wanted passed before the sonarmen concurred that the new sound was a Soviet attack submarine. Finally they had a firm series of bearings. Now target motion analysis had to be conducted before any weapons could be fired. And that meant reversing *Olympia*'s course to obtain a second series of bearings to plot the Russian's course and speed.

Olympia's skipper considered all his advantages—his boat was quieter, his torpedoes had a greater range, and he maintained a special confidence in his shoeless crew. The Russian had the advantage of greater depth and perhaps higher speed. With the anechoic coating on the Soviet's double hull, it would be harder for a torpedo to home and the hit would have to be in a critical area. There was no room for near misses.

Though his torpedoes had a greater range, the American captain knew that firing too soon would be a mistake. Once the Russian knew his location, they might have an equal chance of sinking each other. Though he'd allow the other to come within range, *Olympia*'s CO felt comfortable. The first shot would be his.

But he had to avoid overconfidence. Quietly, he called the officers in charge of each space. He wanted to be able to make that initial shot the only one necessary. He wanted noisemakers ready to divert anything that might be fired at him, even in desperation. And he wanted to be able to take off like a scared jackrabbit. None of that was too much to ask of a well-trained crew, but there was no harm in a reminder as their quarry drew closer.

The musky smell of tension permeated the air. It was obvious to *Olympia*'s crew that the Russian might not know their exact location, but his guess wouldn't be too far off. It became clearer when the other gradually began to increase her depth. That would make the torpedo's search that much harder.

As the seconds ticked cautiously by, another element, one that promised that time was indeed short, became obvious. *Imperator* was closing from the south. She was traveling near maximum speed, making no effort to mask her position.

Olympia's captain ordered warm-up for the torpedo. They now had a firing solution. The range was almost perfect, depth less certain. Tubes one and two had been flooded earlier to avoid detection.

"Make the weapon in tube one ready in all respects." The pressure in the tube equalized with the outside. It caused noise, but there was no alteration in the Russian's track.

"Open muzzle door." More noise . . . too much after so much silence . . . too obvious.

"Muzzle door open." The torpedo was peering into the murk.

The weapons control coordinator reported the presets—speed, gyro angle, enabling run. An optimum depth was inserted. The torpedo had been programmed.

"Recommend course two eight one," came from the weapons control coordinator. "Speed eight." That would be their optimum speed and course to fire at the target.

The OOD brought them to the ordered direction. "The ship is ready, sir."

"The weapon is ready, sir."

"Very well."

They were just about there . . . a matter of seconds.

"The solution is ready, sir." They could fire.

Olympia's skipper was close to giving his firing orders—he was opening his mouth—when a terrifying shout rang out: "I have high-speed screws on the Soviet bearing . . . torpedo in the water bearing two seven six!"

The captain felt the chill surge down his spine and for just an instant he was sure that chill had reached his feet.

Then he reeled off his emergency orders automatically, firing the torpedo, commencing evasive action . . . releasing noisemakers, all of it instantaneous, instinctive.

Andy Reed contemplated the drama unfolding to the north. Sleep had been difficult. Aspirins dulled his headache, but nothing would soothe the rasp in his throat. It was the rapidly developing confrontation that left his symptoms in the background.

The approach was classically Russian. He knew the Soviet would increase his depth long before any weapons were actually employed. It was a standard doctrinal approach that other submarines of that class would follow. Reed also knew that *Olympia*'s skipper would wait until his shot was almost assured. There was no point in giving away position to a faster, deeper-diving target. The objective was to make your first shot your best shot. There was another matter for consideration that Reed hoped wouldn't take place. The Russians were improving their technical capabilities every year and their listening gear had advanced tremendously.

Olympia was waiting too long!

Timing. Just a few extra seconds, but now there were two opposing torpedoes in the water—no longer just a game between hunter and hunted. Each had become a target. There was no room for follow up, no chance to wait breathlessly for a torpedo to strike home. Both submarines were frantically attempting to elude the warheads searching for them in the depths.

Reed closed his eyes. It was easier for him to imagine the next step when he could create the picture in his brain. There was the Soviet submarine, deeper than its counterpart, its torpedo searching upward for the target, seeking an identifiable sound that would draw it toward its destiny. The American torpedo might still be attached to *Olympia* by a long, metal thread, her computer directing it to the last known location of the target. Then it, too, would home on the sounds it had been programmed to search out.

More likely, the wire would break as they took evasive action.

The inner space of the Pacific was no longer quiet. Both submarines were accelerating as close to full speed as possible, racing from a closing torpedo. The Russian would likely be heading deeper at the same time. Both submarines employed noisemakers in their wake to deter the torpedo homing devices.

As the situation evolved, the Soviet torpedo was not immediately attracted by *Olympia*'s early noisemakers. The torpedo, still well below its target, sped in the proper direction before rising to search. It was only as the last of the decoys were ejected from the American vessel that Reed's assumption was confirmed. The torpedo was diverted as it rose, exploding thirty yards from the actual target, and *Olympia* reared upward like a bronco, the shock wave snapping through her entire length. The hydrophone array on her tail was ripped off; a high-pitch whine shrieked from her jarred shaft. But her basic systems survived the near-hit.

Olympia's torpedo detonated just off the stern of the Russian, destroying her propeller and warping the shaft. As water spurted through ruptured seals, the Russian craft, suddenly powerless, had no option but to seek the surface.

Olympia turned, listening for her quarry. The beat of the Soviet's propeller was gone. Compressed air could be heard whooshing into ballast tanks, forcing water out as she struggled toward the surface, her forward motion negligible. There was no telling if she would still fire. Obviously she was suffering. No need to close if there was no forward momentum. A second torpedo was instantly on the way.

The silent ocean carried the harsh squeal of only one high-speed torpedo. The Russian was totally involved in the struggle for survival. This time, *Olympia* enjoyed the luxury of monitoring the progress of her torpedo.

On board *Houston*, Reed had no immediate clue to the effect of the initial two explosions that rolled back to their sensitive listening devices. He only knew that both submarines had fired, both torpedoes had detonated. The sound of a single, third torpedo meant one was going for the kill. This time the computer called the eventual winner before the torpedo ever located its target—the screw-beats were American. The frantic roar of compressed air never reached Reed's ears. There was no way to tell how badly damaged the Soviet was, only that it was once again a target. Reed's heart beat in sympathetic response to the Russian's terrified efforts.

Then the second blast came clearly to them, soon followed by the unmistakable, unforgiving sounds of a submarine breaking up. Though Soviet listening devices were shorter range, Reed was sure that what had just taken place might be just as obvious to the Soviet submarine accompanying them—it should already be evading! He also was sure that the Russians had to have a need for revenge, that sudden, natural desire for a parting shot. They had been prepared for more than twenty minutes. He gave the order quickly. In seconds *Helena* launched two torpedoes at the trailing Russian boat.

There had been no hesitation in Reed's decision. While it was his alone, his original orders sanctioned the act. It would be months before the Russians could prove a thing. Of course, the explosions could be heard over great distances underwater but no one could say for sure what had caused them or what the result had been. As far as Reed was concerned, the mission justified his reaction.

The sounds of battle had been monitored by *Imperator*, and they understood what had taken place ahead of them though there was hardly a soul in the active navy who could remember actual submarine warfare. But they knew that when a submarine was killed, every man went down with her.

Resting in her stateroom, Carol Petersen thought back to the early days of *Imperator*'s planning. Computer-aided design of standard seagoing vessels was an art. The giant submarine, however, had taken shape on a modular basis with various teams creating separate units of the vast ship. They worked on their own, using the specifications provided for their particular module while the consortium's computer oversaw the project on a single, giant scale.

The submarine was longer than four football fields laid end to end. Her reinforced hull was a cocoon enclosing compartmentalized units that other teams never saw. The reactor area and associated engineering spaces were a world on their own, as were human subsistence areas, command and control spaces, the massive storage areas, and navigational and sonar units. The consortium planned that there would be no chance she could be sunk by one torpedo, even two or three. She could sustain damage like the old battleships, and damaged or open areas could be automatically sealed off from the remainder of the ship. This compartmentalization was controlled by the computer to avoid the necessity of having a huge crew to operate her. Caesar managed many of these spaces, and his programs were designed to respond to the possibilities of battle damage. Carol felt increasingly secure as *Imperator* continued to prove the success of her design.

Hal Snow also considered the effects of damage to *Imperator*, but at the same time he was reminded of her ability to annihilate almost any challenge. She was a creature born of futuristic technology. Her hull possessed aerodynamic features allowing previously unimagined underwater speeds, and she was driven through the depths in almost total silence by her propulsor system of shroud-enclosed blades. She became a creature of her environment, an immense shark, sinister and lethal.

Her sensory system, under Caesar's direction, could seek out the slightest variants in the marine world, detecting and identifying anything man-made well before her own presence was realized. This capability was tied into a fire-control system able to react instantaneously to a variety of dangers. *Imperator*'s kill capability was well beyond the range of any known submarine weapons. Her highspeed torpedoes could be fired either directly at a target, or conveyed by rocket over the ocean's surface to a target hundreds of miles distant.

Perhaps the aspect that fascinated Snow more than any

other was her ability to support a battalion-size marine amphibious unit. Missile systems were integrated into the fire-control apparatus to support the landing team with antiair or antisurface fire. *Imperator* was capable of either landing her force via undersea amphibious craft, ejected in the manner of a torpedo, or she could surface, defend herself against attack, and land her team in the normal manner. She carried helos for vertical envelopment, and artillery and tank units to provide close support to her ground forces. To Snow, she was a lethal machine beyond anything man had yet imagined, and her most dangerous quality was her ability to deliver this immense force without warning anywhere on the globe. Carrier battle groups and amphibious forces gave prior warning to their enemy. *Imperator* could literally strike without a sound. By herself, she was dangerous to any country who challenged the United States. If she was successful in this initial transit, the Northern Flank of Europe would be her goal. While Hal Snow and Andy Reed were certain they would be directed there, especially after the message to rendezvous with the amphibious force near the Pribilof Islands, they had yet to receive firm orders.

While Snow slept, down in the depths of *Imperator* Caesar continued a ceaseless vigil. Over a one-hour period his sensory system detected and identified more than a hundred different forms of sea life. Other sounds cataloged included every surface craft that passed within his listening range. Water temperature was recorded every minute, and every fifteen minutes, tiny expendable bathythermographs were fired off to record temperatures surrounding Caesar for a distance of ten miles. The reactor was monitored for the tiniest alterations, climate in select spaces was checked on a programmed basis, and the shift of weight via human or liquid motion was monitored to adjust *Imperator*'s trim. And after the Russian submarines had been dispatched, Snow ordered that self-destruct communications packages be fired to the surface once every hour or that *Imperator* could either send or receive sixty-second messages on a special wavelength.

The computer's most impressive talents were being saved for weapons control. Caesar was Hannibal and Napoleon, Patton and MacArthur, nestled in a gray metal box.

It was not in Abe Danilov's nature to remain morose. There were times that Anna simply had to be dismissed from his mind. Just as there was no place for women on a warship, there were times when there was no room even for memories of them. The underwater transit was boring, like driving a car down a straight highway with no traffic or scenery. It could lull the senses. And when Danilov realized this torpor was allowing his sentimentality to overwhelm his mental agility, he forced himself to react.

He called for a messenger to locate Sergoff—then aware how easy it was to wait lazily for another, he canceled his order. After changing into a freshly pressed uniform, he went in search of his senior staff officer, whom he found dozing in his own cabin, an open book on his chest.

"Sergoff . . . Sergoff . . . wake up," Danilov bellowed. "We're growing lazy."

Sergoff sat upright, banging his head on the bunk above him. Never before had Danilov come into his stateroom when they were at sea. Sergoff shook himself like a puppy. "What is it, Admiral?"

"One of us is going to find a polynya so that we can communicate with home base. Perhaps they already have data on *Imperator* that we can use. Then we're going to play games among ourselves."

Captain Sergoff was loyal to Danilov in the old-fashioned manner. Soviet Navy officers often remained within the same command for many years. An officer on a destroyer or cruiser could gradually rise through the ranks to become commanding officer if fitness reports remained exceptional. The theory that constancy bred perfection was often transferred to the staff of senior officers like Danilov. Sergoff, commanding a submarine years ago in the admiral's squadron, had later been selected for Danilov's staff. And as Danilov rose in power, Sergoff's influence also increased.

Sergoff understood the benefits of such security. He

knew his admiral well enough to know that Abe Danilov made few mistakes. But of even greater significance, the admiral's mentor for more than twenty-five years had been the commander in chief of the Soviet Navy. Sergoff, even during moments of wonder at Danilov's impulsive decisions, remained comfortable.

When Danilov interrupted his nap, Sergoff's surprise was momentary. As a matter of fact, he was pleased to see that Danilov's spirit seemed to have returned. Sergoff knew that Anna was dying, as did everyone on *Seratov*. But there was no single person who could express to Danilov the sympathies of his sailors, not even Sergoff. Because Danilov kept both his love and his sadness so deeply within himself, those around him accepted his reticence and made believe they knew nothing of his problem. They watched his moods, their own seeming to rise and fall with the admiral's.

News of Danilov's return to his old self spread through *Seratov* quickly. Sergoff made sure that it was also passed to *Smolensk* and *Novgorod*. The mood of the leader could easily infect his subordinates, and the abrupt changes in Danilov created a positive attitude for the men in the three submarines passing under the arctic icecap.

The news, however, was anything but good when they rose to a polynya to communicate. Sergoff heard it first and even considered withholding the worst until he was sure his admiral's attitude might remain unchanged. Yet even when he passed on the messages concerning the explosions in the northern Pacific, coupled with the failure of either Soviet submarine to report afterwards, and the disappearance of the intelligence ship, the admiral remained positive—a bit subdued, but still in a much better mood than the past two days.

"Perhaps, Sergoff, that's exactly what happened. The Americans sank them." He paused momentarily, knitting his brows in a curious manner as he peered at his chief of staff. "Though I find it hard to believe that they could dispose of Captain Molikov that easily. He was a tough one. But maybe there's nothing to the reports. The explosions could have been anything. Our ships could be playing a game. After all, their mission is intelligence, not war.''

Sergoff nodded in agreement. ''That's a good point. No need to worry yet—''

''But,'' Danilov interrupted, cocking his head to one side, ''that Admiral Reed is a cold-blooded son of a bitch, and the commander of *Imperator* . . . Snow''—he finally remembered—''he's no better. Read the reports on them if you doubt me.''

''I've seen them, Admiral.'' Sergoff's job, at which he had grown adept over the years, was to let his admiral speculate whenever he desired without interrupting with facts or further conjecture. When Danilov mulled over a situation, he often thought aloud. His words didn't necessarily reflect what he believed. He was simply expressing each aspect of the ideas generated in his mind. Sergoff knew when a good chief of staff should add specifics of his own and when he should agree or keep his mouth shut. Danilov appreciated Sergoff's wisdom and often talked directly with him when the time was suitable.

Then, Danilov spoke up. ''What would you do if you were in Admiral Reed's position, knowing what we both know about him?''

Sergoff did not have to think before he answered. ''I'd sink them both. There's no way anyone can prove what happened right away. By the time *Imperator* completes her mission—if she does—those two submarines of ours will have little import. Yes . . . I'd sink them.''

''Of course you would. I would, too. They'd be a damn nuisance otherwise. That's why we're going to play some games today . . . just like riding to the hunt. And we're going to play the *Imperator* game. No, that's not what I really mean,'' Danilov decided as he looked more closely at Sergoff. ''We're going to play American commander, and I'm going to use my computer to act just like I think they do. In two days, Reed or Snow could be very definitely trying to get rid of us, too.''

Later that day, as the Soviet hunter/killer group passed the North Pole, they conducted wholly original subsurface games. At a little more than three hundred miles from the geographical pole, they cavorted like a school of oversize dolphins in more than two thousand meters of icy water.

Though Danilov had never seen *Imperator*, he entertained visions of her in his mind. According to the limited reports he'd received, she sacrificed nothing in maneuverability to achieve her immense size. The admiral knew that *Imperator* was exceedingly fast. Her hull design included experimental design concepts that imitated the dynamics of a fish. Combining knowledge of Snow's personality with tapes of his style when he commanded attack submarines, Danilov developed a picture of what they might encounter. Contrary to what would normally be assumed, his immense quarry was not necessarily an easier target. Because drawings of her weapons suite were unavailable, he had to assume that her defenses were conducted by a computer that detected and analyzed threats. He then assumed it must counter them from individual defensive sectors along the sub's length.

Admiral Danilov alone decided when attacks were successful or thwarted. Three times before the end of the day, *Novgorod* and *Smolensk* had been sunk. *Imperator*'s retaliatory capabilities remained an unknown, and underestimating them could bring failure. His responsibility was to prepare his commanding officers for the unknown. Yet even Sergoff was unaware that his admiral bore a healthy fear of *Imperator*'s powers.

There is a point in time when media involvement in a sensitive political situation may evolve into acceptance of a fact before it has occurred. It is almost impossible to pinpoint when the turnabout takes place, for it is a state of mind rather than an actuality. This oddity can happen in any country at any time. Two factors are required—the will of the people to believe what they are told, and the desire of the media to control their attention and be accepted. It becomes a matter of suspending belief—or disbelief.

This was happening by the third day of *Imperator*'s

voyage. From the American vantage point, the Russians might just as well have been occupying the Northern Flank. Americans pictured in their mind's eye the Norwegians fighting a valiant, losing battle against Russian hordes sweeping across the country in blitzkrieg fashion. Though there was hardly a footprint in the snow around the Soviet border with Norway, the description of Russian forces poised for battle was enough to make invasion an accepted fact. Television news directors fought for viewers with a "what if" campaign that terrified the average American much as his parents had been in 1962—the specter of mass destruction became paramount.

In the Soviet Union, which possessed total control of media events, the probability that American submarines were moving and would soon challenge Soviet forces in the Arctic graduated into a cross-ocean attack. Once again, it appeared that the Motherland faced a challenge no less fierce than Hitler's strike into their heartland almost half a century before. The Soviet citizen was easily convinced that the Americans were finally making a move against their country.

There was little difference in the manner information was provided. In the free media, analysis of a situation became reality in the competition for viewers' attention. The controlled media was designed to get the people behind their government as a mass reaction to aggression. Both efforts were successful. Both might have been under the same system, because they brought the results that the media forces demanded—control of the viewers.

Citizens of both countries desperately needed to see something positive, anything that might win the day against fear.

— 6

THE DEEP WATERS of the northern Pacific quickly became shallow as *Imperator* rose to the surface for the first time south of the Aleutians. The lights of Dutch Harbor were visible to port when they navigated the shallows near the island city shortly before midnight under Caesar's total control. After a late-night conversation on the underwater telephone, Reed and Snow concurred that *Imperator* would maneuver independently until exiting the Bering Strait into the Chukchi Sea. After the two Soviet submarines failed to report, intelligence monitors indicated the Russians had ordered their other boats to remain to the south, trailing the Americans at a safe distance. The Bering Sea was extremely shallow—no place to conduct undersea battle. *Imperator* would operate primarily on the surface. Cloudy weather that time of year would automatically negate Soviet intelligence satellites.

Beyond the Aleutians, *Imperator*'s sonar identified sounds of surface ships approaching the rendezvous point a little more than a hundred miles to the northwest. Three hours later, with skies turning pale to the east, the amphibious force witnessed the approach of a massive black sea monster. A gray, choppy sea washed against a hull that seemed as long as an aircraft carrier. Any man among them who knew submarines understood how much more lay beneath the waves.

Two amphibious transports were ready to transfer their field-equipped marine contingents to the submarine. In less than three hours, under the protection of a solid cloud cover, *Imperator* received marines and their supplies. Air-cushioned landing boats, mechanized landing craft, and helicopters converged on the submarine, transferring their cargo into well-marked holds that appeared in the massive hull. The submarine swallowed over fifteen hundred men and their equipment as fast as they could be transported. When she was full, the mysterious submarine disappeared to the north faster than any surface ship they'd ever seen. Before the crews of the amphibious ships returned to their bases to report this wonder, *Imperator* would already have completed her mission and would no longer remain a secret.

Gulls from the Pribilof Islands, sensing a foreign presence invading their environment, swooped low. Hovering over *Imperator*'s sail, as curious as any cat, they searched for a life form that might identify this creature. But there was nothing—no animal appeared, there were no sounds. Nothing of any concern to a gull.

Overhead, satellites automatically reoriented to this aberration in the Bering Sea. Infrared sensors detected minute changes in the water and air temperatures, but there was nothing to be gained that wasn't already known. Soviet fishing boats lounged off the nearby Pribilofs and further north by St. Lawrence Island. They would be efficiently nudged aside by Coast Guard patrol craft at the first sign that sophisticated sound gear had replaced fishing nets.

Carol Petersen was aware of Snow standing behind her in the computer center before he spoke.

"You certainly do concentrate, don't you," he exclaimed. "I was outside for a while, wandering up and down in front of these windows, even waving. You were so intent I was actually afraid I'd startle you if I just barged in. So," he concluded with amusement, "I finally barged in—after knocking—and still"—he shrugged—"nothing."

"Pull up a chair, Captain. Perhaps I do get a little paranoid sometimes, sitting down here all alone with Caesar as a companion. It can be rather disconcerting when he's able to answer a question before I'm quite sure how to enter it. I'm beginning to think he's taught himself how to read minds."

"Then he'll know I'm here under false pretenses." How curious, Snow thought, referring to Caesar that way. Ships are automatically women. They become a she to the men who sail them. And here's a computer that's already been christened a male . . . even referred to that way. "Here." He handed her a list. "Caesar's going to conduct surface exercises with me today. From here on there's nothing more than seventy-five meters of ocean under us."

Her eyebrows raised as she scanned the list. "It's easy enough to have Caesar do all this. It's part of his program, but is it a good idea to override him in the middle of all this? Are your OODs ready . . . ?"

"I think so. Anyway, I'll be in the control room as soon as you get started. One of the first things the OOD will do is call me up there. If it looks too bad, I'll ask you to put him back on the line."

"What if any Soviet units approach when his sensors are down?"

"I've already talked with Andy Reed. He's taken over the guard. No problem. If you accept the way I drive submarines, I'll put all my faith in you and your friend, Caesar."

"Fair enough. Let me call up the damage control program." Waiting for Caesar to bring up the detail she requested, the thought that had been on her mind since they left the fishbowl finally erupted. It had been on the tip of her tongue so many times before. "None of you have ever sailed with a woman before, but is anyone going to accept that it's finally happened?"

"Not on a submarine." There was no change of expression.

"That's not what I mean."

"If I have to sail with a computer, I guess I can sail with a woman."

"That's still not what I mean. You know damn well I'm getting tired of the men staring at me. Some of them, the old-fashioned sailors, hate having a woman aboard. Some are curious, and . . . and I suppose some of them are just plain horny. I don't know that I like that . . . I mean I know I can't do anything about anyone's attitude. Oh, I don't know what I mean." She sighed, her eyes still on the screen. "I guess it's a lot like being the only black person surrounded by whites. I'm not scared of anyone . . . oh, do you see what I'm driving at?" It seemed impossible to put into words.

Snow was immediately uncomfortable. His answer was dry and elusive. "The captain's supposed to be available to everyone aboard and listen to every problem." He chewed at his lower lip for a moment. "Frankly—since you're so frank—I was really hoping you wouldn't bring it up, 'cause I wasn't quite sure how to answer it . . . and I'm still not." Snow folded his arms. "Do I bother you . . . personally?"

"No, that's not it . . . not really." The menu ran down the screen before her. She responded by typing more detail on the keyboard. It was easier to study the screen than to look at Snow. "Actually, I rather like you, Captain. And this isn't the place for that, is it?" She poked at the keyboard again, then turned. "That's why I wondered how long you'd been standing behind me. I don't want you to think I'm paranoid, and I don't want you to think I'm standoffish."

Snow's expression was an answer. "Well, that's a different attitude than I've noted among any of the other members of the crew lately. It's almost unheard of for any crew member to tell the captain whether or not they like him. As far as the crew's attitude, it was probably something I would have avoided mentioning for another day or two myself." What the hell else do you say, he wondered? This is why women have been barred from warships . . . what with the navy's Victorian attitude toward women. "Since I am this ship's only captain, I should have an answer for everything you're thinking. I don't," he concluded with finality.

"I'm not the last unicorn, but I've been feeling more like one since we got underway." She looked at him curiously, then turned back to the screen. "Enough said. Caesar says he's ready."

"Start at the head of that list. We'll secure Caesar's transmission lines forward of frame two hundred and try a fire in the forward pump room."

Within moments, the familiar "Captain to the control room" echoed through *Imperator*. By the time Snow arrived in control, the OOD had employed remote control to secure the pump room area. Electrical cross-connections had been completed to check temperatures in the area. The drill was effective. If high temperatures had actually been recorded in any space, automatic sprinklers would have activated until a fire-fighting team took control. At the same time, engineers would have been at work restoring Caesar's control to that section of the ship.

With the crew normally functioning in the after third of *Imperator*, more than eight hundred feet existed that were controlled mostly by a faceless, soulless computer. Remote sensors were therefore critical to normal operations. Computer monitoring became essential. Secondary units provided a backup to Caesar, their main purpose being to signal breaks or interruptions in the submarine's engineering integrity. If Caesar was unable to respond to an emergency, his provisional features included a report to the control room concerning those areas of *Imperator* no longer under his protection.

Snow had always been an authoritarian, one who had determined that the best way to manage a submarine was by leaving no doubt about his absolute control. He was convinced *Imperator*'s size required a captain who exercised his powers without the slightest doubt in his own ability. Snow's talents were legendary in the submarine force and the respect for him when he returned soon expanded into a sense of awe.

Snow's normal method of command was to remain aloof, giving orders when needed, allowing his subordinates generally to manage the ship's affairs. These exercises allowed him to develop a better grasp of each individual's capabilities. It was one of the few times he actually became a part of the crew and involved himself in their exercises.

The commander of the marine unit, Colonel Campbell, joined them in the control room since the forward spaces now became the responsibility of his men. Campbell knew very little about submarines but before the day was over, he left no doubt with Snow that his men could manage the forward section of the ship in an emergency.

Each of Snow's watch sections had the opportunity to respond to fires, flooding spaces, collisions, torpedo ruptures, steering failures, reactor scram, and a shopping list of other emergencies. Operational control was lost three times. Each time Caesar concluded that *Imperator* would also have been lost. He provided a printout of alternate methods to bring him back on-line shortly after he reported the submarine sunk each time.

The final exercise expanded Snow's confidence in Caesar. He was shut down completely throughout the ship. The only access remained down in computer control with Carol Petersen. Communications to various sections of the boat gradually failed. Power winked out. Air grew stagnant. The loss of sensors left them blind to the world outside. Losing Caesar was akin to shutting off the sun. An aircraft carrier of the same size could continue through the wits and courage of the six thousand men aboard. The sixty people who sailed *Imperator* were unable to respond to their ship's needs as Caesar slowly failed.

The sensation was eerie, similar to a large, complex city slowly coming to a standstill—subways, buses, construction, light, sound, everything would eventually disappear until decay hung ominously in the air. The pervasive whisper of silence was the most frightening. Under normal conditions, man naturally integrated with the hum of his environment until it became inaudible. As Caesar shut down, no different than a great city coming to a halt, the sense of doom became overwhelming. There was loneliness in place of confidence; a void supplanted the feeling of protection and well-being. Snow and each person aboard now understood Caesar's significance in their lives. Caesar could give and Caesar could take away. He was their heart and soul. The sense of dependency, even for Hal Snow, was disconcerting.

Soon after Snow secured the exercises that day, a message was copied that had been addressed to Admiral Reed: "YOU ARE DIRECTED TO ASSUME WARTIME CONDITIONS UPON TRANSITING BERING STRAIT. SOVIET HUK GROUP PROJECTED TO BE STATIONED OFFSHORE LIKELY DUE WEST POINT BARROW. DETAIL TO FOLLOW VIA SCRAMBLER 2200."

Captain Sergoff was the ideal chief of staff for an admiral like Danilov. There were some who considered themselves elevated to a military elite once they consorted with men whose sleeves were lined with gold, while others fawned over their admirals like wet nurses. Sergoff treated Abe Danilov as he would have preferred to be treated himself. He was a buffer for personal problems, an analyzer of data, a strategist when Danilov was unsure, and a merciless enforcer of his admiral's orders.

Sergoff was also clever. Years before, of all the Soviet submariners involved in the emplacement of listening devices and mines along the Baltic coast of Sweden, he was the only one to carry out his mission properly and without detection. The others had been either so cautious they failed to locate their equipment properly, or so incautious that they were noted either approaching their area or in setting their mines. Sergoff was eventually given tactical command to complete the operation.

Captain Sergoff also possessed a modest talent for playing the foil to the angry or irritated admiral. When Danilov's temper or patience reached their bounds, Sergoff was available to absorb the venom. Though such a situation rarely surfaced, it allowed others to note that both men were human and capable of adapting to each other's failings. Danilov could do little wrong and his chief of staff seemed destined for greater things under his master's tutelage.

When Washington's 2200 message commenced on the scrambler, *Imperator* was located 150 miles south of the Bering Strait. Her escort of three nuclear attack submarines were slightly ahead, cruising in a half circle reminiscent of an old convoy screen.

One of Sergoff's responsibilities was to screen all messages, selecting only the most critical for Danilov. The ability to intercept American communications via the scrambler system had been on-line for more than twelve months. It had proven valuable at times, though Sergoff often felt the Americans were challenging the integrity of their own system with junk that should never have been classified. He was sometimes amused by what the U.S. considered so vital to keep from the Soviets; so much of it was common knowledge within Kremlin circles.

This time, the message proved of little value, other than the fact that the Americans knew almost as much about them as they knew about themselves. *Seratov* and each of her sisters were clearly identified. Danilov, Sergoff, and each of the commanding officers were covered, and details of equipment capabilities, the experience of both officers and crews, and command patterns were surprisingly accurate. It was nothing to bother Admiral Danilov with, though it was worth pointing out that American intelligence was exceedingly meticulous. Neither man had ever expected to surprise *Imperator*. Nor did they underestimate Andy Reed's capabilities. The only part of the scrambler message that was unintelligible was the data for the computer. There were also times that Sergoff wondered if the Americans knew that their scrambler system had been compromised. Perhaps they did and continued to use it for the benefit of the Russians because it was too complex and costly to send their computerized (and still secure) data through a new system.

Sergoff's final responsibility, one that he took seriously, was to interpret his admiral's moods, to adjust to them or to attempt to adjust them when the situation demanded. He was more concerned about Danilov's high and low points in the past week than he had been for a long time. At times, the man seemed deeply introspective, almost to the point of depression. Yet he could reverse these moods in a matter of hours. Sergoff had long ago accepted Anna Danilov's influence on the admiral's disposition and the chief of staff could accept this because of her continuous kindness to him, as though he was her son. Yet this time it was almost as if the lady were on board *Seratov*. It was unnerving to see the admiral's mood switches.

Perhaps the poor lady has finally died, Sergoff mused. She certainly deserves some relief from her suffering. Or perhaps her ghost is riding with us . . . or with Abe Danilov! The thought sent a shudder down his spine. Women on submarines were dangerous enough. But a ghost, a personal ghost, was . . . He hoped that the current upswing in Danilov's spirit this past day would remain.

Andy Reed blew his nose again. The skin was raw and chapped, and he was careful. Replacing the soggy handkerchief in his breast pocket, he bent over the chart table to read the latest meteorological reports again, anything to take his mind off this interminable cold. The floe ice, sparse enough now, gradually increased until it was a solid mass approximately 150 miles due north of the Bering Strait. There it hung like a massive gray-white curtain, one that would cut them off from the outside world. There were polynyas and leads that would allow occasional communications, and they could break through the ice in certain places. The ice could often be used to their advantage during search or evasion. But, once underneath, they became as equal as enemies could be. Like boxers circling for an opening, submariners depended on speed and judgment.

Reed picked up his baseball cap, smoothing his hair as he set it back on his head. He replaced the weather messages on the proper board, moved the pencils over to the corner of the chart he'd been studying, and announced to the staff watch officer that he was going to rest in his bunk for a while. He was forcing himself to remain awake, yet there was no purpose. Everything that he had been dallying with at the chart table were things that others were responsible for.

Back in his tiny stateroom, Reed flopped on his bunk without kicking off his shoes. He could sleep anywhere without the normal comforts most others required. Little naps of five or ten minutes, sometimes half an hour if he was lucky, left him wide awake and rested. It was simply a matter of losing himself in a pleasant thought. He would be suddenly asleep, often dreaming of the last clear picture in his mind.

This time that picture had been his one and only hobby—sailing. Since his academy days, when he raced on Chesapeake Bay, Andy Reed had been a devout sailor. Nothing pleased him quite so much as a small sailboat and a fair breeze. With just Lucy and himself, it was easily the most peaceful method of relaxation there was. With the kids, it was less so until they grew up enough to crew for him. Then the sailboats in the Reed family gradually increased in size. The fact that he sired a crew for his favorite pastime never ceased to amuse him. He would tease Lucy that if they worked at it hard enough, the Reed family could eventually crew a twelve-meter yacht all by themselves.

They sailed the first boat on Long Island Sound when he was stationed in New London. It was christened *We Two* and was on the water every moment they could find from the early cold days of April until the first northeast storms in the fall. When the first baby was born, it was a joke to cross out the old name and paint in *We Three*. A few years later in Hawaii, the new boat became *We Four*, and that soon became *We Five*. Wherever the Reeds sailed, the crew of the *We Five* attracted new friends with two little children bundled in orange life jackets manning lines, and the baby asleep in the cutty up forward. When they were transferred to Charleston, the next boat was a few feet longer to accommodate six Reeds. It seemed natural to once again cross out a "Three" and a "Four" and a "Five" and a "Six" when the *We Seven* was christened.

The new baby, their surprise, was born when Andy was on shore duty in Washington. Their next sailboat, a handsome twenty-six footer, was purchased when he went out to Pearl Harbor to command a new submarine. Reed simply had *We Eight* painted across the transom. He was sure anything other than that might bring back luck. But that name lasted only through part of their first weekend on the water. When they returned to the dock that Sunday morning, the stern had been repainted with the old *Two, Three, Four, Five, Six, Seven,* and crossed out and an exclamation point next to the *Eight!* And there was no way they would ever be allowed to change that name with the attention they attracted as the eight Reeds came down the pier that Sunday morning for a day of sailing.

When Andy Reed approached the quarterdeck of his new command that Monday morning, there was little doubt who the painters had been. Above the ornately carved shield of the submarine *Cavalla* was a second, handpainted sign *We One Hundred Twenty-Eight*.

That had been seven years before. Back then, Andy Reed had been considered flag material and every sailor he knew looked forward to it. The selection board reached way down to give him his first star. But promotion to flag rank had taken him away from the squadron he commanded and he'd seen too many desks until this mission.

Now, as he fell asleep, his last thought was of the *We One Hundred Twenty-Eight* sign that hung over the mantle in his house. The *We Eight* had been tied up much too long at its berth on the Potomac. As he slept, there were no thoughts of torpedoes or other weapons of war. Andy Reed never worried about the future.

Traveling on the surface, *Imperator* was on an advanced stage of alert. Earlier in the evening there had been a near-collision with a surface object that had never been identified. Even Carol Petersen, who had been taking some air on the bridge, had been unable to see it, and Caesar had reported nothing. It was only in the final seconds that something activated his sensors for evasive action.

Now, an hour before midnight, *Imperator*'s radar printed an airborne contact whose takeoff had been reported earlier by satellite. From an airbase well inside Siberia, the Soviet Badger had climbed to forty thousand feet as it headed east toward the Bering Strait. This particular aircraft, though armed with air-to-surface missiles, was fitted for electronic intelligence. It was a reconnaissance flight, preliminary to any attack.

U.S. satellite recon maintained a steady picture once it was evident the Badger would soon enter air space affecting *Imperator*. A target designation link for the submarine was automatically fed into Caesar's system. At a range of four hundred miles, the Badger began a slow descent, circling to the west and then the south of *Imperator*.

At three hundred miles, the aircraft's active electronic devices went silent. She turned purely to intelligence gathering, a myriad of detectors silently reaching out in the night to analyze the slightest electronic radiation from *Imperator*. A half hour before midnight, Andy Reed requested that Snow radiate signals from a brand new unit—nothing steady, just enough to attract attention, to lure the curious closer.

The Badger turned toward *Imperator* and descended below five thousand feet, seeking the bait of new, highly classified equipment. This was akin to dangling raw meat. Snow activated his laser system as the Badger was drawn into the kill radius. There was never a warning, no indication to the Soviet air crew that they had come under fire. No explosion—nor any shock—occurred as Caesar carefully pinpointed the Badger with a ten-second irradiation.

The Badger's listening equipment noted the event with a high-pitched squeal a millisecond before the unit ceased to operate. Piercing noise deafened the operators, as the deadly sound penetrated through the radio headphones of the pilot and copilot. All equipment ceased functioning—navigation, radar, communications, targeting devices for weapons systems. In less than five seconds, the pilot understood he was under attack of some kind. Yet he was unable to either defend himself or return fire. The last Siberian base lost contact with him as he fought to regain control.

The Badger turned sharply west, climbing once again as it did so. No better than a fish out of water, it flew through the inky night with no idea of true height, direction, or speed. Finding a large enough airfield in Siberia would be the luck of the draw, and approaching any military installation without preliminary identification would be hazardous. Parachuting into the cold Bering Sea was also an unacceptable alternative, since there was no chance of survival. There was no way they could respond to queries from the lazy and often bored radar installations as they closed the Siberian perimeter, but they had become a fresh contact for their nervous countrymen.

Forty-five minutes after the laser attack, the Badger became the target of a missile from a friendly station. The air crew had little idea of their location, and there was no indication of their fate until the starboard wing tank erupted with the detonation. *Imperator* had brought down her first aircraft. Three more times within the next hour, other Badgers attempted to close them. One even fired a cruise missile. All of the aircraft met the same fate as the first. The missile dropped harmlessly out of control into the Bering Sea.

Hal Snow stared at the bland, sand-colored bulkhead in his stateroom, contemplating the Badgers' demise but finding little to concern himself with, since they would have done the same to him. He was pleased with his lethal craft, more so now that they had departed the fishbowl and *Imperator* was proving herself. As he'd watched her take shape over the past year he also understood that there was always time to get out—to return to a safer, saner life. But he wouldn't. Whenever the thought crossed his mind, it was met in an instant by a singular desire to be the commanding officer of the greatest warship afloat. He was willing to acknowledge that they understood his ego at least as well as he did. Yet now, facing increasing danger, he felt the need to talk with someone. It wasn't fear by any means, just the need to talk.

Realizing sleep was impossible, Snow headed for the wardroom. It was empty and the coffee was old and thick and stale. Then he saw a cup with lipstick around the rim perched on the pantry shelf. The stewards often cleaned up stray cups before midnight, so perhaps Carol Petersen had just been there. She'd made the effort to communicate with him earlier in the day . . . why not? Snow had yet to understand that he was desperately in need of a friend.

"I'll bet that's you, Captain," she responded to his soft knock. "Come on in."

It never occurred to Snow to question how she knew it was he. "I'm not disturbing you, am I?" She was sitting at a writing desk folded out of the bulkhead, a blank sheet of paper before her. "Writing a letter home?" he asked when she shook her head to the first question.

"I was thinking about it. You can see how far I've gotten."

"To your parents?"

"Just my mother. Dad died five years ago. She's all alone now. The rest of the kids are just like me—strung out around the world and no better at writing letters."

Snow was lowering himself into the chair beside her desk, but he stood up again. "Really, I'd be happy to leave if—"

"No, please, Captain." She pointed to the chair. "I know enough about you to think that maybe my friend, Caesar, had gotten you down."

"I don't know if it's that so much. Sometimes I have to keep reminding myself—that Caesar's still a machine. I think I can handle that. It's that laser system. I punched in the data to fire on those Russian planes." Snow stroked his chin thoughtfully before looking back at her. "You understand we had to compromise a terrific weapon a little while ago. We should have saved it until the last minute. The Russians will figure out eventually that it was this ship that disabled that recon plane and dumped the others. Submarines don't normally bring down aircraft, but this one did. I wish I'd saved that laser. . . ."

Carol studied her fingernails for a moment, then murmured, almost as an afterthought, "I wonder how much difference it makes whether they know it now, or a couple of days from now."

"It's a matter of how much they know, I suppose. They're not going to take the chance of losing any others tonight. Once the intelligence people on either side have the slightest inkling of something new, they pick away one bite at a time. Odds and ends fall together after a while. This time we left nothing to the imagination."

"Captain, you've been worrying when there's really nothing you can do about it." She paused. "Zapping those planes was just part of what's getting to you, isn't it?"

Snow stood up as if he was about to leave. She said nothing. "Well, I can't drink when things seem to be getting to me . . . and there's no way I can go for a long walk to get everything out of my system." Once again the words he might have said to make her an integral part of his crew wouldn't come to the surface.

She looked up quizzically. "I don't know Captain Snow well enough to offer the answer you're looking for, my friend. I've got an idea about you . . . directly . . . as much as I know about you at this stage."

"I suppose what you should tell me is to get back to the job I was hired for in the first place and stop grousing about it." He moved toward the doorway. He had no idea now why he'd bothered . . . or perhaps he'd somehow made a move.

"No," she answered, "I'm not going to say anything of the kind. I'm going to say instead that I'm willing to talk to you again if you're looking for someone other than one of your old submariners. I'm going to be one of your most valued shipmates, too, and you'd better believe that. Do you understand what I mean?" Her eyes held his as if she dared him to disagree.

"I think so."

"Good. Then we have started understanding each other.

We'll work together. That's more important to me than you can understand. Now, Captain, I do have to finish this letter to my mother. Good night.''

"Good night." Walking back to his stateroom, Snow could not quite imagine whether he felt more in command of his ship, or still at odds with himself.

The object *Imperator* had almost collided with earlier now began to bear more import. Though the Kremlin was aware of *Imperator*'s passage through the northern Pacific, the voyage had yet to be announced to the American people. The master plan was to make the announcement as she surfaced on the opposite side of the icepack days later.

Like so many great plans, however, they failed. *Imperator* had been seen. In the early evening of the fourth day, as a brilliant red sun was tinting the fog banks, the submarine appeared as a great black sea monster to two men in a fragile skin boat.

Their craft, fashioned from walrus skin stretched over a bone-and-wood frame, showed little change through generations of Eskimos. The only departure from tradition as they challenged the frigid arctic waters was the addition of motors. The added power allowed them to extend the range of fishing and hunting areas. But once there, these natives would revert to their ancient ways, paddling by hand into their favorite fishing area or sneaking up on an unsuspecting seal, the motor long since silenced.

Imperator might have passed as a sea monster that evening if the occupants of the skin boat had both been aging Eskimos. The submarine appeared suddenly, immense and threatening as the fog parted, and the monster bore down on them through the floe ice at a tremendous speed. Tons of water rose in a bulge over the submarine's bow, foaming down into hollow gulleys on either side. The Eskimo was transfixed as he peered at the submarine's bulky sail more than a thousand feet to the rear. The creature made no sound. There was only the surflike rumble as the parted waters and ice fell back in white foam. It seemed as if this monster had been sent to claim them. The other man, a research scientist taking a moment to fish with a native friend, was the first to react. Though he had seen nothing like *Imperator* before, he was not superstitious. Dropping the motor back in the water, he yanked repeatedly on the starting cord. Perhaps a healthy, natural fear made him forget to prime it.

The simple act of pulling at the engine was enough for the computer deep inside the submarine. Caesar's sensors immediately located the tiny craft bobbing on the surface directly ahead, and put *Imperator*'s rudder over sharply. The sub could not maneuver as rapidly on the surface as in its natural element, but responded quickly enough to ease away from the tiny craft. As she did, the stern began to swing toward the skin boat. Caesar waited only long enough to ensure they would miss before reversing his rudder angle. The stern moved in the opposite direction.

The Eskimo and the scientist remained seated, staring speechlessly as the immense black creature sped silently past them. It was so close that there was no doubt it was man-made. The scientist could project how much of this submarine must be below the surface. It was the size of an aircraft carrier . . . and there were no markings to identify it. But nothing like this was known to man. It could have passed as a bad dream for the scientist, or an apparition for the Eskimo, if they hadn't noticed a person appear in the sail just before the fog bank closed around them again. The scientist in the skin boat doubted she saw them, but there was no doubt in his mind that he had seen a woman peering in their direction, as if she knew something was out there, but was unable to perceive it through the fog. Then, it was gone, as rapidly as it had appeared.

Since there had been no markings, there was no way to tell who had built this monstrous craft. It could be dangerous to his country, and the natural suspicion in waters so close to Siberia would be that it was of Russian origin. It was unlikely something like that could be built in America without the people knowing of it.

As they tossed in the deep swell left by the passing of the submarine, the scientist remembered to prime the engine before he pulled the starting cord. The motor roared into life instantly, and they were off at top speed for the Eskimo village where the scientist radioed their sighting to Fairbanks.

Within hours the wire services had picked up the story.

On a submarine located 150 miles north of Prudhoe Bay in the Arctic Ocean, unaware of the media attention about to be focused on *Imperator*, another lonely captain was saying good night. Abe Danilov neatly folded Anna's letter after the first reading and lay back on his bunk with one hand under his head.

His good night could not be heard, because his lips never moved. It had been just a whisper from the recesses of his heart. Anna was thousands of miles away, and he toyed with what time it might be at their apartment in Moscow. More than likely the sun was already well into the sky. Natalya probably had arrived to straighten up the apartment and prepare some food for the day, even if Anna would later refuse what was offered. That was more likely at that stage of the disease.

Danilov hoped that somehow she would be able to sense that thousands of miles from her bedside her man had wished her a loving good night. In recent months he liked to believe that couples could develop a special sensitivity— that certain awareness when their mate was thinking of them. There were times he had been sure in the last few days that Anna was actually transmitting her innermost thoughts to him. Now he was responding in kind.

Right this moment, he was acknowledging her letter, silently attempting with all his power to let her know that he was as proud as she was of young Boris, who had just become a doctor. He was their second son, and the last child, born in 1966 when the family was still in Leningrad. Arriving after Eugenia, his fate was already unknowingly sealed by his older sister. No matter what he did, no matter how hard he tried to please his father, there was little room in Danilov's heart to offer equal love to a second son. Anna's letter was much different in approach from the earlier ones because she had begun by saying, "I'm going to tell you who your son, Boris, is and why I have loved him so specially in his short lifetime."

As he lay in his bunk remembering each line of her letter, he wondered why he'd never realized how much Boris was like him. Anna claimed that Sergoff had first emphasized that to her. One night during a dinner party, when the admiral had left the room, Sergoff considered a photograph of the admiral as a young officer in Sebastopol for a few moments. Then he pointed out to Anna how much the boy resembled his father. It was a remarkable likeness. Anna Danilov recognized how similar their mannerisms were, the short temper, an inability to suffer fools that had made the boy so many enemies at school, not to mention neatness, vanity, orderliness—they were both perfectionists.

Boris Danilov imitated his father because he so wanted the man's approval. The boy worshiped his father and yearned for a love that was not forthcoming because it was his older brother who had been chosen to follow in the father's footsteps. Anna had written: "Boris's fate was that you only had room in your disciplined heart for one boy to succeed you and one daughter to be a princess." That was why his son—the best student, the one who never broke his father's rules, the one who ate everything on his plate—finally determined to become independent. Yet even when he had announced that he had an appointment to a special school for the sciences, with the vague hope of shocking his father, his natural ability had still gone unrecognized.

Anna Danilov's time was limited and she was now urging her husband to accept what mattered to her the most—love.

Most important, Abe, when you are next in Moscow why don't you contact some of your friends at the air force ministry and ask about your second son, Boris. You will learn that he is one of the finest students in space medicine. He tells me that two of his class will be selected to become cosmonauts—and he is at the head of the class! Find out who your son is. Learn to love him and his accomplishments, and the pride you show will be returned by a boy who so wanted to please you for so many years.

Before Abe Danilov whispered good night once more, he also sent a message that said how hard he would try to follow her wishes. He understood what she was saying. It was urgent that he settle his business and return home as quickly as possible. She was right. He'd known it for years. But somehow he'd never been able to put it into words.

While not a word was heard from Moscow concerning the voyage of *Imperator*, concrete actions were taken despite the little they knew of her capabilities. There were wise men in the Kremlin power structure who, while trusting Abe Danilov implicitly, felt that he was rushing headlong into the unknown without the power to match it. *Imperator*'s power had already been demonstrated. With accurate, submerged-cruise-missile capability and a destructive laser system, there was little doubt that *Imperator* promised many more surprises.

Six additional high-speed attack submarines were dispatched to positions beneath the icecap to await further orders from Abe Danilov. A Spetsnaz commando unit, trained exclusively in cold regions warfare, was detached to an airbase near Murmansk. They were placed on an arctic jump alert to defend an underwater demolition unit. For some reason, a forward-thinking individual had suggested the necessity of control of air space over the arctic regions.

Tension is a serpent that attacks slowly, so slowly that its effect is unnoticed until it has taken a firm grasp on its victim. Its ability to gradually invest the human body is comparatively similar on a mass level.

The patience of a large segment of the American people was becoming strained by international events. They had learned to be skeptical of their own government during Vietnam, and that distrust had never completely evaporated. Each time a potential international conflict developed far from home, there were certain members of political circles, the media, and the citizenry who automatically cried wolf before they understood all of the facts. Their opposite number would normally identify a complex plot aimed specifically at the United States regardless of the location or nations involved.

Few Americans have been schooled in the significance of the Far North. Anything beyond the Arctic Circle is considered frozen and therefore of little value. Little credence was given to the fact that all of Norway, not just her southern half, was as much a part of NATO as the Mediterranean countries. Furthermore, claimed the detractors, there was little strategic value in ice and snow, not to mention an ocean that was covered by ice and therefore unnavigable. The government, and those few who really understood the Arctic in the Soviet scheme, attempted to explain the USSR's reasoning for their current position.

Tension, invisible at first, managed to infest the general populace. Here was another potentially dangerous situation that once again could burst into warfare with the Soviet Union, and most people immediately anticipated nuclear war. It was much like being a passenger in a huge plane—since only the crew could understand its operation, there was a sense of futility among the passengers, feeling they had no control over their own destiny.

The physical reaction to such anxiety was no different in the Soviet Union. Television news also carried selected messages concerning this growing confrontation. Their news was controlled in that there was only one aggressor, and that aggressor would be challenged directly in this situation. Such bravado brought only one message to the Soviet citizen: The United States possessed nuclear weapons and the desire to use them if the situation demanded such action. While the news belonged to the state, the Soviet citizen shared much the same dessert as his American counterpart—futility, which spawned tension!

And the leaders on both sides had yet to reveal the sinking of *Fahrion*. It was an incident that neither side could be proud of and one that was pushing them both irretrievably to the edge of conflict.

7

ADMIRAL REED'S *Houston* led the way through the Bering Strait with *Olympia* abeam, the latter to continue along the coast on the surface. Her damage was superficial but there was no reason to dive until repairs were complete. *Helena* remained astern of *Imperator* to block any Soviet sub attempting to sneak through the strait for a stern attack. Friendly aircraft, unseen overhead but certainly there, added to his security. Reed was certain there would be no further trouble from the Russians after their Badgers had been downed so easily.

The challenge lay beyond the Bering Strait. Andy Reed anticipated the Soviet hunter/killer (HUK) group somewhere ahead of them. *Houston* moved out on the point. Being considerably smaller, she could dive, even in the shallow Chukchi waters, and act as a forward listening post for *Imperator*. The four submarines communicated freely by radio while cruising on the surface. It was understood that Snow would continue to operate independently although Reed desperately hoped he could locate the Soviets before *Imperator* was able to go deep. The advantage, as in almost any encounter, would go to the boat able to initiate an attack. Once they both were aware of each other, it would become a cat-and-mouse game.

As *Imperator* navigated the thickening ice of the Bering Strait, Andy Reed spent much of his time at the computer. Everything available on Danilov and his three submarines had been relayed by satellite during their surface transit. There was little difficulty in selecting the most obvious route for a submarine departing Polyarnyy. He was uncertain only when they would arrive in the vicinity.

In analyzing Abe Danilov's character and career, Reed found even more that was similar to his own. Their strong family ties seemed to follow the same pattern. Danilov was aggressive, as ruthless as Reed had been when he sank the two Soviet subs the previous day, and he was cunning. It was a mistake to take any competitor for granted. Reed's assumptions were reinforced by the computer.

Danilov's submarines wouldn't surface. That was obvious. They would remain invisible in the safe confines of deep water far enough off the continental shelf. It also would be senseless for the three Soviet submarines to stick together. If the decision was Reed's, he would leave one along the Alaskan coast in deep water and position two well apart to prevent *Imperator* from racing due north toward the pole.

The ice became thick to the north. Floe ice was heavy beyond the Bering Strait and totally impassable that time of year well into the Chukchi Sea. There was no way the Americans would be able to use aircraft to locate the Russians either with sonobuoys or magnetic detectors, nor could satellites pierce the icepack. It would be a simple case of submarine against submarine.

Reed's intent was to confuse the Russians initially. He ordered a variety of time-delay noisemakers dispersed along and well ahead of their route. Where openings appeared in the ice, they were dropped by aircraft. The capabilities of these new noisemakers were unknown to the Russians. They were small, self-propelled units that would take off at high speed once in the water. As their fuel became exhausted, their engines fell to the bottom. The noisemakers remained motionless, suspended at a preset depth. Then, at a predetermined time, they would employ almost every natural sound that existed in that part of the ocean until their batteries died. They were so sophisticated that it would be impossible for all but the best sonar operator to distinguish between the natural and the man-made sound. This tactic would initially offer a confusing, protective sound barrier and would prevent Danilov from recording and analyzing *Imperator* too soon. Reed intended to make it a pursuit of the unknown for as long as possible.

Snow was tired. Though Carol Petersen had insisted that the computer could navigate the Bering Strait with better eyes than any man, he remained on the bridge. He was imbued with the tradition of generations. The night was black and there was very little water under the keel. A captain must remain on his bridge in such a situation. . . .

The Bering Strait was anything but busy at that time of year because floe ice was still thick. Caesar plotted the paths of occasional fishing craft long before Snow saw any of them. Whenever he marked one with the radar cursor and punched a locator number into the computer, the response was instant. At one point, out of curiosity, Snow requested a pictorial surface-situation report. Instantly, an accurate display of the area appeared with *Imperator* in the center, and the narrowest part of the strait just ahead of them. Fairway Rock lay a couple of miles on the port beam and Cape Prince of Wales, the westernmost point of Alaska, stood to starboard. Little Diomede Island, just two-and-a-half miles from Russian territory, lay off the port bow. Ahead, the waters opened onto the Chukchi Sea. Andy Reed's three submarines were still clearly evident.

The air picture was quite the opposite. There were no landmarks but the sky was crowded—with friendly aircraft. The consortium was taking no chances. Choke points were attack points, and the Bering Strait was the most obvious place to stop *Imperator*. Sheer logic demanded that she be protected from any further threat. It was worth forcing an international incident if the Russians attempted to stop her.

From this point, they would follow a course allowing as little of the submarine above the surface as was safe. Once they were in deeper water, *Imperator* would dive and remain submerged.

As the American submarines headed north, a meeting was taking place on the top floor of a high-rise along the Potomac in Alexandria, Virginia. There, not only were the rooms secure but there was less chance of certain members of the group being recognized than if they had met at the Pentagon. Before the chairman convened the meeting, a videotape of comments from various commentators on each network was shown. The network analyses were not unpleasant, for there was little information to work from. But the atmosphere they created was heavy with innuendo, leaving an inference that once again the White House might be involved with a project bearing future military implications without congressional knowledge.

The consortium was a small, intimate group. All were male. The civilians dressed in expensive suits, while the military members were resplendent with gold and stars. No junior staff members from the military were present, nor had any of them ever been to one of these meetings. Decisions were reserved for what the media would call power brokers. Such meetings were held only when circumstances demanded instant decisions.

On the previous day, their strategy had been frustrated by an Eskimo and a scientist in a skin boat. The eventual announcement of *Imperator*'s existence had been carefully planned. But perfect orchestration of the media had evaporated on the day they planned to hand out smoothly designed press releases. Exposure of the unknown had automatically generated suggestions of mistrust. Therefore, the logical response was to reveal nothing. When questioned at a news conference, the president's press secretary said only that the report was being investigated.

There was nothing to be gained by Moscow's reporting

their version of *Imperator*'s true mission. The limited
details provided by a scientist and an Eskimo bobbing
about the Bering Sea in a skin boat provided little to
refute. *Imperator*, regardless of the extent the consortium
might eventually reveal about the submarine and its mission, would remain a contradiction.

Kremlin leaders focused on one clear objective. No
matter what was or was not acknowledged about *Imperator*, their singular goal was to ensure that the submarine
would never again surface once she dived under the icecap. With the head of Service A (the KGB's directorate
controlling disinformation) recently relieved, the reliability
of any propaganda efforts remained at a low ebb. Let the
world think what it might concerning the American submarine. Let the world ponder the facts after *Imperator* was at
the bottom!

As silence echoed through Kremlin hallways, the civilian power structure in Washington grew increasingly con-
fused. While they were angered at being the foils of a
well-kept secret, they were equally concerned with the
speed of the Soviet buildup on the Northern Flank. It was
difficult to sort out the most critical concern facing them.
Was it at home or within the Kremlin? They were shocked
at the alert of Soviet polar commandos. When that factor
sank in, it took little time to evoke a similar response from
Washington. Force would match force.

Danilov snatched the headphones from his sonarman. "I'll
listen," he growled. "It's been too damn quiet—until
now." With little neck to speak of, Danilov assumed a
froglike appearance with the dark-padded phones envelop-
ing his ears. He cocked his head to one side, eyes staring
sightlessly into space, concentrating on the sounds outside
the sub. He made a motion with his hand to the sonarman,
who began to manipulate his dials very slowly, eyes closed,
listening to the same sounds.

The listening device could be concentrated on a very
narrow beam to magnify the sound and isolate its source.

Danilov held up his hand for the sonarman to stop the dial. The admiral listened intently, then said, "Sergoff . . . the recorder. I want this on tape." To the sonarman, he added, "You fiddle with the dials. When each sound is at perfect peak, Sergoff will record it for me."

The process went on for half an hour. Danilov would move his index finger in a small circle, indicating they should go on to the next clear signal. When he put up his hand, the dialing would stop and the sonarman would fine-tune his equipment until it was at its peak for recording.

At one point, Danilov queried his sonarman. "When was the last time you had such perfect sound?"

"Rarely, sir." The man shrugged. "Then again, this water is very cold. Sound travels much farther . . . and clearer," he added as he saw Danilov's hand raise to indicate the next loud, clear signal coming over the sonar.

"The water temperature is much the same in our home waters."

"Yes, sir."

"Have you ever before heard anything like this in Soviet waters?"

The man shook his head. "Never, sir."

"Nor do I think you ever will." When he was satisfied, he removed the headset for a moment. "Now, what we are going to do"—he addressed no one in particular—"is compare these sounds we have to those recordings you train on in sonar school. Sergoff, you too—you have a good ear."

The leading sonar technician also donned a set of headphones, and the four men listened intently as Danilov operated the equipment himself. First, he would switch on the training tapes used in sonar school. Then he would play the one they had just recorded to identify similarities.

After each comparison, Sergoff would just shrug. He could differentiate nothing. Occasionally, Danilov would note a difference, each time attracting the leading technician's attention to it. There was little change in the man's expression. But Danilov was persistent. He insisted on

playing certain comparisons again and again, switching
from the actual recording provided by the fleet sonar school
to those they had just heard.

"Can't you hear it?" Danilov exploded in frustration,
aware that these men were much better trained than he
would ever hope to be. "Isn't it too perfect?"

The leading technician's forehead wrinkled with exasperation. The admiral was correct. "Yes, I see what you
mean, sir . . . but it could just be a freak of nature."

"Can you run a comparison on the computer? You
know—decibels, frequencies, clarity—whatever you people understand?"

The technician looked warily at Sergoff, who only nodded that he should concur. "Yes, sir. I will do everything
I can."

While Danilov waited impatiently, pacing from one end
of the small control room to the other, the loudspeaker was
turned on overhead so that they could continue to listen to
exactly what his sonar was picking up. No matter where
they turned, a cacophony of sound greeted them. New
noises would drown out or replace others on the same
bearing. At one point, Sergoff remarked that what they
were experiencing must be similar to being in a madhouse.

It *is* a madhouse, Danilov agreed silently, once again
moving over to the quartermaster's table to consult his
chart. But this is a man-made one. I am so sure of that that
I would gamble my life. If that computer is as good as we
are told by those greedy swine who build them, then it will
agree with me. Then he paused, grinning to himself. He
despised those scientists in the white smocks who built
those computers and constantly told the Kremlin how wonderful they were. Now here he was, almost insisting that
their computer agree with him.

"Most unusual, Admiral," the leading sonar technician
interrupted. Without a second thought, he laid his printouts
directly over the chart Danilov had been studying. Sergoff
stepped forward, but the admiral, seeing how excited the
man had become, waved him off. The sailor continued

impetuously, "Look at these, sir. The whale sounds. We know how they may vary along a certain part of the frequency spectrum and we can often record it. But look at that." He tapped the figures with a forefinger. "The sounds seem to vary to our ear, but the computer records this all on the same frequency."

The man's excitement was infectious. Sergoff leaned over to see the figures for himself. Danilov's expression was more animated than at any time since they'd left Polyarnyy. In most instances on the printouts, the proof was limited at best, yet there was evidence that the recordings they had just made were of man-made sounds . . . at least, they were emanating from a man-made instrument.

"You see, Sergoff," the admiral finally announced, "it is not a madhouse out there. It is more like a fanfare. These are the trumpets and the banners to announce the approach of this *Imperator*. Admiral Reed quite rightly doesn't want us to record anything of value on our sonar before they are ready to meet us head to head. This is his way of preparing us. And, it is very effective. . . ." His voice softened as he considered how well thought out this ploy really had been.

"What do you wish to do?" Sergoff inquired, already certain there was no answer.

"Nothing . . . nothing at all. Wouldn't you say that he would be planning on our moving to another position to try to locate his great sea monster?"

"I would stay right here myself," Sergoff responded. He knew in an instant he should have added that before Danilov asked him the last question.

"Whenever a man wants you to make the first move, even in chess where you think the gentleman might be very foolish, be cautious," Danilov said with emphasis. "It is to Admiral Reed's advantage to find us before we find him. He would like to drive us out of the madhouse, as you called it. But, he created the madhouse." Danilov was unconcerned that his opponent had made the first move. "So we'll stay right here for a while."

• • •

Hal Snow stared at the clutter of papers on his desk, trying to remember what he'd just read. None of the sentences he glossed over now seemed familiar. How many times had he read them? It was no use. He'd never been a paperwork man before, and it was doubtful that he would change now. *Imperator*, or rather Caesar, was sailing his vessel. The commanding officer was the senior passenger. It was something he would never accept.

Snow turned the chair to face his remote terminal, which had just been repaired. Of all the remote terminals on board, his was the only one that required repair since they'd departed the fishbowl. That hadn't improved his attitude either.

He slipped on the access switch and punched in his code. Caesar responded with a cheery, "HOW MAY I HELP YOU, CAPTAIN SNOW?" across the screen. Snow queried sailing status. The details appeared on the screen without hesitation. There were now 296 feet of water under the keel and their current course was gradually bringing them into deeper water. Checking the time, he knew the watch was preparing for scheduled satellite communications.

When the comm officer reported transmission complete, Snow saw no point in remaining on the surface. They could submerge to a depth safe enough to avoid creating any surface disturbance that might alert curious satellites, and for that matter, the increasing concentration of surface ice would mask their presence anyway. It was time for *Imperator*'s final disappearing act. He punched in the power data to effect their dive, then authenticated his order. The computer responded almost immediately. "CAPTAIN SNOW, DO YOU WISH TO OVERRIDE THE CONTROL ROOM?" Of course not, he realized. That would require an emergency order. Now why the hell did he go ahead and do that? There wasn't the slightest reason to upset the watch at this stage. Lifting the sound-powered phone from the wall box, he called the control room and gave his orders to the diving officer. The computer, he was told, had already projected the increased frequency and density of floe ice over the next twelve hours, and the OOD requested permission to set the upward-looking sonar. That unit was set at a specific depth before entering a solid ice area when ship's depth was equal to the distance to the surface as determined by the sonar. Upon entering an ice area, the sonar recorded changes between the submarine's actual depth and the distance to the surface alone. It was vitally important for *Imperator* to be at perfect trim since even the slightest deviation from zero trim would result in inaccurate measurement of ice thickness. A mark that showed a perfect distance to the surface according to the presetting would identify a polynya, a hole in the ice. It was vital to maintain a constant chart of surface ice and polynyas in case the submarine was required to surface through the ice for any reason.

As Snow silently wondered what else Caesar had been doing in his spare time, the watch officer reported that repairs had been made to a valve seal in one of the forward ballast pumps, a heat detector had been malfunctioning in the magazine next to the number three Tomahawk missile launcher, umbilical readings had reported a low battery on one of the Apache helicopters stored in the forward hangar room, and a radiation detector had malfunctioned in a compartment adjacent to the main reactor. None of the incidents had been noted by the crew before Caesar reported them to the engineering office.

It was eerie, Snow muttered to himself, how an electronic marvel could grate on one's nerves. There was no malice involved—Caesar was incapable of humanity. Yet the fact that Snow was increasingly irritated by this electronic nonentity bothered him. He found himself longing for the old-fashioned comfort of a submarine dependent on the men who sailed her. Malfunctions in those days were reported to the captain at once and details were constantly relayed to him on what repairs were underway, and again when they were complete. *Imperator* had been designed to alleviate that factor. If Snow desired a status report on his command, he could call it up on the computer. The report would be far more accurate and timely than those called back to a captain in his old-fashioned control room by a technician or engineering officer up to his armpits in grease.

There was neither the smell of the old diesel subs nor the efficient quiet hum of the nuclear boats of only ten years before. Sound silencing had become such an art in the construction of *Imperator* that she functioned with the soundless hush of space. The only noises were human, and they seemed to intrude on the efficiency of the wonder that was Caesar, the heart and soul of *Imperator*.

As Snow's fingers ran over the keys on the terminal before him, he realized from conversations with Carol Petersen that there was a limited capability for human psychological response programmed into Caesar. She had assured him it was designed to interpret certain mental problems that might crop up among the crew, similar to implanting a set of medical symptoms in a computer's memory bank. The system could then respond with a diagnosis of the correct ailment.

What, then, would Caesar say about Hal Snow? How would he respond to a man with two failed marriages who often went months without knowing where his offspring were? The navy determined that Snow was fine for their purposes. His record from the day he was commissioned until the day he resigned was nothing but professional. He had always been able to set aside his personal life in favor of professional demands—and the life of a submarine officer was rigorous and demanding. The psychological testing he'd undergone before commanding a ballistic-missile submarine was no different. Hal Snow was in total command of his submarines, able to make life-or-death decisions in every possible situation navy psychologists could imagine without displaying the slightest inconsistencies. You were perfect, Snow, he remarked silently to himself.

Then why the hell am I tempted to talk to Caesar about the things I'm aware of that no navy shrink is ever going to learn? Was it because he'd decided to come back for one more round? That was the mistake of boxers . . . race car drivers . . . test pilots . . . to have to prove it to themselves one more time—the old ego trip.

Or was it Carol Petersen? Why was a man his age so concerned about what that woman thought? No one could ever convince him that a woman had a place on a submarine, yet there had been moments when he felt like a high school jock showing off for some girl in the stands. So while he was considering having this very personal conversation with good old Caesar, he was also worried that Caesar's mistress might get wind of the fact that he, Hal Snow, was plumbing the psychological depths of a computer. What kind of stable mind was that?

He snapped off the terminal abruptly. While the glow faded from the screen, he was able to convince himself there were better things to do than challenge Caesar to a mental duel. The results could be disconcerting. One thing that computer couldn't do was go on a tour of the forward weapons systems with his weapons officer. Snow hadn't inspected that section of *Imperator* since they got underway. It was a good excuse to keep his mind busy, and it was even better to have his officers see him involved in their department.

But the effect Carol Petersen seemed to have on him remained in the forefront of his mind that day.

Abe Danilov's plan for arriving on station at least twenty-four hours before *Imperator* cleared the Bering Strait was based on sound reasoning. He knew listening devices would have been deployed, and that they would be heavily monitored before the American submarine ever entered the shallow Chukchi Sea. Creeping stealthily closer the previous day, Danilov managed to arrive unnoticed.

Seratov and *Smolensk* waited patiently for their quarry, and *Novgorod* had departed after the exercises on the third day to assume station between four and five hundred miles to the east. There she could silently patrol the deeper waters off the entrance to the Northwest Passage. Danilov was positive that *Imperator*'s chosen path would be under the North Pole, but he was covering every alternative. Once Admiral Reed determined that his best choice was a course due north under the ice, then Danilov and his two submarines would be waiting. *Novgorod* would then swing in behind them and contact the additional hunter/killer forces dispatched the previous day.

"Sergoff," he called as he passed by the wardroom, "come with me." The chief of staff reacted with unconcealed pleasure to the broad smile on Danilov's face. The admiral had been brooding again, and this always troubled Sergoff. The best he could expect would be a change of heart, for Danilov reminded him these days of a rubber ball perpetually bouncing from one mood to another. The radiance he now recognized on the admiral's face appeared to be more than a simple change of moods.

In the control room, an ebullient Danilov continued, "Sergoff, I've spent far too much time picking on you about your work on the charts. I apologize. In front of everyone here." His hand swept about the small compartment. "I apologize for my impatience." Waving for Sergoff to join him, he bent over the chart table. "I need your effort now more than ever. It's time to locate *Imperator*."

Sergoff looked into Danilov's face. The broad smile was still evident. "What may I do, Admiral?" he inquired cautiously.

"You've plotted *Imperator*'s position each time we have been able to receive satellite confirmation?"

"Yes, sir." Sergoff's index finger stabbed at the neat notations he'd made on the larger chart.

"You have a fairly accurate concept of her speed of advance depending on her position, depth of water . . . that sort of thing?"

Sergoff nodded. "It's sketchy. But more could be done . . . to analyze her progress . . . determine any patterns, I suppose."

"Exactly. That's exactly what I mean." Danilov's expression remained animated. "It's foolish to sit here waiting to identify a certain sound through that madhouse noise, as you call it, that Admiral Reed has created for us. You've laid out a prospective track for *Imperator*." Danilov ran his finger across the course Sergoff had carefully penciled onto the chart. "So, we know where she was earlier today until she ran into deeper water." *Seratov* had sent up a radio buoy through a polynya to receive message traffic a few hours before.

"She was right here, give or take a few kilometers." Though Danilov's smile seemed to animate his entire face, Sergoff remained serious. He understood exactly what Danilov was coming to, but he would let the admiral announce it.

"Lay out her likely position every thirty minutes on the chart. Sonar will concentrate on a sector in the probable location you indicate. Sooner or later they have to pick her up. The noisemakers must keep drifting." There were pronounced underwater currents sweeping from the north down toward the Alaskan coast, then west into the Chukchi Sea. They would carry the drifting noisemakers with them. Logically, they should pass across any bearing that sonar was keying on. With that sort of movement, it seemed probable to Danilov that sound from *Imperator* would eventually have to be isolated since it would not be moving with the current.

Painstakingly, Captain Sergoff studied *Imperator*'s progress over the past few days. There was a pattern. It would be impossible to determine whether it was the result of Captain Snow's systematic planning, or Admiral Reed's, or even the consortium that controlled them both. Nevertheless, a pattern existed, and he laid out prospective positions for the American submarine every thirty minutes.

From these, Danilov provided a probable bearing from *Seratov* for his sonarmen. They were to concentrate on a three-degree sector. The arc would widen considerably by the time it crossed *Imperator*'s likely track. As Danilov had predicted, the movement of the noisemakers followed the current from east to west. Computer assistance was required in most instances to confirm this motion. The next job was even more demanding—to isolate and track a sound beyond the noisemakers.

It was the old needle-in-the-haystack problem, except this time the only sense they could employ was auditory.

They were blindly groping for a sound they had never heard before. What encouraged the sonarmen on *Seratov* more than anything else was the fact that Admiral Danilov remained beside them. He listened just as intently as each one of his men, conversing with them on occasion whenever the possibility of an alien sound attracted their attention.

With only a few hours remaining on the fifth day, the most junior of Danilov's sonarmen was the one to identify a vague sound that pierced through the torrent generated by the noisemakers. It was distant but steady. Fed into the computer, it was identified as a propulsor system. Nothing in their vast audio collection of identifiable submarines compared to it.

Over the next fifteen minutes there was an increase in pitch detected only by the computer. It was possible the contact could be drawing closer to the Soviet boat, which remained stationary. Sergoff found the general direction coincided with his projected track of *Imperator*.

"Sergoff, search the sectors to either side of that for her screen. Then I want you to run everything we have heard back through the computer. Make a separate recording for a radio beacon and release it when you have an opening above us. We don't have a great deal to go on, but I want to make sure that it's relayed to *Novgorod* when she sends up a listening buoy." Then he turned to the man standing patiently behind him. "Captain Lozak, now all we have to do is find her escorts. What would you do if you knew we were waiting out here?"

Until now, *Seratov*'s captain, Stevan Lozak, had been a mere figurehead aboard his own command. Danilov's presence overwhelmed everyone around him, and Sergoff remained the admiral's right hand. Lozak, having sailed with Danilov before, was accustomed to the situation and content to accept his position until he was invited to participate.

Lozak was a superb mariner. Before he had been given command of *Seratov*, he had worked in the tactical research section of the Leninsky Komsomol. This prestigious school of submarine warfare in Leningrad was charged with developing original antisubmarine tactics for the emerging breed of high-speed attack submarines designed to protect Russia's ballistic-missile force. Lozak had cataloged American submarine tactics, collating them into data for computer projections, the objective of which was to teach Soviet captains what to anticipate from their opposite number in actual combat. He had taken his work one step further by actually devising tactics to meet whatever the Americans might do. After reading about Lozak's work, there was no doubt in Abe Danilov's mind who would command his next flagship.

Lozak responded now without hesitation. "I'm sure Admiral Reed realizes we are waiting somewhere in this vicinity. He's thoughtful, cautious almost to a fault until he is certain of his quarry. I expect he will keep his boats spread out. They'll stay within communication range but he's going to maintain a screen to the north of *Imperator*. He'll want to sanitize her path." He looked thoughtfully at Danilov. "I'd say there was every chance they could sweep this area in the next six hours."

"Would you care to presume where they might be now?" Danilov's smile had faded, but his eyes remained bright and alert. The action was about to start and he was enjoying himself.

Lozak signaled to the quartermaster to get out another chart of the area. "Bring it into the wardroom," he ordered as he beckoned Danilov to join him. The dining table in the wardroom provided the only other unencumbered, flat surface they could use.

When the chart was spread out, the corners secured with salt and pepper shakers, Lozak used a red pencil to show Danilov what he anticipated. "These arctic waters will continue colder and more saline, and I think sound propagation will remain excellent. That's good or bad depending on who is the hunter or the hunted at any given moment. I'd like to have some sound velocity profiles to be sure, but if I were Admiral Reed I'd separate my submarines by about seventy-five miles." He made three imaginary points on the chart. Using a set of dividers, he traced the imaginary path toward the pole of two screening submarines going well beyond *Seratov*'s current position. Then he swung the path of the one closest to the land in an arc until it became a straight line paralleling *Imperator* two hundred miles to the east.

Danilov nodded and murmured, "You're right . . . yes, that seems logical. I'd probably do the same."

It would be likely that one of the submarines would stay to the east, lying in wait for an enemy hovering close to land. Any competent submariner would assume two screening submarines would flush out anything to the north. That third American submarine could easily be near *Novgorod*.

"Exactly," Lozak said. "And look how close one of those heading toward us comes to our current position. We couldn't exactly throw stones at each other. But, nevertheless," he said, chuckling, "I bet one will be in range of our torpedoes within that six hours I mentioned. A rocket could drop one right on top of the American."

"You think I should stay in position." Danilov's response was a statement to himself rather than a question to Lozak.

"Let the rabbit come to you," Lozak concluded.

Danilov picked up the sound-powered phone and called the control room. "Sergoff, when you are finished, commence a passive search fifteen degrees either side of *Imperator*'s projected course. Tell the men to be patient. They'll locate a target in due time."

Andy Reed was taking advantage of *Houston*'s wardroom with her captain's permission. None of the officers had ever been involved in actual combat, never known of a shot fired in anger other than the wistful tale of a navy fighter pilot reminiscing about Vietnam days. So, he'd asked the cooks to bake a few pies to enhance this meeting.

This was Reed's opportunity, in this case perhaps the final one, to impress upon his people the critical phase they were approaching. "How many of you have been playing with the odds for tomorrow?" He paused between bites to blow his nose. His cold was persistent and irritating.

There was a pause at the wardroom table. A few forks remained poised in midair as they considered Reed's strange question. No one wanted to be the first to answer—if they understood what he was looking for. Finally, his eyes locked on a lieutenant (j.g.) near the end of the table and he held the young man's stare until there was no choice but to respond.

"I'm not sure how to answer that, sir," the lieutenant offered as his fork slowly lowered to his plate.

"By this time tomorrow, *Imperator* should be well under the ice." Very calmly he covered another bite of pie with ice cream, balanced it on his fork, then added, "To get to that position, there will be some submarines on the bottom, either ours or theirs." Not a soul around the table had touched his plate from the moment he asked his question. Reed savored the next bite with a pleasant smile as he finally added, "At this stage, the game becomes deadly. Those first two subs were more on an intelligence mission than anything else . . . at least initially they were. Now Danilov has one objective in mind. He's going to try to sink *Imperator*, but to get to her, he's got to get through us first. The odds tend to be in his ballpark to start with. He's the hunter; we're the hunted. He's waiting for us; we're coming toward him. What are the odds? Who gets the first shot or, rather, who takes the first hit?"

Andy Reed's eyes once again fell on the lieutenant near the end of the table. The young man was a foil for his purposes. He would explain that to the boy later, but it was necessary that someone respond. Both Ross and the executive officer had been asked earlier by Reed to remain quiet. Now the young man's initial reply was a feeble, "I see what you mean, sir." Then he grew braver. "You are sure that it's just a question of odds—who fires at whom first?" It was obvious the simplicity of odds troubled him. "I would think a lot would depend on what we do . . . wouldn't it?"

This brought a smile to Reed's face. "It relies completely not only on what we do but how we do it. None of what will be happening has ever been done before. There are no tech manuals, no NWPs, nothing available to explain how you fight other submarines beneath the ice. A great deal has been written about it, but it's all based on assumptions. No one has ever escorted *Imperator* beneath the ice before, and no one has ever actually faced a hunter/killer group from that vantage point.''

Admiral Reed went on talking about what lay ahead, and as he did, the members of the wardroom gradually began to eat again. His encouragement was similar to Danilov's during the Soviet transit from Polyarnyy. There had never been any doubt in Reed's group that they faced an immense task, one unlike anything ever attempted before. But it had never before been put in the words that Reed used that evening.

By the time coffee was served, there was a new level of awareness aboard *Houston*. Her station was on *Imperator*'s port bow to the northwest. *Houston* would be the bodyguard. Before the group had broken away north of the Bering Strait, Reed had given his final orders. *Helena* would move farther ahead, remaining well north of *Imperator* until contact was established with the Soviets. *Olympia*, once again capable of full speed, had effected final repairs as she moved well to the east before commencing her end run to the pole. Reed hoped she might detect any of Danilov's reserve forces if they were lurking to the east.

Reed's strategy was much as Abe Danilov anticipated.

The messages that were directed that day by both Washington and Moscow to Reed and Danilov were increasingly anxious. If the Americans were so willing to sacrifice the little frigate days before just to test a Soviet threat, there appeared no doubt that this mysterious submarine of theirs was no simple show of force. It also seemed increasingly obvious that the U.S. meant to forcibly support the Norwegians with amphibious forces and the unknown power of *Imperator*. Though Danilov's original orders were to stop the American submarine, he was now directed to *expend* all his forces if necessary—no sacrifice was too great at this stage. The communications from Washington did not directly state that sacrifice was necessary, but the idea was implied to Reed. While the verbal posturing on both sides was, in effect, bringing their satellite nations to advanced states of readiness, there was no knowledge of the real threat that actually was about to explode under the arctic ice.

The sound of the phone on the bulkhead above his pillow briefly registered with *Helena*'s captain. Though not fully awake, he was aware there had been but a single buzz. Two meant an emergency. He took advantage of a brief moment for his senses to react to his surroundings, the dim red light above, the whisper of the ventilation duct to his left, the soft touch of the sheets on his back. The captain was the type who would strip and climb between the sheets if he thought there was more than an hour of sleep possible. His clothes lay in order on the chair three feet away. He could pull on skivvies and pants in an instant and hop into his slippers as he went out of the stateroom lifting his shirt off the hook.

He removed the phone from the cradle before it could buzz a second time. "Captain here."

His engineer was on the other end. "I've got a noise problem, Captain. If I had to guess right now, I'd say it was a slight variation on the propeller—just enough to change our sound signature."

"Are we louder?"

"It's possible, sir. It's hard to tell from inside, but I think we may be a bit like an organ grinder out there."

"Are you sure it's the prop, Ed?"

"I'm not sure what it is, sir, only that we're making more noise than we'd like to and I don't know what the hell to do."

"How about changing speeds?"

"There's a direct correlation. When the revolutions increase, the sound does too. And then it seems to level off above thirty knots."

"Once we're over thirty it doesn't matter?"

"Well, I wouldn't say that. I don't think it gets any worse, Captain."

"We'll have to live with it then." *Helena*'s captain replaced the phone, but he did not go back to sleep. In a world where silence was everything, where it could mean the difference between life and death, he was slowly creeping into his enemy's lair. His enemy was awake and waiting for him, and *Helena* was shaking cow bells as she approached.

Aboard *Seratov*, it was Stevan Lozak who eventually understood the unusual noise emanating from an object well ahead of *Imperator*. When the sonarmen had been unable to determine its source, and the computer could not match the sound against its memory, Danilov called for *Seratov*'s captain.

Lozak listened to the recordings, compared them to others in the memory bank, studied the movement of the sound that Sergoff had carefully plotted, then placed a plastic overlay of Sergoff's over his chart.

"You seem to know what you're looking for," Danilov murmured curiously.

Lozak shook his head unconsciously, then looked up with surprise to see that it was the admiral who had addressed him. "I have an idea but I'm not sure."

Sergoff saw what the captain was doing. "Perhaps it's not another of those noisemakers the Americans have been using."

Lozak looked up at Sergoff. "What's the range now?"

"It's much too distant to tell. We haven't got a perfect position on it."

"Its movement seems to be north, a little northeast maybe?"

"It would appear to be north . . . right at us."

Lozak smiled. "It's not moving with the current and it's well ahead of *Imperator*." He looked at Danilov, tilting his head to one side in speculation. "It seems to be following much the same pattern I laid out earlier. But Admiral Reed wouldn't be calling attention to his plans, would he?'' he mused softly to himself. ''I'll wager, Admiral, that we have propeller cavitation sounds now from a submarine that either has a defect or has been damaged somehow. I have to assume Admiral Reed has sent this submarine out toward what he may project as our location. See!'' He pointed excitedly and retraced the projected route of an American submarine along the line he'd pointed out to Danilov earlier.

''Our first target,'' Sergoff murmured.

''Do we want to give away our position by attempting to sink her?'' Lozak asked. Their target was near the edge of the solid ice with open spaces in the floe ice overhead.

Danilov's smile faded to be replaced by a thin-lipped grimace. ''One of the reasons that Admiral Reed would send one of his submarines along this route is because he anticipates where we are. If we let it pass by, then we will have to begin a stern chase. Whether we give ourselves away by sinking this one, or with the racket we'll make chasing them, they'll be able to find us. Better to try a standoff weapon while we have the opportunity. They can't be absolutely sure of the distance it will travel, and we have an extensive lead above us that could close if the wind picks up on the surface. My suggestion is to eliminate this one while we have the opportunity—before it's beneath the pack for good.''

The ice could easily close in above them at any time. The major problem they now discussed was the range to the American boat. Depending on her speed, she might take a few hours before she came within range of their rocket-launched torpedoes. Timing was so vital—it would be very close. The American could very easily be saved by the ice.

Abe Danilov decided to return to his stateroom to rest. It was near midnight and the fifth day was drawing to a close. His tiny stateroom allowed space only for a bunk, a tin commode and sink that both folded into the bulkhead on one side, and a desk that folded out on the opposite side. The latter lay open and was covered with papers, but he was too tired to leaf through them. He sat down heavily on the bunk with a great sigh. Bending over slowly to remove his shoes, he experienced a brief dizzy spell—though it passed within seconds. The damn doctors were right, he thought. Everything should be done more slowly as you get older. But that didn't mean he had to like it!

Tomorrow could be the beginning of the longest day of his life. He paused to remember the disciplined existence at his first naval school, the pressure that was constantly exerted on each cadet to account for every movement every minute of the day. There was a purpose. . . .

After carefully rolling his dirty clothes into a ball and placing them in a bag, he removed a fresh uniform from the tiny closet and lay it carefully on the single chair beside his bunk. He could be called at any time.

Then he removed the next of Anna's letters from the packet in the back of the desk drawer. It was a letter that made him laugh to himself. Severodvinsk! The ends of the earth had nothing on that place. But it was also the shipyard where his first command had been built. Admiral Gorshkov had been kind enough to let Anna and the children journey to that miserable spot with him.

His Anna was a city girl, so she'd looked forward to a new adventure: ". . . let the snow and cold come as long as we're all together . . ." was about what she had said. And winter took hold of Severodvinsk with a vengeance. That winter of 1969–70 had become the longest winter of her life. They were even cut off at times from Arkhangel'sk, the closest imitation of a city in that region. He was sometimes trapped by a blizzard at the shipyard for two or three days at a time, and Anna was left with the children in that little apartment where the steam pipes never stopped clanking and the smelly old lady they shared the kitchen with never stopped talking. Anna reminded him how Boris was still at the diaper stage, how Eugenia whined for six months, and Sergei teased them both unmercifully until his father threatened to deposit him in a snow drift.

Much of the unpleasantness was overlooked as Danilov prepared his ship, the largest missile submarine ever built.

It was an honor to receive that command, and he even had been allowed to bring his family there, regardless of the conditions. What great times those were, he thought, as he turned to Anna's letter.

> I remember the nights you came through the door in your greatcoat, covered with snow, and I always waited my turn while you made a fuss over the children. You'd shake the snow from your hat and place it on Eugenia's head. Sergei would rush for the broom and brush the snow off your coat before you hung it in a corner. Then Boris, who would be jumping up and down and screaming for attention when he wasn't hanging on your pant leg, would be the first one to be picked up. One by one, you'd lift them up over your head and they'd scream in mock terror. I sometimes used to imagine that you would forget yourself when it came my turn and lift me over your head and bump me against the ceiling. You never did. You were a gentle bear. . . .

Severodvinsk was the end of the world, he realized now, but what a wonderful place it was then. When spring came and muddy water ran down muddy streets, he had taken his submarine out for sea trials. Those were days he could never forget—his first command—when it was the pride of the fleet. That's when Anna had told him one night that she had finally realized that there was no doubt in her mind that the parental obligations were now firmly established—she would take care of the children and her husband would take care of the submarines. It had taken Sergei Gorshkov, when he came to Severodvinsk for the submarine's commissioning, to explain to her that this was as it should be, that a man like her husband owed as much to the Motherland. It was refreshing so many years later to consider Anna's remembrances and gain an entirely different perspective on their life together.

While Abe Danilov was occupied with Anna's letter, Sergoff observed the approach of the American submarine with a detachment that belied his excitement. He and Captain Lozak could not explain why their target slowed for a period of time, yet it made very little difference. It would just allow Admiral Danilov a longer rest. The rockets nestled in *Seratov*'s torpedo tubes had a maximum range of fifty miles. Danilov's theory had always been to cut in half any ranges that the technicians claimed.

The noise from the approaching submarine overshadowed the continued use of noisemakers and made tracking much easier. As long as *Seratov* remained in position, it was unlikely the American would ever know she was there. Of course, the rocket bursting from the torpedo tube would give them away, but the solid fuel missile would be over the target in no time.

The torpedo was fast, capable of more than forty knots. Would this damaged submarine be able to reach maximum speed to evade the weapon's programmed search? Would they have the opportunity to retaliate, or would the necessity of evasion require all of their time? Would it be a race, the torpedo faster but limited by its fuel capacity, the submarine able to run forever but limited by whatever engineering casualty it had suffered?

Sergoff said nothing to Lozak, though the mental picture of the attack repeated itself again and again. He saw the rocket nestled in the tube, the charge driving it out and away from the sub, then to the surface where the solid fuel booster ignited in a burst of steam and smoke. It would leap straight up before wheeling over in the direction of the target. In his mind's eyes, he was momentarily looking skyward from beneath the ocean surface as the rocket motor detached, the small parachute billowed, and the torpedo plunged down directly at him. The protective nosecap separated perfectly as it hit the water. As the torpedo dived down toward its target, Sergoff would lose sight of the final search.

Lozak was lost in his own thoughts. They had nothing to do with the flight of the rocket or the life-and-death chase between submarine and torpedo. He was an analytical man. Captain Lozak was more concerned that this would be the last easy shot . . . or as easy as they would ever experience on this mission. There was still a distinct possibility of failure. They were firing through a lead in the ice at a target passing beneath increasingly heavy floe ice. From that point on, it was likely that there would no longer be the luxury of such long-range shots. But this was not a normal situation. Even with all the ice, it was worth the chance.

The rest of the battle would be fought beneath the icepack. The only weapons available would be torpedoes fired from their tubes at a closing enemy. That was the true test of a submariner's skill—there was only one winner.

Both men continued to work quietly as their admiral slept, neither one caring to exchange his thoughts with the other.

Sleep would not come to Carol Petersen. At first, she was sure it was too hot, but removing a blanket accomplished nothing. She turned up the air nozzle on the bulkhead, directing it on her face and chest. Within five minutes she was cold, and the blanket was tucked around her chin. After an hour, she turned on the lights to read for a few minutes. She was a little beyond the page she had turned down the night before when she realized she had no recollection of what she'd been reading. She turned the lamp back out and found herself staring at the dim red light filtering around the edges of the curtain hanging over the doorway.

Carol had always been sure of what kept her awake during those rare nights of sleeplessness. Yet right now she was in a quandary. There was no doubt what the next few days held in store for *Imperator*. She had accepted the danger when she applied to the consortium.

But the other concern weighing on her mind was Hal Snow. There seemed no way she could get him out of her thoughts. It was obvious that Hal Snow's personality altered abruptly as *Imperator* departed the fishbowl that dark night five days before. As the submarine emerged from her pen, Hal Snow had cut himself off from the real world. *Imperator* was the only world he really understood—a man's world. But was he really as superstitious as so many of the others about a woman on a submarine? she asked herself as she lay in that netherworld between sleep and consciousness.

Hal Snow had been jarred by his phone buzzer shortly after he'd drifted into a restless sleep. Caesar had just alerted the senior watch officer to an alien sound ahead of them. The various sonar units throughout the submarine were tied into one of Caesar's subsystems, which controlled the myriad listening devices. Each new sound was automatically isolated, analyzed, then cataloged within a complex reference system. At the operator's request, a sound detected by sonar could instantly be compared to an encyclopedic collection and a printout delivered with every available detail. In this particular case, the sound could not be immediately identified with anything in the reference file, an automatic operation taking place over a period of no more than thirty seconds.

The process of notifying Snow, however, was immediate. Anything unidentified was considered by Caesar to be a threat, so by the time Snow clamped the headphones over his ears, the watch officer had already initiated secondary analysis. The computer acknowledged the sound was undoubtedly from a man-made system. The only known object in the response arc around the sound was *Helena*.

Snow ordered a tape of *Helena* fed into the system for comparison, the signals processed through the computer until background noises on that same bearing were identified as the submarine's actual sound signature. There seemed little doubt that somehow *Helena* had experienced an external defect. The variation could be minor but it would stand out like a red light to any experienced sonarmen.

"Are we still tied to any surface communicators?" Snow inquired.

"Almost ready to secure it, sir."

"How about *Houston*? Can we still raise Admiral Reed?"

The watch officer flipped the switch for radio central. "Chief, would you please patch that communicator into sonar for the captain." Then he turned to Snow. "It'll be touch and go, but let's give it a try."

Snow keyed the radiophone as soon as the red patch light lit up. The range for voice communications was short. It would be by chance alone that he could contact Reed. Once they were below solid ice, the only communications would be at specified hours—and that was only if a polynya was located at the appointed hour. Otherwise, they'd be out of touch until the next scheduled time. If he couldn't raise *Houston* now, whatever might happen to *Helena* would come as a complete shock to Andy Reed.

Snow repeated *Houston*'s call sign until he was rewarded with a faint response. "It is urgent . . . repeat urgent . . . I speak to Admiral Reed."

The wait seemed interminable until a weak voice came back, "This is Admiral Reed."

There was little time to think. Their signal was increasingly faint. "Andy, we've got a problem on *Helena* . . . our sonar located a high-frequency emission on her bearing . . . probably something external on the prop . . . it's broken through your noisemakers . . . if there's anyone out there near her, they're going to pick it up . . . over."

Reed's response was broken. "Understand *Helena* will attract attention . . . is that . . ." His voice faded.

"That is correct. Can we contact? Over."

"Negative . . . ordered to go deep . . . nothing further until . . ." His voice became so garbled that Snow could only assume the admiral was indicating there would be no communications beyond the schedule Reed had ordered earlier.

Snow tried three more times to raise *Houston*. He could hear the static and the other station keying in the background. Reed was trying to respond, but there was no point in continuing. And there was no solution to *Helena*'s problem. All they could do was wait and listen intensely in an arc where the Soviet forces were anticipated. There would be no doubt in Caesar's electronic mind if a rocket or torpedo was fired. It would be a momentary indication of where enemy forces lurked, but similar to locating a needle in a haystack. Somewhere beyond *Houston*, perhaps as many as a hundred miles to the north, a Soviet submarine could be preparing to fire at *Helena*. A full torpedo run would take minutes, but at that range it would merge with *Helena*'s signature anyway. If the Russian used a rocket-propelled torpedo, the sound of firing would be brief, and then once again there would be silence on that bearing. Snow knew it was much like trying to catch a bullet.

8

THE CHANGE IN strategy that day was Sergoff's idea, though the decision was up to the admiral. Abe Danilov took advantage of a few quiet moments to nap while *Seratov*'s attack team plotted the approach of their noisy target. The weapon, a missile carrying a homing torpedo, was taken through prefiring checks by Captain Lozak. Though *Seratov*'s captain was not a bloodthirsty individual, he had a major responsibility in developing this weapons system and now possessed an insatiable desire to prove its effectiveness on a real target. In the Soviet Navy, a great deal of emphasis was based on proving a system and this was a moment that could have significant influence on his career. He knew Abe Danilov would always stand behind him, but successfully dispatching an enemy submarine would also mean a great deal.

Captain Sergoff knew enough not to suggest a change in strategy to Lozak. That decision was up to Danilov. Sergoff was almost certain Lozak would make every effort to get Danilov to support his own contentions. But Sergoff felt his first duty was Danilov's safety. So when the admiral appeared in control yawning and refreshed, Sergoff immediately offered his opinion. "Admiral, it would seem to me that *Seratov* is as important to us, or at least your presence is, as *Imperator*'s is to the Americans. That's why they have a protective screen in front of her."

Lozak glanced at Danilov, realizing quickly that Sergoff's desire not to draw attention to the Admiral's flagship would likely meet with approval.

"What I mean," Sergoff continued, "is that the minute the water slug ejects the missile from the tube, the Americans will have a solid bearing on this submarine. And they know enough about our weapons to know our range within reason—"

"And," Danilov concluded for him, "if you were in one of those American submarines, you'd fire instantly in retaliation." He knew implicitly that American orders were not to fire until fired upon.

Sergoff nodded.

"But this submarine is fast enough to outrun their torpedoes," Lozak responded. "As soon as we fire, I'll go deeper and go to full speed on a reciprocal course."

"*Smolensk* is the same class and she can do that also." Sergoff smiled. "Only, she doesn't have Admiral Danilov aboard." He turned back to Danilov, adding quite seriously, "We are not yet trying to stop *Imperator*. We're attempting to take away her guard dogs. I believe, Admiral, that your seniors would consider it impetuous if you were to endanger yourself even before we have the opportunity to face the real objective. Prudence at this stage is a necessity."

Lozak recognized opportunity fading quickly. Sergoff made too much sense. Lozak's desire to make the first kill was counterbalanced by the argument that the most important man in the operation was standing next to him. While Lozak had no doubt that he could outrun any American torpedo yet to be made, a simple engineering casualty—even one that could be quickly repaired—might be the difference between Danilov's demise and a successful conclusion to the operation.

"Captain Sergoff is right," Lozak concluded unhappily.

"The Americans are still out of range. I'm sure *Smolensk* is doing the same as we are right now. I agree that we should give her the opportunity, sir."

The decision, as rational as it was, bothered Danilov also. He felt briefly like a hunter lowering his gun so that the man next to him could have the first shot. "Permission granted. Send the signal."

The preplanned signal consisted of coded sonar pings directed on the bearing of the adjacent submarine. Three shorts, two seconds apart, indicated that the senior submarine was giving the target to the junior.

"All stop!"

"All engines are stopped, Captain."

"Very well." *Helena*'s captain nodded to the chief of the watch. "We'll drift for the time being, Chief. Hold your depth."

"Aye, aye, Captain." The chief rested his forearms on the back of the helmsman's chair, eyeing the ship's trim as speed began to drop.

"Put some extra men on if you need to, Ed," the captain said, turning to his engineering officer. "Since we've become such a hell of a target, we may have to play scared rabbit for some damn Russian torpedo."

The OOD's expression displayed his anxiety. "Should I attempt to contact Admiral Reed, sir . . . let him know we've stopped?"

"Not yet, Ben." The captain was already following the engineering officer aft to the watertight door leading to the reactor area. "Ed's got fifteen minutes to figure what the glitch is. After that, we'll either try to make contact or just continue on again, sounding like the Fourth of July, I guess," he added over his shoulder.

"Range to target?" *Smolensk*'s captain called out.

"Approximately forty-five kilometers, sir."

"Actual range," the captain barked.

The fire control officer looked cautiously toward the captain after first checking the dials. "The computer doesn't have a solution as yet, sir. Another sixty seconds . . .'' he added, his voice trailing off.

''You've been tracking the target.'' The captain's voice was rising. ''Give me your range!''

''It's hard to be precise . . . I'd say forty-four now, sir,'' he guessed, feeling most uncomfortable with the captain peering over his shoulder. Then his face blanched. He wheeled, almost bumping the captain, to confirm what had just happened with the sonar operator.

''Lost contact with the target.'' The technician frantically rotated the dials in front of him, expanding his search arc a couple of degrees to either side.

''Impossible!'' The captain snatched the headphones from his fire control officer, clamping them over his ears with both fists. He listened, his eyes fixed on a spot on the overhead, while those around him waited fearfully for another outburst. The captain's eyes finally settled on the sonarman, and he shook his head in wonder. The technician shrugged his shoulders to answer, turning back to the sonar console to again widen their listening arc. Removing the headphones, the captain added silently, ''There's nothing out there now.''

''We have a general solution, sir.'' The fire control officer turned brightly. ''It should be accurate enough to drop the torpedo within range.''

''Still too far. We'll wait,'' *Smolensk*'s captain decided.

''Admiral, the target has gone silent,'' Stevan Lozak reported to Danilov. ''She was at about forty kilometers.''

Danilov's face remained expressionless. ''Did you have a solution?''

''Yes, sir.'' Lozak smiled at the chief of staff for the first time that day. ''Captain Sergoff insisted we continue our solution, just in case there was a casualty on *Smolensk*.'' Lozak wondered silently if there really was a special talent in being an admiral's chief of staff. So far, Sergoff hadn't missed a trick. He'd covered every angle. Perhaps he wasn't a threat to Lozak's ambition after all.

''She's dead in the water,'' Danilov remarked.

"Make that correction to your solution," Lozak ordered. "Hold your target at last known position." He looked up at Danilov expectantly.

"*Smolensk* may not have completed their solution. We will wait fifteen minutes for the American to make repairs, or whatever they are doing. Then we shoot at him ourselves. If there's no noise, they're holding position."

Hal Snow was sniffing with distaste at a cool cup of coffee in the control room when the report came from sonar. "*Helena*'s stopped, sir."

"Stopped?" Why? It didn't make sense—not without contacting him or Reed.

"No screw noises on her bearing, sir. I've still got reactor and steam system–related noises, so they're expecting to resume speed pretty soon."

"Christ," Snow muttered. "I wasn't planning to travel with a dinner bell in front of me." He called to the OOD as he left the control room, "Cut your speed for a while. No reason to run up her back. And tell sonar to keep an ear open for anything Russian out front of us. If I was them, I'd take out *Helena* first thing and worry about the rest of us later." He paused for a moment and looked over his shoulder. "Better yet, man battle stations. They'd be crazy not to if they're nearby. If we hear them fire at *Helena*, we ought to be able to squeeze off a couple of shots ourselves. We've got longer range than *Houston*."

When a submarine is prepared for sea, a base-line survey identifies every sound emitted by the boat. Computers can identify those not in the survey so that corrective action can be taken. When necessary, extraneous noise can normally be isolated by use of a stethoscope.

Helena's captain, engineer, and senior chief machinist mate were in the engine room near the shaft alley. The unidentified noise was directly astern, the only part of the submarine that sonar could not pinpoint. It was necessary for the engineers to isolate the source themselves.

"Turn the shaft," the chief engineer ordered over the sound-powered phone.

Very slowly, the shaft began rotating the propeller. The chief, stethoscope against the bulkhead, shook his head.

"Add more turns."

Vibration increased in conjunction with the shaft revolutions. Still there was nothing.

The chief looked up at the captain. "It's nothing to do with the fittings on the shaft, captain. They're secure. Got to be outside on the prop."

"Add more turns."

The submarine was increasing speed with still no extraneous sounds noticeable through the stethoscope until they reached eleven knots.

The chief's hand rose slowly. "Got something here, Captain. Nothing sonar could pick up yet."

"Sure?"

"I'm sure, sir." The chief looked up with a grin. "I listened to it in sonar before we stopped. It's got to radiate with more strength before we can pick it up ourselves."

There was little the captain could say. At times like this, he was at the mercy of his experts. There was nothing to do but wait.

At seventeen knots, sonar reported the sound radiating from astern, and that it increased with the shaft revolutions. Once it dispersed beyond the dead area, there was no doubt that it could be picked up by any good piece of equipment. It was on the propeller. There was no way they could repair anything until they were either alongside a tender or in dry dock. There had been no damage they could determine. It had to be an imperfection in the metal that became evident only after thousands of hours of operation. There would have been no way to anticipate such a casualty.

When the captain returned to control, he called his operations officer. "We have to get out of here. We're a hazard. Contact *Imperator*. She'll relay to *Houston*."

"Roger your last. You're still faint, *Helena*, but we copy.

Understand noise problem is external. Over.'' While
Imperator was able to receive messages over vast distances
on her refined underwater telephone, ''Gertrude,'' other
submarines remained unable to hear her transmissions. The
sonarman aboard the giant submarine waited for a response. There was only silence.

He called Snow in the control room. ''Captain, I have a
voice transmission from *Helena*—about her noise problems. No way I could get back to her. I'll bet she'll repeat
in a minute.''

Sonar was just off the control room. In seconds, Snow
was seated next to the sonarman, headphones in place. It
was less than a moment before the message was repeated.
This time, it was more extensive.

''*Helena* is dropping out of formation to the south.
Severe external noise problem diagnosed as propeller casualty. Noise increasing. Consider myself a hazard to your
transit. Request you forward status to *Houston* at best
opportunity. I am unable to receive from you at this range.
This is my last transmission. Out.''

The voice transmission from *Helena* could not be heard by
the Russians well to the north, but there was no doubt
concerning the source when the same propeller noise began on the exact bearing as before. Aboard both *Smolensk*
and *Seratov*, the tubes had been flooded, pressure equalized, and the outer tube doors opened in anticipation that
their target would turn away from the formation.

''Solution?'' *Smolensk*'s captain bellowed anxiously.

''Thirty seconds, Captain. There was slight drift after
they went dead in the water. Perhaps they are in a turn
now. . . .'' His voice faded away as he attempted to concentrate on the reports from his attack team. The initial
solution appeared accurate. It was a matter of rechecking,
insuring the solution was in the torpedo's memory, and
ejecting the missile from the tube. Fifteen seconds . . .

''Will we wait until he's out of range?'' The captain's
anger was rising.

''Ten seconds, Captain.''

Smolensk's captain began counting on his fingers. His breath was now unpleasantly warm on the fire control officer's cheek as he studied the maze of dials before them.

"Standby."

The captain's arm was involuntarily in the air and it dropped as he was told. "Ready to fire, Captain."

"Shoot." His fist hit the chart table resoundingly.

Every man aboard *Smolensk* felt the ship shudder against the ejection of the missile from the tube. "Come about to course zero, zero, zero—speed two zero," the captain ordered joyfully.

"Nothing from *Smolensk*?" Danilov inquired calmly.

"Perhaps their solution wasn't complete," Captain Lozak answered.

"Have they reversed course?"

"Can't tell yet, Admiral. They're too far away."

"Do you have an accurate solution?" Danilov asked.

"Almost perfect, Admiral," Lozak answered.

Danilov looked toward Sergoff. "We don't want to lose him, do we?" He grinned.

Sergoff smiled first at Danilov, then at Lozak. "You may shoot, Captain."

"Shoot." *Seratov*'s deck trembled as the missile burst from the tube, then all was quiet.

A voice from the sonarman broke the stillness. "I have something on *Smolensk*'s bearing . . . identified as . . ." There was a pause. ". . . missile fired . . . I'm sure they also fired, sir."

"So," Danilov replied to the silence in the control room, "we have two birds in the air. That makes it even more unlikely our quarry will get away from us."

"Admiral, I would suggest we take evasive action." Sergoff could be the master of understatement. "I doubt their *Los Angeles*-class boats can touch us right now, but *Imperator* seems to have advanced capabilities. There's no harm now in being safe."

Danilov nodded and turned to Lozak. "Captain, select a

course to the north and increase your depth, but do it as quietly as possible—no more than four knots. I don't think they will be able to track us at that speed. We have given away one position, but I don't intend to inform them of the next."

Snow was still eavesdropping in sonar when the missiles were fired to the north. To the untrained ear, the sound of a missile ejected from a torpedo tube was indistinguishable from the other noises in the ocean.

"Did you hear that, Captain?"

Snow looked curiously at the sonarman and shook his head.

"Let me replay it. I'd swear someone was firing." He reversed the tape recorder until he was ahead of the sound he'd identified. "Now listen to this, Captain. There'll be sort of a thumping sound, like slapping your hands under-water, then a rushing noise. That's the bubbles created by the missile bursting out toward the surface." He punched the replay button.

Snow vaguely heard what the man was talking about, but only because he had been instructed to listen for something specific. They came one on top of the other, at such a close interval that they could barely be distinguished even then. "Both from the same boat?"

"I don't think so, Captain. One was a hell of a lot softer than the other."

"Can you get a range?"

The sonarman shook his head. "I don't think so. Let me run that through the computer." He was interrupted by a new sound in his earphones. "Don't go away, Captain. This is a hell of a lot more interesting. I think I got an Alfa here, same bearing, moving out like hell—sounds like a bucket of bolts."

"Range?"

"Could be as much as fifty miles . . . let me have another minute to play with it."

"Feed it into the fire control system." Snow was already through the sliding door into the control room. "Mr.

Lyford, set up for an attack . . . couple of birds in the air." He reached for the Gertrude mike. "*Helena* . . . *Helena* . . . go deep and secure prop . . . go deep and secure prop . . . you are under attack . . . you are under attack." He handed the speaker to a sailor. "Keep repeating just what I said, son. There's a chance they'll hear you . . . a slight chance," he added wistfully.

Snow wasn't sure that *Houston* could have picked up the missile firing with her gear, but he knew Andy Reed would say there was no point in letting them get away. Snow wasn't giving up his location. There would no telling the type of submarine firing back—if the Russians could hear a missile pop at that range.

In the background, Snow identified the process as the torpedo doors were opened . . . pressure equalized . . . the ordered litany of reports to the fire control coordinator until he heard, "Captain, we're capable of firing, but our solution is still kind of hazy."

"Put in six hundred feet. It drops off fast just ahead. I don't think they can pump out one of these missiles from much deeper than that," Snow answered. "How much longer?"

"We've got a deviation here. Fire control has a range variation of about six thousand yards from Caesar's. Which one do I take, Captain?"

Snow reached for the phone to the computer center and pressed the buzzer.

"Petersen here," came the response.

"Carol, we've got a range differential on the target. We—"

"I see it on the board, Captain. Wait one . . ." He could overhear her breathing in the background. "Okay, Caesar's adjusted for a speed of close to twenty knots until the torpedo hits the water. Take his—"

Snow never heard her finish. He was already ordering. "Add six thousand yards to your solution . . . manual input . . . firing point procedures . . ."

"Solution!"

"Shoot." There was no sensation in the control room as

the missiles erupted from *Imperator*. The tubes were situated so far forward that there was nothing to indicate they were off. Snow's gamble—that there would be open water for weapon entry—would be considered later.

"Missiles away, Captain . . . flight time should be about four and a half minutes."

Snow called down to Carol Petersen again. "Can Caesar figure flight time of those Russian missiles to *Helena*?"

"That an Alfa that fired on her?"

"Sounds like it to us."

"Caesar said they should be firing sixteens . . . just a second."

Snow drummed his fingers against the bulkhead. In the background, he could hear the sailor still broadcasting his warning to *Helena*. That was a slim chance, a very slim one, but anything was worth a try.

"Sir," the sonarman called in to him, "*Helena* is making a hell of a lot of noise. Sure could be a terrific target . . ."

Snow lost the last of his words as Carol Petersen came back. "Seems like about another two minutes in the air, Captain. No more than that."

We used to be able to hear a torpedo from the beginning of its run until the end, Snow thought. At least you knew when someone was after you. Now, *Helena* had no idea of what was headed her way—not until she heard the splash of a torpedo hitting the surface followed by the sound of its screws.

Imperator would have heard the warning if she had been the target. But voice transmissions attenuate rapidly under water and *Helena* did not. The lone submarine was racing off in the opposite direction in an effort to leave *Imperator*'s whereabouts a secret. There was no doubt in the minds of any man aboard that they were playing the rabbit, drawing attention to themselves. They also understood that the Russian's singular response to their presence had to be a torpedo.

Heading back toward the Bering Strait in an arc away from *Imperator* was her only choice. To continue north would compromise the mission, and the waters to the east and west offered no safety. Yet the water would become shallower as she headed for the strait. Instead of going deeper, the most natural protection for a submarine, she would be gradually decreasing her depth. Her captain kept her keel as close to the sea floor as possible. It was a long shot, but bottom return might just confuse a homing torpedo; yet *Helena*'s unique noise signature, now made even that suspect.

There was no hesitation in the sonarman's voice when he called out to *Helena*'s control room, "I have an object that just hit the water abeam to port, sir." There was a pause, an interminable one for each one in earshot. The man's voice became higher as he continued, "Can't figure out what that is . . . something breaking away maybe . . . wait . . . torpedo in the water . . . bearing two eight zero relative."

"Right full rudder all ahead flank," the captain bellowed automatically. He punched the button for maneuvering. "Give me everything you've got. . . ." His voice drifted off as he listened to the continuing sonar reports.

"High-speed screw . . . it's in a search mode . . . not a hell of a lot higher off the bottom than we are . . ." The man's voice droned on, reporting in exactly the same manner as he'd been trained, until he broke off excitedly. "Captain, something else just hit the water . . . same sounds . . . dead ahead . . ."

There was nowhere to run! One was astern, searching. They'd turned away from it. Now there was another in front of them. "Left full rudder." There was no choice. They had to turn in some direction!

"Both still in search mode . . . wait one—" There was another pause, no more than seconds. The sonarman strained, his eyes closed, his whole being concentrating on the sounds in his headphones. "First one's range gating." The torpedo had ceased circling in search of the distinctive sound it was programmed for. It was now aware of its target. "It seems to be on the same course we were before turning . . . maybe it's after our cavitation . . . now it seems to be turning this way slightly.''

Helena's noise level was a red flag to a listening torpedo. ''All stop. Breach the ship!'' The torpedoes were too close, the captain reasoned. They were coming out of their search modes at a depth of two hundred feet going after a high-speed target radiating horrendous noise. Emergency surfacing was the only chance. There was no way those homing devices would stick to the bubbles from *Helena*'s prop for long. His one remaining choice was to go silent—hope that the torpedoes would lose contact. He felt the deck angling upward. Noisemakers now! ''Launch the after signal ejector.''

In the background, the diving officer was speaking calmly to the planesmen. ''Increase your angle.'' They were going up too slowly!

Helena's captain closed his eyes momentarily, separating the sounds around him. The sonarman was reporting, ''. . . second torpedo has turned in our direction . . . she's range gating, too . . . closing . . . second torpedo is also turning . . .'' For a second he was quiet, then he added, ''Captain, I think the second one's locked on the first, coming right up its tail.''

''More angle!'' he shouted, but the bow refused to come up properly. They were losing speed rapidly. The engines had been stopped to silence the noisy prop. With the loss of forward motion, the diving officer was unable to maintain an up angle— soon they would start slipping backward. There would be no choice. Before they plummeted straight back down, they would have to blow all the main ballast tanks! That in itself would create almost as much noise.

The captain grabbed for the polished chrome bar, shouting, ''Emergency! Blow all main ballast tanks!''

''Down angle on the planes,'' the diving officer barked as the ship's control party fought to maintain the proper up bubble. A deep rumble of high-pressure air venting water from the ballast tanks was overpowering.

''Torpedo closing . . . now at about sixteen hundred

yards . . . range gate . . . second appears to be following the first . . . noisemaker seems ineffective . . .''

The depth gauge read one hundred feet. The diving officer had brought the planes to a slight up angle. Lost forward motion was regained as the ship's positive bouyancy propelled *Helena* toward the surface. Now they were roaring upward on the vented tanks.

"Fire more noisemakers!"

"Captain," the sonarman called out, "I've got both torpedoes in a one second ping interval. . . ." The tenor of his voice was increasing as he called out the progress of the two homing weapons.

"Fifty feet," the diving officer called out. "Prepare to surface." No one in the control room was moving. Each was caught up in the chase. There was no time to escape. There was only time to wait, to see if the torpedoes would pass below them.

"First torpedo's in a continuous range gate. Captain, she's onto us for sure." His voice was now a squeaky, high-pitched tremor, fear overpowering his training. "The other's lost in the return from the first . . . it's following . . .''

"We're on the surface." *Helena* burst onto the rough Chukchi Sea like a balloon, floe ice rearing into the air before crashing down on her hull. An observer would have been overwhelmed by the sounds that echoed across the silent water—*Helena* breaking the surface, the roar of ice falling back on the hull, and then the deafening blast as the first torpedo detonated fifty feet forward of *Helena*'s stern. Seconds later, it was followed by the roar of a second, which had burst somewhere inside the hole blown by the first.

The initial blast opened the engineering spaces to the ocean. Water poured through fractured bulkheads, rolling the submarine clumsily to port. The second torpedo lifted *Helena* by the stern, her bow disappearing below the surface. Water rushed through engineering spaces on all decks, covering machinery, filling the reactor space, shorting out electrical wiring, ripping away successive bulkheads.

In the control room, men were tossed about like rag

dolls with each blast. None were spared. Handholds vanished, dumping men on top of each other as the bow plunged under the surface. Then, the submarine slipped backward, the flooding aft hauling her stern downward. Emergency lights briefly illuminated the chaos to those still aware before they were tumbled backwards. The captain's skull had been crushed when he was thrown into the periscope. But there was no longer any purpose for orders. The final sounds were screams of pain and fear as *Helena*'s bow rose quickly at a sharp angle. The control spaces filled with water as the submarine rolled to starboard, holding just for a moment on her side before she turned belly up, and slid backward out of sight.

The picture of *Helena*'s demise was quite accurate in *Imperator*'s control room. While a detached voice from sonar described the submarine's frantic race with the torpedoes, Caesar displayed an animated projection of the entire sequence on the holographic imager. The silence that descended through the control room was all the more pronounced by the horror pictured for them. The idea of surfacing at the last moment to avoid the closing torpedoes was not entirely original—it had been theorized in the past—but it had never before been attempted by a nuclear submarine. The one argument against making this last-minute effort was simply that the noise created by high-pressure air rushing into the main ballast tanks could be as attractive to a homing warhead as that of the propeller.

Caesar was not programmed to picture how a submarine would appear as it was breaking up. For the sake of everyone in the control room, Hal Snow thanked his lucky stars. The final horror was difficult enough for those listening on the sonar.

For those in the engineering spaces of *Helena*, it was a quick death. Any survivors must have been killed by the second blast. It would have been longer in the forward spaces if the watertight doors to the engineering spaces held—at least for those who survived the battering as the submarine tossed about in her death throes.

Snow studied the chart, slowly circling the approximate spot where *Helena* had gone down—no more than three hundred feet! God—if the watertight doors held, there was a chance some of those forward could still be alive. The hull would hold at more than five times that depth. He asked his XO very quietly, so that no one would overhear them, to send a communications buoy to the surface giving *Helena*'s coordinates. Perhaps something could still be done.

Snow gradually became aware of a change in the atmosphere of the control room. His spirits were buoyed by the familiar words from the fire control officer, ". . . torpedo should be separated and in search mode now." While he had been overcome momentarily by a part of the submarine world he'd never before experienced—the death of a boat—*Imperator*'s missiles had continued on their programmed track. Now it became a mission of revenge.

Quite similar to the Soviet missile in operation, the American weapons separated from the rocket and drifted by parachute to the open water below. As soon as the protective nose cone had broken away, the torpedo went into its search mode, actively seeking the target inserted in its memory banks.

"Do you hold the torpedo?" Snow called out.

"Negative, Captain. All I've got is a Soviet Alfa charging away from us."

"Carol," he called down to the computer center. "Have you got anything down there?"

"I don't think we're going to get anything but the Alfa on that bearing, Captain. Caesar agreed with you and sent those birds just ahead of the Russian. They should have plunked down in a lead about three thousand yards directly on his bow. The Alfa should be between the torpedo and us. No way to hear it now—"

"I got something here, Captain." It was the sonarman shouting above the commotion in the control room. "That Russian just turned on the horses. Can't tell yet, but I'll bet he's just about lying on his side trying to turn away from that fish . . . probably diving, too."

• • •

The Alfa had been distant enough from *Helena* so that there was little she could hear during her torpedo's attack. *Seratov* must have fired also, for there was no doubt that two torpedoes had detonated. Then they heard the telltale sounds of a submarine in peril . . . and finally the propeller sounds that had first attracted them were silent.

The euphoria overspreading *Smolensk*'s control room was short lived. A panicked sonarman, his string of words repeated constantly, was shouting, "Torpedo dead ahead . . . torpedo . . . torpedo . . ." The man echoed himself, screaming the word long after the captain had thrown his rudder hard right and called for a crash dive.

"Stop him," the captain bellowed at the top of his lungs, jabbing his finger in the direction of the sonarman.

An officer clipped the man in the side of the head with a closed fist, knocking him to the deck. Another placed the headset over his own ears, eyes widening as he stared back at the captain. "It's locked on," he shouted over the commotion about him. The submarine seemed as if it would stand on end as it dived at high speed to evade. "Turning with us . . . must be same depth . . ." His eyes grew wider as he realized there was no escape. Their forward motion as the torpedo entered the water gave the weapon the advantage. By the time the Soviet submarine began evading, the torpedo was already too close. They couldn't accelerate rapidly enough. It was a catch-up race . . . but the torpedo won.

The torpedo hit amidships with a violent blast that rocked *Smolensk* sideways. Bursting lights darkened the control room, then emergency lighting snapped on to reveal bodies strewn about the deck. The captain rose to his knees, shouting, "Damage reports!"

Silence was his only answer. Then the groans of the injured began, rising in volume as they comprehended their situation. *Smolensk* was still diving. "Up angle," the captain shouted.

There was no movement. An agonized scream from the other end of the room increased the frenzy, squelching any further orders from the captain. He dragged himself over to the control panel on a broken leg, yanking back on the diving planes. Still there was no movement. He jerked harder but the resistance was steady and he was too weak. He glanced up at the depth indicator. Nothing—the glass had been shattered, the dial jammed near five hundred meters. Impossible! It wasn't that deep here.

They were still going down.

"Back engines," the captain bellowed. He was greeted only by the sounds of agony and fear. He pushed the annunciator to "Back Full."

He thought that there seemed to be an answer from engineering. He listened for the high-pitched whine of reversing engines . . . but there was nothing. *Smolensk* was plummeting toward the bottom, her angle and speed increasing. In a moment . . .

That was his last thought as he was catapulted forward into the fire control panel. The glass shattered around his face as *Smolensk* impaled herself on the ocean bottom, her seams tearing open to admit the icy waters. . . .

Smolensk's death throes were evident in *Imperator*'s sonar room, as each of the telltale sounds described in detail how the Russian sub died. The Soviets had exhibited great confidence in their Alfas. They felt they were the equal of any American submarine they came in contact with. They'd never cataloged the abilities of *Imperator*.

To the north, another Soviet submarine had been listening to those last fateful minutes. Abe Danilov and the men in *Seratov* had recorded each event that had taken place to analyze later. There was no doubt that both missiles, *Seratov*'s and *Smolensk*'s had hit their target. The noise emanating from the wounded sub's prop had been akin to waving a red flag. But the shot that had gotten *Smolensk* was something else to consider, beyond the fact that finding open water was pure luck!

Imperator was more than fifty miles away, so her listening capabilities had to be fantastic if she sensed *Smolensk*'s location, and her missiles even more amazing if she had been able to hit an Alfa at that range, one that was running full speed in the opposite direction and diving. The evasive tactics executed by both submarines were unknown to Danilov; they had been too distant to hear anything but the final moments. For Danilov, this was his first brush with the new American submarine, and it was impressive, teaching him two things: *Imperator* could detect an Alfa as if they were next to each other, and it could strike at unknown ranges with an uncanny ability to locate openings in what should have been an almost impenetrable ice pack.

Danilov ordered Lozak to take *Seratov* deep and to increase his speed very slowly. The best way to remain hidden was to remove any possibility of detection from an enemy he now held increased respect for.

The torpedo blasts had been just as obvious to the men on *Houston*. There was little difficulty in determining the outcome. But there had been two torpedoes that destroyed *Helena*—and they had come from separate sources! Sonar had been unable to determine their exact bearing, but the missiles burst from the tubes at different ranges, both to the north. One submarine had turned tail and run loudly. The other—the wise one . . . and the more dangerous— seemed to have tiptoed into the Arctic depths.

Reed ordered *Houston* to close *Imperator*. Snow had already given away a good deal of her capabilities, and now it would be wise to change tactics before their next encounter. It seemed to Reed that the submarine he had been ordered to protect might soon become his benefactor.

Andy Reed had poked an antenna above the surface to receive satellite pictures of the ice fields ahead. What had been broken floe ice six hours before was now a solid sheet of white, up to five feet thick in many places. A long lead, an open body of water, appeared about fifty miles to the north, northeast. He called to Snow over Gertrude to rendezvous there in two hours.

Neither submarine was required to surface. Instead, buoys carrying antennae for extremely short-range communications were floated to the top. They could be neither seen nor heard unless an errant satellite had appeared directly overhead.

"You gave away a lot of the beans, Hal," Reed began.

"Didn't have a choice. At least, not from my point of view. I had a good target. There was more than one of them out there . . . just trying to even the odds a bit."

"Don't bother yourself with excuses. Sooner or later, they had to figure out your range capabilities."

"I can do a lot better than that," Snow replied impatiently.

"Keep it to yourself for now. They've got more attack boats coming over the pole. You're going to have plenty to keep you busy. Have you been in touch with that other Alfa?"

"Never did have it," Snow answered. "You sure that's what it was?"

"We picked up something on him, maybe because we were still ahead of you."

"Anything now?"

"Went silent after he fired. What little we had on him disappeared after we decided to get together with you. Sonar thinks he went deep, probably stayed under four or five knots."

"I can't figure out why we didn't hold him," Snow wondered.

"You picking up a lot of biologics?" He was referring to the sound of sea creatures, like the clicking of shrimp.

"Just a second," Snow responded. He was back momentarily. "Yeah, quite a bit up ahead . . ."

"That's him," Reed interrupted. "Tell your boys that there's very little life under the icepack, just ice noise. If they compare what they're hearing now to their tapes, they'll find out it's man-made—some new kind of noise-makers, kind of similar to ours. Danilov's just screening himself while he beats it off a little farther. I'll bet you convinced him that he'd better sneak up next time."

"Like a cat," Snow concluded. He paused for a moment, then inquired hesitantly, "You still going to let me proceed independently, or do I have to tail you?"

"We're going to stay close enough so we can talk again if we have to. It's crazy for *Houston* to stay out in front now that Danilov has an idea what you can do. We're going to play with the computer here, try out all our ideas with two subs now instead of three. We'll stay about twenty-five miles on each other's beam for the time being. When you pick something up, then I'm going to cut around one side or the other—sort of flanking them," Reed added.

"I'm going to be your eyes and ears," Snow concluded matter-of-factly.

"Until there's something to shoot at, yes."

Andy Reed's plans to review his arctic strategy on the computer changed somewhat after his conversation with Snow. Their discussion had troubled him to a degree. *Imperator*'s captain was the most dependable man the consortium could have appointed. He possessed a natural ability to command literally anything, according to his psychological profile. His talent with submarines and men was legendary in a peacetime navy. Never in his career had he broken the chain of command or questioned his orders, though it was well known that he would later say exactly what he thought about the performance of others, a lack of political sensitivity that might have contributed to his inability to achieve flag rank, critics said.

Imperator had destroyed Soviet forces in the air and on the surface, and now had dispatched a Soviet submarine. In accomplishing the latter, Snow had compromised his own position, the sensitivity of his sonar, and the range and accuracy of his rocket-assisted torpedoes. There had been two Soviet submarines firing on *Helena*—one now understood exactly how dangerous *Imperator* could be and had gone silent, waiting, hoping Snow might be drawn into an impetuous act.

The decision to fire had been Snow's. No one had dictated when he could use his weapons systems. Andy Reed admitted to himself that he'd considered launching if he'd acquired a firm target. But he could not have found that lead in the ice without phenomenal luck. There appeared to be no cut-and-dried answer to that one. When you have been taught all your professional life to destroy targets of opportunity, especially when you might be the next target, how could all the positives and negatives be balanced?

What concerned Reed more was the truculence that had been evident when he questioned Snow's rationale for firing. Snow had just been too matter-of-fact. There had been no discussion with his senior, no explanation of the factors involved in making the decision. That was so unlike the Hal Snow he'd known over the years that Andy Reed determined to keep a much closer watch on *Imperator*'s commanding officer. Every submariner was on his own in a situation similar to the one Snow had faced, but Reed knew a great deal of soul-searching should be involved in a mission such as this before revealing one's position.

Novgorod was about four hundred miles northeast of Prudhoe Bay, heading quietly eastward just below the ice. Her mission was to prevent *Imperator* from turning toward the Northwest Passage as an alternative route, and to make sure that none of the American submarines attempted a sweep to the north along the arctic islands to get behind the Russian forces.

The water near the surface was less saline and extremely cold, and sound waves tended to bend upward as a result. Therefore, a submarine hovering just under the ice possessed an advantage. It was much easier to detect another at a lower depth and, in a shooting match, torpedoes had much more difficulty detecting a target when the background was obscured by ice. Sea life was limited that far north, making for superb listening conditions. What extraneous noise existed came from the ice itself. It could grind or break with a pop, a splash, or a fizz. Sonarmen classified the sounds with such names as "bergie seltzers" and "growlers."

Novgorod had been cruising independently since Danilov detached her days before. The submarine had poked her antennae to the surface in polynyas at the designated times for her message traffic, but she had sent nothing but her own position reports. A recent message from Danilov indicated that there was now a distinct possibility that one or more American submarines could be sweeping in her direction. The result had been a series of boring lectures from the political officer concerning American designs on the homeland and the necessity of stopping the American submarines before they got beyond the pole.

Novgorod remained as silent as possible. Nothing was allowed that might create extraneous noise, and no maintenance could be performed without the commanding officer's permission, which then usually required another officer to supervise the process directly. Meals were of the simplest kind, prepared with the intention of eliminating any sound that might pass through the hull.

"Captain, sir." One of the sonarmen appeared in the control room and saluted. "We have a contact to the southeast."

"Classification?"

"I am sorry, sir. We have nothing specific at this time. My officer insisted that you should be informed as soon as anything—"

"Very well," the captain interrupted. "You have done the correct thing. You may return to your duty." As the man turned on his heel, the captain added, "Fifteen minutes. Inform your officer that I want classification in fifteen minutes. He will report to me personally."

The political officer insisted on remaining by the captain's side. He had no doubt that he knew almost as much about submarine warfare as most of the other officers on board, having been with this commanding officer for more than two years. The captain had no interest in discouraging him, since the political officer really did little to interfere. While he had so far concurred with the captain on all decisions, he was required to report directly to his own superiors after each cruise on the activities of each officer.

Those "higher-ups" in the party had great influence in furthering the careers of captains when they became too senior to stay aboard submarines. It was worthwhile letting the political officer participate.

"Do you assume it is an American?" the political officer inquired. He had already determined in his own mind that it must be, but he never committed himself without first discussing the matter with the captain.

"None of our own boats are in this area. Nothing can travel on the surface. The Canadians operate nothing here." He traced a lightly penciled line on the chart representing the rough bearing from *Novgorod* that sonar had reported. There was nothing in that direction. The pencil passed into the wilderness of Canada's Northwest Territory. "If there is a true submarine contact on that bearing, it has to be an American."

"I couldn't imagine anything other than that myself. My recommendations would be to attack as soon as identification is conclusive."

"Thank you." The captain might have been sarcastic but political officers were meant to be humored. He paid little attention to a report that sonar had lost the contact momentarily.

A small, dangerous fire in *Olympia* had been controlled quickly. It was an accident. The cooks normally kept a tin of oil near the grill, a practice approved by the executive officer during sea trials, but in this case, one of the copper kettles had been balanced precariously on a shelf above the grill by one of the mess cooks. When another had been shoved onto the same shelf, the first one slipped off. A frantic grab for it dislodged a third kettle which had tipped the fat onto a red-hot burner. Luckily, no one was injured. They'd all been through the drill so many times that the fire was controlled within moments. But in that time, the most precious item in a submarine—air—had been consumed beyond the ability of the equipment to replace it quickly. A most dangerous addition to the environment had also been added—smoke.

The precipitators had worked overtime to remove particulate. Oxygen had been regulated quickly, but the stench hung heavily in the air. Eventually the submarine would cleanse itself—it was designed to do so—but there was nothing like fresh air and the captain decided that he would poke the sail above the surface in a nearby polynya.

It took no more than half an hour to retrace their steps to an opening in the ice. *Olympia*'s sail stuck just above the ice, enough to satisfy their needs. The captain was alone on the bridge, wrapped in arctic foul-weather gear, when a call came from the control room. "Captain, we've picked up an unusual signal on the ESM gear off to the northwest."

"Any idea what it is?"

"Hard to be absolutely sure. A couple of the technicians claim they've listened to similar recordings in school. They seem to think it's one of those high-speed transmission buoys the Russians pop up to the surface to send messages."

"Aren't those directional? Straight up to a satellite?"

"Right, Captain, but they do bob around a little bit. There's some spillage and we're damn sure down here we got the right reading . . ."

"And," the captain responded to the pause.

"And if it's a Soviet submarine taking a normal message break, then he can't be that far away. The technician on the set says he doubts that we could have picked that up much more than thirty miles away from the transmitter."

"What else could it be?"

"Nothing else, I'm told." Some louder voices echoed in the background. "Out here, Captain, there's practically nothing else they pick up on the ESM gear to begin with. When they get a signal, these guys move pretty fast . . . and they said that was strong enough so that it had to be pretty close. Nothing on that frequency travels any distance horizontally, even under the weirdest of conditions."

"They pretty sure they got a live one then?" He was sure, but he wanted to hear it confirmed first.

"Stake their lives on it, Captain."

"The hell with airing the wash. Prepare to submerge.

And man battle stations.'' He leaped through the first hatch. There had been nothing to secure on the bridge.

Abe Danilov was increasingly displeased with himself. Before departing Polyarnyy, he'd understood how vital his mission was, but he had also seen it as one in which he would quickly finish off anything allowed to transit the Bering Strait into the Chukchi Sea. It was hard to imagine that a submarine, regardless of its size or impressive capabilities, could not be destroyed within the first few days by Soviet forces. The methods of terminating its voyage had been planned well ahead of time in the Kremlin, so he was not as yet sure why each of their carefully planned attempts had failed. He was willing to give *Imperator* credit for being a magnificent instrument, but he gave even more credit where he felt it was due—to Admiral Reed for seeing that his charge was safely protected.

Scant days before, Danilov had envisioned a one-on-one situation as he lay in his bunk. He admitted that his speculations were somewhat childlike, for he was imagining great feats that he would perform to the adulation of his peers. What he now faced were men equally as able as he and a machine that possessed capabilities yet to be tested.

He was sure that *Houston* was still with *Imperator*, and also suspected that his earlier assumption had been correct—that there was one American submarine heading east to guard the Northwest Passage. That alone justified sending *Novgorod* there. While he couldn't imagine navigating something the size of *Imperator* through those narrow, ice-jammed stretches that time of year, this move would also prevent any sweep of an American submarine behind his own forces.

Now, Abe Danilov found himself in the position he might have dreamed about just a few short nights before. *Seratov* was alone now, maneuvering to interpose herself between the oncoming American behemoth and the homeland. *Houston* was still escorting her charge while *Seratov* was at a slight disadvantage after the loss of *Smolensk*.

Danilov rarely, if ever, weighed the odds for or against him. While most naval experts would give a *Los Angeles-*class submarine like *Houston* the nod over a Russian Alfa, Danilov felt perfectly comfortable facing one at any time. Even against the formidable *Imperator*, he wouldn't have bothered himself over rumored superior abilities. But against the two of them, and considering the talent commanding them, Danilov was wisely reassessing the situation.

There were another half dozen Soviet attack submarines racing under the icepack to support him. They would be able to provide aid by the end of the next day. It made excellent sense to accept the advantage of numbers—even though he ached for the opportunity to personally destroy *Imperator*.

But, too often now, as he considered his situation, another factor intruded to curtail his planning—Anna, his wife. Her patient endurance would be considerably shortened if he could dispatch this invader now and return to their cozy apartment in Moscow.

He was interrupted by a burst message just arrived from *Novgorod*—she had what must be an American submarine under surveillance; they would evaluate the contact and prosecute as necessary. Providing the American was sunk, *Novgorod* could rejoin him by the next day. Danilov was reluctant to lose any precious moments with Anna, but a wiser mind would wait for backup.

Danilov would let *Novgorod* keep *Houston* busy on her return.

The decision to wait, to be cautious, won out for the time being over the childish dream of facing the dragon—slaying *Imperator*.

Novgorod's captain relished his haughty position on the raised platform in the center of the control room. He glanced for a moment at the political officer who stood next to him, then glared back down at the navigation officer as if he'd broken a cardinal rule.

Just minutes before, the navigation officer had asked for and received permission to utilize the forward-looking sonar. Traveling as close to the ice as they were, it was standard navigating procedure to activate that sonar for several sweeps every ten minutes to ascertain the likelihood of any ice keels in their path. The last time, approximately eight minutes ago, they'd had a return almost two thousand yards dead ahead. At six knots, they would cover that distance in ten minutes. "I reduced speed when you first identified it," the captain finally responded. "We shouldn't be there yet."

"Captain, sonar has reported numerous times that the ice is shifting around us. We are almost on top of that contact. It could be a deep pressure ridge." When ice floes ground together, one piece would inevitably ride up on another. Current and wind could play havoc with the process, forcing tons of ice downward to create a hazard to any submarine just below the ice pack.

The captain turned to the political officer, who nodded his agreement, though he never stopped glaring at the navigating officer. "Very well . . . one ping."

"Thank you, sir." The navigating officer gave the order and the forward-looking sonar was activated for one ping. The result was a solid mass across the scope.

"Two hundred yards . . . dead ahead . . . recommend—" began the navigating officer.

"All stop," the captain ordered.

"Recommend all back, sir. There appears to be a major ridge close on the bow."

"All back one-third," the captain responded. "Give me a new course," he growled quietly.

"I . . . I'm not sure, Captain. It covered the scope. Recommend coming right about ninety degrees . . . but we must then activate the sonar again . . . just once," he stammered, "to make sure . . ." He was unused to this type of badgering and assumed that it was caused by the political officer. The navigating officer was never hesitant working directly with the captain.

The captain gave the necessary orders, followed by a final warning to the navigating officer: "Just once . . . just to make sure. The next time I prefer to go deeper rather than use sonar. I don't want to broadcast our position to the Americans.''

The sonar made one final ping. A clear track lay ahead. The navigating officer recommended a revised course toward the target and was relieved that he had another ten minutes before he was required to interrupt the captain and the political officer again.

The captain called into the sonar room, "Nothing more on that contact?''

"No, Captain,'' the sonar officer reported. They had picked up enough sporadically on tape to identify the contact as a *Los Angeles*-class submarine. There had been other sounds, an alarm of some kind in the interior of the contact—maybe for an exercise but that was foolish in these waters unless it was an emergency. Then the contact had apparently reversed course. That was followed by sounds of surfacing a short time later. The operations officer had discussed the events with the captain, both men coming to the same conclusion. It was quite probable an exercise had been conducted in which the American was required to find a polynya and surface. Since there was no reason for patrolling this particular area, they assumed it would resume its course toward Lands End on Prince Patrick Island. They laid off its projected path on the chart.

The captain turned to his operations officer. "Where should he be now?''

"Almost thirty points off the starboard bow, Captain, perhaps twenty kilometers distant.''

The political officer looked at the captain with apprehension. Neither one could imagine why nothing more had been heard, especially at that range, unless somehow they *had* been heard. . . .

A hush of anticipation spread through each space in *Olympia*. This crew had destroyed a Soviet submarine just days before in the Pacific, yet they also knew their limitations. They had almost been sunk themselves and the realization was sobering. There was no direct order, nothing passed by word of mouth, that silenced them. Rather, it was a return of excitement and terror coupled with mature understanding after their first experience. And there was that feeling common among submariners that allowed no room for a mistake. Another few yards on that last Soviet torpedo, and they might all be dead now! Luck certainly wouldn't visit them twice.

"Got 'em!" The chief sonarman seemed to whisper the contact report under his breath. "Port bow . . ."

The captain moved the short distance into the sonar room, leaning over the chief's shoulder. "What have you got, Chief?"

"Ice did it." His voice was still a whisper. "Got 'em twice. Once when they were boxed in by a pressure ridge. They turned . . . clear sailing . . . if we'd been closer they might have picked us up."

"Any range?" Now the captain's voice had become a whisper to match the chief's.

"Hard to say, sir. I know it's one of their forward-looking sonars . . . heard 'em before . . . don't quite know their range . . . maybe twenty thousand yards . . . maybe a bit more . . . no less."

"No machinery noise, Chief?"

"Quiet as hell, Captain. Must know we're out here." He looked up to catch the captain's eye. "They're getting better, sir. When they get this quiet, they're hunting."

The captain stroked his chin for a moment before looking down at the chief. "Would he pick us up if I took her up another four or five knots?"

The chief nodded without hesitation. "Like I said, sir, he's probably hunting. If he knows roughly where we are, he'll be listening right around our bearing." He spread his hands, and shrugged. "Hell, Captain, there's nothing else out here but us . . . no sea life . . . nothing. Anything that makes a sound is going to be us as far as he's concerned."

The captain clapped him on the shoulder. "That's what I figured." He turned back as he was leaving the darkened room. "I promise I'll stay just as quiet."

Olympia's captain went directly to the weapons control

coordinator. "I want you to prepare for an attack now. They tell me in there"—he jerked his head in the direction of sonar—"that the other guy knows where we are, but he's not about to give us another chance to hear him, either. Do everything you have to do now—warm up two torpedoes, flood the tubes slowly, open the doors . . . and see if you can get sonar to help you. That ice upstairs is making some noise. Wait until we've got a growler if you can, especially when you open the muzzle doors. Let's try to keep all that racket to ourselves."

Then the captain moved over to the plotting table, beckoning the executive officer with him. A quartermaster was already making a paper overlay with the approximate position of the Soviet submarine in relation to the lighted bug representing *Olympia*. The two men studied the relative position of their vessels, the XO waiting for the captain to speak.

"He heard us first. Maybe he got enough to get some sort of course before we went completely silent." He nodded to the quartermaster. "Why don't you lay off a projected course for us for about fifty or sixty minutes . . . same speed as now," he added.

The two men watched as the line for their course was laid out with a straight edge. Then the quartermaster used a compass to mark their distance every ten minutes. "He's probably doing this right now himself," the captain muttered. "Trying to figure what I'm up to." He stroked his chin.

"I'd take odds he was going to try to come right up our butt," the XO commented.

"Good bet . . . I wouldn't take it," was the answer. The captain tapped his finger on the thin overlaying paper. The Soviets' course would eventually intersect their own on the port quarter. "He's got to be under six knots, probably no less than four . . . give him five. Lay out a course for him to intercept us at that speed." When the two lines intersected, the captain wondered aloud, "What's the perfect range for those torpedoes he's shooting? Maybe six or eight thousand yards?"

"For a sure shot." The XO had picked up the compass and was drawing a half circle behind *Olympia*'s projected position representing about eight thousand yards.

"Yeah," the captain murmured. Then he smiled. "He'll want to make sure his first shot's his best . . . cause he knows we'll be firing right after we hear the tiniest sound."

The quartermaster had anticipated the next step. As the two officers watched, he laid out the progress of each submarine in five-minute segments until the Soviet boat was just a hair's breadth from the eight-thousand-yard half circle. He checked his watch to ensure his times were correct, then wrote the time projected for the other boat to reach that semicircle. "About thirty-eight minutes from now, Captain."

"Great! Good work, son. That's exactly what I wanted. You read my mind." He offered the thumb's up sign as he stood up straight. "What the hell do I need a computer for if I've got quartermasters? Now you just keep rechecking what you've got there son, and if sonar picks up anything you mark it right away and let me know if he's off that track of yours at all."

"No problem, Captain. We'll get him." The quartermaster had never looked up. His eyes were glued to the track he'd laid out for the captain.

The weapons control coordinator looked up as the captain returned. "Torpedoes are warmed up, sir. Do I have enough time to wait for a little noise outside before I finish the rest?"

The captain nodded. "You will be firing in approximately thirty-five minutes . . . unless sonar picks up something and tells us different. I'd estimate your target will be at about eighty-five hundred yards, still hovering just below the ice. Give him a speed of about five knots. He's going to be coming right down the throat because I'm going to turn around a few minutes before and wait for him."

The fire control coordinator's eyes lit up. "He'll be figuring to come up behind us, hiding in the baffles, won't he?'' The baffles, directly astern, were the only area where a submarine could be considered deaf.

The captain nodded with a smile. ''Sounds like a perfect shot for us, doesn't it?'' After a pause, he added, ''Nothing ever is. I want to fire two torpedoes . . . and I hope to hell the wire holds on at least one of them because he's going to be moving faster than hell as soon as they leave the tubes. You may have to feed some steer into those fish, you know.''

The fire control coordinator nodded. They'd rehearsed the same sequence innumerable times.

''Well . . . the sooner the better,'' the captain concluded. ''It all sounds too easy to me. If you don't have enough outside noise in the next twenty minutes to complete your sequence, then get it all ready anyway. We'll just have to take our chances.'' He smiled, adding mostly to himself. ''Of course, they won't be too good if he fires first.''

Novgorod's captain expressed his displeasure. ''They're not that quiet, damn you.'' One of the sonarmen clapped his hands over the earpieces to shield the noise the captain was making. The pressure of listening for an elusive microsecond of sound at a time like this was overwhelming. Men had been known to have a nervous breakdown, even in fleet exercises, when another submarine was running an attack on them.

The political officer touched the captain's sleeve tentatively, after noting the sonar officer's eyebrows raise in despair. ''We can't do anything to help them. They're trying very hard,'' he offered. The tension had gripped even him in the last moments. The knowledge that another submarine was waiting for the slightest hint of their position, anything that would justify firing a torpedo, had overcome the confidence he had been exuding up to that moment. His armpits had inexplicably grown cold. Perhaps it was the fuzzy picture of two dark submarines that clouded his mind. They were vague forms suspended like puppets in a liquid environment—each one seeking the other, each intending to shoot and run before the other might grasp the opportunity.

The half smile the captain had managed as he entered the control room turned brittle as he saw the navigating officer bent over his chart table. "They must have heard us ping. That pressure ridge . . . that damned pressure ridge may have given us away." Others in the control room turned at his outburst, only to find him suddenly silent, appearing moody, thinking. All that single ping could provide the American with was a rough bearing, and confirmation that *Novgorod* was operating close to the ice. There was nothing he wanted to alter yet. No point in changing depth. The ice provided too fine a background screen to mask them from a torpedo.

The more he considered his options, the more he realized there really were very few. They each had a reasonable idea of where the other was, and neither would take a chance of revealing his actual position. They could each stop and hover in place until the other made a mistake and gave his location away. But there was no time for that . . . and the American submarine was quieter than his own—he had to admit that. No, he'd much rather attack. That was his strength . . . and he was in the best position.

Moving to the plot laid down by his navigating officer, the captain studied the assumed position of the American in relation to his own. He was approaching the American from the port quarter. He should be difficult to hear at that angle. It wasn't a matter of chasing after the American. They were converging if the plot was reasonably correct. There was only one answer: prepare three torpedoes. It would be wiser to waste one. Fire the first before they were really in position. No need to have a target solution. Just fire the damn thing. The American would hear it. Then he would either have to fire his own without preparation, or commence evasion immediately. Either way, the captain would be ready to fire at the first sound the other made with his two remaining torpedoes. It might not take two, but two were a much better precaution.

He moved about the control room giving orders in preparation. The navigating officer worked furiously at his figures to determine the optimum time for firing the initial torpedo.

Olympia's quartermaster called out softly, "Recommend coming left in thirty seconds, Captain."

"Thank you." The captain, his measured voice matching the others in the control room, moved over beside the diving officer for the third time in as many minutes. "Don't do any trimming, but try to grab a bit of an up angle as we come about. I'm going to slow down at the same time—can't take a chance on any sound." Not moments before, he'd explained the same process to the engineer. He wanted his ship as quiet as possible, yet he expected them to accelerate like a horse coming out of the starting gate as soon as their last torpedo was in the water. Absolute silence wasn't entirely possible. Steam flow in the turbines and engine noise could be picked up even at this speed in close quarters.

"Make it a slow turn," he added to the sailor on the helm. "We've got the time."

"Recommend coming about now, Captain."

"Come left to course three one zero . . . easy now," he added to the helmsman.

"Coming to course three one zero, sir . . . very gently."

In the background, the captain could hear the diving officer coaching the planesman. Checking the engine revolution indicator, he saw that they were slowing gradually, exactly as the engineer had explained they would. There really had been no need to rehearse the process once the captain described his plan. Each man who listened to him repeat himself understood his intent exactly. *Olympia* had to have the first shot!

"Passing north, sir."

"She's risen about sixty feet, Captain . . . about all I can get out of her. Our speed's too slow . . ." The diving officer paused for a moment. "Two hundred forty feet between us and the ice."

"Making turns for two knots, sir."

The weapons control coordinator had reported ready before they began the turn. The torpedoes had been warmed, the tubes flooded and pressure equalized, muzzle doors opened—each completed as the ice above provided masking sound. All the presets had been entered according to the captain's wishes: target course, speed, range, aspect, optimum depth. *Olympia* was ready to fire once she steadied on her new course.

"My course is three one three, Captain. I've lost steerage way . . . no forward motion."

"Zero bubble, sir . . . we're steady."

"Dead in the water, sir."

"The ship is ready, sir."

"The weapon is ready, sir."

"Solution ready."

"Shoot on generated bearings."

No sonarman ever misunderstood the sound of a water slug, not the sudden, powerful burst used to eject a torpedo. Even before its propellers started, he cried out, "Torpedo in the water . . . dead ahead."

"Range?"

There was a hesitation. "About five kilometers . . . maybe a little farther. I have screw beats now."

Novgorod's captain had exercised almost exactly the same preparations as his enemy. His first torpedo was ready to fire. The presets were a bit off, but not too far if they could change it with the wire guidance. He had to force the American to dive before he could get off an additional shot. "Fire!" he shouted.

"Our torpedo is running, sir," sonar reported.

"The American torpedo . . . range?"

"The range seems to be about—" He never bothered to finish his analysis. The captain didn't really care at that moment. "Probably close to four kilometers."

"He was closer than we thought. What speed?"

"I have nothing on him . . . dead in the water . . . our torpedoes seem to be head on to each other."

"No evasion yet?"

"Nothing, Captain."

Novgorod's captain turned to his fire control officer. "Do you have the solution for the second torpedo?"

"Almost complete, sir."

"Standby to fire." The captain called to his executive officer. "Noisemakers! Tell engineering to prepare for evasive action."

No more than thirty seconds had elapsed. During that time, the political officer had not moved from his position, nor had he uttered a word.

"Firing point procedures!"

"Solution ready," *Olympia*'s fire control coordinator responded.

"Noisemaker in the water, Captain," another reported.

"Very well." The presets had been inserted as soon as sonar pinpointed the Soviet water slug. There had been little to alter. *Novgorod* had been very close to the quartermaster's projected position.

The captain called over to the chief of the watch, "We're going to go deep right under him. Make all the noise you want with the trim pump as long as we go down like a rock."

"Their torpedo is still searching, Captain. I think it started out too deep."

"Shoot!" he called out. He felt the jolt of the water slug through his feet.

"I have a second torpedo in the water from the Russian!"

The captain waited. He couldn't go deep as quickly as he hoped. The wire attached to the torpedo should remain until they were sure it was running correctly. This was the consummate moment when seconds became hours . . . the waiting . . . knowing another torpedo was actively searching for you. His hands gripped the shiny railing beside the periscope as he sorted out the reports from each sector of his ship.

"Unit's running properly, sir." They could break the wire now!

"Very well . . . all ahead full . . . make your depth six

hundred feet." He had to change the aspect he was presenting to the Russian. "Right full rudder."

Olympia's deck slanted downward, the angle increasing
perceptibly as the propeller bit into the water. With the
rudder hard right, she began to bank slightly with increasing speed. The feeling of motion—forward, downward,
starboard—was exhilarating. Now they were making their
escape.

The political officer heard each of the reports. He knew
the American had fired first . . . that *Novgorod* had answered within seconds . . . then had fired again . . . that
the American also had two torpedoes in the water . . . but
he was unable to move. His feet were glued to the deck.
His hands gripped the side of the chart table. He was
aware there was no way he could assist the captain, but in
such moments he also understood that the captain didn't
want his help. All along, he had been humored by the
captain . . . and he now realized the amount of patience
the man could exhibit to an important party member.

"Captain, their first torpedo is range gating!"

"Is it locked on us?" the captain called out frantically.

"I don't know yet . . . it could be the ice . . . a
noisemaker . . . us . . . I can't tell, Captain, I'm not sure."
Fear was cracking his voice.

There was little point in maintaining position, waiting
foolishly to determine if they were a firm target. The
engineers were ready. "Ahead full . . . right full rudder,"
the captain barked.

A warm feeling surged down his back as the submarine
responded. Noisemakers! That was it. Screen himself! If
he was now going to create so much noise, he had to put
more decoys in the water. He knew how much noise an
Alfa generated. Glancing briefly at the political officer,
whose eyes stared blankly into space, he called for more
noisemakers over the din of reports from each department.
He knew the American was also underway now, more than
likely scrambling just as he was. No point in precision
when you may be blown up any moment.

"Torpedo closing . . . port quarter . . . locked on us." The sonarman's voice had changed from fear to a high-pitched cry as the torpedo propellers screamed ominously into his headset.

Olympia's sonarman had been reporting the Soviet torpedo's approach in a dry monotone. This changed instantly to a shout of glee, "First torpedo appears to be locked on a noisemaker . . . passing astern."

The captain tried to restrain himself. "Number two . . . where's the second?"

"Still in search, sir . . . may be too shallow . . . they may have programmed it for a different depth after own first one."

"Hold that angle, Chief," the captain called out. "We can stay under it . . . make your new depth eleven hundred—"

His voice died with the distant explosion that needed no sonarman's identification. The sharp blast cracked across the depths, penetrating *Olympia*'s hull, into the ears of each of her crew. It was the most terrifying sound a submariner could hear—a massive underwater detonation.

The silence in *Olympia* endured for perhaps five seconds. Each man stopped whatever he was doing—pondering his own good fortune, considering the fate of his opposite on the other submarine, desperately hoping that his own destiny would not be settled within seconds.

It was the captain who broke the silence. "Confirmation on that hit . . . did it impact the target?"

"It's a mess out there, Captain—hard to separate. I think I still have cavitation on that bearing. . . ." His voice trailed off as he strained to differentiate the full spectrum of noise through the rolling waters. The grinding of disturbed ice floes magnified the confusion.

"What about their other fish?" The captain's voice was demanding.

"Still in search well above our port quarter. They could have been depending on the wire when our torpedo hit."

The second sonarman interrupted. "No chance. They'd

already turned on the horses and were changing course. Wire had to be busted before.''

''Own speed eighteen, Captain.''

''Passing through nine hundred feet . . . decrease your angle,'' the chief whispered to the planesman. ''We're still gaining speed.''

''My rudder is straight, Captain. Do you have a new course?''

''Is that fish still searching up there?'' The captain was sensing victory—not that his enemy was sunk, but that he had also escaped the second torpedo.

''Still circling . . . no change in depth.''

''Chief, level off at twelve hundred . . . what course are you passing now, helm?'' The captain's breath was coming in short gasps. He could feel his heart thumping. Could he have held it when they started maneuvering? Hell, no. He'd never stopped talking—just good, healthy fear.

''Now passing one one two, Captain.''

''Steady up on one three zero.'' That would be almost a reciprocal course from the torpedo's origin.

''Captain, I still hold the Alfa. I have a burst of cavitation . . . also sounds like she's going deep.''

Olympia's torpedo had burst directly above *Novgorod*'s port bow plane, the pressure of the blast forcing both bow planes into a full dive position. With the submarine increasing speed, she instantly pitched into a sharp dive.

Her captain was one of the first to pick himself off the deck after the shattering explosion. Emergency lights outlined a crumpled pile of bodies thrown to starboard by the blast. The men handling the control surfaces remained strapped in their chairs. The political officer, who never once moved from his white-knuckled position by the chart table, had been flung against a stanchion. Blood now flowed from an ugly gash on his forehead across his neatly pressed uniform. The slant of the deck was increasing quickly with the planes at the full dive angle. They were falling rapidly from the relative security of the ice overhead.

"Up angle," the captain shouted, "up angle . . . up angle."

"I can't, Captain." The planesman was straining at the controls. "They're jammed."

"Help him," the captain shouted, pointing at a sailor struggling to his feet. "He can't do it by himself." He waved his hands in the direction of the control panel. "Help him."

He stared impotently for a few seconds as the two men struggled over controls which would not respond. The angle was now critical. Those trying to regain their feet slid across the deck, frantically grabbing for any handhold.

"All back full," the captain called. "Blow the forward main ballast tanks."

The diving officer rose to his hands and knees, crawling to the controls that would blow high-pressure air into the ballast tanks. There was no roaring sound of water flushing from the tanks. Again he went through the motions before he cast a desperate glance over his shoulder. "I'm getting nothing, sir . . . main ballast blow system doesn't respond."

Novgorod's angle was beyond anything she'd been designed for. She began to shudder as the backing engines turned a propeller that struggled furiously against the downward flight of thirty-five hundred tons. Not a man had been killed by the impact of the torpedo. Some bulkheads had been fractured, but it was not a killing hit. Yet *Novgorod* was passing five hundred meters, her bow long past the critical angle for survival. Her ballast tanks remained as full of sea water as before. Now the rumble of her turbines and the high-pitched yowl of her single shaft desperately straining against gravity could be heard for miles through the icy waters.

Her captain refused to relinquish his grip. By then, it was as if he was swinging from a bar above his head. He had seen the depth gauge pass six hundred meters . . . eight fifty . . . a thousand. "Impossible!"

He could sense the hull rupturing. The immense pressure of the depths cracked *Novgorod*'s once-powerful hull like an egg. He was aware of the screams about him as the submarine exploded inward. And then there was nothing as the crumpled junk drifted to the sea floor almost four thousand meters below.

Olympia remained on the same heading until the executive officer came over to the captain and rested a hand on the man's arm. "Captain, do you intend to remain on this heading for the time being?" The answer was obvious but it was the easiest way to start.

The captain looked down at the reassuring hand, then peered about the control room. No one else was nearby. Each man seemed to have a specific job to accomplish. "Negative. Do you have a recommendation?"

"Suggest we resume course and speed as recommended by Admiral Reed, sir."

"Very well. Secure battle stations. Set the normal underway watch. Check our current location. We may just have some catching up to do so that Andy doesn't have to wait for us . . . and you should have the comm officer prepare a short action report for me when we surface for messages."

Stevan Lozak remained in his control room as *Seratov* moved away rapidly to the north. He had followed Danilov's wishes and taken his submarine deep, over six hundred meters, and eventually he had sped away behind the distraction of noisemakers that no listening device could penetrate. Abe Danilov understood that although *Imperator* might be as fast as the Russian Alfas, she could travel only as fast as Admiral Reed's *Los Angeles*-class submarine. Not even the awesome *Imperator* would be allowed to race boldly into the lion's den without Reed nearby.

For Abe Danilov, this was an opportunity to rest once again. It seemed that those doctors in the Kremlin were correct. At his age, men in his position required more rest, more time to prepare mentally for the taxing work that lay ahead. He hated to admit it, but mental exercise was growing more tiresome each day they were at sea. There was no problem with his strategy. His ability to sustain a mental picture of the vast stage they were covering, and placing the surviving submarines in their appropriate positions, was better than he remembered. Mission awareness was simplistic as far as he was concerned. He understood what Reed and Snow were attempting, and had no doubt in his own mind how they intended to go about it.

Though Abe Danilov remained a bear when it came to analyzing an enemy's strategy, he also possessed a comparative weakness—he failed to comprehend at this stage his increasing dependency on Anna's letters. Her neatly handwritten memories redeemed choice events of his past, rekindling a desire to return to the happiness of those days. He now desperately wanted to partake of the joys that he had so often missed because of duty, even if he was limited to exercises of the mind. He realized what kind of father he had been, returning home each time as a hero to his children—yet he was a father they really never knew. He saw himself as he must now be in their eyes: an authority figure in a greatcoat covered with snow. But he never really knew them. He loved them and they loved him, but much of his affection had been distributed in choking doses over short periods of time.

He lay in his bunk as *Seratov* raced northward, comprehending more fully how much he had actually missed of a family that had grown up successfully under Anna's direction. As he memorized each word of her earlier letters, he came to the realization that he didn't want to miss another moment of that life, even if it involved only himself and Anna.

But Anna was dying, and he had no options other than this tiny, cramped bunk in another man's stateroom. He must complete this mission quickly! It was vital that she understand that her message had gotten through to him, vital that she know he would continue her efforts to hold the family together.

Danilov removed the packet of letters, taking out two of them. It was almost the end of the fifth day, and he knew he would not sleep again until the sixth—and then he would be so busy. Perhaps it was cheating Anna, but he would read both of them now.

She told him of another stage in their life that required more of his time away from the children. It was his first major command—the newest, fastest attack submarine in the fleet. He had helped to develop it during his time in Leningrad, and his reward after the mud and blizzards of Severodvinsk had been to take the sub as his own. Anna related how jealous she had been—it was no more than a machine, yet she had become increasingly irritated by it. And when they returned to port, all he could talk about was his submarine. He would go through the motions with the children, spoiling Eugenia, encouraging Sergei's military studies, putting up with Boris's competitive spirit. But never, she explained, never loving them regardless of what they were or would be. They were tough days for Anna and he marveled now at how sturdily she had faced them. What a powerful woman—her love had remained while he blithely took advantage of both worlds.

The second letter related their experiences in Moscow. Admiral Gorshkov had obtained orders for him to the Voroshilov General Staff Academy, where only prospective flag officers were sent. Those were the days of special privileges, the stores where only important government officials and high-level officers could shop. They were invited to the parties that the average citizen only suspected might take place, and they attended the opera and the ballet and so many other events that Anna loved. He attended because they were supposed to be there.

The special privileges were overwhelming. Abe Danilov grew more impressed with himself than others around him. Once again, it was his Anna who gradually awakened him to the fact that he was becoming enamored of another mistress—his own self-importance. That was not something she would ever love in a man. She picked away at it each week until he was able to understand exactly what she was driving at. He would destroy himself with his own self-indulgence and pride. There were other, more senior officers who had been through the same thing. She explained how they stood back in judgment of the younger ones as they experienced the same temptations.

He returned her letters to his drawer, briefly wondering why he had allowed himself to go out on this final mission. His place was beside Anna as long as she remained alive. He cursed himself momentarily for being coerced into going after the giant American submarine, until he acknowledged that it had been his own decision. There was no way he could have gone back!

Anna understood his strengths as well as she forgave his weaknesses. She would not have wanted him to remain in Moscow, however much she needed him. He would come home again soon, just as he always had before.

There have been moments in the past when two countries facing the probability of armed conflict finally come to the realization that some form of truth may be the best solution to mutual problems. It is not necessarily the whole truth they intend to utilize nor is there any rule that says it has to be anything more than as they see it. Truth is subject to interpretation. It can follow a variety of courses and usually does on the international level. It can often become a weapon.

The Kremlin was not about to allow the sighting of *Imperator* in the Bering Sea to pass without taking advantage of magnifying a mystery. Over the following thirty-six hours they projected a scenario of American aggression about to take place that increased international suspicion of U.S. intentions. While Washington was in the process of countering the movement of Soviet Spetznaz units toward the pole, the Soviets were documenting the fact that American Spec Ops and SEAL teams were already en route to arctic airbases. They were even successful for a period of time in convincing the media that the U.S. was pushing Moscow to the breaking point.

The White House countered—they felt justified in stretching Soviet intentions on the Northern Flank into the final step before the invasion of Europe. Russian denial to the contrary, the concept of a possible Soviet invasion of

NATO countries became more feasible . . . a specter that invalidated Soviet hints of arctic warfare only hours before. Stated Soviet intentions of only defending their country against American encroachment, first in the Norwegian Sea and then in Soviet waters themselves, were lost in an American publicity barrage.

The Kremlin valued stretching the truth themselves, again emphasizing the terrifying possibilities of the deployment of U.S. attack submarines into the Soviet arctic bastion. While Russian ballistic-missile submarines were intended as a last resource, now they were exemplified as a means of maintaining stability in a frightened world. Their sole purpose was to avoid a nuclear holocaust at the instigation of the U.S., and the main thrust of the Soviet argument was quite simply that an American attempt to dislodge the missile-carrying subs could be the beginning of an attack on the Soviet Union itself. And an attack on the USSR would precipitate a war that would draw in every peace-loving nation. The result would be unthinkable.

While there was never any doubt in a single Soviet military mind that the Northern Flank offered vital protection to the homeland against the American fleet, there had been no consideration of invading any NATO country. That would precipitate a war the Politburo could not afford. But it would be hard to convince those European countries bordering the Warsaw Pact nations, given the maneuvering of Russian forces on the Norwegian border.

Conversely, world leaders were horrified by the concept of the Arctic as a battlefield. Many would agree that the Soviet SSBNs in the region provided a rational balance to their American counterparts in the Atlantic and Pacific. The idea that the Americans might actually be in the process of challenging Soviet SSBNs in the Arctic created a noticeable stir in the UN and almost every world capital. Not only could a horrifying nuclear imbalance be possible, but the Russians also introduced the concept of a nuclear explosion in the Arctic that might create devastating environmental results.

The war of words manipulated truth as a shield to

deflect the realities of their expanding confrontation. The Russians used Murmansk as a staging area for their special operating forces while the Americans had transferred their own to Thule Air Force Base on Greenland's west coast. As far as either country was now concerned, reinforcement was brief hours from the North Pole, where their submarines seemed to be converging.

What neither power could do was communicate with their submarines long enough to explain the complexities of their evolving strategy. They were limited to selective data relayed in burst transmissions. Content was mostly reassurance of the placement of special operating forces as a backup. It became purely submarine against submarine.

As Andy Reed sat before *Houston*'s green wardroom table an hour before midnight, he understood the inner conflict other commanders had faced in past wars. His elbows were planted firmly to either side of a mug of cold coffee, and he massaged his temples with the fingers of both hands, his red-lidded eyes shut tightly against their demand for sleep. The cold he had inherited from his youngest son had shifted from his head to his chest, and the headache had disappeared, to be replaced by a hacking, dry cough that made breathing uncomfortable. His voice had grown deeper, a prelude to laryngitis, he was sure. He'd read many biographies of famous admirals and was sure that not once had history ever recorded whether or not colds had influenced the outcome of a battle. He wasn't sure why.

Reed never noticed one of the junior officers enter the wardroom, seat himself at the other end of the table with a mug of coffee, then think better of disturbing the exhausted admiral. Rising quietly from the table, he tiptoed silently out. Beside one elbow was Reed's message board containing the brief action report from *Olympia*. That had changed his outlook tremendously. He knew that Danilov had been sent out with three submarines, and that two of them were gone. Six other attack submarines had been dispatched by the Russians. He was sure that there were no others to the east and that *Seratov* was alone. That allowed him to accelerate *Olympia*'s speed, sending her directly across the top of the world. His orders were for her to transit in deep water north of the Queen Elizabeth Islands until reaching a point opposite Perry Land near the northernmost tip of Greenland. Then she was to head north with the intention of coming in behind the additional Soviet submarines.

His greatest concern of the moment was not Abe Danilov or any of the Soviet attack submarines. He was sure that Danilov would attempt to keep a reasonable distance between himself and *Imperator*, delaying any attack until his reinforcements were closer. The Russian admiral already understood more of *Imperator*'s capabilities than he should have—and that was the crux of Reed's problems. Hal Snow's too-quick decisions and instant retaliation had spawned a gnawing concern in the eyes of his commander.

Since *Imperator* was a task force within a single hull, it had originally appeared easier to command that task force from another unit, and distance offered the advantage of added perspective. But the more Andy Reed considered Hal Snow's reactions to date, he wondered whether he shouldn't be sailing with him. Reed was positive that if there was any weakness on *Imperator*, Abe Danilov would be searching for it. It meant a great deal for *Imperator* to move cautiously on cat's feet. At one time, Snow would have been the man almost everyone in the sub force would have chosen for the job. Andy Reed wasn't so sure he was that man today.

Hal Snow was restless. *Imperator* could go faster than they now were moving, but he was limited by *Houston*'s speed. Snow desperately wanted to catch up to Danilov, sink him as rapidly as possible, then look for more Russians. To him, that was his singular goal and there should be no deviation. Sweep away anyone in the way, and charge on in to finish the job!

He climbed out of his bunk, slipping on wrinkled trousers and shirt, and wandered down to the wardroom. It was deserted. All the old magazines had been neatly stacked before someone headed for his own bunk, and there had been no one in there recently to mess things up. Snow had no interest in disturbing the watch. Finally, he decided to stop by Carol Petersen's room. She'd been pleasant enough the previous evening.

The curtain had been pulled over her doorway, and no light peeped through. He considered calling her name, but that seemed a crude thing in the middle of the night, nor was there any reason to disturb any of the others along the corridor. Finally, he tapped lightly on the bulkhead, hoping she might also be having trouble sleeping. There was no answer. Snow decided there was no further reason to bother anyone. He shuffled back down the corridor in the direction of his own room.

As the footsteps disappeared down the linoleum passageway, Carol Petersen relaxed with a soft sigh of relief. She sensed how troubled Snow was, but there was no time now to comfort him—nor did she care to encourage his attention.

Only the watch section remained awake through the artificial night induced by *Imperator*'s computer. Caesar drove the immense submarine through the icy arctic waters toward the North Pole with only the slightest hum, one that her crew had become quickly inured to. There was no sound for them—there were watches, drills, periods to eat, periods to sleep. With the exception of normal security patrols that Snow had begun, as a sort of backup to the time that Snow feared Caesar might fail, most of the crew remained in the after section of the ship.

If *Imperator*'s length could be divided into four football fields, the hindmost would take up the engineering and propulsion spaces; only those who ran the equipment entered that area. The control and living spaces were ahead of that section—the thinking, fighting part of the ship, as Snow liked to say. Ahead of that was the main storage compartments; here were the tanks and helicopters and armor belonging to the marine contingent. Though Caesar also watched over this area, Colonel Campbell had established duty sections to patrol his heavy equipment. Like Snow, he could not be convinced that Caesar was able to control everything. From the day he was commissioned, it had been drilled into him that marines protected their own weapons, and it would be no different now. It also kept busy a marine unit that had little idea why it had been transferred at sea to a monster submarine that was taking them to an unknown destination. Colonel Campbell had explained to Reed that these marines were no different than any others—they were always ready to fight, but, if they didn't know where or when, they had to be kept busy. So each marine stood one-in-three watches, having no idea what lay in the after half of this immense ship or what unknown element guarded them as they patrolled their spaces.

What no one else understood was that the captain sensed the eeriness of the situation as much as they did.

_ 9 _____

ANDY REED HAD been captivated by maps since he was a
kid, learning early on that they could make the world come
alive. His father often explained that it was impossible to
read a book about a place you'd never been if there was no
map. Once the shape of a place could be pictured—the
lakes and rivers and mountains, the locations of cities and
the roads that connected them—then the actions of the
characters in the book could be pictured with clarity.

As Andy grew older and sailed with his family in the
summers, charts became just as appealing. He learned how
to navigate his sailboat among the coastal islands and
rocks, or into the harbor by sighting the church steeple and
the water tower on the highest point in town. He could
also imagine the ocean bottom in bold relief just like the
landscape on a map, picturing in his mind the offshore
trenches, the rocks where the lobstermen dropped their
pots, and the broad banks where fish schooled.

Now, as Reed leaned over the chart table in the rear of
Houston's control room, he studied his position in relation
to the North Pole and the land masses to the south and
east. The chart displayed no land whatsoever, the closest

being Ellesmere Island almost six hundred miles away.
Overhead was solid ice broken only by occasional polynyas or leads that might close at any time. The floor of
the Arctic Ocean was six thousand feet below as they
raced northward five hundred feet under the ice.

Chief Quartermaster Gorham leaned on the opposite side
of the chart table, watching Reed with obvious interest.
The admiral was experimenting with various courses and
speeds, plotting positions in relation to a Soviet submarine
that had yet to be located. His methods were decidedly
old-fashioned, at least to a quartermaster who had always
located his position with the aid of satellites and computers
and digital displays. This admiral was using a compass, a
protractor, and his imagination. Chief Gorham had never
served in anything other than a nuclear submarine and had
no concept of balancing on a wildly gyrating bridge to
shoot a star or take a noon sun line, more or less plot it
manually in a tiny chart house to fix a ship's position.
There had been stories about submarine officers doing that
even as recently as the sixties—but nothing like that in his
experience.

Finally, the chief could contain himself no longer. "Can
I give you a hand with anything, Admiral?"

"No . . . no thanks. Just playing, Chief." Reed's voice
was still hoarse and he cleared his throat. After a pause, he
added, "Gives me a sense of place . . . time . . . I know
it's deep as hell out here, but it's always been a habit."

It wasn't a custom for quartermasters to chat with admirals, but Reed appeared interested in continuing the conversation. Enlisted men knew only what they were told
when it came to where they were headed and what the
ship's orders entailed. The scuttlebutt that passed for information was regarded with more suspicion after each promotion until chiefs generally realized the worth of rumors.

"I still like to study the bottom and figure out where
roads would go and where I'd build a house for the best
view if it was all above the surface," the chief offered.
"I've started some very nice developments if I do say so."
He handed Reed a sharpened pencil.

"Well, what do you know. The only other guy I ever knew did that was a friend of mine on the *Will Rogers*."

The chief pointed his finger knowingly at Reed with a wink. "Commander Folger . . ."

"Yeah . . . Brud Folger. That's the guy, Chief. We were at the academy together . . . he was funny as hell then. Used to do comedy routines making fun of all the instructors."

"Used to do the same thing, Admiral, when I rode the old TR with him. Hell of a funny guy." The chief shook his head from side to side. "Captain caught him one time ashore doing an imitation of the commodore and almost busted him. Got any idea where he is today, sir?"

"You wouldn't believe it, Chief. He started doing the same type of routines after he retired. You know, I wouldn't tell on him if he was still active"—Reed pondered for a moment—"but he did a bit for some ladies' group at an officers' club somewhere around the District, and brought the house down. It seems the CNO's wife was there and she passed the word around so now he's in demand every weekend."

"Mr. Folger sure was a funny guy." The quartermaster looked down at the chart that Reed was contemplating. "Fine navigator too, sir. He was the one that taught me how to make believe the ocean bottom was actually above the surface. Said it was the best way to imagine where a submarine might hide if you got in a tight place. Sometimes late at night on one of those dull boomer patrols— running around inside a box—he used to teach me how to design underwater highways and that sort of thing."

"You were only on boomers with him then."

"Yes, sir, just the TR."

"He served on attack boats, too. He was the one who taught me how to look at the bottom of the ice just like he taught you to look at the sea floor. Did he ever explain that to you?"

"Sure did, sir. But it's a son of a bitch trying to do the same thing when it's on top of you . . . sort of like standing on your head to figure out where you are."

Reed had been hoping he wouldn't have to interpret it alone. "Do you think you could do it again if you had to?"

"You mean turn upside down . . . look at the ice like a highway?"

Reed's expression changed perceptibly. "That's right, Chief, and navigate that highway overhead just like your life depended on it."

The quartermaster's expression never changed. There was still a smile on his face as he said, "I'll bet my life does depend on it, doesn't it, sir?"

"Sure does. Mine, too. You see, we're going to have two OODs doing the driving, one just to make sure we don't hit anything, and the captain's going to be looking for targets with me. I need someone who can work with all of us. If you think you can help the OOD navigate, no matter how fast we want to go, and at the same time tell me where I want to go if I'm leaning over your shoulder, you're going to become a super chief before you hit the beach next time."

Now Chief Gorham's expression altered slightly as he rubbed his jaw thoughtfully. "I guess I never should have mentioned Mr. Folger's name . . . right, sir?"

"Wouldn't have mattered." Reed grinned. "I checked all the service records and decided maybe the two of you knew each other." He tapped his forehead with an index finger. "I figured I didn't have time to do it all myself, and if Brud Folger taught you, I figure I can run around those ice fields without a second thought."

The captain's stateroom had become Reed's for the length of the voyage. It was the one place on *Houston* where he could be alone with his thoughts. Every possible element that could possibly affect the submarines under his command was evaluated, then reevaluated if he were to fulfill his responsibilities to each man aboard.

This was more than a simple showdown with a man he'd encountered twice at sea but never met—Abe Danilov. While each man understood his country's strategy was the focal point, much more was required of them. Since Abe Danilov had to face a secret weapon—*Imperator*—his superiors were ensuring that he would face the unknown with superior numbers. Andy Reed, on the other hand, had to learn *Imperator*'s limits against those odds. In addition, control of the environment above the ice pack could be as important as that below, so each country was prepared to launch aircraft for inserting their specially trained arctic forces depending on surface conditions at the time.

While the weather below the ice never changed, that above now became a critical factor. There were two purposes for inserting combat teams. If a submarine was damaged, the only chance for survival might involve surfacing through a polynya or a lead to either vent smoke from a fire or make limited repairs. Whichever country controlled the area where a submarine surfaced would be able to protect their own or finish off an enemy. There was also the possibility of technical assistance during undersea combat. Though it had never before occurred, a surface support group could place either noisemakers or mines below the ice to give their own submarine an added advantage.

As Reed considered how long a combat team could be sustained, and studied the regional weather reports, he experienced a feeling of insufficiency. He understood submarines and how to fight them, but the vagaries of arctic weather were beyond him. He knew that navy SEAL teams could be inserted wherever he decided that Abe Danilov would stand and fight. They would be within range to assist him as long as they could survive the climate. Their odds of being extracted might be poor.

A chart of the Arctic Ocean was taped to the bulkhead above the desk. He stared at it until his eyes smarted. They were traveling at just over thirty knots on a course that would bring them close to the North Pole shortly. They were currently passing over the Lomonosov Ridge, a subsurface mountain range rising as much as nine thousand feet above the deep Arctic Ocean. Beyond was the Fram

Basin and ten to twelve thousand feet of water almost to the edge of the ice pack.

As hard as he tried, he was unable to imagine how best to determine where Danilov would turn. Again, it was dependent on the surface weather. Intercepted reports indicated that Soviet strategy was little different from his own, and their weather analysis was equal to his. It all finally came down to plotting a larger area than desired where aid might be provided from the surface.

What would his old friend, Brud Folger, have done at this point? How would the master navigator balance the data on his charts with the weather in the Arctic and the wiles of an experienced Soviet submariner?

Reed slowly massaged his eyes and temples until relaxation overspread his body. It was an acquired habit and the end result was always the same—he began to doze and dream. Brud had been a sailor, too. They'd crewed together at Annapolis, and a few times in later years whenever they were stationed nearby. He remembered the time he and Lucy had agreed to vacation together with the Folgers. A yacht had been chartered in the Bahamas for a week, but at the last minute Brud's submarine had been kept at sea and the Reeds were left with a yacht too large for two people to handle. What would they do with that big boat for just the two of them? It had already been paid for and this was the last time he'd be able to get away for a long time. Lucy Reed had made the decision—we need a crew, she said, why not the kids? All six had been sailing since they were six weeks old, and even the littlest could follow simple directions.

Was she ever wrong about something like that when her mind was made up? he mused. Lucy arranged a small loan from the local bank to cover plane tickets for the kids, helped to prepare early homework with their teachers at school, and the day before they were ready to leave she had them all packed and ready. And it ended up being the most glorious vacation the Reeds had ever experienced.

Andy had fond memories of one moonlit evening in particular. They were anchored off Eleuthera. Their oldest had finally given up trying to stay awake and unrolled his sleep mattress by the bow. Andy went below and mixed the final Anejo punch of the evening. Then he and Lucy sipped and watched the moon reflect off the white sand along the shore.

"Here's to Brud," Lucy murmured. "He didn't know it—and he's probably still blaming the U.S. Navy for his troubles—but he's done more for this family than a million dollars ever could."

"Brud, wherever you are, we hope you know the Reeds are thinking of you with affection . . . for not being able to make it," he added with a soft chuckle.

Lucy looked into his eyes in the moonlight, her face as serious as it ever could be. "We'll never be able to do this again, will we? What I mean is that we'll never have a chance again to get to know our kids like this . . . or for them to know us." She wet her lips thoughtfully. "Do you know what I mean, Andy? It's never like this at Christmas or any other holiday, and Timmy will be off to college next year. It's hard enough to get kids to do anything with their parents when they're teenagers—and we've got three teenagers with us!" she exclaimed.

Nonetheless, it was a wonderful week. The Anejo rum seemed smoother each time, complementing the fresh lemon and lime juice so perfectly that he could have put away a dozen of them that night. That vacation had been a little over three years ago, but it came back so vividly. His daughter, Tammy, had decided after only a couple of turns at the wheel that she was never going off to college—the life for her was the sea. She was going to go into her own charter business and spend all her time sailing through the Bahamas and the Caribbean. At thirteen, what could be more romantic?

Dick had been fifteen at the time and nothing around home had ever suited him. It didn't matter whether it was having to make his bed, or putting his dirty clothes in the hamper, or mowing the lawn. Nothing was ever right and nothing was ever his fault. There were days when it was hard for Andy Reed to live in the same house with him.

Yet out here on the ocean, he'd changed overnight. He took his turn at the wheel with gusto and there was never a complaint about handling the sails, washing down the deck, or any of the constant chores that had to be done when eight people lived so closely together on a small craft. He even volunteered to help with the more difficult work, anticipating the moments when his father would need help.

The oldest, Timmy, was the quietest. But when they were out of sight of land, he was the one hanging over his father's shoulder to learn how to pilot the boat through the islands. He'd become quite a navigator in just a short week. He managed to replace the great navigator, Folger, who would never let anyone else help once he'd laid out his charts. But Timmy Reed became equally proficient in those seven days, challenging his father to contests to see who'd be the first to sight a landmark or pick the correct moment they'd drop anchor each night. He usually won.

Now, both Timmy and Dick were off to college. Neither one had any desire to follow their father to Annapolis, but that never disturbed Andy as it did so many of his peers. Considering his situation now, racing toward the North Pole five hundred feet under the ice pack, he was sure they'd all made the right decision.

The big fish had been the highlight of their final days on the water. The youngest, the unplanned-for Kevin, became the fisherman of the Reed family during that trip. He was the one who loved to run down to the nearest stream wherever they lived to fish for sunny and bullhead. As soon as they were in open water in the Bahamas, he was the one who used to troll for hours from the stern, his bare feet dangling over the side. Kevin had the patience of Job. He would sit there forever, occasionally reeling in so that one of his brothers could put on a new plug for him.

The big fish had struck the last day. Andy remembered the screams of excitement from the stern. It sounded as if someone had fallen overboard, but when he poked his head through the hatch he saw Timmy with his arms already around his little brother's waist. Little Kevin held tightly to the pole while the line fairly screamed out. Lucy was at the helm and he still remembered her words as he stared dumbly at the scene on the stern. "For God's sake, Captain, do your duty and get aft and help the boy. Something big just jumped back there."

It had taken more than an hour and Kevin needed help from each of them, but Andy had finally leaned over the rail and gaffed a handsome sailfish. When they entered port that night, all the people wandering the docks had come down to take pictures of the little boy who happily posed with the fish that stood twice as tall as he. It was something Kevin would never forget all his life, and it was a picture that Andy Reed still carried in his wallet. Whenever he settled into a wardroom, every junior officer had heard that the first thing to do was ask the admiral if he had a picture of his son with the big fish.

Each of the children had experienced something they would never forget. As he dozed now, he realized that it would be one of the happiest memories he and Lucy would retain. How he missed her now! Remembering things like that brought back so much . . . and it was always Lucy who was smiling back at him through those memories. It didn't matter whether it was a simple picnic on a Sunday afternoon or the traditional meat loaf dinner she prepared whenever he was getting underway. Always—always Lucy was smiling, never asking when he was returning. Just sending him off with "all the love he could handle" were usually her last words when she said good-bye.

How could any man be so lucky?

"Admiral." The sharp voice competed with the knuckles rapping on the bulkhead. "Sir, the captain sent me down to inform you we just copied our normal message traffic. We have a position report on a Soviet burst transmission, probably a sub, no more than two hours ahead. The captain said he sure could use your help in the control room."

"Thank you. Tell him I'll be right up just as soon as I get a little cold water on my face." Cold water—that would clear his head. He had to find out how much time had elapsed since that Soviet transmission. Danilov could already have chosen where he planned to make his stand. A weather update in the last traffic might answer that. There was no doubt that if the Russian made a move from Murmansk, the U.S. would make one also from Thule.

Refreshed, Reed dried his face and ran a comb through his hair. Staring back at himself in the mirror, he wondered if perhaps the decisions had already been made for him, though it wasn't of great concern if they had been. The first thing he would do would be to make final contact with Snow. As he sauntered down the passageway to the control room, he could sense the up angle of the deck. The captain had certainly anticipated him. If Danilov was already searching for them, they wanted to hover just under the ice. No need to give the other guy the advantage.

Hal Snow studied the red numbers on the digital display— one seven nine degrees four six minutes west, eight eight degrees five six minutes north. *Imperator* was just to the east of the International Dateline and would soon be on the other side of the North Pole.

"Captain, we just got a call from *Houston*."

"Patch it into the number three speaker."

"No need yet, Captain. Admiral Reed just requested us to close him near a polynya about twelve miles to our west."

Reed's instructions were simple when they talked between the communications buoys. They followed his original plan of sending *Houston* out on what was assumed to be Danilov's flank. *Imperator* would continue directly toward the pole. Weather data indicated a fair area in the region ahead and that it should remain the same for the next forty-eight hours. *Olympia* was expected to be approaching from the opposite flank within the next twelve hours. There was no need for further discussion. The stage was set. As they severed communications and each submarine submerged, they were on their own.

Carol Petersen entered the control room just as Snow was about to call her. "My sixth sense tells me that you are planning to wear out Caesar in the next day or so.'' Her smile was friendly and professional.

Snow forced a thin smile in return. ''I'm going to use the hell out of him. Come on over here.'' Without explanation he directed her to the chart table, where he picked up a pencil to outline what he was about to say. ''Admiral Reed should be about here right now. I want to get a reasonable position on him as soon as you're back below. Insert a course about like this.'' He drew a rough of *Houston*'s projected course, and jotted down an average speed for a submarine operating just below the ice. ''You're going to lose him from time to time and I want Caesar to know where to expect him to reappear.'' He drew a circle near the pole. ''Danilov ought to be somewhere in that sector. Sonar has a tape on every possible sound a Russian Alfa ever made. Plug that into Caesar if you haven't already. Danilov's going to be hugging the ice, too, but we might pick up a chance peep of some kind before he wants us to hear him.''

''Back to the old needle-in-the-haystack approach?''

Snow shrugged. ''No choice. He's got the upper hand for the time being. What Andy asked me to do is toss out some of those new noisemakers of ours. Since Danilov knows we're coming after him, he's going to have to sort us out of a number of different contacts.''

''Can't he figure out where we are just from the sound patterns of those noisemakers?''

''We're going to run a little zigzag for a while. And have Caesar insert time delays on most of them so they won't begin to radiate until we're well away from them.''

She nodded, saying nothing.

''*Olympia* should be coming up here.'' He marked an area to indicate where the other submarine would be approaching. ''I can't take a chance on sinking her . . . because''—he enclosed *Olympia*'s circle with an even larger one—''the Russians have another half dozen probably moving in somewhere beyond the pole. Alfas, Victors, Sierras, Akulas . . . they all produce different signatures from a 688-class.''

"That's one thing you can bank on. Caesar knows the difference." She bit her lower lip before adding, "Captain, why don't you come below with me to see how I'm going to go about telling Caesar everything that he's supposed to do." Frustration had replaced the pleasure and excitement of just a few minutes before. Hal Snow could be so damned condescending!

Snow glanced at the fingers of his right hand beating a tattoo on the chart table. What the hell made her talk to him like that? The answer was evident even before he looked up. "You're right. Nerves . . . can't imagine why Caesar didn't tell you that was my problem," he added weakly. His thin-lipped grimace was replaced by a slight grin. "Why don't you just tell me whenever I'm asking too much . . . which I don't think will happen."

"Great," she answered. It was admittedly a weak, meager apology. "There's got to be more . . . right?"

Snow was amused by her flip response. She reminded him a lot of himself in years past. "Sure. There's no way I can use missiles anymore. Even if I found a hole up there to fire through there's no chance I could hope for it to come back down on anything but solid ice. I've reloaded every tube with torpedoes. Since I'd much rather fire too soon than too late, I'll expect firing solutions on any sound we come up with, even before we identify it. But don't let me fire too soon. . . ." His voice trailed off at the end, almost as if he anticipated the possibility of crossing over the fine line of self-control. It seemed more difficult to maintain each day.

"Between these people"—she indicated his fire control party—"and Caesar, you've got everything under control. The only thing that can happen is if you try so hard to confuse the Russians that you do the same to Caesar."

"Understood, ma'am." The wry grin playing at the corners of his mouth was completely out of character compared to the touches of anger he had shown only moments before. "Can Caesar provide me with a visual on the ice above us from the inputs from sonar?"

"Just call me when you need it. I can put it on the holograph."

"I'm going to need contacts plugged in there, too."

"I can handle all that, and more. What I'm more curious about is how do you plan to creep up on Danilov when you're driving four football fields of submarine."

"On cat's feet," he murmured softly. He tore the paper off the chart table and handed it to her. "On cat's feet . . ."

Abe Danilov's hand ran up and down the shiny chrome support pole on the platform overlooking the fire control suite. He could feel the adrenaline surge through his system—once again he felt like a young Turk rising through the ranks of the Soviet submarine force! In those days, it seemed that nothing could stop him, and today he was equally invulnerable. They would make contact with the Americans today, and he could hardly wait. He was imbued with a sense of invincibility.

Such anticipation also convinced him of the necessity of placing his concern for Anna in proper perspective—that much he owed to *Seratov*'s crew! Before he dropped off to sleep, he was positive that he was once again spiritually in contact with her, and he slept happily because she understood he would not be back until his mission was complete. When he awoke four hours later, he couldn't remember the last time he'd felt so rested. For the first time on this cruise, he never considered the doctors' orders a burden. He felt so good that he was positive he would feel even better by following their instructions.

He'd stretched until every muscle seemed to tingle throughout his body. Sitting up on his bunk, he breathed deeply, his mind alert to the day ahead. He realized he wasn't the least bit concerned about the purpose behind it all. Abe Danilov was going to show his seniors that he still had a long way to go in the service. As he shaved, checking the messages that had come in during the last burst, he admitted that he felt even better because he had followed the doctors' instructions.

The breakfast he consumed in the wardroom was huge,

and he ate it with a gusto none aboard *Seratov* had seen since he boarded. His ebullience spread through the submarine. The same atmosphere had developed on other submarines Danilov had ridden in the past. His enthusiasm was infectious.

Sergoff was delighted with the change in the admiral as he entered the wardroom that morning. He had been awake a good deal of the time Danilov was sleeping, and his mood, he knew, would be based that day on how the admiral felt.

Seratov was now meandering through the ice pack, keeping no more than fifty feet between the top of the sail and the bottom of the ice. The forward-looking sonar was activated to warn of imminent danger ahead. The upward-looking sonar charted the thickness of the ice above, carefully recording those areas that were suitable for surfacing in an emergency. Speed was kept at a minimum to avoid noise. There was no longer a need to outdistance their enemy. Instead they were waiting . . . waiting for the Americans to give themselves away.

"Contact!" The red light winked on above the fire control board. "Relative bearing two one six."

Danilov nodded pleasantly to the fire control officer, who glanced over in his direction. "That's right. That's close to where they should be coming from." He relaxed as they maneuvered to get an accurate plot on their contact.

"Contact appears to be moving east to west. Speed about eighteen knots. Classified as probable American *Los Angeles*-class. . . ."

More details followed. As he listened, Danilov's smile disappeared. They should be coming toward him . . . they should be hugging the ice when they knew he was ahead of them, and they shouldn't be radiating all that noise. He sent Sergoff into sonar to have them go through the identification process again. He was sure the Americans—Reed—wouldn't come charging right at him.

"Contact . . . bearing one seven one." Again, the process was the same as the first. Another *Los Angeles*-class! Impossible, Danilov surmised. There was no way the one off to the east could have come back this close so quickly. This contact moved more slowly and was making a zigzag path, according to the sonar officer. It didn't make sense.

A half hour later, another contact was reported—another *Los Angeles*-class! The strategy became obvious to Danilov. The Americans weren't going to come to him waving a red flag, and to have expected that possibility would have been foolish. The first contact fooled him, the second planted the seed, the third confirmed that they were toying with him. Sonar insisted that their classifications were accurate and there was no way he would dispute their analysis. It would take an expert to sort out the difference between the noisemaker and the real thing. He was sure *Houston* wasn't equipped with such a device, nor could it move about so agilely to release them without being located herself. No . . . this had to be *Imperator* coming directly toward him!

Danilov turned to Stevan Lozak and said softly, "Captain, that submarine of theirs may well hear us before we can sense it. Stop your engines."

"All stop." Lozak turned expectantly. "Secure the active sonar, sir?"

Danilov nodded, appreciating a man who anticipated him. "Let's have a look at that chart of the ice we've been developing."

Properly laid out, the portion of the ice pack under which a submarine had passed should read like a map. In addition to the thickness of the ice, they also recorded obstacles, especially the pressure ridges, which could easily sink a submarine. However, the ice pack is an unstable element that can be affected by the weather above. Wind and current can push the ice together, forcing pressure ridges as much as a hundred feet below the surface. A submarine drawing not much more than thirty feet of water can hide behind such a deep pressure ridge.

Danilov studied the sonar chart carefully. Finally, he selected a spot with his finger. "Right here." He tapped the spot repeatedly. "Bring her here, Captain. I don't mind if it takes a couple of hours. Just don't make a sound while you do it. I want to hide behind this ridge as long as we can. If it disappears, so what? By then he may have given himself away." He turned to Sergoff. "See if you can find any consistency to those decoys he's using. Perhaps we can locate him through his efforts to confuse us."

The warning light on the sound-powered phone caught Snow's attention before the buzzer sounded. "Captain here."

"Caesar picked up something dead ahead of us—very faint. Hard to classify but it appears to be man-made." Carol Petersen's voice was hesitant.

"Sonar didn't report a thing."

"I know that. I already checked with them. That's not their fault. This is apparently below the threshold of even your best sonarman, Captain. Caesar can pick up a lot that he can't identify, a lot that the human ear wouldn't know was there. That's what this was. It was only there for thirty seconds, and for some reason it stopped."

"Probably the ice."

"Negative. This was man-made," she insisted. "Caesar can differentiate that much."

Snow was ready to dispute her comment without thinking. "What the hell—" But then he remembered how many times the engineers back in the fishbowl had extolled the superhuman features of their computer—and one of the items that had been repeated was its ability to distinguish sound, even if it could not classify what it heard. One of them even went on to say it could save his life some day.

"Captain, it was on a bearing dead ahead . . . right where you expect them. I'd—"

"Sorry," Snow interrupted. "I didn't mean to discourage you. Call your bearing up to sonar and have them work it too. The only man-made thing in front of us is that Russian submarine."

"Wait a minute, Captain. We've got something again dead ahead . . . very faint—"

"Does sonar hold it?" Snow shouted impatiently across the control room.

"Negative."

"Whatever it is, it's very faint. Caesar's barely holding it. If it's a submarine, it's either a hell of a long way off or dead slow."

"Is it man-made?"

"No doubt about it . . . but we can't classify it."

"Roger . . . see if you can get a track on it."

Snow closed his eyes tightly, imagining what he might do if he were in Danilov's shoes. The man knew his Alfas made a great deal of noise, and that *Imperator*'s sonar ranged beyond the human state of the art. No doubt about it—go silent, as silent as possible, and wait. *Imperator* also possessed exceptionally long-range torpedoes. She could take the chance of using active sonar to obtain the Russian submarine's range. Then fire before Danilov's torpedoes would be effective.

The Russian admiral was known for his brilliance; he wouldn't leave himself out in the open. More likely he would hide behind a pressure ridge. Snow kept his eyes tightly shut as he contemplated Danilov's options. They were limited. It was probable the Russian would fire first if he could hide successfully. Get wire-guided torpedoes in the water—*then* steer them, Snow realized. He gave the order to stand by the evasion devices forward. Caesar would fire them automatically if the ship appeared to be in danger.

Admiral Reed sat disdainfully before the computer console eyeing the blank screen. He had been intent on playing the game "what if" when he sat down, but never touched a key after switching on the terminal. Instead, he readily acknowledged that they were beyond the war-games stage. They were no longer struggling for position. It was now a matter of who would fire the first shot and which submarine would be the first to plunge to the bottom of the Arctic Ocean.

It had become apparent to Reed from the messages directed to him, and what little he could garner of the political situation that existed, that both Washington and the Kremlin were willing to settle things beneath the arctic ice. At this stage, the threats and counterthreats would continue on the international level. The United Nations, and those countries who understood the stakes involved if either country dug in its heels, would attempt to mediate by keeping the conflict on a shouting level.

Since the sinking of *Fahrion*, Reed and Danilov knew that they were not really pawns being moved about on an international set. Few people in their own countries—none among their allies—were aware of the scene evolving under the arctic ice pack. Andy Reed understood that it was being left to him and to Abe Danilov, two men who had met twice before, to settle matters. If *Imperator* was able to complete her journey beneath the ice and surface off Norway, the United States would have succeeded in supporting NATO and maintaining a hazardous neutrality on Europe's Northern Flank. If she did not, the Soviet Union would control what she considered rightfully hers— the arctic seas—and she would be able to maintain her tenuous threat to America by keeping her missile submarines beneath the ice pack.

By nature, submarines and their commanders were given sanctions that other leaders with more powerful forces never entertained—once submerged, their decisions were their own. Whether they eventually were right or wrong would be determined long after they had been made and ships and men lay on the ocean bottom. Andy Reed and Abe Danilov, and each of the men who commanded the submarines under them, would settle the international squabbles taking place above them over the next thirty-six hours.

Danilov had wisely removed himself from the scene north of the Bering Strait when he realized that his odds were unsatisfactory. Now he had reached the depths near the pole, intent on a fight. Having reacted prudently before, there was no reason to believe that he now was throwing caution to the winds. He must feel that the odds were back on his side and that could mean only one thing—his reinforcements were nearby.

Six additional attack submarines had been sent out to assist him. There was no logical reason to imagine they would remain together. Sometime during the past twenty-four hours Danilov must have been in contact with them. A plan would have been formulated, a loose one because submarine warfare was an individual game—but it had to be taking shape as Reed sat staring at the console. No, there was no way to insert Danilov's mind into a machine and expect to have definitive answers. Submarine warfare was conducted on experience and instinct. With the possible exception of an outrageous mistake, the best man won.

Reed picked up the sound-powered phone and pressed the button for the control room. When the captain came on, he said, "Turn ninety degrees to port and stop engines. Concentrate sonar on an arc about thirty degrees either side of the bow. I'm willing to buy a round for every man aboard if we aren't being flanked ourselves right this minute. I'll be up shortly."

The concept had come to Reed as cleanly as if he had planned it himself. Of course—if he had six submarines coming in as a backup he'd form them in a rough half moon to avoid being flanked.

Andy Reed considered Danilov's tactical ability equal to his own, and that's essentially what he would have done. No matter what flank the American 688 class was on, he would be caught in a pincer. So the thing to do was to pick off the outboard submarines one by one. Using the North Pole and Danilov as the center of a rough maneuvering board, Reed devised probable positions for each of the six Russian submarines. When he was satisfied with what he had done, he left for *Houston*'s control room.

"Ross." He beckoned the captain over to his side, laying out his projection. "This is the pole, right here. How about inserting a current position for *Houston* on my chart?"

The captain noted their position on the navigation gear, measured it off on a nearby chart, and came back to mark the same spot for Reed. "Those your Soviet subs?" he inquired, pointing at the six marks forming the half moon.

"No doubt in my mind—attack subs, each looking for us right now."

"That one's pretty close." He winked at Reed. "Could be within sonar range, I'd say."

"Want to bet on thirty degrees either side of the bow?"

"Wouldn't touch that bet for the life of me." Then he added, "Unless he had us before we were silent, he could end up on top of us before he knew what hit him."

"Come on," Reed said. "We're not doing ourselves any good standing here staring at the watch. I'll buy you a cup of coffee."

There were freshly made doughnuts on the wardroom table. They were almost finished with the second, after a short discussion on waistlines, when the wardroom phone buzzed. The captain conversed briefly in monosyllables with the OOD, then replaced the phone, explaining, "Looks like they got an Alfa on the starboard bow, Admiral. Nothing certain for range yet, but they're maneuvering and ought to have something by the time we put away the last of these doughnuts." He winked again and grinned. "Glad I'm not a betting man." He glanced down at his watch. "It's less than an hour since you told us where we'd find 'em."

Back in the control room, the fire control tracking team was already set. "It looks like he's about thirty miles away," noted the executive officer. "That's an early mark. Give them a little more time to confirm. Seems to be heading toward us at a little more than five knots—trying to be quiet, but those Alfas just seem to broadcast over three knots. His aspect has him passing somewhere on the starboard beam if he holds course."

Reed nodded, a smile of satisfaction on his face. "He wouldn't be so quiet if he didn't expect we might be nearby. Danilov figured exactly what I'd do."

"We've got enough time, Admiral, but I'm going to initiate the attack sequence. No telling how he might change in the next hour or so."

Reed nodded. "The best idea would probably be to just sit here and wait for him. But that takes time and I don't want his buddies to think we're easy. Now that we know where he is, let's close him very slowly on a reciprocal course. He's not going to hear us yet and I want to get up closer to the ice. No need to be firing at the entire ice pack from down here. Let's take away any advantage he has.''

Abe Danilov had done much of what Hal Snow anticipated from *Imperator*. The scenario that Snow expected with *Seratov* hiding silently was correct, except that Danilov had no intention of firing a torpedo. As *Seratov* nestled behind the pressure ridge, the admiral explained exactly what he intended to do to Stevan Lozak, then asked the captain to pass the word through every compartment that he expected absolute quiet. Every piece of machinery that could possibly be secured was silenced. Even if Snow's sonar had heard them, the Russian submarine would now essentially disappear from the Arctic. The only possible way they could be detected would require that *Imperator* come around the pressure ridge and either run down the Alfa or locate them with active sonar, and Danilov knew that the Americans wouldn't be using that.

There were indeed six Soviet submarines that had received orders from Danilov and they had spread themselves across a wide range. But they were not exactly in a half moon. While two were well out on the flanks, two others were assigned to stations between the flanking submarines and the last two, who remained a good distance from *Seratov*. The latter two were almost a hundred miles astern of Danilov, and they had gone silent. Their orders were to wait until an unidentified submarine came in contact. Beyond positioning themselves they would do nothing to give away their location. While a pincer was in effect, there was also a box into which Danilov hoped to draw *Imperator*. There would be five submarines surrounding the giant sub within hours after she passed by *Seratov*.

Abe Danilov depressed the button on the side of his watch, just as he had done innumerable times that day to assure himself of the date. If he could dispose of *Imperator* before this day was through, he would be able to keep his promise to Anna. He would be home on the tenth day.

• • •

Hal Snow fidgeted with the instruments on the chart table, then paced from station to station around the control room, peering over the shoulder of each man. Since that initial contact, that single faint indication that *Seratov* was somewhere ahead of them, there had been nothing.

He came to the sliding screen that separated sonar from the control room, stared at it for a moment, then slid it open a few inches. Hesitating, he glanced at the men hunched over the equipment, headphones dwarfing their heads, taking no notice of his presence. His sonar officer looked over, squinted against the glare, trying to recognize the intruder, then put his index finger to his lips for silence. Snow slid the door shut.

Striding over to the sound-powered phone, he buzzed the computer room. "Come on, what's wrong with that computer of yours," he asked before Carol Petersen could speak. "First you think you got him—then nothing. Either he's out there, or you were imagining it."

"Caesar has no imagination, Captain," she responded calmly. "Remember, I explained to you once that we couldn't program human qualities . . . and he can't develop them himself," she added, hoping to shield the unpleasant inflection in her voice.

"There was a submarine out there—" Snow began.

"There did seem to be one, Captain. We held a man-made sound for a very short time, though it could not be firmly identified. Since that report, we have identified nothing similar."

"Maybe you're experiencing an electronic casualty."

"If there was any electronic gear inoperative, Caesar would report it automatically. Everything is working. Captain," she began, "it's possible for a submarine to go silent and nothing could pick it up at long ranges or under certain conditions if it didn't want to be heard—"

"So much for engineering marvels," Snow interrupted sarcastically.

"Captain, sound does strange things in cold regions. What we heard could have been something very loud and very definite that traveled over a long distance. That's possible. Sound waves also bend in this region. What we had could have been attenuated after a second. There are too many possibilities to begin to consider.''

''Okay, okay, I'm not patient. Forget it. I'll just wait here,'' Snow finished with exasperation as he hung up the phone.

Beyond *Imperator*, in the icy arctic waters, the only sounds that sonar could identify clearly were those of the ice itself, cracking, sliding, fizzing. Sea life was almost nonexistent beneath the pole.

''Range twenty-one thousand yards.''

Reed's hand rose involuntarily in the air. ''Stop,'' he murmured softly to the captain, almost as if he might be heard by the approaching submarine.

Houston glided to a halt. ''Sound off if you have trouble holding trim,'' the captain said to the diving officer. ''Any change in the contact?'' he asked the fire control officer.

''I don't think he's about to change anything now. He seems to have increased depth.'' The Soviet had secured his navigating sonar, which likely meant he'd lowered his depth at least 150 feet. ''He's still moving at about five knots . . . and you can be damn sure he's straining to hear us. We could take him now, Captain.''

The captain turned to Reed, eyebrows raised in question.

''Negative, Ross. Give him maybe . . . another twenty-five minutes. At eight thousand yards, he shouldn't be able to dodge any torpedoes no matter what he hears. And when he turns on the horses to run and makes all that racket, the better for your fish.''

Minutes ticked by more slowly, each one seeming longer as the Soviet Alfa closed them. What if he'd tracked *Houston* before they were silent, each man wondered privately. Just enough data to plug into a torpedo? Maybe he'll fire half a minute ahead of us and turn tail before we have a chance to put our fish in the water. Then we'll be on the defensive. . . .

The torpedoes were warm, their tubes flooded, pressure

equalized, muzzle doors open, when Reed said to the captain, ''Don't let a soul make any noise, Ross. Just take her through the steps until the solution is ready, nice and easy . . . let your crew feel this is the easiest thing in the world . . . there's going to be more . . .'' He was whispering.

The captain silently registered the reports through to torpedo presets, checked to ensure that his target appeared to remain at the same depth, made sure that *Houston* was at the right angle to the target, and finally turned to Reed. ''We're ready, sir. Request permission to shoot.''

''Your discretion, Ross.''

The captain glanced over at the fire control coordinator, who gave him the thumbs-up sign. ''Shoot on generated bearings.'' The sound and sensation of the water slug as the firing key was depressed was felt in every corner of the submarine. The second torpedo was no different.

''Standby decoys,'' the captain ordered. It was second nature to anticipate return fire.

''Torpedoes running . . . wire continuity good.''

There was no time at this range for the Russian to initiate a firing sequence. Escape was the single, vital requirement of the moment. Just in the time that it took for the Russian to achieve enough speed to increase his turning angle, the American torpedoes had covered that much more ground—while the Soviet forward motion brought them even closer.

''Hull popping,'' sonar reported. The creaking, crackling sound of hull compression was clear as the Soviet boat increased depth rapidly. ''And she's really turned on the horses. Her aspect's changing fast.''

Reed watched with a professional eye as the technicians aboard *Houston* continued their individual functions. The attack did not cease after firing. The wire attached to each torpedo was an umbilical still connecting it to the womb, the fire control computer. Changes in the target's actions could be transmitted to the torpedoes to avoid a programmed search pattern before they were within acquisition range. The operation ran smoothly, sonar reporting the Alfa's evasive actions while continuous data was transferred to the miniature computers within the torpedoes.

Houston had succeeded beyond even Reed's expectations, waiting until the ultimate moment. Their enemy had been unable to pause long enough to develop a target solution. There was no need for evasive action.

"She's got decoys in the water . . . one . . . two . . . three . . . four of them . . . all running off in different directions . . . torpedoes still operating normally."

Reed nudged *Houston*'s captain. "Looks like a good shot, Ross."

The captain smiled. "Seems to happen whenever we have an admiral on board." He was in awe of Reed's tactics and could think of nothing else to say.

"Alfa's changing aspect fast. . . ."

"Wire's snapped on number two. . . ."

"Alfa's like a dog chasing its tail . . . aspect's changing again. . . ." The reports from sonar were increasing in intensity. Each man was creating a mental picture of the submarine and the torpedoes. The sonarmen added further reality with verbal accounts of the sounds of the chase, which they had developed to a maximum sensitivity. It was akin to the nose of a hunting dog on a trail. Sound heightened the image of the hunt.

"Captain, number one is on to him . . . I'm sure . . . seems to be range gating . . . I think it's locked on."

A tremendous explosion echoed through *Houston* as a torpedo detonated.

"Captain, if this trace from the fire control system we've got here is close to right, he almost ran right into that fish." The fire control coordinator tore off a sheet of paper and brought it over to show the track of the torpedo and the submarine. "What do you think, sir?"

Reed's smile grew as broad as anyone had seen it the entire trip. "I think he swallowed it. What does sonar have to say?"

"Hard to say, sir. Got a hell of a mess . . . can't find any screw beats . . . wait . . . wait one—oh Christ, we got him."

The sonar officer removed the headphones momentarily and called out to Reed. "Must have torn her up forward. I can hear her engines now, sounds like she's backing down at full power . . . must be filling up forward."

"Can you estimate her depth?"

"Negative, sir. We could try to ping her."

"Go ahead. She's not going to do anything to us."

Within seconds, the Russian sub was illuminated by sonar. She was losing depth rapidly. Her forward spaces had been opened by the blast. Her engines backing full meant that the engineering spaces were still intact. But she was unable to control flooding.

"I can hear her trying to blow tanks, sir . . . still have her going down!"

"Still using the engines."

"Christ, she's tearing herself apart, sir."

"Poor bastards must be scared to death."

"Past two thousand and she's a goner," Reed said matter-of-factly.

"She must be past test depth," the captain noted, checking the time since the blast.

"They're dead," Reed remarked. "Nothing's going to back all the way up that hill they just tumbled down." He held the captain's eyes with his own, his expression hard as a rock. "Fine job, Ross. They would have loved doing the same thing to us."

"Should we be looking for a polynya to get off an action report?"

"Don't give anybody a hint about anything." Reed was amused now by his own callousness. "I suppose the last submarine left will send out a final report."

Abe Danilov was sipping a hot cup of tea when *Imperator* passed at a range of approximately six kilometers. The black tea was strong enough to compensate for the coffee he had acquired a taste for many years before—another pleasure the doctors had taken away from him. It interfered with sleep and they indicated that too much of it would damage his reactions. So he had gone back to tea again, insisting on a strong brew.

Seratov's wardroom was no bigger than that on the American boats. Danilov relaxed at the table, thumbing through the pages of a magazine. Stevan Lozak watched him with an admiration bordering on irritability. How could the man sit there so calmly when the most magnificent target they would ever encounter was just then slipping by, mere minutes from their torpedoes?

Lozak had calmly argued the point soon after they'd ducked behind the pressure ridge. How could any submarine hear them preparing to fire, even to the point of identifying the sound of their muzzle doors, with so many tons of ice between them? It would be like sniping, Lozak asserted, if we prepare four torpedoes. With four of them in the water, how could any submarine do anything else at that range other than try to evade? The American submarine would run for her life, and that would give them time to fire again if she needed finishing off.

Very calmly, precisely, Captain Sergoff explained everything they knew about *Imperator* to date, and then filled in the blanks, as Danilov had done the day before with him, to encompass her fantastic capabilities. So much was still unknown. The range of her torpedoes was beyond anything known to any navy. There were laser weapons aboard, and who knew what else that could destroy them. To take on the American submarine by themselves would be the most foolish act possible. There was a plan and Admiral Danilov would attack when the time was right.

As he watched Danilov sip his tea, Lozak remembered his earlier years when his father had taken him hunting with the dogs. He remembered the feel of a leashed dog when they were just about on top of the quarry. Their straining, slobbering, howling need to attack came back to him now—he thought of himself as one of those dogs and sincerely hoped that Danilov did not have the same vision.

Lozak knew that the admiral respected him. Why not just say what was on his mind? "Have you ever been hunting, Admiral?"

"Hmmm?" Danilov looked up from his magazine. "What kind of hunting?"

"In the forest, after deer . . . with the dogs."

Danilov put his magazine down on the table. "When I was a boy, yes. But that was so long ago I have forgotten just about everything. I can't even remember how to load a rifle anymore." He was enjoying Lozak's anguish.

The captain looked at Danilov and took a deep breath before he made his admission. "I think you understand how anxious I was to go after this *Imperator* right away . . . just now as she passed us . . . and Captain Sergoff explained to me that you have other plans, as I'm sure you told him to do. Well, I was just thinking now how similar the situation is. And I was thinking how you must see me as one of those dogs straining to race after the buck. If the hunter lets them go at the wrong time, the animal would get away and there would be no hunt."

Danilov was nodding his head slowly as Lozak blurted out his innermost thoughts, smiling slightly to show the captain that he was interested.

"Hunting is an interesting comparison, but I promise I don't see you in that light, Captain. If you were out here all alone—or even with another submarine—I would consider you a coward if you hadn't gone after the American with everything you had. There would have been no other choice. Here, now, we have a choice, and I think I can explain what I intend to do so that someday you might be in the same position." He leaned forward as if he was involving Lozak in a secret. "That *Imperator* is so powerful that I'm sure we might be heading for the bottom of the sea now if we went after her by ourselves. Instead, I hope maybe she will be plunging down before the end of the day. You've seen the approximate placement of the six submarines that have joined us. There are two out on either flank, two not too far ahead of us, and the other two are well away. *Imperator* is going to sail into a box, which all of us will tighten from the outside. Soon she will realize that she has some targets. I don't particularly care who fires first as long as I know what the American does after she is fired upon, and then what happens when she fires at one of our boats.''

Lozak understood only too well. He was young enough to overlook the possibility of death. ''You don't expect all of the submarines to return after today,'' he stated woodenly.

''No.'' In a way, it made Danilov's job more interesting, for it would be a test of his captains. Though he knew intuitively who was more capable and who might be sent ashore during peaceful times, it was more likely that none of them would return. ''In order to understand our quarry, there may be certain sacrifices necessary. No man will knowingly sacrifice himself or his ship, but it will take place,'' he concluded grimly. ''As far as *Seratov*'s concerned, I don't think the American can fire at all of us at once.''

''I was too anxious.''

''I would have been more sorry if you weren't,'' Danilov answered, remembering his own eagerness as a young skipper. He had been lucky then. Those were always exercises when he was younger. Today, Stevan Lozak could have died from his impetuousness.

Danilov took another tentative sip of tea. It was getting cool, and strong tea turning cold lost its attractive bite so quickly. He glanced up as Sergoff knocked on the entrance to the wardroom.

''Admiral, there has been an explosion astern on our flank. A submarine appears to have been sunk. There were no other blasts—''

''And do you have any clue as to who is the winner?'' Danilov was irritated because Sergoff hadn't begun the conversation by answering that first.

''There is no confirmation. According to your orders, there was to be an identifying code from any of our submarines that scored a success. There has been nothing of the sort over sonar.'' He paused. ''The other submarine is active and appears to be moving in this direction, though sonar has nothing absolute for identification . . . I think it is an American *Los Angeles*-class.''

''Why didn't you just explain that as soon as you came

in here?'' He had been counting on surrounding *Imperator* without any outside threat. ''I can do without the suspense.''

Sergoff had experienced Danilov's outbursts for so many years that he knew there would be more. ''Admiral, there is no confirmation. We are still waiting for something firmer, since it is a long way off. But I think you should join us in the control room . . . both of you,'' he added, nodding to Stevan Lozak.

The sun never set at the North Pole that time of year. There were twenty four hours of daylight, and when the sun was at its apex the temperature might soar above freezing. It marked a changing of the season. At midday, puddles formed where everything had been frozen solid for more than half a year. Such weather also affected the ice formations. Open stretches of water showed more movement. Pressure ridges formed and disappeared more easily. There were few weather fronts in the spring, and day after day there would be nothing but brilliant sun and cloudless skies. The endless intensity of cold was being transformed into constant change. This was the time of year the polar bears moved off the ice to summer on land.

It was superb weather for flying and just as perfect for satellites to sense anything out of the ordinary near the earth's surface. Neither the Russians nor the Americans expected to insert special operating forces without the other's knowledge. It was simply a matter of who would be the first to launch their aircraft and how much time it would take to counter the other's move.

The consortium decided it really had little to fear from that sighting of *Imperator*. The press was wholly involved in the posturing between Washington and Moscow. Only days before, there were few people on the street of any major city in the world who could have answered any questions about the Norwegian border with Russia, more or less know that it existed. Now, any human being with access to television or radio understood not only its location, but the details of what was taking place there and the impact it had on the entire world. The Northern Flank became as familiar as Korea or Vietnam or Lebanon. Once again the superpowers were involved in a situation that might drag the rest of the world into their private disagreement.

Word was received in Washington that the Russians had dispatched their aircraft carrying special arctic troops—even before the satellite reported it! That meant that the Thule-based American forces were off the ground shortly afterward. Then the president of the U.S. contacted the Kremlin offering to turn his planes around if the Soviets would do the same. When neither side could agree, the press soon unearthed the details. *Imperator* was all but forgotten, much to the relief of the consortium, because the actions of submarines beneath the ice were limited to speculation.

Both the Americans and the Russians made an effort to relay details of these events to their submarines. But this time, the only submarine that was able to find a polynya and surface for regular message traffic was *Olympia*. She was approaching a point between the pole and the Lincoln Sea, off northernmost Greenland, at maximum speed. Once her captain understood the implications of the message he had just received, he turned on a more direct course for his rendezvous point just beyond the North Pole.

Score one for Caesar, Hal Snow muttered under his breath. Sonar had obtained two contacts well ahead of *Imperator*, beyond where Snow had anticipated them. While the sonarmen strained to identify them, Caesar's printout appeared satisfactory. Both the Akula- and Sierra-class submarines were newer to the Russian fleet than the Alfas, and what they may have sacrificed in speed and depth, they made up for in quieter running and improved listening devices. And they were no less dangerous. Their mission was to seek out and destroy enemy submarines and their designers had learned much from the Americans.

"There's no way that Alfa could still be ahead of us." Snow was calling from sonar to Carol Petersen. He wanted everyone to understand exactly what it was he feared. "We must have passed him. Are you sure there's no casualty in the towed array?'' He was concerned about the hydrophones they were towing at the end of a long cable.

"It's operating normally." Carol interrupted before anyone in sonar could answer. "Caesar has double-checked it. It's electronically perfect. As a matter of fact, it's doing quite well on our own noisemakers, Captain. Caesar has identified them right down to the company who made them. I also removed all traces of them from his memory and had him start over. Same printout. There's no casualty. We passed the Alfa. He was dead quiet.''

"Well, sooner or later he's got to come out if he's trying to box us in. Once he does we'll hear him." Snow really hadn't intended to repeat what was running through his mind. There were tinges of uncertainty in his voice. "And with all the noisemakers we keep throwing out, I think we're going to confuse them all on which is the correct target.'' That was his purpose—but you couldn't fool a good sonarman for long.

"One thing to keep in mind, Captain: the Akulas and Sierras have a lot better ears than that Alfa. They're going to be able to pick us out better than he will.''

"At least we know where they are.''

He was interrupted by one of the sonarmen. "Wait one . . . something new to starboard." His hands fiddled delicately with the dials in front of him. "Submarine contact.'' The hands finally stopped, suspended in midair, as he leaned back slightly to listen, eyes closed. "Yeah, it's a submarine all right . . . still a long way off . . . no range for a while, Captain . . . but I'll bet it's another Alfa.''

"You got that one, Carol?''

"Got it, Captain. He's right . . . almost beat Caesar on that one. He estimates it at close to ninety miles just aft of the starboard beam. Only an Alfa would sound like that at that range.''

"We have one more advantage," Snow concluded resolutely. "*Imperator* can still travel at slow speed less than five miles from them without being detected by listening gear. They'd have to ping on us right in their backyard to be sure where we are. So we're going to light off everything. We'll put on a show they can't overlook. Then go silent."

Snow moved back into the control room, a renewed look of determination on his face. In retrospect, he wondered why he sometimes began thinking as he had in the past. He was slipping—automatically assuming the limited capabilities of the older submarines. Was he wearing himself out? What he had under his feet now was beyond the imagination of any Soviet captain out there. If he recognized the reasons for his own letdown, then it was time to change the attitude of the others. Their reactions would be a mirror of his own.

He called down to Carol to join him with the other department heads in the wardroom. When they were assembled, they found yet another version of their captain. This time, the nervousness and eruptions of anger of a short time before had been dispelled.

He radiated confidence as he explained that they were going to go active with every piece of equipment that might appeal to the Russians for the next hour. Although he assumed they might be boxed in, it was a large box. They would examine this box at top speed, in an expanding circle until they knew every inch of ice above them. At the same time, their effort to attract attention should draw the Russian submarines closer. They should be able to develop a consistent track and identification on each one as a result. The computer would store a record of every polynya, lead, pressure ridge, and any thin ice that could be used for surfacing.

"Then, we're going to let Caesar take over for us. There's no one on board who can outthink five attack subs tightening the noose at the same time. And I apologize to each of you for trying to be the genius I thought I was." He looked around the table, waiting for a response.

"I don't know why it won't work, Captain," the weapons officer responded. "That's what we're designed for."

"We've been training around Caesar for over a year

now.'' The operations officer looked at Carol with a grin. ''Let's draw them into the trap.''

Snow smiled. They were reacting to a feeling of uncertainty, partially because they had fallen into the same trap he had—remembering the old submarine, when they faced adversity. ''What the hell,'' Snow continued. ''After Caesar finishes his analysis, we'll know exactly where we are and the Russians will be coming into an area without the advantage of knowing the ice. They won't be able to stay close to the surface either . . . be better targets, too, if they have to come down to our level.''

Within minutes, *Imperator* had given up any pretense of silence. She moved at full speed in expanding circles, charting the ice above. There was no letup in dropping noisemakers with built-in time delays. They would switch on at various times over the next twelve hours, if they were needed that long.

When he was satisfied, Snow would order absolutely silent running with *Imperator* changing course and depth under Caesar's control on a totally erratic basis. The only method the Soviet submarines could then use to locate her would be active sonar. And unless they were on top of *Imperator*, they would open themselves instantly to Caesar's attack.

''What the hell . . . ?'' *Houston*'s captain asked as they listened to *Imperator*'s wild gyrations. ''That's crazy. . . .''

''Every once in a while, Snow comes out of a funk and does something unpredictable,'' Andy Reed answered facetiously. ''He can be moody as hell, drive everybody crazy, then comes up with some genius idea. But he has to be driven into it sometimes.'' He shook his head. ''I'd imagine he finally figured out that Danilov was a little bit slyer than he anticipated.''

''But he'll draw them all in on top of him.''

''I suppose that's what he's intending, Ross.'' Reed was doodling with a pencil. ''Look at this.'' He indicated the possible submarines around *Imperator*. ''I'm not saying that's exactly what he sees . . . but the way we tracked him in circles meant he was giving everyone a chance to locate him. So perhaps he sees himself surrounded. If you don't know where everyone is, you'd be crazy to go after them one at a time, because the guy behind would try to get you. So, he's going to try to draw them all in . . . which gives us a chance to go after another.''

Ross nodded his understanding. ''You figure the one that has to be closest to us is going to get sucked into that mess, too.'' It wasn't really a question. He saw exactly what Reed had meant. It made excellent sense. ''But the one near us has got to be on his toes. He knows we're behind him. He can't just turn tail—''

''We'll just have to listen and see what he does. He sees safety in numbers near the pole . . . or he may figure the best thing to do is let us run up his back.''

''The Americans have an expression for it,'' Sergoff remarked. ''I think they call it a bull in a china shop . . . or something to that effect. Whatever the exact words are I think that is a very apt terminology.''

''Crazy. That's what it is—crazy!'' Stevan Lozak had refused to believe his sonar officer and took the headphones for himself. He decided a child could have figured this one out. ''Why, he's a madman . . . giving away his position . . . giving away everything we had hoped to hear.''

''Maybe he's crazy like a fox.'' Abe Danilov chuckled. ''That's another expression I like,'' he said to Sergoff. Then he turned to Lozak, clapping him on the shoulder. ''No one does what he is doing without a purpose. He is inviting all our friends out here to dine with him.''

Captain Lozak saw little to find humor with. Like Danilov, he knew there was a purpose in *Imperator*'s wild display. But for the life of him, he couldn't figure out why a submarine commander, who had engaged in stealth for so many days, would now seemingly go on a rampage.

Sergoff enjoyed analyzing the impatient Lozak. The man was wise in the ways of the sea; he knew submarines as well as, or sometimes perhaps better than, any captain afloat. But his patience was limited. In wartime, such men either lost their boats early or became heroes—often dead heroes. Danilov, on the other hand, was a study in contrasts. His impatience stemmed from boredom, the lack of an objective, in this case a live contact to prosecute. Once he found his quarry, he became the picture of moderation. Satisfaction reigned once he was sure his objective was within sight.

"Range to the American?" Lozak called out.

"Approximately sixty kilometers . . . although he is moving away from us now." They had been tracking *Imperator* using computer projections.

"I recommend we follow, Admiral." Excitement radiated from Lozak's eyes.

"Admiral, I suggest we establish the position of our other submarines first." Sergoff employed his diplomatic talents as he added, "There is no need to expose our own location until we have a better idea of the perspective the American gains of our own forces. After all, a little more time won't hurt us . . . especially if it's to our benefit."

Lozak and Sergoff both looked to Danilov—Lozak for concurrence that the aggressive stance was necessary, Sergoff that further analysis of the situation was required.

"Would you be kind enough to provide us with an analysis of all contacts?" Danilov asked *Seratov*'s sonar officer. "We have the time," he added pointedly to both officers.

Imperator's indiscretions had generated exactly what Andy Reed and Abe Danilov anticipated. *Seratov*'s sonar officer constructed a visual picture of five Soviet submarines cautiously closing, based on their earlier projected positions. The American *Los Angeles*-class identified as *Houston*, the one they'd tracked intermittently since the loss of their first submarine, was moving away from *Seratov* at an angle that would eventually intercept *Imperator*. A Soviet Alfa was between them. The two submarines Danilov had placed on the opposite side were certainly attracted toward *Imperator*. The two he had placed at the far end of the box had generally been masked by *Imperator*'s actions, though sonar occasionally identified their signature. There was little doubt they, too, were drawn toward *Imperator*.

"I don't understand the American's reasons, but I recommend we close this end of the box," Lozak insisted.

"No need," Sergoff stated calmly. "If, for some reason, he decides to escape in our direction, we are here . . . waiting."

"I'm sorry, I can't—" Lozak began.

"We wait," Danilov responded firmly. "You see, Captain Lozak, we appear to be the one submarine *Imperator* has lost." The admiral's face was expressionless now, though his features grew hardened as he sensed time was becoming precious. "The American knows this is my flagship and that is why he came directly at us. Every officer in every military organization in the world understands from his earliest days that the primary target is the leader or the radio . . . that is *Seratov*! If he hasn't already guessed that we have fooled him, he'll know shortly. There is nothing quite so frightening as the unknown . . . and I intend to remain the unknown." His heavy eyebrows rose and he extended his hands, palms up. "Relax, Captain. I have no objections to your desire to sink him. It's just that Captain Sergoff has been with me for years and understands my methods. We will wait and watch."

"Man your battle stations again, Ross. Let's see if we can open one side of that box for Hal Snow." Andy Reed found himself enjoying the taste of blood much more than he would have expected.

"Same process as before, or do we just go in balls to the wall?"

"No need for hide-and-seek. He's been aware we're somewhere behind him since we blew apart his buddy—maybe hoped he'd find some safety among his friends." Reed was sensing the spirit of the hunt. "I'll bet he feels less secure since Snow started running around in circles. All of a sudden, I wonder if this one doesn't think maybe one of his friends on the other side will help him."

"Range to target," the captain requested.

"About thirty miles, Captain . . . just a little aft of the starboard beam now. It looks like he may be picking up some more speed . . . and his aspect's changing some now."

"I want a course to intercept," the captain explained to the OOD. "And a time to firing position."

"I don't know, sir. If he keeps upping his speed, he's going to outrun us—"

Reed interrupted. "*Imperator*'s still in one of her mad circles, isn't she?"

"Seems to be, Admiral. She should be coming toward us again soon."

"Watch our target. See if he doesn't inch away when he sees that huge submarine turning right at him . . . even if she is a long distance off. When you don't understand the other guy, you give him a little space."

Less than ten minutes passed before sonar reported that the Russian seemed to be turning toward an intercept course with *Houston*. "He knows we're coming after him, Ross. You may have to waste a fish to keep him on his toes. As long as we fire first, I think we have the advantage . . . he's got to be nervous."

"We'll be in position for a shot in thirty-five minutes, Captain."

"No more than thirty if he decides to turn more toward us. Make it twenty-five . . . and have that fire control tracking party of yours ready to shoot in less."

Olympia's captain watched with a studied interest as the sonar chief transferred to paper the projected locations of the sounds he had been interpreting in sonar minutes before. They were based on a jumble of sound and satellite transmissions of Reed's last analysis, now three hours old. At that distance, a good deal more than fifty miles to the closest one, he estimated, there was little difference in bearing. They were all dead ahead a few degrees either side of his bow. *Imperator* was identified with a solid black mark. There was no doubting her signature. On the far side of her, he had readings on what could be two submarines. The two between *Olympia* and *Imperator* appeared to be Alfas, though one might be an Akula. They bore many similarities.

"No doubt they got her pinpointed," the captain mused. "I guess we ought to go after these two," he indicated to his XO. "They're closer. What do you think? If we run that reactor for all it's worth, we ought to be on top of them in at least three hours if they remain in that area?"

The XO nodded. "I don't see why not. No one's going to be leaving *Imperator*. Of course, at flank speed, we're not exactly going to sneak up on them."

"We're not supposed to. Andy Reed said that when the Russians started making noise, we all better." What had seemed absurd at the time now made a great deal of sense. "We'll man battle stations when we're about thirty miles out."

When *Imperator* ceased her wild circling, she possessed a contour map of the ice above her that read like a road map. She had also located and identified each Soviet submarine. With her nose now pointed toward the nearby North Pole and her stern toward Murmansk, she held to the rear a Sierra and an Akula. They were closing cautiously, hugging the ice and keeping about forty miles between them. There was nothing directly ahead, though Snow had hoped there would be some sign of Danilov's position. Somehow *Seratov* had disappeared into thin air—yet there was no place to go with ten feet of ice above.

On his starboard bow and running aft toward his beam were a Soviet Alfa and Andy Reed's *Houston* closing both of them. On the port bow were two more Soviet submarines, an Alfa and an Akula, both separated like those astern and closing very cautiously. Caesar had reported that astern of them *Olympia*'s signature was evident, approaching at flank speed.

The holographic imager presented a three-dimensional picture. All the participants were oriented to the center stage where *Imperator* bobbed and weaved quietly on the erratic path devised by Caesar. Those on the outside advanced, hugging the ice, twisting around ice formations as they moved inward with an occasional ping for safety. It was a puppet show in slow motion.

Carol Petersen was now in the control room, at Snow's request, in touch with the computer from a remote console. "Once again, this computer seems to agree with you, Captain. The Alfa to starboard is the least of our worries now. *Houston* appears to be in an attack pattern, according to Caesar."

"How about the two to port?" Snow experienced a weird fascination in comparing his estimate of the situation to the computer's. The latter depended on a complex program in contrast to Snow's years of experience and a sixth sense that rarely had failed him.

"The closest—the Akula—could present a problem when he nears torpedo range. But it looks like they've got to worry about *Olympia* within an hour or so at the speed she's making. They should turn in her direction—if for nothing more than the integrity of Danilov's strategy, according to Caesar—in order to avoid penetration of their artificial perimeter."

"I can't argue with that either," Snow concluded. "So I suppose he says I ought to go after those two astern first?"

"That's a decision, Captain. Caesar never makes decisions. I've been asking him to evaluate the threat. He concurs with you in that regard. As far as how you should imperil your command, that's up to you." She looked over her shoulder teasingly. "I could tell him the captain is unsure of his next step, but Caesar would just query the statement since he's not programmed to make strategic decisions for you. But he can run a hell of an attack with his eyes shut!" She immediately regretted the last statement, sure that once again Snow would be provoked.

He laughed instead. "The only thing that computer can think about for me is where the hell that *Seratov* is hiding." He pondered his situation for a moment before adding, "We'll reverse course toward those two astern." Then, with a coarse, almost unpleasant laugh, he asked,

"Which one should I take out first . . . in Caesar's opinion?"

Carol knitted her brows as the response finally appeared on the screen. "Hard to tell, Captain. They're both new and reasonably fast—not as fast as an Alfa. Both the same size . . . both equally dangerous. If we didn't have that ice above us, the Sierra might be a bigger problem. But there's nothing she can do with her cruise missiles down here."

"We'll take the first that comes in range. Sooner or later, they've got to go active on their sonar to find us. They know we're within certain coordinates. All they're going to be looking for is enough data for a firing solution."

"Captain!" Snow's XO was indicating the holographic imager. "Look at the one near *Houston*. She's turning out to attack."

"Alfa's turning, Captain."

"Range?" Ross glanced toward Andy Reed, who was engaged in conversation with the chief of the watch.

"Thirty-eight thousand . . . closing at about thirty knots."

"Torpedo status?"

"Tubes one, two, three, and four warmed and flooded."

"Firing point procedures tube one."

"The ship is ready, Captain."

"The solution is ready."

"Presets entered . . . she's right at the edge of the envelope, Captain." The target was barely within a realistic range of the torpedo.

"Doesn't matter. Open the muzzle door tube one."

"The door is open, Captain . . . weapon is ready."

"Shoot on generated bearings."

"Unit is running. Wire continuity is good." The enabling run was high speed.

The captain nodded to the OOD as soon as the torpedo was far enough away. "Left full rudder . . . tell engineering I want maximum speed. Chief," he called to the diving officer. "Take her down according to the admiral's instructions."

"Twenty degree down angle," the chief ordered quietly. *Houston*'s deck canted down and to port as she responded to the orders. Hands reached out for support as she dived away from her target.

"Wire's broken," the weapons officer called out.

"Torpedo's running normally."

Reed established the mental picture in his mind. The Alfa turned toward them on an intercept course. *Houston* had fired soon after that, and her torpedo would be leading the Russian submarine. Once the torpedo's course was evident, logic and doctrine called for the Russian to turn away to starboard and dive at high speed. At that range, the Alfa would outrun the torpedo. But if *Houston* imitated the same evolution to port, the Russian would be coming directly toward *Houston* if she completed a three-quarter circle.

"Alfa's aspect is changing rapidly."

The chief studied the depth gauge closely. They were coming up on a thousand feet. "Ease back on your planes . . . slowly now . . . slowly." *Houston* passed twelve hundred feet. "Zero bubble . . ."

The chief was trimming for neutral buoyancy at the new depth. He closed the valves as she settled close to 1,250 feet. Reed had indicated he wasn't as concerned about the exact depth as long as they reached it fast—and they had.

The OOD was also meeting his rudder. They had come around 270 degrees. By the time *Houston* settled on her new course, the engines had been stopped. She was as silent then as she had been noisy a few minutes before.

While they were maneuvering, the captain had muzzle doors opened on tubes three and four. *Houston* lay ready, coasting to a dead stop at thirteen hundred feet.

"Captain, the Alfa's evaded beautifully. That fish is somewhere off in the boonies."

Neither Reed nor the captain had ever expected that first one to succeed. Now, as they listened to the sonar reports, the Russian came out of her turn at flank speed. Her emergency maneuver completed, she was on a course that would have her pass off *Houston*'s bow at about three thousand yards.

"She's cutting speed, Captain."

Just as Reed hoped, the Alfa had come out of the maneuver looking for her attacker. Though she had heard *Houston* move away at high speed after firing, there was no indication of the American's position now. The only solution was to go silent herself and listen.

"She's almost dead in the water."

"Last range?"

"Seven thousand."

Reed was beside the captain now and smiling. "Beautiful job, Ross. He's right where you want him."

"He's about four thousand yards away from where you wanted him."

"Doesn't matter. You got a solution?" Reed glanced over to the fire control coordinator.

"Yes, sir." He reported his current solution on the target.

"By the time we settled down snug right here, we had a bead on him," the captain said with confidence.

"Go ahead, Ross. Don't let me get in your way."

The procedures were the same as for their first shot. Ross's voice echoed through the control room as the reports of weapon ready for tubes three and four came to him: "Shoot on generated bearings!"

There was an unnaturally long pause between sonar's confirmation that both torpedoes were running normally and the report that the Alfa had suddenly come to life and was evading. At seven thousand yards, it would take the torpedoes less than three minutes to reach their target. The dead time between recognizing the threat and commencing evasion cut maneuvering time to even less than that.

The Alfa did turn, accelerating when they realized she had been attacked head on at close range, but there wasn't enough time to outrun a torpedo closing so quickly. Nor could she dive a great deal more. Sonar reported decoys in the water. But that was too little, too late. Reed's concept had been remarkably accurate. Two torpedoes barreled into the submarine within seconds of each other. However she had been hit, sonar reported that there was no chance of survival. After the impact, there was never a sound from her engineering plant, and the pitiful echo of collapsing bulkheads came to them as the Alfa dropped like a rock.

Abe Danilov's eyes were shut tight. He was concentrating, willing himself to run Anna's letters back through his mind—but they remained hazy. One might swim into focus, then wash out just as quickly, as if a receding wave had pulled it away from him. He knew Sergoff and Lozak were alert to every development even though *Seratov* remained an integral part of the immense ice ridge. While he should have been able to rest for a few moments, discipline would not allow it. He'd been straining mentally, almost willing himself into another dimension when . . .

"There's no way she can escape . . . not with two torpedoes . . ."

Then the sound of two distinct blasts rumbled across the frozen depths. Danilov's eyes did not have to open to know that Stevan Lozak was approaching or that Sergoff was close behind, having failed to dissuade *Seratov*'s captain.

"Admiral, the Americans have succeeded in opening up one side of the box. There's no doubt that *Imperator* could escape now—"

"Sergoff," the admiral interrupted, his eyes opening slightly to irritated slits, "where is *Imperator* now?"

"She has turned toward *Tambov* and *Orel*."

Danilov's head nodded imperceptibly as he murmured, more to himself, "They are fast and tough. Let's see what this *Imperator* can do in such a situation." To Lozak he said sincerely, "I understand your enthusiasm, Captain. It's not time yet for us to interfere. Be patient . . . please be patient and you will learn."

Snow was perched like a vulture on the edge of a stool, elbows on his knees, hands dangling as he studied the motion of the little submarines on the imager. It was a projection of what existed according to Caesar's analysis of sonar rather than an exact picture. It could not depict the destruction of the Russian submarine by *Houston*. The image of that Alfa simply winked out soon after the computer indicated that it had been destroyed. And then there were seven, Snow mused. Although that was correct according to the imager, it was also incorrect. There were four Russians—he was closing two and there were two others on his starboard quarter. Then there were *Houston*, *Olympia*, and *Imperator*. But there was one more—*Seratov*! Once she'd gone silent, there was no way Caesar could account for that one. So the man, not the computer, knew there were eight.

The two ahead of him began to split to either side. That was normal. He would have done the same. It seemed like an out-of-body experience to see the larger craft within the image approaching the Sierra and Akula as they spread out on either bow. *Imperator* dominated that three-dimensional image and Snow could almost pinpoint where he now sat, staring into this holographic world. He knew that if he could open the hatch in the sail and look straight up through the frigid water, he would see the exact ice formation above that now appeared in the imager over *Imperator*.

The Akula appeared to be closing more rapidly. Snow surprised some of those near him as he thought out loud, "We'll take the one to port first. I'll use Caesar for the attack, but"—he grinned, biting his lower lip—"I can't imagine how that goddamn computer can do every last little thing." Then, unaware his inner thoughts had been heard through the control room, he said to the XO, "I want the torpedomen to recheck all the tubes and all the loads. Can you imagine what Andy Reed would say if I told him I missed a shot because the torpedo that Caesar said was in perfect order was a dud?"

"All tubes, Captain?" It seemed so unnecessary. They'd been tested less than twelve hours before.

"Right . . . just one more time. And make sure they check those reserve fish. We may have to use everything we've got."

The XO peered at the imager, as fascinated with the

reality of the picture as Snow. He pointed at the closer submarine, his finger seeming to touch the image. "Are you planning to back up with the battle stations party?" he asked diplomatically.

"No doubt about it. They're going to run exactly the same sequence . . . just in case."

Snow remained lost in his own thoughts until sonar reported, "The Akula was pinging, Captain . . . three of them . . . he's reaching for us."

"Has he got a range on us?"

"Absolutely . . . found us on the first. The second and third were just to make sure he wasn't fooling himself . . . and to get a firm aspect on us."

"Since he knows that we've got him, too, he's going to start on the decoys, and keep up with them until he improves his range." Let him get as close as he wants, Snow reminded himself. Don't play games.

He straightened his back and stretched before he was aware of someone behind him. "Just kibitzing." Carol Petersen smiled as he turned nervously. "Before they complete another one of these monsters, we ought to point out that a terminal should be right next to the imager."

"You're within shouting distance over there," Snow remarked irritably.

"Fine for you. You can see and give orders. I can't see and I have to take them."

"Drag a stool over if you want."

"I will, right after Caesar goes through the precheck—"

"I'm having it done now."

"I know. It came up on the screen. If you think it's a good idea to back up the computer, I guess it's just as good an exercise for the torpedomen."

"I can go along with that." Snow's mouth spread in a smile, but the expression in his eyes never changed. "What kind of range do we have now?"

"About forty thousand . . . closing. He's not going to fire for a while and he's probably going to try to get lost in the ice . . . confuse your torpedoes."

"That'll be interesting."

"You've got longer range in your fish . . . lots faster . . . definite advantage."

"As far as I'm concerned," Snow answered dryly, "I've got all the advantage. I'm going to let him fire first unless he's still holding at twenty thousand."

Aboard *Orel*, a fast, sophisticated Akula-class, the captain was ill at ease. No one had ever run an attack on this monster before. He had no intention of taking any chances. He would use two tubes and had two more ready. He'd checked and rechecked his equipment relentlessly . . . until his own crew was as nervous as he.

Orel didn't possess all of the advantages of her quarry, though she was one of the most advanced Soviet attack submarines. Her listening gear was more sophisticated and her speed and maneuverability were superb. Even the creature comforts, of little concern in Soviet ships of the past, had been improved. But her listening devices lacked the range and efficiency of the Americans, and her torpedoes were just a bit slower and less reliable. The Russians had sacrificed silence for speed and a defensive double hull, so it was no surprise when *Orel* was forced to activate her sonar to locate a quarry that had been silently tracking her for quite some time.

Her pinging had been tentative, and *Orel*'s captain knew *Imperator* would alter course and depth immediately, but at least he knew where she *had* been. Presets were entered in the torpedoes. Each process was approved by the captain before it was carried out, then reported back to him when it was completed.

At a predetermined time, he estimated where *Imperator* might now be in relation to his own position, conned his submarine to the estimated angle for firing, and activated his sonar again.

Snow heard the ping through the speaker in sonar before the report could be made verbally. "Range?" he called out.

"Ping steal range—nineteen thousand."

Orel's captain had guessed incorrectly. He was turning slightly to improve his angle of attack.

"Give Caesar control of the attack," Snow ordered.

The Akula in the imager was still altering course. Snow studied the movement of the two submarines, the Russian as her captain sought the proper alignment, *Imperator* as the computer aligned for a technically perfect shot.

There was no sensation as two torpedoes departed *Imperator*, nothing other than the acknowledgment from Carol Petersen that Caesar had fired. Then they appeared minutely in the imager as they were tracked by sonar. Two torpedoes appeared simultaneously moving through space toward *Imperator*, followed by two more thirty seconds later.

The similarity in attacks ceased at that point, for the Russian had overreacted. Realizing that it had also been fired upon, the Soviet submarine had snapped off the second two torpedoes, then broken all four wires as she automatically altered course, speed, and depth, and discharged decoys. *Imperator* did nothing of the sort. Rather than evade, she adjusted her direction toward the Akula, commencing a stern chase that would soon astound the Russian. *Imperator*'s speed increased to compensate for the rapid acceleration of the Russian.

"Well, if Caesar picks now for a casualty, we are in deep, deep shit I would say." Snow's attempt at humor failed. His voice was as serious as before.

Imperator's noisemakers traveled at a higher speed than any known previously. One of the Soviet torpedoes was drawn away by a perfect imitation of *Imperator*'s signature, but the other three bore down on their target. The tiny underwater missiles (ATMs) that Caesar discharged next were invisible on the imager but there was no doubt among the sonarmen that they were underway. Their tiny, high-speed propellers emitted an ear-piercing screech as they raced out at a tremendous speed. Homing rapidly, they impacted two of the Soviet torpedoes, detonating the warheads harmlessly at four thousand yards.

The final Russian torpedo was now bearing down on

Imperator. Although sonar reported it now in the final homing mode, Caesar relentlessly drove *Imperator* closer to the fleeing *Orel*.

One of Snow's torpedoes was drawn away by a noise-maker, exploding well away from the Akula. The second continued to close, but the race seemed to benefit the Russian. On the imager, it appeared as if *Imperator* were actually moving as fast as its own torpedo.

As the last Soviet torpedo bore down on the huge sub-marine, a tiny light flared in *Imperator*'s bow. It winked once . . . then again . . . then one more time. While the power of a laser was severely attenuated underwater, the beam controlled by the computer was aimed directly into the intricate guidance mechanism in the warhead. It was a last-ditch defense, one that had been designed to destroy a torpedo far enough from the submarine to avoid any dam-age. The warhead, thinking it had impacted a target, deto-nated harmlessly ahead of them. *Imperator* raced through the roiling water of the blast.

Orel's captain reacted with astonishment when sonar insisted the American sub was bearing down on them. The blasts from their torpedoes had been heard in the control room—yet there was no change in sonar's reports. The unmistak-able *whoosh* of *Imperator*'s propulsor was clear. There had been no change in pitch. She had been unaffected by the three torpedoes that appeared to have been homing directly on her. Perhaps two of them, the captain admitted, could have been destroyed by some kind of new weapon. A shrill squeal had come through clearly. But the fourth—there had been no indication whatsoever that it had been fooled by a decoy, nor that it had done anything other than impact the target. Yet *Imperator* was closing the distance between them.

As his eyes met those of his other officers, he recog-nized the same fear that was surging through his own body. This wasn't submarine warfare—it was a dogfight! It was as if they were two fighter planes screaming high above the earth, jockeying for that one shot to destroy the other. Yet *Orel* was not jockeying for anything. She was racing away as fast as her engines would take her—and this monster was closing the gap.

The captain was no longer concerned with *Imperator*'s second torpedo. Somewhere in the recesses of his mind he knew that his weapons officer had discharged additional decoys, and he was positive sonar reported that the torpedo had detonated behind them. Had he recognized the explosion? Or had it been his imagination?

Orel continued on without interruption and he acknowledged to himself that she was still unhurt . . . but a voice also nagged at him that his time on this earth was fast coming to a close. He was momentarily blinded by a deep sense of impending doom before he was aware of the political officer shaking him roughly. The captain stared about his control room. Every eye was on him, fear replacing the trust that had been there since the day he took command.

The captain heard himself shouting orders instinctively—the same he would give if he was evading a torpedo. Yet there were none in the water. He was running from a great monster intent on swallowing *Orel*. They dived steeply. Any change of the planes at that speed brought an instant reaction from the submarine. His rudder was over sharply. The Akula banked at a steep angle.

"The planes . . . the planes . . ." the voice came from the political officer. "You're going too fast for a full dive." Then he lost his footing, dragging the captain down with him.

"Up angle . . . up . . ." His words were drowned out by the shouts of the diving officer, frantically yanking at the controls. As the planes eased back, he wheeled about to open the valves that would blow his ballast. *Orel* continued to career downward, speed and gravity pulling against the up angle of the planes.

"Rudder amidships." The captain's mind was strangely rational once he accepted the fate they were nearing. The ship was his responsibility . . . he had to save the ship. His eyes searched out the depth gauge—almost seven hundred meters! They were beyond test depth and still going down.

"Torpedoes!" A voice from sonar repeated over and over, but the words seemed to blend into one with a new awareness—they had yet to control their own ship while this *Imperator* chasing them had fired more torpedoes!

With the roar of high-pressure air entering the ballast tanks and the shrill voice of the diving officer repeating depths in a frenzied cadence, they plummeted toward the bottom.

What was that other noise? the captain wondered. Recognition came slowly—it was *Orel*'s engines backing. Someone had ordered the engines reversed to stop their dive. Had he done that? He didn't remember.

The last fact that registered in his mind was the depth gauge—the dial was well into the red at eight hundred meters. Screams of terror were the last sounds that came to him as the torpedo struck *Orel* just outside the control room. The blast, magnified by the tremendous pressure, crushed *Orel* like an egg. Exploding inward, she rolled end over end toward the bottom of the Arctic Ocean.

Snow held *Imperator* at twenty-one hundred feet as he listened to the death throes of the Akula. Her shell had fractured with a sickening tearing and crunching. The silence that had followed, punctuated only by the bubbles rising to the surface, was as shocking as the rending of *Orel*'s hull.

He looked over to the imager out of curiosity, noting that the Akula had already disappeared. Whether or not she had yet reached the bottom, Caesar's efficient brain had removed her as an entity.

Caesar, the computer . . . Caesar, the brain . . . Caesar, the instrument programmed by man to assure *Imperator*'s survival, had done a thorough job. Like a mad dog, he had chased down his enemy, hounding it until nothing remained. He was a superb killer.

"The Sierra," Snow inquired without looking at the imager. "Where's the Sierra now?"

"Hiding, I think," whispered Carol Petersen, still in awe of Caesar's efficiency.

"Or waiting for us to come looking for him," countered the XO. "She's back near the ice . . . snug in among some pressure ridges." He indicated a series of ice formations plotted earlier. "Must be a lot of motion on the surface. The ice is moving together, creating a lot of little pockets. It's a hell of a maze where that Sierra is now."

During the period *Imperator* had been prosecuting the Akula, sonar had remained in constant contact with the other submarine, following its progress until it rose to the protective camouflage of the ice. Never disappearing, it meandered through the ice, seeking a secure location to lie in wait for the American submarine.

"I'll take back control," Snow said, tapping his code out on the console. "Let's see if I can do as well as a computer on this next one." A deep insecurity weighed heavily on Snow as he retained control of the submarine for the next phase. The computer could function without error, yet it could not deny control to a human being. Its power was solely in the hands of the operators. Snow denied the little voice in the recesses of his mind that occasionally rose to remind him that he was not as capable as his machine. He was unable to suffer silently with inner voices hinting any weaknesses on his part.

As he conned *Imperator* in the direction of the Sierra, he realized there was little reason for a silent approach. The sounds emitted by *Imperator* and the Akula would have awakened Neptune himself from a drunken stupor. There would be nothing possessing a reasonable listening device within a couple hundred miles that had not heard the short, swift battle that had just taken place.

Andy Reed understood that *Imperator* was now bent on destroying the Sierra and he had no doubt she would. That would open two sides to the box that Danilov had established. Therefore his attention was drawn to the two submarines on the far side, still well off *Imperator*'s starboard quarter as she headed for the Sierra.

"What kind of chance do we have of keeping quiet if we move in on those two?" Reed inquired of *Houston*'s sonar officer.

"They all know we're out here after our last kill. I really think the only way you're going to sneak up on anyone, Admiral, is to stay silent—and there's no way you can do that and still get within range of them."

"What's their range now?"

"Maybe seventy miles." The sonar officer sketched a few short lines on a pad of paper and added, "Maybe fifty to intercept. Sometime along the way, you're going to have to use some speed, and then maybe you can stay quiet after you're nearby—"

Before he could finish, Reed had turned to the captain. "Let's turn it on now, Ross, and catch up with the show. All Snow needs is one casualty and he's just like the rest of us . . . with a few major exceptions."

A shaken Captain Lozak was obediently taking in every word of Danilov's explanation of what probably happened to *Orel* when Sergoff interrupted. "Pardon me, Admiral, but we've picked up an American submarine moving fairly rapidly toward the center of the box. It originated from the area of the earlier sinking. Sonar has just about definitely classified it as Admiral Reed's."

Danilov wagged a finger in Lozak's face. "You see . . . you see." His features seemed almost cherubic as a smile overspread his face, his eyes squinting out under his heavy brows. "A little silence goes a long way in our business."

Lozak nodded his assent, his eyes fixed on the chief of staff. He sensed nothing. Captain Sergoff had seen too many young submarine captains eager to outguess Danilov. He paid little heed to their youthful transgressions, or their negative feelings toward him. Danilov enjoyed his role as a mentor tremendously and it was not Sergoff's place to interfere.

"Well, what do you think, Captain?" Danilov inquired of Lozak. "Should we challenge this American now . . . or should we tarry a little longer?" The admiral was enjoying himself immensely at Lozak's expense. The loss

of the other submarines was already a thing of the past as
he contemplated the opportunity to destroy his counterpart.

"I think at this point, Admiral, I should defer to your
judgment. You have been correct at each stage."

"How about you, Sergoff. You're a wily one. What
would you do?"

"The American admiral can't have any firm idea of our
position. I wouldn't allow him the pleasure of discovering
us now." Sergoff paused, then added, "This *Imperator* is
a formidable weapon, though, and I would hate to see us
face her without more assistance. If *Houston* continues
her present course, her objective would seem to be the
other two submarines. I would let *Houston* pass." Before
Lozak could say a word, he concluded, "But then I would
attempt to sneak up behind her."

"That is exactly what I would do," Danilov agreed. "That
is exactly what we will do, Captain," he indicated to
Lozak. "We will remain deep enough only to avoid any
ice damage. I have no intention of using any active sonar
to give us away."

Olympia had made no secret of her presence, approaching
at high speed. The two submarines intent on creeping up
on *Imperator*'s stern were left with no alternative. The
Alfa, faster and deeper diving, came about. Leaving a
pattern of noisemakers to distract the American, she went
silent near the surface.

Olympia's captain appreciated the Soviet strategy. He
was being forced to make the first move while the Sierra
turned toward *Houston*. As he altered course to close his
range with the Alfa, he was interrupted by a call from
sonar.

"Captain!" The sonar officer's voice was pitched a
shade higher than normal. "I'm getting a malfunction . . .
some kind of a variation in power. The computer's having
trouble sorting out the incoming signal."

"Make it simple, Peter . . . simple." Lieutenant Merry
was intrigued by details. He would have been a good
lawyer.

"It's just like a phone conversation, Captain, when you can only hear half of what the other guy's saying. I've got his noisemakers—they're mobile. But I can't distinguish a pattern. And it sounds like the Alfa's changing depth . . . probably going up."

"Are you able to hold the Alfa?"

"Negative . . . that is, not all the time. Every time we start to get a good picture, the signal cuts out. Then we have to start all over again. And there's a lot of movement in the ice up there. If he gets below three knots, he'll be pretty well masked."

"Last range?" The captain's voice was soothing.

"Between nine and ten miles . . ." the fire control coordinator responded.

"Speed?"

"He's cut down to about six knots . . . staying behind that screen of noisemakers."

"Are you able to hold him enough?" he asked the sonar officer.

"Hell yes, Captain. When my gear is operating right, no problem." Lieutenant Merry qualified everything.

"Just checking, Peter. I'm not worried yet. Just keep your technicians humping. Could he be close to firing soon?"

"Maybe, Captain. But he's right on the edge. He wouldn't have a great solution . . . but it would be better than anything fire control can give you now."

"And there's no way he can tell that we've got a sonar casualty?"

"No way . . ." There was a long silence, and the captain was about to speak when he heard, "Christ, that was a long one. Chief, could it be in the sonar dome, or—" He was interrupted by a voice in the background. Then he was back on the speaker again. "We lost it for almost thirty seconds on that one. The chief is sure the problem's somewhere in this equipment, Captain."

"Recommendations, Peter?"

He was faced with another long pause before Lieutenant Merry answered. "I . . . I don't have any, Captain. All I

could think would be to . . .'' Again there was silence
before he concluded hesitantly, ''. . . to get the hell out of
here. But we could be in his range now.''

The captain had already waved over his XO. ''All stop.
Let's get some decoys out—double fast! And . . . I guess
we're going to have to generate some noise. I want all
tubes ready for firing, on manual input if we have to.''
Better to have his torpedoes warm and muzzle doors open.

The images creeping into the captain's ordered mind
grew more unattractive by the minute. He could picture a
Soviet Alfa loitering near the surface, using the movement
of the ice for cover as he closed to torpedo range. And if
the man possessed a sixth sense, he might begin to wonder
why the American had held off firing torpedoes for this
long . . . perhaps a casualty to take advantage of. The
minutes seemed hours as they closed their target with often
erratic contact by sonar.

''Torpedoes in the water!'' The cry from sonar was
urgent. ''Two of them . . . our gear was down again. We
never heard anything until it came back on.''

''Snap shot . . . tubes one and two. Whatever input
you've got, shoot on generated bearings.'' The captain
signaled to his XO with his hands to dive and go to flank
speed as he shouted into the speaker, ''Sonar go active. I
need a range.''

''About eight thousand yards . . .''

Damn! He'd crept at least five thousand yards since the
last firm range. He'd let the Russian sneak right in. As the
thud of the last torpedo leaving the ship came to him, the
deck was rolling to starboard and falling away. *Olympia*'s
props slashed the water. Alternatives raced before the
captain's eyes. He knew more decoys had been fired and
that *Olympia* was reversing course and diving as fast as
she could. But, it would most likely be maneuvering that
would save them.

Two torpedoes fired at that range and they'd never heard
a thing . . . not the telltale sound as the muzzle doors were
opened after flooding tubes . . . not a goddamn thing!
Just the report from sonar that they were victims of their

own inoperative gear. And the Russians had the advantage—good target solutions in their warheads!

Olympia had performed so perfectly the past few days, killing quickly and efficiently. And here she was running . . . running when she should have been attacking. The captain had no idea how much data they'd been able to insert before they shot, but he was afraid it wasn't enough. Torpedoes were like little spaceships, miraculous instruments but almost directionless without the simplest of instructions. Each bit of information made them that much more intelligent. With proper input, they could be as accurate and deadly as a rifle. His single advantage was that an Alfa moving at high speed simulated the sound of an express train—or at least that's what his sonarmen indicated.

"Are we able to get a range on the nearest torpedo?" The captain's voice was loud and sharp, but there was no fear evident.

"They're both still in search."

"What is Alfa doing?"

"Same thing we are, Captain." For a moment, Lieutenant Merry's voice was tinged with humor. "Running like a scared rabbit. He's making such a racket that the ice isn't giving him the least bit of help now. Hell, if anything, it's reflecting all that sound." But the Soviet torpedoes were still closing.

Olympia's decks canted sharply. The diving officer kept her planes on the edge of a full dive. The rudder was hard left, after first turning to starboard. Her speed was still building.

The captain, gripping the shiny chrome railing, noted a sensation completely foreign to anything he'd ever experienced in the past. Everything he'd ever anticipated in all his years aboard submarines—assuming he was ever fired upon—no longer seemed to be important. Two high-speed Soviet torpedoes were bearing down on him, and the fears and the systematic orders he'd once memorized no longer mattered. Each situation had to be unique. Intuition was everything in successful evasion—that and a little luck, like having perfectly operational equipment.

Those torpedoes bearing down on *Olympia* had been programmed to chase after a diving, evading submarine—and they were doing just that.

"Their torpedoes are past that first batch of decoys."

"We did fire more?" The captain glanced over his shoulder at the XO for confirmation.

". . . ought to be in the middle of them now . . ." The XO's response was lost as sonar reported one of the Soviet torpedoes apparently veering away . . . attracted by one of the decoys.

But one more was still closing, its electronic brain intent on an American 688-class submarine making enough noise in its escape attempt to attract them.

Olympia's captain shifted his rudder again as the diving officer leveled off near test depth. They were approaching maximum speed now. The captain was gambling—hoping to confuse the torpedo with radical course changes. The addition of the noisemakers might just turn the trick.

"Range . . . two eight hundred . . . range gating . . . damn . . ."

The sudden silence was ominous. Then the words droned over the speaker, ". . . sonar's cut out again . . . we're sure it was homing on us. . . ." Then, ". . . got it back again . . . it's on to us, Captain . . . definitely homing . . ."

"Decoys—spit 'em out." This course and depth were no good. They couldn't go deeper. And with the torpedo still above, they couldn't head up . . . the only option was to make it a stern chase. The captain altered course, then ordered the diving officer to add five hundred more feet. That would take them below test depth—but it also would make it that much more difficult for the torpedo. *Olympia*'s deck tilted sharply once again.

Reversing course cost more precious seconds. Even at top speed, the new Soviet torpedo was more than twenty knots faster than a 688-class. *Olympia* became the rabbit for a torpedo that would not be deterred by their decoys.

The Soviet torpedo detonated in *Olympia*'s reactor compartment as she plunged beyond test depth in her frantic effort to escape certain death. Those who weren't killed by the blast in the after third of the submarine died within seconds as bulkheads were crushed by the intense pressure of the water. Those in the forward section behind the watertight doors survived . . . until *Olympia*'s hull was shattered like an egg as she plummeted past crush depth.

None of them lived to hear the blast as one of their own torpedoes was attracted by the express-train sounds of the Russian Alfa, detonating after a glancing blow. The outer hull fractured behind the control room. Power was lost when the shock wave rolled over the ship driving the rods into the pile. The scram was momentary. The engineers reacted instinctively, quickly bringing the reactor back on-line. The Alfa would have been unable to sustain a second hit. Many of their instruments had been shattered. Only experience kept her operating within reasonable limits.

She turned to rejoin her sister ship, seeking protection while she licked her wounds.

Abe Danilov's eyes remained tightly shut, as if he were in a trance . . . scarcely breathing. But Sergoff knew better— and Stevan Lozak had learned to appreciate these eccentricities as never before.

What Danilov perceived behind those closed eyes was much like what was depicted on the holographic imager in *Imperator*, but it was within his mind. He was withdrawn from the picture, gazing down on it well away from *Seratov*. He had mentally erased *Orel* when she was mercilessly destroyed by *Imperator*, and he had dismissed *Olympia* in the same manner. The Alfa that had been damaged, *Poltava*, reversed course and limped after her sister ship, *Ryazan*. On the far end, *Tambov* huddled among the ice floes, hoping to remain hidden until *Imperator* blundered too close.

Through all of the day's action, he was as tempted as Lozak to venture forth to assist his sheep. Yet Admiral Danilov remained aloof to their needs. He was in sole command and his orders were to destroy *Imperator*. He had not been expected to return with every man and submarine under his command . . . only to destroy what appeared to be the greatest threat to his country. He was doing it the best way he knew how.

Carol Petersen, curiosity piqued, remained in the control room, but well away from Hal Snow. Though Caesar continued to provide data to all weapons systems, Snow retained control. There wasn't a trace of doubt in anyone's mind that he would now show that he could complete the next attack as efficiently as the computer.

Snow was again perched on his stool before the imager. The representation of *Tambov* was vague, almost to the point of fading. Sonar no longer held contact, and only Caesar's memory bank provided an image of the Soviet's last known position. A series of pressure ridges had formed in that location, deep clefts of ice forced downward by the clash of immense floes above—tons of ice temporarily forced fifty, seventy-five, sometimes more than a hundred feet below the surface by unimaginable pressure.

It was a dangerous retreat at best, but worth a chance after the harsh destruction of *Orel*. Her captain was sure that there was no passive sonar able to detect him amidst the crush of these untold tons of ice. He had no doubt of *Imperator*'s intentions. She had turned at high speed from her destruction of *Orel* and headed immediately in his direction. Revised target data were continually inserted into his torpedoes. Once the range was right, he would increase his depth, maneuvering for a proper angle on his target to empty his tubes. He was sure that lurking between the pressure ridges vastly increased his odds.

Glancing out of the corner of his eye, Snow noticed Carol hovering in the background. He motioned her forward with a wave of his arm. "Grab a stool. More than enough room to watch the fun from here."

She'd been hoping he would notice her, hoping his mood would remain positive. She made a concerted effort to be as casual as she could. "You and *Imperator* are finally getting a chance to—"

"Oh, no bother about the ship. We both knew she could do it." He was totally engrossed in what they were doing, yet seemed quite pleased she was there. "See . . . the Sierra, right there." He pointed toward the pressure ridges.

"If that's where Caesar left him, I'll go along with you."

Snow frowned momentarily. "He's there," he repeated conclusively.

"What do you think he's planning?" The question sounded stupid when it came out.

"He's hoping we don't know where the hell he is . . . just snuggled in there waiting for us to come looking . . . waiting until we're in range," he mused, almost to himself. Then he added with more certainty, "It's a damn good idea. I'd do the same. All the racket up there from the ice would give the average sonar fits. But, then, you know your equipment." He grinned, patting her shoulder without looking away from the imager. "It was designed to do just what it's doing now. Even though we don't hold him on sonar, the memory has him in the last known position . . . and it's one hell of a good one."

Carol nodded. She'd programmed Caesar, first attending all the courses on tactics that the navy offered. Then she spent time with the war games people so she could understand how battles evolved in the past and how today's warriors studied them in relation to modern weapons.

Snow spoke before she asked the inevitable. "Of course, I'm not going to let him come out and take a shot at us. We're going to remove his hiding place instead." This time he held her eyes with a satisfied grin. "We get to try those new fish, the ones with the sodium heads." When sodium came in contact with water, it almost exploded with a violent reaction of hydrogen bubbles, burning with an intense yellow heat. It had been designed specifically for under-ice warfare.

"Remove the walls he's built . . ."

"Mirrors," Snow responded quietly. "It's just like a mirror up there. We're just going to shatter his mirrors so he's standing there naked."

When *Imperator* came within range, which remained beyond the effective range of the Soviet submarine's torpedoes, both Washington and Moscow soon understood that a violent confrontation was taking place on the Russian side of the North Pole. Infrared satellites detected tremendous amounts of heat. Boiling water roared skyward through fissures in the ice pack from the explosive contact of sodium and water. Nine separate blasts were recorded, the last four tracing the outline of *Tambov* as she frantically attempted to escape from the plunging cakes of ice ricocheting off her hull.

The "eye in the sky" satellites—the ones that could identify a postage stamp in the snow—relayed photographs that could have been taken at Yellowstone. Tall geysers of steaming water continued to burst into the arctic air, propelled through ice fissures by the violent reaction of the sodium as the warheads burst open against the pressure ridges. Icebergs the size of churches leaped skyward as they were released by the pressure of overriding ice floes, their pinnacles magnificent spires reaching for the heavens.

The satellites could record only what existed within their capabilities. They could not see what happened to the Sierra-class submarine that had been nestled between these pressure ridges. *Tambov* reared upward from the initial blasts, three at about the same time. Her captain had made no effort to evade the approaching torpedoes because he assumed there was no way a homing torpedo could seek them out—*Tambov* was secure and silent behind the protective ice.

Not until the final seconds did her captain become concerned with their true purpose. His suspicions, though well founded, were too late. Not a soul aboard *Tambov* understood what was happening to them. They hadn't been hit by a torpedo, nor was there any explosion near enough to cause them damage. Yet they found their craft leaping uncontrollably upward from a force beneath them.

A combination of pressure and immense broken chunks of ice keels attacked from beneath. Other bursts to either side rocked their craft. Beyond the impact of the blasts, the sound rolled through *Tambov* as if they were locked

inside a bass drum. Ice breaking, ice grinding against other
suddenly free chunks, ice leaping beyond the surface only
to crash down again, the millions of bubbles created by the
constant reaction of sodium and water—all this perpetual
sound created a waking nightmare within *Tambov*. So
horrifying was this experience that each man seemed driven
within himself by an unnatural fear—the terror of the
unseen! Not a one seemed capable of moving. They could
neither hear nor follow orders. The unknown encased them
in a living hell.

Above and around them, the Arctic became a boiling
cauldron. The sudden geysers of water created by new
fissures were followed by immense waves that leaped into
the air as great chunks of ice tumbled back to the sea,
driven deep by their own weight. Icy water ran across the
broad white expanse of the ice pack, puddling in depres-
sions that increased to pond size until the ice broke away
from the weight of the water.

One huge mound of ice pitched across *Tambov*'s bow,
scraping heavily down one side, twisting the bow plane
closure into a sealed compartment. Another fell against the
sail structure, crushing the periscope opening and ripping
the upper bridge access hatch away. The outer hull had
been rent with dents and jagged holes from bow to stern.

As the initial chaos subsided, her captain gained enough
control of himself to give the orders to get underway. To
remain where they were was suicide.

It was preferable to face *Imperator* alone than to face
elements that were beyond their understanding. Valves
were opened and trim tanks began to fill as *Tambov* gradually settled away from the surface. It was at this stage
that the captain found his diving planes were inoperative.
All navigational sonars had been destroyed by the ice. A
single hydrophone continued to function.

The only option left to *Tambov*'s captain was ninety-
nine percent suicidal, but he held little doubt that he would
soon be dead anyway. As his submarine increased her
depth, he ordered two-thirds speed ahead and turned in
Imperator's direction. His tubes were loaded. If any of his

electronic gear had been able to absorb the pounding of moments before, there might still be data in his torpedoes. Perhaps his active sonar might work. He wanted just one return ping, just one confirmation of *Imperator*'s position before he fired everything he could.

Imperator had drifted to a crawl at a range of eighteen thousand yards, a safe distance from the chaos ahead and a perfect position for firing on their target if it survived the sodium torpedoes. At two-thirds speed, the damaged hull of the Soviet submarine began to radiate a steady signature above the chaos around her that pinpointed them as a target for *Imperator*'s guidance systems.

To Carol Petersen, *Tambov*'s final charge at them was akin to a railroad train rushing headlong toward a solid rock headwall. Snow was as cool and detached as the captains in the novels she read in her youth. He saw no reason to use more than two fish—after all, their target was beckoning for them.

"Just like a gunfight," Snow commented. "Only I have all the guns . . . I shot theirs right out of their hands. All they can do is throw a few stones at me."

The last words were murmured as sonar reported a total of four torpedoes fired from the doomed Sierra. They meant nothing to Snow. His weapons officer was already energizing the same defensive mechanisms that had been so successful before. Soon, the miniature homing devices that had worked so well against *Orel*, the deadly ATMs, were exploding against the Russian torpedoes. The range was so close and the solution simple enough that the lasers were never activated.

As the last of *Tambov*'s torpedoes exploded prematurely, the Soviet submarine was hit by both of *Imperator*'s. With her pressure hull already damaged, there was little protection for the inner hull or the delicate mechanisms that kept her afloat. She spun out of control, spiraling toward the bottom at two-thirds speed, as the control room opened to the sea. Her captain had been right that his headlong charge toward *Imperator* would be suicidal. He had been wrong about his one percent chance. There had never been any chance at all.

The destruction of *Tambov* answered the initial question in both Washington and Moscow: the location of *Imperator* and, likely, those submarines remaining involved in the under-ice confrontation. Moscow had no immediate answers to the eruptions that damaged the ice pack. Washington understood exactly what had happened and emphasized that *Imperator* was continuing her mission.

The consortium's position was elevated in the eyes of the White House power structure and, on their advice, Washington issued an ultimatum to the Kremlin: Remove all equipment and personnel one hundred miles from the Norwegian border over the next seventy two hours, and relinquish all demands that U.S. or NATO vessels remain south of the Norwegian Sea. In exchange, the destruction of *Fahrion* would be forgotten, an unfortunate international incident. Discussions would be opened that summer to discuss positioning of ballistic-missile submarines in restricted waters.

The demands were too stringent for the Kremlin to accept. It meant admitting defeat in a war that had never taken place—not in the eyes of the public! There was no purpose in accepting such terms—"capitulating" was the word some used, while others in the Kremlin called it "negotiating"—not until Abe Danilov reported back to them. Dawn was breaking in Moscow when the Kremlin refused further discussion.

10

Reed licked his lips. "We'll take the cripple first, Ross." Better to get rid of that one before he went after Danilov.

"Roger, Admiral." Ross's tone of voice reflected a lack of enthusiasm.

"You don't want to take that one, do you?" Reed stated flatly. There was a fine line between following orders smartly or quietly accepting something you didn't want to do. Ross was near that line.

"It's a feeling," *Houston*'s captain stated flatly.

"What do you feel?"

Ross's eyebrows rose. He shrugged. "Someone's behind us."

"Danilov?"

Again Ross shrugged. There was nothing that could justify his feeling. "I guess so. I don't know how he got there."

"You've got more than a feeling."

"Nope. Just the trace of our path over the last eight or ten hours." He led Reed over to the table where their course had been recorded. "Remember, it wasn't so long ago yesterday that Danilov was in front of us. Now look at this swing of ours, way out to port, sunk one, hung out there for a while, moved back in toward the middle of that box, sunk a second on the way. Now we're going after a cripple and there's still no sound out there that would indicate someone's going to help it.'' He was leaning on his elbows, tracing their path with his index finger as he spoke. Now he looked up and held Reed's eyes. ''There's a lot of space between where we began that big swing and where we are now . . . and it just seems to me that Danilov ought to be somewhere in there.'' He tapped it with his finger. ''Look at all that water, Admiral. At one time, there was a bunch of submarines. Now four are gone . . . just two left and one a cripple . . . and we haven't heard from Danilov since he disappeared back there—''

''And Abe Danilov is one foxy character,'' Reed interrupted. ''Right?''

''Right.'' Ross nodded. He looked up again. ''Worth thinking about?''

Reed held the other's eyes for a second, then called over his shoulder, ''Range to the cripple?''

''Twenty-two thousand. He's making about ten knots, Admiral.''

''In a little more than an hour, he'll be just about on top of us if we wait right here,'' Reed noted. ''I can't imagine he's got much left for listening gear. I'll go halfway with you, Ross. How about if we just shut up for a while? We'll sit here, and we won't make any noise to speak of. Try to rise slowly so we're in line with that cripple. We'll listen sharp for anything else. At ten thousand yards, we'll put two torpedoes into her, then we'll go looking for Danilov.'' He cocked his head to one side, searching for agreement in Ross's eyes. ''We'll still have a few tubes ready if she should sneak up on us,'' he added.

Ross smiled halfheartedly. ''I guess if I can convince you to meet me halfway—'' He never finished the sentence, his expression changing rapidly as he realized that he'd won a moral victory. ''Sounds better to me than before.'' As he turned toward his OOD, Ross still had a

feeling that something was missing. *Houston* was his ship.
But the Admiral had given as much as he was going to.

Abe Danilov sipped at a cup of steaming black coffee. The
hell with the Kremlin doctors! He loved his coffee at times
like this, and if there was ever a time to indulge in one of
the few luxuries he felt he could still enjoy, this was it.

He had paid his silent respects to Anna once the chro-
nometer indicated a new day had arrived. Perhaps it was
for the last time . . . since he realized that the terrible
efficiency of that killing machine, *Imperator*, was drawing him further away from ever being by Anna's side
again.

Houston had accounted for two of his submarines; he
laid the blame at the feet of both captains. But *Imperator*
had destroyed two more, and he couldn't censure either of
his commanding officers for those losses. *Olympia* had
been sunk by *Poltava*, though he had little hope that she
would survive the next few hours. He also had doubt about
the chances for *Ryazan* beyond this day—she had turned to
challenge *Imperator*. Now there was *Houston* sitting out in
front of him. She was an attractive target.

Danilov eyed Stevan Lozak carefully. While the efficient Sergoff continued to perform his duties quietly as they
waited silently in the lee of the pressure ridge, Lozak had
hopped about the control room like a brightly feathered
bird with his tail on fire. *Seratov*'s captain was a fine man
operationally, but Danilov was now sure that the man
lacked the patience for senior command. Get in a fight, he
thought to himself, and there's no finer man to have at
your side than Lozak. But get in a corner, and it's the
Sergoffs of this world who save your neck.

Danilov eased over to Lozak as he would to an old
friend. "Captain, we are ready to get underway. Before
we do, I would like to emphasize a few points again. If we
projected their path of advance correctly, a little more than
thirty kilometers from us is a *Los Angeles*-class submarine
that has already killed two others just like us. They are
very good fighters . . . and they have ears like bats!" He

hung on the last word, stretching it out. "There is no reason for them to hear the slightest thing at this range."

"Of course not, Admiral—"

"I'm not finished, Captain." Danilov's attitude was so different from anything Lozak had experienced in their many cruises together. The admiral gripped his elbow tightly. "Of even greater concern to me is that *Imperator* may be as close as sixty or seventy kilometers. She has the ears of a thousand bats . . . and she destroys submarines . . . in ways no man has ever experienced before."

Lozak nodded slowly. While he may have command of his *Seratov*, Danilov still had total control.

"Both Admiral Reed and this Snow . . . the one who commands *Imperator* . . . are ruthless men. They have no concern—none whatsoever—about how many more hours you live."

"Nor do I feel any different about them, Admiral," Lozak interrupted.

"Now, to extend the number of hours we plan to continue living, we don't make a sound. We let Reed finish off *Poltava*." He paused to allow Lozak to digest that bit of information. "While Reed is concentrating on taking one more of our submarines out of the picture, we are going to depart our little nook ever so silently. We are going to remain as near to the ice as possible, but there will be no use of the navigational sonar. We'll assume there will be no pressure ridges of more than fifty meters' depth. If there are . . ." He shrugged with a fateful grin. "Proceed at three knots. By the time any other submarine picks us up at that speed, we will have fired on them. Send a messenger around to each space on this ship—don't miss a soul—and make sure there is no unnecessary movement, no talking, no leaving station for any reason—if someone has to piss, use a bucket."

"Right away, Admiral." He was no longer a party to the decisions. They had been made without his advice. If there was a single positive note to his exclusion, he assumed that Sergoff had not been included either.

But on that point he was dead wrong. Sergoff had even

insisted, politely but firmly, how Danilov should handle his impetuous young captain.

The captain of *Ryazan* had no idea where Admiral Danilov was lurking. He assumed that his commander had chosen to go silent to evaluate the situation and that he would appear at a moment he deemed critical. The one thing the captain understood at this moment was that he was the only opposition facing *Imperator*. For what little he had gleaned from copied messages and his sonar's interpretation of far-off battles everything within the giant submarine's path was ruthlessly eliminated.

Ryazan's captain had been brought up through the officer corps under Abe Danilov's tutelage and he had retained a single, vital lesson—never copy someone else's mistakes. He knew he could not survive if he tried to escape, or if he sought refuge among the pressure ridges. Head on, his enemy seemed invincible.

It appeared that his only opportunity was to go silent and allow *Imperator*, now moving rapidly in his direction, to pass. *Ryazan* would be most difficult to detect astern of her. If he could somehow escape detection, he would fire a full spread of torpedoes at her stern. Though he had no idea if she was equally impervious from the rear, he was sure that strategy had yet to be employed. It was worth a try. And, after all, he was also following his mentor's dictum—"You will never meet a live Soviet submariner who has successfully run from his enemy."

Ryazan hovered silently near the ice with each of her crew glued to their stations. They were lost in their own interpretation of eternity.

"Range to contact now?" Snow called out, noting the increase in his heartbeat with a touch of pride. The spirit of the hunt was exposing a hedonistic self he'd been unaware of. Never in his entire career had he fought in any battle. But now that he had experienced the taste of blood, new sensations within his body had come to the surface for the first time. His blood was racing faster—he was sure of that. He could almost imagine it pounding through his veins, just as the books explained it. It was adrenaline—pure and simple.

"Last range was thirty-eight thousand, Captain."

"What do you mean, last range?"

"That's when we lost contact, Captain."

"Lost contact . . . what lost contact?" Snow sputtered.

"Sonar reported it a minute or two ago," the XO offered tentatively.

"I didn't hear a thing—" Snow began.

"That's correct," Carol Petersen interrupted. "Look at the imager. It disappeared as soon as sonar lost him." Her finger circled the space the contact had occupied within the holographic imager.

Snow stared dumbly at the spot. It was empty! He could see *Imperator*; *Houston* was near the damaged Soviet submarine. But there was simply nothing where the next target should have been.

"Forget it . . . never mind," Snow began. "My mind was somewhere else . . . give control back to the computer. We'll have to depend on the memory until we regain contact."

Carol punched the data request into the terminal. Within seconds the image of a tiny submarine returned. "That's the exact location where we lost contact," she said. She tapped at the keyboard again and added, "We'll have projected motion in a moment."

As she finished her last words, the image of the Soviet sub darted to a new location as if encouraged by an invisible hand. "Projected range . . . thirty-one five if she maintained course and speed."

Snow studied the picture cautiously. He had to avoid the snap decision he had almost made. Contact could have been lost for any number of reasons. The Soviet could be exactly where he was projected . . . or he could have gone dead in the water, deciding silence was the best of all possible worlds. He couldn't have continued at the same speed or they wouldn't have lost contact at that range.

There was no indication of equipment casualties. The Russian must have understood what awaited him. If it was my decision, Snow concluded, I'd let my enemy come to me.

Carol studied Snow's face closely. His facial expression, which had been so animated by anger moments before, recovered its original perspective. The muscles in his face relaxed, his features softened, and his eyes grew distant as he attempted to project his mind into that of the Soviet skipper. Caesar could not think for him. The computer would again become irreplaceable if contact was regained—but for the moment they depended on a single human being.

"Put him back," Snow requested softly. "The Russian submarine . . . instruct Caesar to move him back to the last known position. I think . . . that's where he is," he concluded more firmly. "What would his range be when we're on his beam . . . if he remained in position?"

Carol read figures from the screen: "Ten thousand three hundred."

"Too close." Snow turned to his OOD. "I don't want to get too far inside his torpedo range. At about twenty thousand yards, let's start a wide swing to starboard. Then we'll double back. I'll keep an eye on it." He smiled guiltily. "I promise."

Carol had been observing Snow with interest. He was becoming the perfect example of a split personality, one minute a captain closely integrated with his crew, the next reverting to his own image of a warrior who thoroughly enjoyed the killing. It was a new side, one that had appeared only after departing the fishbowl. Andy Reed had once explained to her that the consortium had decided on Snow because of his consistency. With all his problems in managing his personal affairs, his ability to captain a naval vessel remained constant. A shudder coursed slowly down her spine as she considered what might have altered this uniformity that had been such a strong part of his career.

Then she trembled involuntarily, aware his eyes were suddenly holding her own. He'd caught her staring! She was unable to look away, yet she was scared for some reason to hold his gaze for too long.

Snow solved her problem. "We'll get him, just like the others. But I don't want to take any chances. *Imperator*'s tough, but we're not totally invincible. Every once in a while, these man-made wonders need a little help from their masters."

Ryazan's captain waited and watched. His own sonar team recorded an accurate picture not only of *Imperator* as she neared them, but of *Poltava*'s anticipated execution astern of them. What the captain desired was the impossible— some action, some sound, some natural occurrence that would distract *Imperator* for just long enough so that he could empty his tubes. He had no idea of what that miracle might be, but his patience was superb—he had no other option.

Though he had never before participated in an attack that would result in only one winner, he did understand that there was no such thing as creeping into an attack. Success came only to those who pressed home their attack with ferocity, and that would eventually mean revealing *Ryazan*'s presence to *Imperator*.

He wished there was an opportunity to write a last letter to his wife—even though there would never be an opportunity to post it. It would have made him feel better.

There was nothing left to chance, nothing that might give them away. Captain Lozak enjoyed the confidence and loyalty of his men and they performed flawlessly as *Seratov* made preparations for emerging from her hiding place. Lozak beamed with pride when Admiral Danilov commented on it.

"If your crew can continue to operate in this method, I . . . I just might be home in time," Danilov said. The remark was more to himself.

Neither Sergoff nor Lozak responded. It was a personal comment that had escaped his lips quite by accident.

"Rudder amidships," the helmsman responded to Lozak's query.

"Make revolutions for three knots," Lozak ordered. There was the slightest shudder as the propeller pushed against the icy water, gradually increasing the number of turns until *Seratov* eased away from the protection of the pressure ridge. "Left ten degrees rudder. Hold it there," he added. "I'll tell you when to bring it amidships." He would wait until sonar had obtained reasonable contact with *Imperator* and *Houston*.

"We've got a good picture down here, Captain," sonar reported shortly.

"Rudder amidships. All stop." To the diving officer, he added, "Sound off if you have any trouble holding depth."

Danilov smiled and nodded when Lozak turned in his direction. To Stevan Lozak, that was a great improvement over being lectured to with his elbow in that iron grip.

"Range fourteen thousand, Admiral."

Reed was leaning against the stanchion by the number one periscope, his arms folded. "Move in closer so there's no doubt. Even cripples have a way of fighting back."

The tubes had been flooded, the muzzle doors opened, the torpedoes prepared, when sonar reported, "She's picking up speed . . . must've added at least three or four knots in the last thirty seconds."

"You're sure?"

"Hell, yes. With the racket she's making with that busted pressure hull, that bucket of bolts sounds like a whole bathtub full now. You can't hear anything else."

"Nothing?" A note of concern crept into Reed's voice.

"Not a damn thing. Sounds like a herd of elephants."

"Speed up the firing, Ross. I don't know how the hell she's doing it, but I'll put money down that the son of a bitch is attacking."

In less than thirty seconds, *Houston*'s first torpedo was on its way. A second followed shortly afterward. With the

Russian slightly less than ten thousand yards away, both torpedoes were running properly.

"Turn away, Ross." There was something very wrong with the Russian's last moves. "That all made me very unhappy." Reed called down to sonar: "You got anything else out there besides our own torpedoes?"

"Admiral, if there was, we'd have a hell of a time sorting it out right now. She's covering that entire bearing—hell, it looks like ten degrees either side of the bearing with all that racket. I don't know what she can hear from us with all the problems she's probably having with her own noise, but she hasn't reacted to our fish yet."

"Goose it, Ross. I don't care if *Seratov*'s sitting on our tail." He glanced involuntarily over his shoulder as if he could see something approaching behind *Houston*. "And let's add some depth, too."

Reed was still pacing the control room when, thirty seconds later: "Contact . . . contact . . . breaking away from the same bearing." Then, "Yeah, there is something out there." Everything from sonar could be heard in the control room. "No . . . no . . . isolate . . . see if you can squelch the background . . . sounds like screws to me . . . high speed." Then a voice was heard above all the rest. "Torpedo in the water . . . two of them . . . both torpedoes range gating in a three-second interval. . . ." The reports continued in a staccato fashion.

"Pull the plug," Ross howled. At this range it was more a matter of luck than technique. *Houston* dived. Her speed increased as fast as possible. The diving officer fought to avoid too steep an angle. Ross used his rudder to alter courses. The objective in such close quarters was to confuse the torpedo's homing device enough to send it off after the decoys now in the water.

"One's locked on . . . no doubt on that."

While sonar recorded the dual blasts from their own torpedoes that finished off *Poltava*, a frightened voice continued to reel off the shortening ping intervals as the Soviet torpedo bore relentlessly down on them.

In a last-ditch attempt, Ross threw the rudder sharply in

the opposite direction at the same moment more decoys were released. It seemed futile to him at the time. *Houston* was at flank speed, making more noise than any decoys could ever hope to imitate, but it may have saved them.

"Still on us," came the detached voice from sonar. "Closing hard . . . stand by . . ."

A deafening explosion rocked *Houston*. Darkness followed instantly combining with the crash of equipment and glass and frightened shouts of her crew.

The emergency lights revealed a tangle of men on the port side of the control room. Reed still grasped one of the support stanchions, but he had been thrown against the periscope and his forehead was covered with blood. Only one thing was certain—the lights proved they hadn't yet sunk.

Damage control reports streamed into the control room. Forward spaces were still secure, with minor flooding from cracked pipes. Sonar was still functioning forward; the towed array wasn't responding. The control area had experienced normal shock damage. The torpedo had detonated aft, somewhere off the stern—probably caused by one of the decoys. The hull remained solid, though cracked pipes in the engineering spaces were causing minor interior flooding. The engineering report was more critical—there seemed to be external damage to the propeller. *Houston*'s speed would be under fifteen knots. Steering problems cropped up a few minutes after and it was assumed they were likely the result of bent or broken control surfaces.

Reed tied a handkerchief around his bleeding head. "Run her through her paces, Ross. See what we can get out of her if we use a little force. Maybe if we wind her up, everything'll straighten out."

The planes worked properly and the trim system remained solid. But *Houston* literally shook herself apart at any speed beyond fourteen knots and the rudder responded only to wide, gentle turns. There would be no chance for her to maneuver under attack again. While she could still fire torpedoes, any attack on her would prove fatal.

"What's the range to *Imperator*?" Reed asked unhappily.

"A little over thirty miles."

"Steer for her," he ordered.

Ryazan's political officer had to say something. The tension was proving too much. Words, any words—they didn't have to make sense—would release the pressure. He stated in a much louder voice than anticipated, "They know we're out here." He then felt much better. He also felt stupid for having uttered it.

"Of course they do," the captain growled. "Submarines don't evaporate. The American knows that as well as you do. He's already isolated a patch of ocean, and you can be sure we're in it." He knew the reason for *Imperator*'s wide circle around their position was to remain on the outer limits of their torpedo range. He experienced a brief sense of futility—his back was against a cliff and the wolf was circling, sniffing the air . . . inching closer.

"Perhaps he's had a sonar casualty," the political officer commented.

"Perhaps," the captain responded, without really paying attention to his answer. He was sure *Imperator* was functioning normally. No, there was no outside chance that they could advance on the American and fire without knowledge of their approach.

Ryazan was able to identify every sound emitted by their nemesis. They knew *Imperator*'s tubes had been flooded . . . they knew the muzzle doors lay open now as the American craft closed the half circle cautiously.

The captain was increasingly impressed with his own patience. Never before had he exhibited such calm. He had often hoped to be an example for his crew, the single thin thread that maintained discipline in the face of certain death. The captain marveled at this new side of himself and wondered if he would ever have discovered it under normal conditions. Or was it something that surfaced in a man only when he faced death? Or was it perhaps a condition that was reserved for those who had the opportunity to prepare themselves for it? After all, most men in his position never experienced the luxury of preparing for their fate; it came suddenly for most.

Like the letter he wished he could write to his wife, this was another discovery that he should have been able to relate to someone—this discovery of inner peace. No, he concluded, this is all foolishness. No man waits bravely to die. He may know that he must die, but he waits to get even!

And that is what *Ryazan*'s captain really desired more than anything else, more than the chance to see his family once more—he wanted to get even with the object that was taking all that he loved away from him forever.

So he was willing to tarry as long as he had to for an opportunity that might never appear. He was hoping for that unanticipated distraction that would give him an advantage over *Imperator*—just enough time to strike a blow before *Ryazan* was destroyed.

The mood in *Imperator*'s control room couldn't have been more jovial. Everything in their path had been wiped out. Now, the remaining Soviet submarine in the imager was within their grasp. True, it was a projection from Caesar's memory indicating that vessel's last known position, but Snow knew that if they hadn't heard it, it hadn't gone far. Target solutions based on that memory had already been inserted in the torpedoes. The fish were warm, the tubes flooded, muzzle doors open. All that remained was to shoot at the first confirming sound.

"Captain." It was sonar. "We've got something coming from *Houston*'s bearing. Can't figure it out yet."

"Computer's working on it, too," Carol Petersen echoed.

They already knew the alteration in her sound signature indicated damage. But she seemed able to move at a sustained speed—somewhat lower than normal—in their direction. It had just been a matter of carelessness, Snow said. Otherwise *Houston* would be rejoining without a scratch.

"What's the problem?" Snow inquired irritably. "How far away is she?"

"A good twenty miles, sir . . . and she's making a lot of noise with that screwed-up prop—"

"Captain," Carol interrupted. "Caesar holds that new sound as a voice print. *Houston*'s trying to contact us."

"Christ, you can't transmit voice at that distance. Andy Reed knows that." He didn't want to break off the attack now.

"Must be some kind of emergency," the XO commented.

"What can the computer do with it?" Snow asked.

"Caesar's working at it, but I'm afraid . . ." Her voice drifted off as she waited for a response on the screen. Then, ". . . nothing . . . still too far off . . . too much interference from our own ship's noise. We've got to close her a bit more."

"I thought *Houston* was coming right toward us," Snow retorted.

"Negative. She was on a sort of intercept course but now she seems to be drifting off . . . or else we're . . . yeah, we're still in a wide circle around that target, and now we're going slightly away from that intercept point. *Houston*'s course is steady."

"Want me to set a course to intercept, Captain?"

"Negative. Not yet. Have we passed the closest point of approach to *Houston* yet? Is she going away from us?"

"Still closing, Captain. We just won't intercept. That's all."

"Then concentrate on *Houston* and see what the trouble is. I don't want to lose this last target. Recheck that firing solution every sixty seconds," he barked at the fire control coordinator.

"If we can straighten out our course for a few minutes, I can toy with one of the hydrophones. We should be able to copy *Houston* a few minutes after," Carol explained.

"Go ahead," Snow grumbled to the XO. "But only a few minutes. We are going to get that Russian out of the way before we do anything else." He jabbed a finger emphatically at *Ryazan*'s location within the imager.

Ryazan's captain considered the slight change in *Impera-*

tor's course. Everything at this stage was a guess on his part, but this could be the moment he hoped for. He knew he would be dead shortly if he was wrong, but he also assumed he would be dead within hours anyway. What difference did it make? It was too late for the world to appreciate his discoveries over the last few hours. The party would take care of his family whether he died now or tomorrow, or even if it had been yesterday.

The captain nodded to the XO, who called aft to the engineer. Ever so slowly, *Ryazan*'s prop began to turn. The rudder was put over to bring her to a course directly in line with *Imperator*. Noisemakers were prepared as they picked up speed. Perhaps they might provide enough distraction to give them another couple of seconds.

The familiar thrum of the deck under his feet gave the captain a feeling he'd never imagined before. His spirits were high. He was charging directly toward his fate. He was a paladin, a knight pounding across the field of combat. Though his final battle would never be seen, he had accepted that as his fate. Pride surged through his veins. When it seemed their approach had to be obvious, he ordered the political officer to play the national anthem over the PA system.

Imperator had been at the maximum range of the Soviet torpedoes when *Ryazan* got underway. The distance closed rapidly from that moment on. The first two torpedoes were fired while the national anthem echoed through every compartment. The second two left the tubes sixty seconds later. As soon as the first reloads were ready, they were fired. A total of eight torpedoes had been expended before sonar reported that *Ryazan* had been fired upon. Past experience told the captain there was no need to undertake evasive maneuvers. Instead he chose to go deep on the chance that one more lucky break might come his way.

Abe Danilov's eyes were once again tight with concentration. He carefully added each report to the expanded mental picture he was composing. Unlike the holographic imager on *Imperator*, his mind did not include the ice above, but he was able to establish an image of each submarine. They existed in their exact location in relation to *Seratov*. His concentration was powerful enough to cut out all extraneous voices. He heard only the reports from sonar.

Poltava was gone, but the admiral also knew *Houston* had been damaged in the process. Her speed was limited by a propeller casualty and, since she failed to alter her course at all, he was sure her steering gear was also impaired. But that was an assumption he would wait on until there was absolute proof. His sonarmen also knew that Reed was trying to send an urgent message to *Imperator*.

He opened his eyes briefly, knowing Sergoff was nearby, and gave the signal to get underway. He was sure *Houston* had enough trouble of her own that it would be difficult to pick up *Seratov* now. With all of *Imperator*'s wizardry, he was still confident that there was too much to occupy her time with *Ryazan* and *Houston*'s emergency.

Stevan Lozak was pleased that they were once again moving, but his curiosity had yet to be satisfied. They were less than twenty kilometers astern of *Houston* and probably no more than fifty from *Imperator*. He had no idea what Danilov was planning and, if Sergoff knew, he was saying nothing. Each time that he impatiently queried Sergoff about their next move, the chief of staff would smile and lay a calming hand on his arm and explain that Lozak would know almost at the same time he did.

"Come ten degrees to port." The calm voice jarred him from his thoughts. He was surprised to find Danilov's eyes open and fixed on him. "You may keep her at four knots . . . no more. I think we have the luxury of time."

Luxury of time! Lozak couldn't believe his ears. After all the hours they had spent huddling behind that huge ridge of ice while the other submarines attacked each other so savagely! Lozak had no doubt that Danilov would live to a ripe old age with so much patience. If only he would achieve such a level of calm—if ever he reached that age.

Snow was caught by surprise. Everything before had been so easy. One after another, the Russian submarines had fallen before *Imperator*. Now he was actually under attack by the one he had been circling! The message that *Houston* was trying to send had occupied his time, only for a few minutes, but that was long enough to lose what he considered the proper picture. He was forced to relinquish control to Caesar.

Eight torpedoes in four salvos! Incredible—it was beyond comprehension that the Soviet submarine could have maintained such discipline knowing that her final strike would be suicidal. Yet somehow her captain had enforced absolute silence until *Imperator* had been momentarily distracted. It was almost as if it had been part of a master plan. But Snow was sure that was impossible. It was luck.

Snow had been ready to fire as he circled the Russian. Now Caesar automatically sent two torpedoes at him. There was no chance for evasion at that range. The Russian had made a headlong charge as his torpedo tubes were reloaded, and fired again. It was just a matter of time. He'd chosen sacrifice in his attempt to destroy the American submarine.

Caesar deployed decoys with electronic precision. These were followed by the high speed antitorpedo missiles (ATMs) as he kept track of each incoming torpedo. One that broke through the defensive screen was illuminated by the laser and disarmed. While the computer coordinated the defense with uncanny accuracy, it was a malfunction by a decoy that allowed the only casualty sustained by *Imperator*. One of the Soviet torpedoes was drawn away astern by a decoy and altered its course slightly to home on the noisemaker. However, a casualty to the decoy's sound-transmission system had silenced it. The torpedo, losing target contact, returned to a search pattern. Caesar's memory no longer carried this torpedo that had gone after the decoy. The Soviet fish now became a maverick, unaccounted for by the computer now defending the giant submarine.

That torpedo was in a long spiral when it sensed *Imperator*'s propeller signature. Once again, the guidance mechanism slipped into a homing mode. At a little over a thousand yards' distance, Caesar was unable to reprogram the lost torpedo in time to destroy it from astern. It struck just outside the computer room.

The impact was felt in the control room but the immense hull absorbed much of the concussion. It was much like hitting an aircraft carrier with a bomb or torpedo—distant parts of the ship were basically unaware of the trauma at the scene.

Imperator continued on its course with no change in speed. Reports from most departments came in an orderly manner indicating no damage. Engineering found minor leakage in compartments nearer to the blast but basically size and honeycomb design prevented the hit from becoming a tragedy. There were no human injuries.

The smile on Hal Snow's face was widening to one of triumph until the initial indication of a major casualty became evident—"I've got trouble here!" It was Carol Petersen, and her voice carried a note of fear Snow had never heard before.

Snow had been studying the imager closely, a triumphant expression growing as the track of their torpedoes neared the Russian submarine. He was waiting for the little narrow images to merge with the larger one when the imager began to flicker. The Soviet submarine vanished, then returned in a slightly different location. *Houston*, little more than twelve miles distant, jumped out of position, then vanished. The ice pack, for so long a secure roof above, rippled and fluttered, then disappeared altogether.

As Snow stared, speechless, the holographic imager went blank. He moved his hand through it, like a magician proving to his audience that there were no strings attached.

Carol was frantically working at the console, attempting to isolate the casualty. "Caesar's reporting failures in his equipment room . . . we've got troubles . . . bad . . . switching to manual on all systems." The screen blinked out before her, reflecting a neutral green haze, like the surface of a pool table.

"Damage control," Snow managed to sputter into the 21MC.

"Automatic," Carol interrupted. "When the computer

identifies a casualty, it appears automatically on Damage Control Central's Board. They'll already—''

But Snow had flipped the switch to DC Central before she could finish. "You got anything on the computer yet?'' he bellowed.

"I got men on the way, Captain. Give them a minute to hook up a phone. I'll get back as soon as I have something.'' There was a pause with many voices in the background before he added, "We've got water down here . . . don't know whether it's salt or fresh yet . . .''

Snow was momentarily distracted as sonar, still operating normally, reported, "Two torpedoes . . . two hits, Captain. No way that Russian could have escaped from that . . . he's a goner for sure.''

The report registered with Snow—it meant that there were no longer any Soviet contacts to prosecute—but he had more vital problems. The brain that controlled this monster of a submarine had flicked off.

"Captain.'' The light on the 21MC speaker indicated it was DC Central. "We got fractured valves down there and flooding. Pressure to the pipes has been secured, but we had to do it manually. The automatic valves failed to function.'' Of course—they couldn't! They were controlled by the computer that was being flooded! "Water hit the electrical conduits, too, and we're fighting some electrical fires now. Got a lotta smoke spreading down there—''

"Can you control the fires?'' Snow interrupted.

"No problem there. Nothing's going to run away on us, Captain. The problem's in shorting. A lot of small fires. Lots of smoke, too. We're going to need to ventilate.''

"How bad's the smoke?''

"Don't know for sure. We got men with masks in there now. But that smoke's gotta go somewhere.''

That was it—one of the most feared hazards in a submarine, smoke! It was near-impossible to fight a submarine efficiently if the crew was wearing breathing devices over their faces. Smoke had to be removed, but there was nowhere for it to go in a submarine. Smoke could be pervasive, trickling from one compartment to the next.

The precipitators could eventually clear it. But the only quick way to get rid of it was to surface and ventilate the spaces.

Andy Reed was analyzing readouts from the navigational sonar with the quartermaster, Gorham. It was a time-consuming process to compare their projected path with their past course, and they both knew it could be futile because of the shifting ice above. They were searching for thin ice or a polynya or lead because Reed wouldn't allow the use of any active sonar yet. They weren't in that bad shape, or at least that was the attitude Reed was projecting. They might even navigate all the way home if they had the time and patience. Besides, there was a missing submarine in the vicinity—Danilov's—and Andy Reed was sure it hadn't been sunk. The man he had been leery of even before they got underway had become his nemesis once *Houston* was damaged. He desperately needed *Imperator*'s protection until they could surface for repairs.

"Anything yet from *Imperator*?" he asked as he worked at the chart.

When there was no answer to his question, he looked up from the chart table irritably, only to discover Ross standing beside him, his face drawn. "No, Admiral. Nothing from *Imperator* yet. That's still a pretty long distance to read voice with all the background noise we're making, even in these waters. She's had another tussle . . . her and that last Russian. I don't think there's any doubt that that Alfa's on the bottom, but we picked up an explosion separate from the other—a torpedo—a few degrees from the Alfa. *Imperator* could have been hit . . . we don't know yet," he hastened to add. "But she's dead in the water, all engines stopped for the time being."

"Keep at it, Ross. I don't want to have to take this thing to the surface without someone standing guard for us." Andy Reed was sure that if such a thing as a sixth sense existed, they were being watched now.

Abe Danilov opened his eyes and rose to his feet in a fluid

motion. "That's it. We are the only s̶
often amazed him how advanced a su̶b̶
devices had become since he first joined ̶
training of the sonarmen, coupled with a̶d̶
and the ability of the computer to separate ea̶
sound in the ocean, had turned sonar into an a̶ ̶televi-
sion. It allowed them to "see" for hundreds of square
kilometers around them and know exactly what was taking
place. They knew how many torpedoes *Ryazan* had fired
in her headlong charge at *Imperator* and they knew how
the American craft had returned the fire. They knew the
relative locations of the battling submarines, how long it
would take the torpedoes to reach their mark, and they
could tell instinctively that *Ryazan* was ripped apart.

Of equal interest was that *Imperator* also appeared to
have sustained a hit. Though they could only imagine the
extent of damage, it was evident she'd experienced some
negative results. The American boat had gone dead in the
water, either to lick her wounds or to discover whatever
damage had occurred. The critical factor—the most vital—
was that *Imperator* was not immune to attack! She could
be hurt—and if she could be hurt, Danilov had no doubt
she could be sunk!

"Is *Houston* still trying to establish voice contact?" the
admiral inquired.

"Yes, sir." Sergoff knew exactly what Danilov's next
question might be. "We are not close enough to translate.
Even speaking our own language, we are still too far
away."

"Has *Houston* turned toward her?"

"If I had to interpret her problem, I think one of them
would be damage to the steering gear. Her course shows
little variation. There could be extensive damage to her
exterior surfaces if that propeller is any indication . . ."

"She needs to surface," Danilov interrupted, his face
brightening.

"Quite possibly . . ."

"And more likely than not, she wants *Imperator* to
protect her while she makes repairs." Danilov's face be-

. animated. "Admiral Reed knows we're out here. .and he knows we'd pounce on a cripple just like he did." He noticed Lozak listening intently, and added for the captain's benefit, "We could run right in after him now . . . but I think Reed would like us to use him . . . as the decoy, Captain Lozak. While we concentrate on him, *Imperator* blows us out of the water."

"A possibility," Sergoff agreed.

"A very good possibility," Danilov smiled. "No. I'm not ready to go racing in for the kill quite yet. But, Captain, add turns for another knot. We'll close them slowly. I really would like to eavesdrop on Reed's problems. They might make all the difference in the world as to how to prosecute our attack later on."

Sergoff had been studying Stevan Lozak. Perhaps he really was maturing. Never once did he interrupt, and he was listening intently. Lozak should have understood that Danilov was adding one more knot, playing with the threshold of noise that could identify him, only because *Houston* was creating so much noise herself; and, she was concentrating on contacting the other submarine. Danilov desperately wanted to determine the extent of her damage. That would influence the where and when of his attack.

"Captain, we've got the fires under control but we've still got a lot of smoke, especially from the insulation in the equipment room. We're going to have to ventilate sooner or later."

"Can you isolate the compartments?" Snow asked.

"Sure . . . but are you going to want to use this computer again?"

"That bad?"

"Captain, we've sealed off the vents in that area. But that means that smoke stays where it is. No one can get into those spaces for repairs. Look at your board. It's so bad, you can't see where it's still smoldering." Snow glanced at the colored sections on the damage control emergency board in front of him. "No matter what we do, eventually we've got to stick our nose above the ice."

"Wait one." Snow snapped off the speaker to DC Central. He turned to Carol Petersen in agitation. "What's it going to take to get that computer back on the line?"

"I don't know," she responded helplessly. "The unit that analyzes casualties to the system is off-line. I can't tell until I can see the damage. It could be simple. Maybe just a matter of replacing some component trays . . . but right now no one can get into those compartments." Her face became firmer. "Captain, I know you don't want to surface, but that computer's going to remain inoperative until someone can get into those spaces. We've got to ventilate them somehow."

Snow licked his lips nervously. *Imperator* on the surface was akin to a carrier submerged. Neither could perform their mission. Like Andy Reed, he knew there was another Russian submarine in the vicinity, and that it had to be Danilov. There wasn't another as cunning as the Soviet admiral . . . and what would be a better time for him? No, the decision to surface wasn't going to be his. "Turn toward *Houston* and close Admiral Reed. It's safe to establish contact now," he said to his XO.

"*Imperator*'s rogered us, Admiral. They're in communication range."

"Are they standing by to open a hole in the ice for us?" Reed's impatience was obvious.

"Captain Snow insists on speaking with you, sir."

Andy Reed moved the few steps into sonar and spoke irritably into the mike. "Hal, we don't have a hell of a lot of time. If you haven't figured it out, there's one more Russian out here. We need an open space or a soft spot to surface for some quick repairs, and we need it on the double. You can dive as soon as there's enough ice-free space for our men to function outside the hull."

Snow's voice came back with the eerie, hollow echo of a human voice transmitted through the water. "We're not much better off than you. I took a near-hit, Andy. The hull's still solid, but I've got ruptured piping in the computer spaces. The flooding set off fires . . . Caesar's down

. . . have to surface and ventilate smoke before commencing repairs. You'll have to decide how we do this.''

Reed considered the few options that existed. A little more than an hour before, nothing beneath the ice could have stopped them. Now, with casualties to both submarines, they were forced to protect each other from a Russian submarine that was certainly nearby, yet had succeeded in disappearing behind a cloak of silence. However he had done it, Danilov held the upper hand for the time being in a situation that might never have been programmed in a war game.

"We need Caesar . . . badly." Reed's impatience had been quickly subdued.''

"Agreed," Snow answered.

"What's your estimate on repair time."

"We can't even get in there to find out what has to be done."

"Okay," Reed decided. "How confident do you feel about Danilov's last known position?"

"Wait one . . . can't even use the goddamn memory." There was a long pause, then, "The best we can do is"—he read off a set of coordinates—"but that was hours ago."

"Probably good enough," Reed answered. "Not more than a couple of miles from our own estimate. That means he was astern of us . . . toward the pole. I'll tell you what—I need some open water if I'm going to be any use . . . and we can't do anything until you bust up some working space for us. I can't get on more than four degrees rudder . . . and I want to have my torpedo tubes in Danilov's direction when I hit the surface. Give me a position, something that I can make a wide turn for so that I'm facing the pole when I reach open water. You surface and get some fresh air while I'm making the turn, then pull the plug again. No need for you to stay up top while you're making repairs . . . you can stand sonar guard while I've got men outside."

"Roger. We've got a location one one zero degrees

relative, about four miles. You can maneuver into that one easily. I'm on my way unless—''

''Take off, Hal. No telling about our competition.''

The competition had indeed crept close enough to record the transmission between the two submarines. The electronics officer ran the tape through a masking device to blot out background sound, transferring it to another tape for an interpreter. Much of the conversation was available.

The interpreter typed out the transmission, leaving spaces where the speech was unintelligible. Then he analyzed what he had on paper, inserting the most likely words in each case. Once he was satisfied, he retyped the Americans' conversation and delivered it to a pacing Danilov.

''Plot that breakthrough position on the chart,'' the admiral growled at Lozak, hoping they were closer than he estimated. His eyes brightened when he understood the extent of damage to *Imperator*'s computer.

''We were right in the middle of the positions each of them had for us,'' Lozak said, laying the chart in front on Danilov. He marveled at the efficiency of the American sonar, for they had been tracked at excessive ranges until their speed dropped under four knots. ''Even now, if they were searching carefully, they might pick us up at this speed.'' But his voice dropped off as he noticed the admiral clap his hands in delight.

Danilov considered the relative position of the American submarines. *Imperator* was eighteen kilometers distant. *Houston* stood between them off *Seratov*'s port bow, sounding for all the world like a garbage truck with her howling propeller. She was successfully blocking *Imperator*'s sonar across that bearing. *Houston* would have to effect a wide turn to position herself beside an opening in the ice another eight kilometers beyond the giant submarine. Considering *Houston*'s infirmities, there was no need for a charge, nor anything that might be suicidal. Abe Danilov was convinced he could stop both of them.

Stevan Lozak was unable to contain himself a moment longer. He could picture the thought processes taking place behind the admiral's eyes and he was anxious to be a part of it. "Should we get the big one out of the way first?"

"No." The rapid response interrupted Lozak before he could explain himself. "Even damaged, *Imperator* could occupy all our time . . . if we were lucky enough to find an opening in her defenses. But she is going to be making a lot of noise when she surfaces, especially when more than a thousand feet of submarine is breaking through all that ice. *Houston* shouldn't be able to hear a thing at that point, and she probably can't hear much beyond her own propeller anyway."

Danilov rarely made a decision that failed to appeal to Sergoff. The chief of staff had often wondered, as he read the history of submarine warfare, if the greatest captains and leaders were actually as sound under combat conditions as they were when they participated in exercises—from which everyone went home and drank vast quantities of vodka after they were through sinking each other. Danilov had been brilliant but cautious in peacetime, and Sergoff was thankful that these traits followed him into combat. He hoped they would not end up like the others—brave and dead.

"I want a course that will bring us roughly six kilometers from where they intend to surface and I want to keep *Houston* between us and *Imperator* as long as possible. If they are going to place their bows in the direction of our last known position, I will settle for a position on their sterns." That way, Danilov figured, *Houston* would remain unable to hear them and she would continue as a screen between *Imperator* and *Seratov*.

Imperator was almost in position. The lead charted earlier had closed slightly, but the ice around the edges was relatively thin. *Houston* had now swung through the arc that would bring her into position bow first, and she was closing from astern.

The two American submarines were methodical in carrying out their plan, for they appreciated how valuable each moment was with an enemy submarine lurking somewhere nearby. Realizing how wide *Houston*'s turn would have to be with only four degrees of rudder available, Snow brought his submarine's bow into position as quickly as he could to keep his torpedo tubes in Danilov's estimated direction. He kept his muzzle doors open and torpedoes ready for a snap shot until the last possible second before touching the ice.

For his part, Stevan Lozak marveled at the ease of *Imperator*'s movement. It seemed impossible that anything that large could move with such grace—if that was indeed the word for the motion of over twelve hundred feet of submarine. Yet for men inured to life beneath the ocean surface, man's machines were a picture of engineering grace.

Seratov took advantage of her enemies' weaknesses . . . of *Houston*'s howling propeller . . . of *Imperator*'s maneuvering. When the giant craft brought her bow around toward the pole sooner than anticipated, Lozak assumed that was to keep her tubes open to the potential threat and was forced to increase his own speed to avoid sonar detection. He was even more respectful when Snow backed the final few thousand yards into position. Lozak maneuvered to keep *Houston* as much between himself and *Imperator* as possible. There were ominous moments of anticipation in the Soviet control room, knowing how capable the American sonar was in detecting an Alfa at that speed. A quick snap shot would put *Seratov* on the defensive. But the howling from *Houston* masked their maneuvering and they crept into position astern of her, where there was only a minimal chance of being identified.

When Sergoff indicated they had reached the desired position, Stevan Lozak realized for the first time that he had maintained a death grip on the shiny chrome bar behind the helmsman for the entire evolution. Now, as he released his grasp, he could feel the pain of tightened muscles relaxing. There was little color in his hands—his knuckles were pure white.

"Okay . . . gently now," Snow ordered. His sail area

would surface in open water, but he hesitated to come up too quickly. There would still be heavy ice all around them. Easing more than a thousand feet of submarine through a small hole in the ice was a complex process. Surfacing too quickly would increase the chances for external damage. The entire process was a matter of increasing their bouyancy, blowing sea water from their ballast tanks while maintaining their stability as they slowly rose to the surface.

"Easy now . . . easy . . ." The diving officer was talking to himself, oblivious to anyone else in the control room. He was doing the job originally designed for a computer. It seemed to Snow, as he tried to visualize from a position somewhere well above the ice, that it was like running a carrier up a trout stream. It didn't seem possible that the sweating diving officer was handling the entire thing by himself.

"Heavy ice contact forward." That meant the bow would hold for an instant while the stern continued to rise. He shifted water to his trim tanks aft to make the bow lighter. Bouyancy accomplished the rest. "Ice contact starboard quarter." The submarine rolled slightly, enough so that the motion could be felt in the control room.

"Ice all sides, Captain," the diving officer reported. "My keel is level. Request permission to blow all main ballast tanks." There were beads of perspiration on the man's forehead.

"Go ahead." Snow smiled. "Do it your way. You earned it, Fitz."

There was a rumble as high-pressure air forced the water from the ballast tanks. This was followed by an even steadier sound as *Imperator* rose upward through the remaining ice. Huge chunks broke away, rattling down the hull into the water. The sharp splashes echoed through the submarine. It seemed as if they were maneuvering in a tank after days of almost total silence under water.

The submarine continued to rock slightly even after the sound subsided. "On the surface, sir."

"Captain," the electronics officer called out, "I've got

all sorts of stuff in the air—their aircraft, our aircraft. I got military radio circuits going a mile a minute.''

"Do you read anything in the immediate vicinity?'' Snow queried.

"Negative. It's all up in the air . . . nothing I can find on the surface.''

"Keep a sharp eye . . . report if anything seems to be closing.'' To his XO, Snow indicated the ladder up into the sail. "Come on, let's see what the North Pole looks like.'' He was halfway up the ladder before turning to Carol Petersen. "Have DC Central report to me on the bridge as soon as they know how long it will take to clear those spaces. We don't belong up here.''

When *Imperator* broke through the static cold of the arctic ice, satellites silently eyeing the great white expanse activated warning systems in Washington and Moscow. Only one object that large could possibly have been under the ice pack—*Imperator*. In Washington, not a soul could fathom why she would possibly breach the surface at that moment. In Moscow, no one paused to wonder why she'd reveal her position—at least they now knew where the monster was.

Messages went out to aircraft in both countries. Until the moment *Imperator* surfaced, there had been no information for either side concerning what had taken place beneath the ice. Now, one of the combatants had appeared. The Russians wished to dispose of it. The Americans raced to *Imperator*'s defense.

Houston slowed at four thousand yards. Reed intended to give *Imperator* plenty of room to maneuver when she prepared to dive. At three thousand yards, he checked on the underwater telephone to determine how much longer they'd have to wait.

At almost the precise moment *Houston* secured engines, one of the sonarmen cried out, "Torpedo . . . port quarter . . . closing fast.'' Up to that moment, with the raucous sounds they had been emiting themselves, coupled with the ice rattling off *Imperator*'s hull, there had been no chance to identify anything else. It had seemed so dangerous that Reed commented only seconds before to Ross that this was the perfect time for an attack. At this recognition of the fact, he'd stopped the propeller to listen—and they'd been greeted by the most terrifying report a submarine could hear.

"More than one . . . two definite . . . both range gating . . . three-second intervals . . ."

While the Americans had been creating their own sound effects, Abe Danilov observed Lozak with pride as the captain eased *Seratov* into a perfect position. There had been more than enough time to creep stealthily the last few thousand feet. The only errant noise had been the flooding of the tubes and the muzzle doors snapping open, but that had taken place during their approach while *Houston* was still making noise. Abe Danilov even commented to Sergoff that it was the simplest of firing exercises designed for cadets in their first year—one had only to hit a standing target! Two torpedoes had been fired. A third and fourth were ready for emergency use while the other two tubes were being reloaded. There was no need to dive. It was an old-fashioned straight shot.

Houston's choices were limited. The high-speed Russian torpedoes gave them less than ninety seconds to evade from the moment they left the tubes. Yet she was unable to turn adequately in either direction, *and* her speed was limited! It seemed that any maneuver would just offer the torpedoes more opportunity. *Houston* was just below the ice, perfectly trimmed, ready to move into position to surface. Reaction time was *negligible*.

With reports of the closing torpedoes ringing in Reed's ears, the realization came to him that there was nothing—nothing at all—they should be doing. Flooding the ballast tanks would just be an assist to the Russians; they would sink a little faster. "Blow your main ballast tanks, Ross . . . quick . . . give it all you've got."

"I don't—"

"Never mind . . . no way we can get away now . . .

collision alarm,'' Reed shouted as he switched on the PA system. Somehow, he had to get to *Imperator*! "We are under torpedo attack. We will try to surface. Prepare to abandon ship.''

The crew in each space heard the last words repeated over and over again. Most were unable to understand his meaning. No one abandons submarines! Either everyone survived or everyone went down with the ship. But no one abandoned. . . .

The first torpedo hit aft, blowing a hole directly into the reactor compartment. Seawater shorted out the electrical system. Only those on the upper deck survived the blast or flooding. The second one hit low, bursting into the torpedo room. Water flooded through the vast rupture in the hull. The last torpedo malfunctioned at the final moment, diving erratically beneath *Houston*, mercifully prolonging her final agony.

Houston had been rising toward the ice as water rushed from her ballast tanks. The second blast lifted her more quickly. The bow pointed gradually higher from the weight of the water flooding aft. Then her nose crashed through the ice at an awkward angle. *Houston* resembled an immense sea lion as her entire bow struggled to climb up on the ice. Then she slid backward until less than the first fifty feet poked from the water; a section of her sail appeared above the surface, gracelessly canted to one side.

Inside the hull, fear and darkness were eased by emergency lights. The force of the blasts flung the crew about the confined spaces like so many rag men. The luckiest had been hurled into each other. Many others were unconscious or dead from violent contact with heavy and sharp-edged equipment. Ross had been thrown sideways into the first fire control console. He lay in a heap, his forehead crushed, blood flowing from his mouth and ears.

Reed lunged for the interior phone. "Engineering . . . can you give us any power?''

He was greeted with silence.

He tried other spaces . . . but there was no answer from any of them. The interior communication system was dead.

Then *Houston* rolled another ten degrees to starboard, slipping further backward. She was being dragged down by the rapidly increasing weight of sea water flooding her spaces.

Supporting himself on a railing, Reed recognized the quartermaster gripping the chart table, his eyes fixed on Reed. "Abandon ship," Reed called to him, pointing at the 21MC speaker behind the man. "All stations . . ."

The quartermaster stared dumbly, wiping blood from the corner of his mouth before the concept dawned on him that the admiral was giving an order. He turned slowly, as if in a dream, and called in a husky voice over the ship's general announcing system, "Abandon ship . . . abandon ship . . ."

There was little time to do more than scramble as *Houston* again slid backward. There were four hatches in a 688 class, but only the forward one and the sail were above the water. There wasn't a soul who escaped the engineering spaces.

It was light near the pole during the wee hours of the morning, but the temperature remained below zero. Sailors leaped toward the ice dressed only in dungarees and T-shirts. Some fell back in the icy water, struggling against instant numbness for a handhold. The injured men lucky enough to be near the forward hatch were passed out to others on the slanted deck who were forced to push them into the water, hoping someone would get them to the edge of the ice. *Houston*, groaning against the weight of her rapidly filling hull, was again wrenched violently backward until water first lapped at the edges of the forward hatch, then cascaded through the opening.

One of the last to emerge was Andy Reed. The sail seemed at an impossible angle when he struggled through the tiny hatch and leaped into the open sea. He thrashed through the numbing water to the edge of the ice, where grasping hands reached to pull him out. He was half dragged, half carried away from the open water as the submarine's bow pointed higher into the air. When they were no more than fifty yards away, *Houston* lurched once more. This time she pointed her nose directly at the clear sky above, before slipping rapidly backward. Huge air bubbles erupted on the surface. Floe ice crashed about with a roar. And then there was nothing but surface debris among the chunks of ice.

Seratov—Abe Danilov—had been rewarded for patience.

Snow slammed his fist against the metal side of the sail. Come on—get tough, he wanted to shout. But he couldn't, not with the XO staring in wonder at his captain's outburst. Why the hell was he giving in to his emotions now? He pressed the button to the control room and bawled into the speaker: "Break out one of those helos forward, on the double. Tell Colonel Campbell he's in charge of *Houston* survivors. No time to arm . . . just get the closest one on deck and into the air. I'll have orders for the crew by the time they're warmed up." An involuntary shudder coursed through his body. Why was he having second thoughts?

He should leave *Houston*'s survivors where they were . . . there should be no other choice. Wasn't that right? Weren't they all in danger? His first responsibility was to *Imperator* and her crew—and the mission. He should pull the plug right now. But he could help those men . . . and he had to ventilate that computer area. God, how he needed Caesar!

It wouldn't take more than a few moments. Get Andy Reed back with him—then send the bird back—just the fuselage of the helo would suffice to protect the others until he could surface again. Once they were inside, there would be warmth and some medical supplies.

He snapped on the speaker to control again. His first decision had to be right! "Double the medical supplies aboard that bird. Just toss in some extra kits. We'll worry about what's in them later." His entire body shook now . . . never before.

A wounded man, Snow reasoned, who was about to freeze to death, wasn't particular about the quality of his medical supplies. He peered impatiently over the top of the sail as the gull-wing doors folded back to reveal the helo rising on the elevator. Two crewmen were already unfolding the rotors. A third was cramming additional supplies inside. The pilot and copilot could be seen through the front, already strapped into their seats. Colonel Campbell waved toward the bridge.

Snow flipped the switch to sonar. "What have you got on the Russian? Is he closing?" *Imperator*'s active sonar was on the bottom of the hull, a hundred feet below.

"Negative, Captain. He probably went deep . . . lots of decoys in the water. He sure as hell wants to confuse things."

"A course . . . direction . . . anything!" He knew the shaking would stop once they had contact. "Where's he headed?"

"He started to open his range slightly when he pulled the plug . . . then he seemed to reverse course. As best as we can figure, he may be circling toward our stern now."

"Okay, sonar, call me with anything, anything at all. We've got survivors on the ice." Snow switched to the control room. "Is Miss Petersen in the control room?" He'd almost said "Carol!"

"Negative, Captain. She went below as soon as they vented the equipment room."

"Can you get her on the 21MC?" Carol . . . and Caesar . . . working together.

"No communications down there as yet, sir."

"Send a messenger down. Have her call the bridge immediately." There were so many factors—too many. He turned to study the *Houston* survivors with his binoculars. There were a half dozen of them stumbling through the snow and ice, waving their arms at him. It was a bizarre sight—men in pants and shirt sleeves near the North Pole . . . and he could sense their fear. Too many factors . . .

"Captain, I have a flight of aircraft approaching on radar—very low. There's no response from them on the interrogator. I don't think our own people have picked them up yet."

"Range?"

"About one two five miles . . . closing at about four seven five miles per hour . . . still no answer on the interrogator."

"Roger, stand by the lasers . . . starboard section. Anything in the sky knows who we are already, so these probably aren't our guys coming in on the deck."

"Roger, Captain, preparing starboard lasers."

"DC Central—how much more time do you need? We're running out up here."

"Can you spare another five minutes, Captain? We still have some insulation smoldering down here."

Snow could feel the tension in every muscle of his body. Aircraft coming in on the deck, men beginning to freeze to death on the ice, a Russian Alfa somewhere below intent on destroying him . . . and Caesar was inoperative! "Make it fast. I may have to pull the plug any moment. Status is changing fast up here." Too many factors . . .

With a roar in the silent arctic air, the helo lifted off and banked sharply toward the frantic survivors. Snow watched through his binoculars as they tried to run, but their feet sank into the hard snow or slipped on ice hummocks invisible in the whiteness about them. Their energy was disappearing so quickly in the frigid air that panic already enveloped them.

Survival was primary to all of them, all except Andy Reed. As he shuddered violently against the cold, he yearned for revenge against the man who had just sunk *Houston*.

Carol Petersen waited anxiously outside the entrance to the computer spaces. The protective mask she wore was tight around her face. Little drops of perspiration collected at the base. She was uncomfortably aware of the hissing sound she was making with each breath.

A damage control party pushed their way past, dragging a power cable. She was forced back against the bulkhead by a burly sailor who shouted something incomprehensible at her. But the smoke was gradually clearing from the passageway, and the emergency lanterns were almost as clear as the normal lighting. The shadows they cast were strange and frightening in the organized confusion around her.

She jumped at the hand that grasped her shoulder from behind. "Okay to go in now, Miss Petersen . . . detectors are reporting clean air . . . but don't take off your mask right away."

Carol nodded as the sailor loosened the dogs around the hatch and pulled it back. She found perhaps an inch of water covering the deck as she stepped inside. Leaning back through the hatch, she saw that the damage control party had already moved on to the next compartment. Forget it, she said to herself. Nothing serious at this point. She'd catch up with them as soon as she checked each of the systems. With no power to the space, there wasn't an immediate hazard.

But as she worked, moving from unit to unit, she noticed that it was getting deeper—not quickly, but it was sloshing over her shoe tops as the ship rolled gently from side to side.

Abe Danilov was close to completing his mission. Only one object remained in his path. Then he could return to Moscow and his Anna. Anna . . . the name excited him as it flickered through his mind . . . Anna . . . the loyal wife who had written all of those letters, one for each day . . . the dying woman who was trying to live long enough for him to come home one more time . . . and there were only two days left!

And then her name vanished from his mind, willed away by another name—*Imperator*, the most dangerous of all, the immense weapon that posed such a threat to his homeland.

"Range to *Imperator*?" Danilov called out.

"We're at approximately six kilometers and opening slightly. Should be on her port quarter," Sergoff added. "I don't think she's moved."

"Well, there's no doubt that she probably holds us,"

Danilov remarked softly. The active sonar from the American submarine echoed continuously through *Seratov*. It was an astonishing instrument, the largest ever built, so powerful that it was piercing the boiling water, where *Houston* had disappeared. Its sheer power was evident by the terrifying sound heard clearly by every man aboard.

Seratov had reloaded immediately after firing on *Houston*, but there was little point in wasting a torpedo at this stage. There was too little chance of accurate homing as long as the target remained on the surface with all that ice surrounding it, scraping against the hull; too much that would confuse or distract a homing device. No, they had to wait until *Imperator* was getting underway. Let her begin to drop below the ice and commence some sort of movement. Then Danilov would make sure they fired everything in their power before she could maneuver freely.

"Those noisemakers . . . will they have any effect?" Lozak inquired cautiously. He was unable to fully grasp the admiral's tactics at this stage. Everything seemed to be the opposite of what he might have done.

"Their only effect is to confuse . . . maybe to anger just a little bit. No, they don't really have a specific effect on what *Imperator* is going to do. The only purpose I can imagine is to antagonize them a little bit." Danilov's countenance grew hard as he spoke. "If there is one sonarman, or one person in their control room, or perhaps even an individual involved with their computer who hesitates for a split second longer than he should have, then there is a definite reason for those noisemakers. And"—here he grinned at Sergoff, who he knew would appreciate his grim little joke—"if they have no effect at all, then we are all dead and there is no further need for them—we will have justified the government's expense for them." He chuckled long after Captain Lozak had given up trying to understand his humor.

"Admiral, I'd say we're at the range to turn. Snow is aware of our location and he's got to commence his dive anytime. The smoke has to be gone by now." Sergoff had planned the details of this attack himself, following Danilov's

outline. They would fire the moment there was any indication *Imperator* was preparing to dive. The noisemakers
should mask *Seratov*'s preparations. The additional noise
generated by *Imperator*'s diving—the sound of the props,
the flooding of ballast tanks—hopefully all of that would
combine to hide the sounds of the torpedoes enabling run.

Danilov placed an encouraging hand on Lozak's shoulder. "Make your turn and commence your run. Sergoff
will assist. And, Captain—the Americans expect you to
make a run at them. Accept the fact that they're going to
take evasive action and use equipment you are unfamiliar
with—and probably fire back at us. It's a fact of life. Do
you agree?"

Lozak understood. This was what he would have done
earlier—bore in on that giant submarine, fire everything
. . . destroy it as soon as possible. There was no reason to
wait. "Yes, Admiral." He was exultant now. He would
be patient, just as they insisted, until the sounds of *Imperator*
getting underway came to them. Then it was full speed,
right down the throat!

"Standby to get underway," Snow called down to control.
"We'll submerge in four . . . no, less than that . . . about
three minutes. Where the hell is Carol Petersen? Has she
got an estimate for us yet?" He had to have some sort of
confirmation. Even if Caesar wasn't back on line . . .
something . . . anything to justify . . .

"Negative, sir. They're jury-rigging a line now . . .
should have communications with the computer room pretty
quick."

The XO interrupted from control. "Captain, those aircraft are at ninety miles now. Definitely unfriendly . . .
just painted us with target acquisition radar."

"Then do the deed . . . illuminate them." Snow heard
his orders repeated in the background. "Anything else out
there to worry about?" Anything else to confuse the issue?
To keep *Imperator* helpless?

"There's some others, but they're a hell of a distance.
Nothing to be concerned about if we're pulling the plug."

''Have radio try to raise the nearest friendlies. Tell them to sanitize this area. We'll be back to pick up *Houston* survivors.'' Never before had so many extraneous factors . . .

The light indicating sonar appeared on the speaker. ''Captain, *Seratov* has turned. He's on an intercept course . . . maybe making six to eight knots . . . range under five thousand yards.''

''Fire control, have a solution ready. We're about to submerge. Weapons Officer, prepare torpedoes. Target closing from astern. As soon as we have the sail below the ice, I will be turning to port for attack. They will have fired on us by then. Now, dammit, where the hell is my line to the computer?''

''Still rigging, Captain. Messenger reports there's no way you're going to have Caesar on-line for this attack—'' The last words were drowned out by the roar of the helo landing forward. Snow watched as three men were gently lifted out onto the elevator. Andy Reed waved up at him weakly. Then the helo was lifting off again, banking toward the remaining survivors.

The gull-wing doors slowly began to fold back into *Imperator*'s hull.

''I want rig-to-dive reports on the double,'' Snow called down to control. He watched the helo return the short distance to the patch of ice where the forlorn figures huddled. At least they'd be inside the helo until he could get back.

''Helo deck hatch, secure . . . engineering ready to answer all bells . . . diving officer says give him the word to submerge.''

Snow strained his eyes in the direction of the approaching enemy planes. ''How about the aircraft?'' It would be foolhardy to dive if there were incoming missiles loose.

''Gave 'em five seconds irradiation twice, sir . . . just to make sure. We counted six incoming. There's four heading in the opposite direction. Two just plain dove into the ice.''

''Roger, I'm securing.'' I'm doing exactly what they used to do fifty years ago, dammit!

Snow double-checked each of the sail hatches as he slid down the ladder. Jumping the final half dozen feet into the control room, he called out, "Submerge this ship . . . double fast. Prepare decoys . . . stand by defense systems . . . we have to be under attack."

A variety of orders echoed through the control room in rapid succession as *Imperator* began settling. The sail had to be under before they could maneuver. Without the computer, there was no picture in the imager. Each station in the giant submarine was functioning on its own, reporting directly to Snow, taking their orders from him as he evaluated the situation. Once again, they were operating like the old attack submarines he remembered from years before, except this one was four times bigger and much more difficult to maneuver.

Then Snow felt power surge through his entire body—this was as it should be! He was no longer competing with a computer. They were diving . . . toward security.

Unlike the attack boats of the past, there was no rumbling as *Imperator*'s tanks filled, no tilt of the deck as she settled. Snow waited calmly, once again at peace with himself, until the words he was waiting for came: "Sail is clear of the ice . . . ready to maneuver."

"Left full rudder. All ahead full . . . firing point procedures . . ." He was captain—there was no question in his mind who controlled *Imperator*.

To each man—Stevan Lozak, Pietr Sergoff, Abe Danilov—*Seratov*'s approach was the culmination of their careers. They had been offered the opportunity to take part in the final action that would decide the fate of their country's national strategy.

While the closing rate of the two submarines increased rapidly, the three men pictured the event as if they were involved in a movie. It was a slow-motion race for each of them, the film seemingly halting at each frame rather than portraying the impending battle as a high-speed duel.

Lozak heard each of the reports from his battle stations team, responding to each with a curt "very well." He was unaware that they were strung together in rapid fire. Each of his men had been ready and their responses matched the speed of the weapons system they commanded. While Lozak was sure that he took the time to evaluate each report and ensure that it was proper, his responses were synchronized with their own. His breathing became rapid as he gave the order—"Shoot!"—for each weapon. When the final torpedo was in the water, he was sucking in deep gulps of air.

Pietr Sergoff studied the process with a detachment that surprised even himself. He had done everything possible to prepare for this moment, and it was not his place to interfere as *Seratov*'s captain fought his ship. There was no thought in his mind of surviving this action. And, he surmised as he reflected on the crisp efficiency of the attack, there is really no reason to return home since I have served my country as I was trained. Perhaps it was an honor . . .

Abe Danilov experienced a feeling of warmth coursing through his body. It was a pleasant sensation and he attributed it to the fact that his hunt was over. The culmination of his efforts was the destruction of *Imperator*, which would be final in the next few moments. Lozak had run a picture-perfect attack . . . and now there were four torpedoes racing for the American submarine. There was still a chance that he would be home in time. . . .

"Torpedoes in the water, Captain. They're locked on. Four of them . . ." *Imperator*'s sonar officer shouted into the control room.

Snow let the defense stations take individual action. Decoys would already have been fired. They would be followed by the tiny ATMs. Anything that got through would still have to survive the laser.

"How's your solution?" *Imperator* was turning to face her enemy.

"Target closing at three nine zero zero yards, broad on our beam now . . . she's still picking up speed. We have a solution . . . just need to get the bow around faster so we have the right firing angle."

"Engineering, give us all you've got. We're not turning fast enough." More than twelve hundred feet of submarine . . . more speed . . .

A voice from sonar pierced the control room. "Torpedoes are in a three-second ping interval . . . antitorpedo missiles deploying . . ." There was a pause and then, in a higher voice, sonar added, "That submarine is coming right at us at flank speed, Captain . . . following those torpedoes like they were dogs in heat . . . like he was going to ram us."

Carol Petersen's voice came over the speaker. "Captain, computer equipment room's a mess. The main unit next door is okay, but it's going to take more than an hour to cross-patch some of these cables just to get back in working order—"

Snow depressed the switch to cut her off. "Can it. Save it till we're finished up here. We're under attack." He had no use for a computer now.

"Almost there," the XO called out. He was peering over the weapons officer's shoulder. "Another ten degrees and we're clear to fire."

"Still coming at us?" Snow yelled.

"No change . . . flank speed. He's no more than a thousand yards behind his fish . . . ATMs are almost on top of them and . . . bing . . . scratch one fish . . . scratch two."

"Ship is in position," the XO called out.

"Match generated bearings and shoot!" Snow's voice rose over the other sounds in the control room.

The weapons officer's voice echoed Snow's as each torpedo left the tubes. He counted them off, "One . . . two . . . standby three and four . . . Christ, right down the throat. He can't be more than two thousand yards away . . . there's hardly time for them to finish the enabling run and arm the way he's closing." There was a pause, then, "Three and four clear . . ."

"Right full rudder," Snow called. "Six hundred feet—

use a thirty-degree down angle.'' It seemed the only choice if the Russian really intended to ram them . . . but it took so much longer to put twelve hundred feet of submarine into a steep dive. He could still catch the after section . . . possibly.

''All our torpedoes are running properly. Two of his got through the ATM barrage . . . too little time. Stand by lasers . . .'' The weapons officer was ready to employ his last resort when he noticed the bow angle on *Imperator*. ''We're swinging away from him too fast. We can't use the lasers, Captain.''

Oh, my God, Snow muttered to himself. Caesar would have picked that up! The lasers were trainable only on a limited azimuth. When he threw his rudder over, he'd forgotten that he was pulling his lasers away from the closing torpedoes. ''Shift your rudder.'' Caesar . . . Caesar would never have done that. Another shudder . . .

''Two Soviet fish at eight hundred yards . . . closing. I've got a wall of decoys out there . . . don't know if it's going to—'' His voice was interrupted by an explosion close enough to shake the control room. ''That's one of them . . . second one's through . . . coming right up our port quarter.''

Caesar and his systems had been designed to survive heavy casualties to the ship. It had been automatically assumed that *Imperator* could take a certain number of torpedoes, experience flooding and power loss, and still regain almost total capabilities within a reasonable amount of time. The computer contained residual backup systems to compensate for loss of ship's power so that Caesar could go back on-line at the exact stage required.

Smoke damage affected only the external elements: instruments, display units, and the giant screen. The only casualty that could critically damage Caesar would be water, and Carol was more aware than ever of the water rising ever so slowly. She called for one of the damage control party to help her.

Together they covered the compartment inch by inch

until the water source was located. Carol was the first to discover the tiny bubbles welling up from a crack in the bulkhead near the deck in one corner of the space. The sailor found the other, in the same location on the opposite end of the bulkhead. It was the same type of weld. Sometime during the construction of this compartment, there had been a welder who was having a bad day—he had made the same mistake twice. Now his error was endangering the heart of the ship—Caesar. But of even greater concern was the adjoining space, a void between the compartment and the hull. Somehow water was seeping through the hull into the ship from that last torpedo, enough to build pressure in the void and force water into the adjoining compartment.

"I'm sorry, ma'am," the sailor explained. "I have to seal off this compartment again—just in case . . ." His voice trailed off. The just-in-case was the possibility of another torpedo exploding nearby. If the hull was weakened that much more, this space might also flood. It had to be sealed to protect the rest of the ship.

Carol understood immediately, but time was precious. Snow needed the computer. "That's all right. After you seal it, let control know I'm still here."

The harsh sound as the hatch was sealed from the outside sent a chill down her spine. Its resonance was transmitted by the metal, then magnified into a dirge as she noted the water lapping around her feet. Had the depth increased some more? Or perhaps there was no change from last time. Knock it off, she commanded herself silently—no time for such thoughts.

But it was hard to think of anything else as she went through the mechanical procedures that she knew she could complete if she were blind. The last she remembered before leaving the control room was that the Russian was closing—he would be shooting at them anytime. It could be minutes . . . maybe just seconds. The defense systems would have to be activated manually until she had Caesar back on-line.

There! She wasn't imagining things. There was no water

around her feet. But it was a short-lived reprieve, because she saw that it was now all in the forward section of the compartment. Of course . . . they were diving! But, at an angle like that, *Imperator* must be evading—a torpedo!

This time it was fear that mastered the tingling sensation running down her spine. How many torpedoes? She tried to remember the design of the Russian Alfa. Four—it had to be four! She thought she remembered that there were four tubes forward in the Alfa. To attack *Imperator*, Danilov would be insane not to use four torpedoes. She knew she must hurry. Snow needed Caesar so badly at this stage. The entire battle-station team in the control room was qualified to operate each of the defense mechanisms. But, she knew, one mistake—just one mistake—and *Imperator* could be hit. One torpedo wouldn't be fatal to a ship of this magnitude . . . but she could imagine how—

The blast knocked her off her feet, hurling her against the main console. Something in her back snapped with a report that seemed to deafen her . . . or was that sound her back? There seemed to be no pain . . . but she couldn't move. Then she saw the outer bulkhead open inward. There was no feeling as the torrent swept down on her.

Captain Sergoff was positive that he had become a human missile as *Seratov* raced toward its target. In the last seconds, he had dismissed the possibility of ever again seeing his family. *Seratov* was hurtling along at flank speed, following its own torpedoes toward their target. The resolute Danilov remained perched on a stool, lost in his own thoughts, eyes shut tight as he once again envisioned the world beyond the hull. He'd remained absolutely silent since the torpedoes had been fired, lost in the picture he saw developing as he listened to the reports about him.

Danilov saw his four torpedoes launched as *Imperator* sank below the ice. They were well on their way before the giant submarine could begin to challenge him. He knew *Imperator* was turning to shoot and smiled inwardly at his wise decision to come in from astern.

He opened his eyes and uttered one word, *"Dive!"* as loudly as he could. It would be their only chance. He knew *Imperator* was diving also. At this speed, they would go down quickly—though he had no idea whether it would be fast enough to avoid the torpedoes bearing down on him. Strangely enough, he was not the least concerned with survival at this stage. His entire being was concentrated on eradicating the foe threatening the Motherland—halting it in any manner possible . . . including sacrificing himself.

Seratov felt as though it was standing on end as the bow planes wrenched them into a sharp dive. Lozak shouted a warning to the men in the control room as the deck fell away from under them. Loose gear clattered across the deck.

"Range to torpedoes?" Danilov shouted.

"Seven hundred meters."

"Can we get under them?"

"No . . . maybe . . . I don't know . . ."

An explosion, representing the last of their torpedoes, was clearly audible. "That's a hit," shouted the weapons officer. "A hit . . . a hit . . ." His voice faded as he peered about the control room at the others tightly grasping the nearest handhold. Not a one of them had ever experienced such a sharp dive.

"Captain, my angle is getting too steep. I . . . I have to pull back on the planes." The diving officer was already changing the angle as he called out to Lozak. "Too close to losing control . . . is it all right?" he finished tentatively.

Lozak turned to see Danilov nodding his head rhythmically in agreement. Either they had evaded . . . or they would be dead shortly. Even Steven Lozak now accepted his fate calmly. Danilov's desire to destroy *Imperator* at all costs had now infected him. It no longer seemed to matter if they returned to base, or if he achieved all the promotions he dreamed of. He was comfortable with the concept that it seemed much more important to sacrifice for the homeland. He found himself totally involved in Danilov's objective.

The deck mercifully began to return to an acceptable angle.

"Torpedoes appear to be passing overhead. Probably too close to reacquire us—" The report was interrupted by a tremendous blast that sent almost every man reeling off his feet. The lights blinked out as *Seratov* rolled viciously to starboard. For an instant, darkness and terror ruled. Then the battle lanterns came on, revealing a control room without a man still at his station.

Steven Lozak was the first to return to his feet. One arm had been wrapped about a support bar as they dived, preventing him from flying across the room. He saw by the dials that *Seratov* was still moving forward; her engineering spaces seemed to be intact. One of the planesmen slid back into his seat, reaching instinctively for the wheel in front of him. Without a word, he nodded over his shoulder to Lozak that it appeared to be functioning.

"Stop all engines—hold your depth." Lozak was in control and felt strangely calm.

The political officer moved quickly to the executive officer's position and called over the ship's speaker for damage reports—the torpedo had hit forward . . . heavy damage in the torpedo room and living spaces . . . no fire . . . but flooding was out of control forward.

"We're taking on water too fast," the political officer said. "We'll have to surface." His hand was gesturing upward as he spoke.

Lozak shook his head. "Not yet." He looked about for Danilov. The admiral had been thrown across the control room and had come to rest in a sitting position near one of the weapons control consoles. His left arm hung limply at his side. A deep gash across his forehead poured dark blood down one side of his face. "Admiral, are you able to speak to me?" Lozak moved tentatively in his direction, fearing the man who controlled everything in his life might be unable to function.

Danilov did not move. His eyes looked up to the advancing Lozak and he opened his mouth as if to speak, but no words emerged. He blinked his eyes, then shut them for a moment. His forehead wrinkled in pain. When he opened his eyes again, it appeared to those around him as if he was more in control. His lips strained to form a sound— then the words came out fitfully, "Sergoff . . . is that you, Sergoff?"

"It's Stevan Lozak," the captain answered softly, kneeling beside the admiral.

"I can't see you, Captain. Are you in front of me?"

"Yes, Admiral."

"I can't see anything." Danilov sighed. "Are we . . . are . . . what is the ship's status?"

"We've been hit forward . . . taking on water rapidly at about two hundred meters. We have to surface, I think, if there's any way to save the ship."

"Sergoff. Where's Sergoff?"

Lozak peered about the control room. He recognized one of the sailors kneeling by Sergoff. He beckoned another over to help him and they rolled the limp Sergoff onto his back. One of the men felt for a pulse; the other held his hand by Sergoff's nose. There was no indication of life. Then the second pointed at his neck. The first looked back at Lozak and shook his head.

"Captain Sergoff was severely injured, Admiral. I'm afraid he's dead."

"Oh . . ." Danilov squeezed his eyes tightly again as if he would be able to see when he opened them. He stared sightlessly back at Lozak. "*Imperator* . . . what has happened to the American?"

Lozak glanced about as if searching for the answer. He spotted his weapons officer and called out, "What does sonar have on the American?"

"We have only the hydrophones on the port side, Captain. We are having trouble."

"We were both diving at the time," Lozak snapped back sharply. "We were both close, no more than seven or eight hundred meters at one time. You must hear something."

They were interrupted by the crash of a bulkhead collapsing against tons of seawater. The political officer's face was pale now as he restated the obvious. "We have little time. Either we try for the surface now or sink."

Lozak reluctantly began the orders to surface. He knew they were taking grave chances maneuvering with so much weight forward, and that they would increase that weight as they moved upward, but there was no choice. There seemed so many reasons to go along with the political officer. Lozak was responsible for the safety of his submarine. He was also defenseless. The torpedo room had been destroyed.

His only other choice would be to do what he was sure Danilov was intent upon as they charged toward *Imperator* moments before—ram? Who was he responsible to? He looked again at Abe Danilov, the finest man in the Soviet Navy.

"Captain, we have contact with the American . . . quite clearly. She seems to be close aboard . . . port bow. She must be near the same depth . . . maneuvering very slowly."

He knew exactly what Danilov would do.

The Soviet torpedo had opened a large hole low in *Imperator*'s port quarter. With no computer to automatically seal damaged compartments, seawater flooded the engineering spaces until it lapped at the main switchboard. The blast that followed touched off an electrical fire creating a dense pall of smoke. Under emergency lighting, the damage control parties finally closed off much of the port quarter spaces. Steering had also been lost instantly. The submarine was now maneuvering under an emergency system that left *Imperator* wallowing grotesquely.

Pumps were unable to keep up with the water. Without the computer, much of the damage control had fallen to a small party of men incapable of managing the valves and watertight doors that had once been under electronic control.

As Snow watched the XO manually list the compartments now sealed off, he asked quietly, "The computer areas —did they receive any further damage? Carol Petersen . . ."
It seemed to Snow that he was floating . . . transported

to a place beyond his body where substance seemed unimportant.

The XO looked up gravely from his list. "All the spaces in the computer complex were just sealed off, Captain. Bulkheads were collapsing." He looked back down at his list. "DC Central said no one was able to get in to see if there were any survivors. The entire space is flooded now," he added softly.

"Very well." Snow turned away, biting his lip involuntarily before he felt the pain. Carol Petersen—he was sure he'd made a friend. There hadn't been many over the last few years. And she *had* made an effort to be nice to him. . . . "Very well," he muttered again. It was requiring all his effort to maintain his mind within his body, almost as if the emotional part of his being—was that what some called the soul?—would soon depart forever.

"Captain, sonar's back on-line again. That Russian's awfully damn close . . . not more than seven or eight hundred yards away. . . ."

But Snow found himself unable to concentrate. There was an emptiness he could not explain. His mighty vessel, the invincible *Imperator* . . . controlled by a computer that made her superior to all comers . . . was severely damaged. The one new friend he thought he'd made in so many years was dead, probably floating against the overhead in a space cluttered with icy seawater and debris. Somehow, he found the battle over. At least . . . his own battle was over.

"Hal . . . Hal . . ." Someone was coming through the forward hatch.

The voice was familiar. At first it seemed a long distance away. Then it was by his ear. "Hal . . . are you all right?" A hand grasped his shoulder.

Snow turned to look into Andy Reed's eyes staring back from a haggard face. "Andy . . . I thought they'd socked you away into a bunk somewhere."

"Never got me there. Not now—not a tough old bird like me. When I got some strength back, I managed to talk my way down to the wardroom for some hot coffee.

Then . . ." He studied the XO's long list of damaged spaces. "Then we were hit. I've been fighting my way through watertight doors. There was no alarm when I opened them."

"There's no computer, Andy, and no power." Snow's eyes had a faraway look, the look of a man who no longer cared. "But we'll survive . . . *Imperator*'s tough."

"*Seratov*?" Reed snapped anxiously.

Snow's eyes turned to a point on the bulkhead and he pointed slowly. "She's out there about eight hundred yards away, getting ready to sink, I guess." It occurred to Snow that sonar had regained contact when Reed entered the control room and they had reported *Seratov* out of control. "Status on the Russian?" he called out.

"Badly damaged. Moving again . . . very slowly. Sounds like she's trying to surface. We can hear a hell of a lot there, Captain. She's fighting a losing battle."

"Can you ping on her?" Reed asked, noting the faraway cast to Snow's eyes.

"Sure can." There was a moment of silence as the weapons officer spoke into his mike, and then, "She's at about seven hundred yards, sir . . . what's that?" he inquired into his mike. "She seems to be turning toward us . . . she's closing. Got no speed to speak of, but she's creeping in our direction."

"I know Danilov," Reed said. "That son of a bitch is going to try to ram us if it's the last thing he does. Get out of here, Hal. Crank it up."

"All ahead one third," Snow ordered. To his XO, he added mechanically, "Inform DC Central that we're underway . . . emergency . . . we need steering bad." His voice was a monotone now. Snow was following orders, instinctively directing his ship, but his emotion was drained.

"Range?"

"About four five zero yards. Sounds like she's had her front end opened up, Captain. I doubt she can keep up for long. We can identify interior bulkheads collapsing."

"DC Central says we have sporadic flooding aft. We can't control it while we're moving," the XO reported.

Snow was staring at the control panel as if he were

about to give another order. His mouth dropped open but there were no words. Then he closed it, his eyes still fixed on the panel.

"Come on, Hal . . . we're moving with Danilov." Reed's voice was a whisper just to one side of Snow's ear. "Turn . . . you've got to put your rudder over."

Snow turned his head slightly to stare at Reed. The admiral knew his words had failed to register. Reed had no other choice.

"This is Admiral Reed . . . I have the conn. Tell damage control I need starboard rudder—instantly. Tell them if they give me enough rudder they might live to see the surface again."

The wait seemed to last forever before the report came back from damage control that the rudder had been jacked to starboard.

"We seem to be opening range slightly." The voice from sonar was animated. "Up to five hundred yards now."

Reed turned to study Snow. *Imperator*'s captain remained in the same position, his eyes still fixed on the control panel. This time, when his mouth opened, the words came slowly, so much so that Reed had to lean near to hear them. "I really didn't know what I lost, Andy. . . ." His voice trailed off as he turned his gaze on Reed. "I gotta get off this thing, Andy. I'm not fit to—" His words were drowned out by another report from sonar.

"Five five zero yards . . . opening slightly . . ."

Somehow, staring despairingly at Snow, Reed understood that his sixth sense had been correct when he insisted on heading for *Imperator*'s control room. As cold and miserable as he was, his instinct had told him that there was trouble. He had come to warn Snow that Danilov would do anything to destroy *Imperator* as long as there was a breath left in him. Abe Danilov was an old-school type—he thrived on stubbornness. He wouldn't be finished until his submarine lay on the bottom.

"Russian seems to be losing the bubble!" The excitement in the voice from sonar spread a hush over the control room. "Sounds like he's coming apart."

Sonar detailed the sounds of the last minutes of the Russian submarine. Andy Reed was able to contain his joy only because he saw that Snow heard nothing. When he finally returned to Washington, he knew he would have to review all of the profiles again—he would have to find out what element had slipped by the experts . . . and what it was that might have triggered this reaction.

"Bring your planes up . . . full rise," insisted Lozak. "We're going deeper."

"They are full, Captain. There's too much water forward. We need to blow—"

. "No way to blow anything . . . more speed," he shouted into the speaker to engineering. Besides, how could you blow flooded compartments?

"You've got everything we can give you," a hollow voice responded from engineering.

"I have everything," murmured Lozak to himself. "I have nothing," he added as he studied the depth gauge. They were falling more rapidly. He turned in Danilov's direction. "We aren't going to succeed, Admiral. They have way on . . . they're pulling away. We can't hold our depth . . . we . . ."

"I understand." Danilov smiled back through sightless eyes. "Shh," he added calmly, "I can hear her." His finger was at his lips. "Shh . . ." His great head tilted to one side. "Good night, Anna, good night . . ." His voice became fainter until Lozak could no longer hear his words, though the lips continued to move.

Stevan Lozak experienced the first traces of loneliness. Admiral Danilov had transported himself elsewhere. Sergoff, who really wasn't a bad sort, was dead. Of those men who managed to return to their stations, a few blindly remained at their posts. Others whimpered silently as the diving officer read off the depth every twenty-five meters.

Captain Lozak remained in his favorite position, one arm around the polished chrome stanchion near the periscope. He continued to study all the instruments until the hull burst in about him.

Andy Reed waited until sonar confirmed *Seratov*'s death before he gave the orders to surface in a nearby lead. *Houston*'s survivors needed them—and it was time to establish contact.

His action report to Washington was beamed off a communications satellite in plain language so that the Kremlin would receive it at the same time. There was no need for further loss of life. There had been a winner . . . and a loser. Washington and Moscow would surely want to discuss details in the next few hours.

Imperator could be jury-rigged by her crew so that she might continue her mission. It was safe now under the ice, and finally she could surface off Norway for the world to see.

— _Epilogue_ ————————————

ON THE TENTH day, _Imperator_ surfaced in bright sunlight off Norway's North Cape. Her arrival could have been recorded by satellite but the navy wouldn't have it that way. The media had been flown out to gaze in awe at her power as her immense bulk broke the surface of a calm Barents Sea. Her injuries had been patched by a repair team parachuted to her near the pole. _Imperator_ radiated a venerable lethality to those who looked down upon her from the skies.

The gull-wing doors were opened forward. One after another, her helicopters deployed with troops for exercises near Hammerfest. Tanks and field artillery were ferried ashore—and all of it was filmed for the world to see.

There was no reason to expect that the Russians would attempt to harm her. Agreement had already been reached— NATO observers were overseeing the complete withdrawal of all Soviet troops and equipment near the Norwegian border; American attack submarines had been recalled from a certain faceoff with the Soviet missile fleet; the government in Oslo had been assured that American marines would be airlifted out in forty-eight hours; both the United

States and the Soviet Union had agreed to a series of meetings in Geneva, sponsored by the United Nations, to discuss withdrawal of military forces from the Arctic Ocean. Collectively, the world powers had condemned the Far North as a battlefield.

It was on the tenth day also that now-retired Admiral Sergei Gorshkov stopped by the Danilov apartment to pay his respects. There had been no parades for the loser, no state funeral, nothing made available to the general public that a great Soviet admiral had fought his last battle and in losing had perhaps saved his nation from a bitter defeat. The admiral found Anna Danilov sleeping peacefully forever. She was clutching a single red rose, the last one from the bouquet Abe had given her the night he left for Polyarnyy.

The *We Eight* was a good size, able to handle the entire Reed family comfortably. With just the three of them, each one could stretch out and enjoy the sun as the sailboat moved down Chesapeake Bay at a leisurely clip. There couldn't have been a more perfect midsummer day for a sail.

From the moment they turned through the gates of the academy and headed toward the launch area, Hal Snow had experienced a warm feeling. The buildings, the roads, the statues, and then from the water the old landmarks. Tolly Point drifted off to starboard, then the beautiful old homes gradually faded in the distance as they moved down the bay. Snow closed his eyes and listened to the soft ruffle of the wind in the mainsail.

"Here, you take over the driving for a while," Lucy Reed whispered, gently placing Snow's arm over the tiller. "The old captain's asleep," she added, nodding at her husband, "and it's time to break out the stores."

There was no opportunity to refuse. Lucy had transferred the responsibility with an ease that sent a thrill through him. There was no need for her to add any other words. It was simply implied that since she had something else to do, and Andy was dozing, that Snow was perfectly competent to control the situation—she had total confidence in him. As she moved down the ladder into the tiny forward cabin, she turned back and winked.

At first he experimented. He loosened the line to the main sheet and let the sail swing farther out until it began to luff. Then he hauled in until the wind was as perfect as it could get. Gradually, he shifted the rudder, turning first to port until the sheet again luffed and the *We Eight* began to flatten out. When he pushed the tiller in the opposite direction, the sail again filled and the little craft began to heel. God, it felt good! *We Eight* was just under thirty feet, but Hal Snow was experiencing a sensation that he was afraid might have died weeks before under the arctic ice. He felt in control again!

A champagne cork popped in the cabin and Andy Reed stirred. He glanced over at Snow, smiled comfortably, and stretched. "I'm going below to give the chef a hand. You can hold this course if you like . . . or come about and head for Kent Island. We're game for whatever you want to do." And with that, he ducked below to help Lucy.

Snow grinned to himself. You've got the conn, old man. No sense in following a rhumb line on such a beautiful day. "Coming about," he shouted happily.

Lucy's lunch was superb, the crackling cold champagne so good that they downed a second bottle. Neither of the Reeds touched the tiller for the remainder of the day as Snow tacked back and forth across Chesapeake Bay. And when he brought the little craft alongside the pier that evening, the landing was perfect.

That night, Snow was effusive, dredging up many of their old memories, regaling them with stories that had magnified over the years, recalling old jokes. And over coffee, he offered simply, "I'm going to leave the navy Monday morning. I hate to . . . but it's time." He was free again. He'd sensed it on that first tack, known it as they docked.

"No need to," Reed said.

"I know that. It's just time."

"When will you be back?"

"I don't know. I'm going to call my kids. We have a lot of time to make up."

"When you come back, there's a job waiting here for you." Reed's stare was level and expressionless.

Snow hesitated. "Not a navy job . . ."

"Whenever you want."

"I've always heard that three strikes and you're out." Snow paused, a flood of arctic memories momentarily overwhelming him. "I'm not interested in taking the third. . . ." His voice drifted off.

Lucy Reed reached over to squeeze his hand. "There was never a second strike—you know that, don't you?" She held his hand tightly, her eyes moving from his to her husband's.

"She's right, Hal," Andy Reed nodded. "You pulled off the impossible up there. You won't have a thing to do with the Washington types—but they're still in awe of what you did."

"Thanks . . . both of you, thanks," he added hesitantly. "But I still can't come back."

"You don't have to, Hal. But the door's open as long as you need it."

"I'll remember that." He pushed back his chair and stood up. "But I think I'll give the kids a call now. There's a lot to do."

— *Afterword* _____

SOVIET TECHNOLOGY is achieving giant strides in submarine development. Over the past decade, they have introduced a dozen new designs and by 1990 it is predicted that future classes will attain the low noise levels of our current 688 *Los Angeles* class. Specifically designed for under-ice operations, their titanium hulls are going to withstand crush depths in excess of 1,000 meters, their engineering plants will be capable of speeds over fifty knots submerged, and the compartmentalization and double hulls will require more than one hit to sink them—that is *if* the torpedo can catch the target and *if* that occurs before imploding at such tremendous crush depths.

We have yet to achieve the necessary sophistication in materials or technology to send a ship of *Imperator*'s size to sea, but naval architects and engineers have experimented in designing such craft for oil/LNG transport. However, it is becoming clearer that the United States will eventually need a submarine with *Imperator*'s capabilities if we are to continue to maintain seapower in the true sense of the word.

Bestselling Books for Today's Reader

___ **THE GENERALS**   08455-7/$3.95
   (Brotherhood of War VI)
   W.E.B. Griffin
___ **CATCHER IN THE WRY**   09029-0/$3.50
   Bob Uecker and Mickey Herskowitz
___ **EIGHT MILLION WAYS TO DIE**   08840-4/$3.50
   Lawrence Block
___ **THE MAN CALLED KYRIL**   07633-3/$3.50
   John Trenhaile
___ **RAMBO: FIRST BLOOD II**   08399-2/$3.50
   David Morrell, based on a screenplay by
   Sylvester Stallone and James Cameron
___ **RUBICON ONE**   08050-0/$3.95
   Dennis Jones
___ **A VIEW FROM THE SQUARE**   08102-7/$3.95
   John Trenhaile
___ **DISTANT REPLAY**   08762-9/$3.95
   Jerry Kramer with Dick Schaap
___ **THE MICK**   08599-5/$3.95
   Mickey Mantle with Herb Gluck
___ **THE CORPS BOOK I: SEMPER FI**   08749-1/$3.95
   W.E.B. Griffin
___ **THE TOUCH**   08733-5/$3.95
   F. Paul Wilson
___ **MANHUNT**   09014-X/$3.95
   Peter Maas